Their Cemetery
Sown with Corn

Praise for *Their Cemetery Sown with Corn* ...

This extraordinary tale is not quite history but a semi-fictionalised account by Frank Binder, a Germanophile who spent the Great War in Dartmoor Prison as a reward for conscientious objection, and lectured at Bonn University between 1921 and 1933. John Arnold is simply his fictional vehicle. Forced to leave the country in 1937, he returned to England penniless and became a foreign language teacher at Scarborough High School for Boys. The discovery and publication of this manuscript is the work of one of his former pupils, Michael Rines, who is to be congratulated on bringing to us this moving, colourful and evocative account of the rise of Nazism in the Rhineland.

Robert Gildea, Professor of Modern History, Oxford University,
review for *History Today*

*   *   *

Binder's novel is helped by the brilliance of the language and the author's ability to portray so realistically the dilemmas faced by very ordinary folk in extraordinary times. Every school child now studies Nazism and this book goes much further in explaining how it all happened than any of the conventional history textbooks.

Christian Wolmar, *The Oldie*

*   *   *

I am struck with the authenticity of this account of the Nazi government's impact on a single village in the Rhineland ... I cannot in a few sentences describe the subtlety of the author's analysis of village society under stress; it is a sophisticated account that is wholly convincing. The importance (not to say significance) of a book written by a contemporary English observer of intelligence and sensitivity, one who spoke and understood the language, and who loved Germany, cannot be over-stressed. Frank Binder taught at the University of Bonn from 1921 to 1936: he was, therefore, a first-hand witness of the rise and triumph of Nazism (which he detested for its corrupting effect on all that was good in Germany). It is fortunate that he was capable of a deeply felt, acutely vivid description of what he witnessed. He was the right man in the right place at a terrible time. His book may very well be unique.

Professor Colin Richmond, Emeritus Professor of History, Keele University

*   *   *

I find this book particularly impressive ... What makes the novel quite unique and valuable in my estimation is that it was written as early as the end of the war, when memory was still fresh and without the superior knowledge of hindsight. It was, moreover, written in a spirit of understanding and compassion.

Having been a member of the same department as Frank Binder at the University of Bonn for three decades, I am struck by the subtlety, fairness and authenticity of the description and the profound insight in the local manners and ways of communicating. The story is told with genuine liveliness, sympathy and literary distinction, quite apart from its political relevance. The book will also make a most valuable contribution to the mutual understanding of a comparatively little known aspect of Anglo-German history.

Dr Dieter Mehl, Emeritus Professor of English, American and Celtic Studies,
Bonn University

*   *   *

Their Cemetery Sown with Corn offers insight into Nazism, based on first-hand experience, which could appeal to many who are interested in the topic but perhaps not keen to read through an extensive non-ficitonal literature.

Professor Sir Ian Kershaw

Their Cemetery Sown with Corn

An Englishman Stands Against the Nazi Storm

FRANK BINDER

Edited by Michael Rines

Pen & Sword
MILITARY

Published in Great Britain in 2012 by
PEN & SWORD MILITARY
An imprint of
Pen & Sword Books Ltd
47 Church Street
Barnsley
South Yorkshire
S70 2AS

First published in Great Britain in 2010 as *Sown With Corn*
by Farthings Publishing

Copyright © Elsie Binder and Michael Rines, 2012

ISBN 978-1-781590-083-6

Typeset by Concept, Huddersfield, West Yorkshire.
Printed and bound in England by CPI, UK.

Pen & Sword Books Ltd incorporates the imprints of Pen & Sword Aviation, Pen & Sword Maritime, Pen & Sword Military, Wharncliffe Local History, Pen & Sword Select, Pen & Sword Military Classics, Leo Cooper, Remember When, Seaforth Publishing and Frontline Publishing.

For a complete list of Pen & Sword titles please contact
PEN & SWORD BOOKS LIMITED
47 Church Street, Barnsley, South Yorkshire, S70 2AS, England
E-mail: enquiries@pen-and-sword.co.uk
Website: www.pen-and-sword.co.uk

Dedication

Dedicated to the memory of the late Frank Binder

(1893–1962)

Contents

Editor's Introduction

The story of a remarkable book and a remarkable man

The title *Their Cemetery Sown with Corn* comes from a pogrom in 1353 in which a Jewish cemetery was desecrated, ploughed up and sown with corn. But more than 500 years later the Jews in Germany were facing a much more sinister persecution.

This novel tells the story of an English student at Bonn University during the rise of the Nazis. Its author, Frank Binder, was himself a lecturer in English literature at the University during that same period. The book, which is written in the first person, is therefore almost certainly at least semi-autobiographical and has an intense realism born of the author's first-hand knowledge.

Binder's own story is as remarkable as that of his book's hero. He graduated from Liverpool University in 1915 and became a conscientious objector. For this, he was imprisoned on Dartmoor, smashing up rocks, for the duration of the Great War. But by 1921 he was lecturing at Bonn University, sharing the privations of his students. 'We, who had nothing but the paper of German poverty in our pockets, were reduced to a ration of black bread, meals without meat, and to a sugarless coffee of burnt corn', he later wrote.

He stayed in Germany until shortly before the outbreak of war, when he was forced to flee the country, either because of his open opposition to the Nazis or, possibly, because he had been acting as a British agent.

The hero of his book, John Arnold, has lodgings in a large village just outside Bonn called Blankheim in the book, but in real life probably Wesseling. There, two Jewish sisters are the wealthiest residents. Arnold is therefore able to track the parts played during the spread of Nazi influence, not only in the rural community and among the academics of the university but also in the nearby city of Cologne. The story is thus a microcosm of what happened in Germany generally, and it enables us to understand how such a cultured, civilised country could have descended into barbarism.

At first, many, including some of the country's Jews, welcomed the emergence of the Nazis, believing that 'a Hitler regime with economy, work and discipline as its first and foremost principles would do Germany a world of good.' They thought it would bring some order to the desperately disordered country, but they were soon disillusioned.

The book is notable for its rich cast of characters and for the different ways they develop in the face of oppression. Not the least of these characters is Arnold himself. He starts off a detached, perhaps naïve, academic, but is gradually drawn into the German predicament. He has to confront and overcome in himself an instinctive element of anti-semitism, and, though he abhors lying, he has to ask himself whether it is lying to tell an untruth to those who have no respect for truth. By the end of the book he has become an even better manipulator than the Nazis themselves, albeit in good causes.

Though the story is occasionally grim, it is lightened by the way Arnold outwits the local Nazis and by the courage of the few who refuse to give in to bullying. Its narrative makes the book a compulsive page-turner, and the author's writing brings scenes vividly to life. Above all, Binder's love of Germany and the pleasure he takes in the streams and hills of the Rhine valley shine through.

I can only guess why the book was never published in Binder's lifetime. Perhaps it was due to the paper shortage just after the war, which severely limited the number of books published. Perhaps nobody wanted to read about the rise of the Nazis at that time, especially not a book that showed some sympathy for the German people. Or perhaps it was simply that Binder was not good at selling his work.

Their Cemetery Sown with Corn needed some editing, in particular to keep the narrative flowing. But though the richness of Binder's writing style is very different from that of today's novelists, it is of its own day and helps the reader to immerse himself in the world of an academic living in the era in which the story is set. Above all else, it reflects Binder's passion for the glories of the written word, and that has been fully respected

The richness of the prose in two books written during his time in Bonn, *Journey in England* and *Dialectic; or The Tactics of Thinking*, is probably unmatched in twentieth-century English literature.

Journey in England was published in 1931 to excellent reviews, and his second book, *Dialectic; or The Tactics of Thinking*, in 1932. Both were published by Eric Partridge, at the time one of the leading authorities on English language and literature. In *Usage and Abusage*, his own highly respected book on the English language, first published in 1947 and still in print (Penguin Reference), Partridge said that Binder and G.K. Chesterton were the century's 'two great masters of alliteration', but that 'Binder was the more rhythmical and euphonious, the more sophisticated and yet the more profound.'

He remained at Bonn University until 1933, earning a glowing testimonial from his head of department which, tellingly, included the following:

Having stayed for more than ten years at one of the best and most famous universities of Germany and in the centre of the Rhineland, he acquired a very thorough knowledge of German conditions, of German culture and history. He speaks German like a native of this country and writes it perfectly. His great interest in economics will make it easy for him in consideration of German affairs to use (sic) the commercial relations between the two countries, in a theoretical or practical way, if he wished to do so.

After leaving Bonn he is known to have spent a year (1935–1936) on a course at the university in Besancon. Apart from that, he claimed to have been wholly engaged in literary work in Germany. However, I can find no evidence of any such literary output. So what he was doing until shortly before the Second World War is not clear.

He did later admit that he had been approached by the Secret Intelligence Service to act as a spy, and his testimonial from the university shows he was eminently well qualified to be one. Another hint comes in a letter to his widow from Eric Partridge, saying: 'He was a brave man and a very distinguished writer.'

Binder denied that he had been a spy. He said that when he was approached by the SIS he had asked what would happen if he were caught. When told he would be disowned he claimed to have turned the offer down.

When I asked SIS if Binder had been in its service I got the stock reply: 'It continues to be the long-standing policy of the Government neither to confirm nor deny whether any information is held on an individual by the Security and Intelligence agencies.' By the same token, if Binder had indeed been a spy, he would have been duty-bound to deny it. What he did not deny was that he was hostile to the Nazi regime.

In 1937, not long after his marriage to a German-speaking Pole who had been one of his mature students, Binder was forced to leave Germany in a hurry to escape arrest for his criticism of the Nazis and for repeatedly refusing to say 'Heil Hitler!' He had written to *The Times* pointing out that from his window he could see that the German military was breaking the terms of the Versailles Treaty and, though the letter was not published by the then pro-German paper, he became convinced that a copy had been passed to the Gestapo.

It has to be said that drawing attention to himself by such actions as these was hardly the behaviour one would expect from an undercover agent, unless it was a very elaborate cover.

When he fled to Britain he had to leave everything behind, arriving in London penniless, a plight relieved at one point only when he got a cheque for an article he had written. He still remembered years later: 'I went straight to the bank and cashed it, bought all the good things I could and sent them off to my starving wife and child (by this time they had been evacuated to the country), then pulled the latest copy of the *Daily Express* up to my neck and slept soundly for the first time since leaving Germany.'

He took a temporary job teaching English to Jewish refugees, before getting a place as a foreign language teacher at the school I attended, the Scarborough High School for Boys – an intellectual letdown from his stimulating days as a lecturer in Bonn.

And what irony that, because he had lived in Germany – and perhaps because his wife spoke English with a German accent – he received threats, and had bricks thrown through his house windows. If anyone knocked at the door, the family hid and kept quiet, much as Jews did in Hitler's Germany.

It was during his time in Scarborough that he wrote *Their Cemetery Sown with Corn*.

Binder had loved Germany, Germans and German culture, and had watched with sadness the country's slide into Nazi barbarism, so when he arrived at the Scarborough High School for Boys in January 1940 he could have been a desperately disillusioned man. Instead of teaching bright undergraduates he was teaching mere schoolboys in what he described as an 'intellectual cul de sac'.

But though he undoubtedly resented his demotion, and was by now aged 46, he threw himself into his new task with the same determination a fellow prisoner on Dartmoor said he had shown when breaking up rocks. Those of us who were his pupils had no hint of this balding and slightly portly man's history, but even the most junior recognised the force of his personality, his originality and his passion for ideas and learning.

In addition to his teaching, Binder ran the school Chess Club, in his words, after the frustrating effort of trying to turn us into scholars during 'a hard and dunderheading day, prostrated in that battle in which the gods themselves engage in vain.' And it was his chess club reports in the school magazine that gave us the first hint that we had a giant in our midst.

Even though Binder said that in chess 'there are no drums and trumpets to attract the giddy crowd', his account of a game of chess between a couple of schoolboys sounded like a mighty clash of arms, and endowed the combatants with the power and pomp of historical heroes.

As schoolboys, we readily recognised the alliteration used in his writing, but we were not conscious of the additional use of assonance (the repetition of the same vowel sounds, as in 'back-cracking thwack'), which is one of the features of the reports. This assonance might have been what led Partridge to the view that Binder's writing was more euphonious than Chesterton's. Nor did we recognise the brilliant use of antithesis to create rhythm and balance, as in the sentence 'How changed into so much sounding brass the one-time seeming gold' in another report.

But it was when one of the sixth-formers told us of the entry on alliteration in Partridge's *Usage and Abusage* that we became aware of the true stature of Frank Binder as a master of English prose. Partridge quoted passages from his two published books at considerable length to justify his judgement on the author's command of alliteration.

Impressive though Partridge's tributes to Binder were, and frequently though I regaled my friends over the years with the glories of the chess club reports, I had no opportunity to appreciate the full range of his literary genius, because both *Journey* and *Dialectic* were long out of print, and searches for second-hand copies went without reward. Then, some forty years after I left the school, I got hold of a copy of *Journey*. Here, I found much more than mere mastery of alliteration, assonance and antithesis. Every sentence is a gem.

Binder's *Journey* describes, in gloriously extravagant style, a tour of parts of England by train and on foot, starting with his journey from Bonn across north Germany to Harwich. He went on by train to see the great churches and other historic buildings at Ely, Peterborough, Lincoln, Liverpool, Chester, Stratford-on-Avon, Leamington and Warwick, then on foot through Kenilworth, Oxford and Thames towns and villages such as Reading, Maidenhead, Bray, Windsor, Stoke Poges, Windsor and Runny-mede, before hitching a lift into London.

Journey is not, however, a travelogue, and his descriptions of the historic towns and buildings are couched not in architectural terms but reflect rather the emotions and philosophical thoughts they arouse in him. The book is, indeed, as much a vehicle for Binder's philosophy as it is a travel book. More than that, it is a literary treasure.

Journey got good reviews, in publications such as the *Sunday Times*, *Manchester Guardian*, *The Spectator*, *New Statesman* and *Punch*, but they have not stopped it from being forgotten. Prophetically, in view of the unfair failure of many of his contemporaries to recognise him in his lifetime, he concludes that 'it is a precarious prosperity that comes of embarking the spirit on the instability of syllables and sounds.'

I reasoned that such a fine writer – and one who so much loved writing – must have written more than two books. So I managed to track down his daughter, Elsie Binder. I met her at her London home, and found that she had kept all his unpublished work – typescripts in piles of yellowing paper, some bound, some loose, some in box files. And when I left I took with me a suitcase full of his works, together with a copy of *Dialectic*. There were two novels, one of them was *Their Cemetery Sown with Corn*. The other, *The Wisdoms of Ramadan*, was a quite prescient sci-fi book. There was also a second massive volume on dialectics, *The Principles of Controversy*, five plays and several volumes of short stories.

Frank Binder was one of the finest prose writers in English literary history, but is unrecognised today, and his two published books forgotten. He was a deeply erudite scholar and brilliant thinker, but ended his days in obscurity; the only people who remember him are his daughter and some of his former pupils.

There was no obituary when he died in 1962, except in the school magazine. Over his untended grave a small headstone stands askew, and his name is all but weathered away. No plaque adorns the wall of the tiny terraced house where he lived in Scarborough. There is no mention of him in any of the reference books on English literature, other than in *Usage and Abusage*, and the recognition that should have been his in life is also denied him in the grave.

If what I have written and the publication of *Their Cemetery Sown with Corn* brings him belated recognition it will right a wrong and repay in some measure the pleasure his writing has brought to the privileged few who have been able to read his books.

Michael Rines
Woodbridge,
Suffolk,
IP12 1LG

Acknowledgements

Grateful thanks are due to Elsie Binder for permission to publish this book and to Julia Jones for her enthusiastic encouragement and valuable advice.

Cast of Characters

The Engels family
Engels, Johann: the father, a retired farmer
Engels, Joseph, his son: jeweller in Cologne
Klebert, Klara: Johann's daughter
Klebert, Captain Karl: Klara's husband
Paul and Else: their children
Nauheim: cook, and Frau Nauheim: housekeeper
Weichert, Tilde: their maid

In Blankheim
Barth: Rektor
Brechner, Alex: plumber, and Kurt, his son
Cohen: doctor, and his son, David
Danker: policeman
Dorlich: tobacconist
Fenger, Johann: failed tobacconist
Fischer: police superintendent
Frenzel: land agent
Gerster: Editor of local Rhineland newspaper, *Landwirt*, his wife,
    Gertrud, and son, Albert
Hamman, Peter: on Gerster's staff at *Landwirt*
Heinrich: Sexton
Hempel, Kurt: farmer
Kiel: original landlord of The Golden Hind
Kemp, Friederich: sanitary engineer
Klassen, Karl: schoolmaster, and his son Ludwig
Kollas: insurance agent and owner of lock-up company
Lambert: solicitor
Matthias: barber
Müller, Friedrich: farmer
Porten family: one of the poorest in Blankheim
Stenzel, Johann: new landlord of The Golden Hind
Wessel, Alfred: builder
Wolff, Rebecca and Rachel: Jewish sisters

Zech, Johann: postman
Zimmerman, Hans: former plumber and communist

In Bonn and Cologne
Boden: doctor, and his wife, Johannah
Bürger: economics lecturer
Hillesheim: philosophy lecturer
Klein, Otto: student
Levy, Geheimrat: professor at the university
Metzenauer, Rosa: student
Reimar, Hans: student
Rosenbaum: Professor of Economics
Sanders, Waldemar: Professor of Protestant Theology
Wagner, Otto: a lawyer

In Neuenahr
Hermann: District Organiser, Nazi Party
Weichert, Herr and Frau: Tilde's parents
Zeller, Johann: Nazi schoolmaster

The SA and the SS
The SA (*Sturmabteilung* – stormtroopers) was a paramilitary organisation
of the Nazi party. It played a key role in Hitler's rise to power in the 1920s
and early 1930s. SA men were often called 'Brownshirts' because their
uniforms were brown. It was superseded by the SS in 1933.

The SS (*Schutzstaffel*, literally Protective Squad) originally provided
bodyguards for leading Nazis. The Nazis regarded the SS as an elite unit,
the party's 'praetorian guard', with all SS personnel selected (in principle,
anyway) on the principles of racial purity and unconditional loyalty to the
Führer and the Nazi Party. The SS military branch, the *Waffen-SS*, evolved
into a second German army in addition to the regular German army, the
Wehrmacht.

The SS was in charge of the Holocaust.

Frank Binder aged 24 in 1918.

Frank Binder in Italy in the mid-1930s.

Frank Binder, in a boater, with some of his Bonn University students.

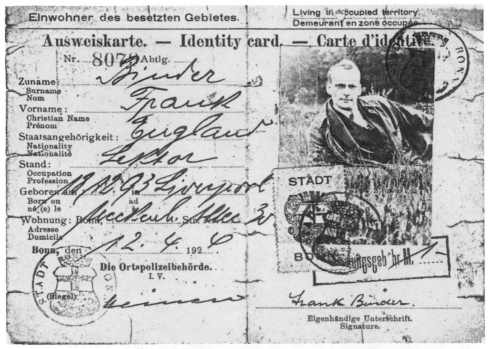

Frank's identity card in allied-occupied Germany, 1924.

Frank Binder on his retirement.

Photograph taken by Frank Binder of his wife, Marianne, kneeling in the snow before the Auge Gotte (Eye of God) Shrine referred to on page 297.

Chapter 1

The Festival of All Souls

Yes, I shall write about my life on the Rhine when the Nazis were in power and when the war that wasted Europe was looming dimly ahead. It will not be easy. No phase of my life is so far off, none so veiled in the farewell air of something that will never return. The war seems to have trampled on it all.

And yet, on dreary winter days or in reflective hours by the fireside, how near those days still seem, clearly limned amid the murk of years, luminous and living as ever amid the reek, dust and tumbling rubble of total war. After all, my youth was in them. And what days are nearer to the memory than those when hope was young?

I was a student at the time, deep in studies, and it is surprising how much and how little I saw; surprising how aware I was, though wholly unaware of the silent stride of the times, which appeared in all their plainness only when they had passed away. But most surprising of all was how I went astray in my judgement of intimate friends.

Under stress of terror there is little honour and little faith. When a tyrant raises his ruthless hand, every man beneath him raises his hand as well, ready to strike where the tyrant strikes, and to add his approving blow – even against his dearest friends. If only one could speak across the years, waken one's forgotten self and whisper a warning word. But there is happiness in illusion, and perhaps it is better to leave one's youth in its dreams.

I lived in the village of Blankheim, which, with its long straggle of houses, lofty church, factory, school and lonely rural station, lay at a sharp bend of the Rhine. My rooms were in a fine old farmhouse, which must in years gone by have stood in pastoral isolation, but houses of a later humdrum style had crept along the road and cramped it in on either side until only its inner charm recalled a freer and grander past. To step across the threshold was to step into a bygone age.

It was a fine half-timbered building, with heavy oaken doorposts, open staircase and massive beams across the whitened ceilings, all of which I could touch with my loosely uplifted hand. To me it was a haunt of the quaintest shadows, and I was glad to linger at odd moments in its half-forgotten nooks and corners, and to study the century-old prints of the Rhine that hung obscurely here and there.

1

In true keeping with this air of long ago, with the cumbrous chest on which I often sat, with the dresser and its array of pewter and with the relics of the chase that adorned the walls, were the lantern lamps that hung from the joists or crowned the newels of the staircase that led to the galleried landing above. Most pleasing, however, was the impression of peace, and this was weirdly deepened by the solemn tick of the clock and by its slow ponderous chime, which raised an echo in every room.

In the deep peace of the house it seemed that time and life itself lay suspended in every note. Leaning on the banister, I would listen to each stately stroke and not until the last echoes had died away did I enter my little study. Here I could close the door on anything but my own thoughts. Here I had my bookcase, my work table, my couch and a spot for dining alone when I chose.

But the glory of the room was its two little casement windows. They looked out to the north-west over what was once the farmyard, now green with the grass and weeds that sprang between the cobbles. On either side of the yard were the empty stables and barns, though these were partly screened from view by two heavy chestnut trees. Beyond the wall ahead, however, was a far prospect of farms and fields, which stretched away to the greyish haze that hung above Cologne. On clear days, I could see low down on the horizon a tiny indefinite blur that marked the great Cathedral. And at night a soft glow from the city illuminated the clouds above.

I remember my first glimpse from those windows. It was All Saints Day, 1932, a day of rest and prayer in the village, and wondrously quiet on the Rhine. There, the barges lay at anchor and the only thing moving was the water as it lapped idly past the deserted ferry. I opened the casement and looked out over the grass-grown yard and the lane that ran beyond.

It was late afternoon, and the russet tiles of the barns and stables were touched with the fading glow of the setting sun. The evening greys were deepening fast, enlarging the shadows and blurring the distant trees and fields, which were soon lost in the veiling haze. Right opposite, on the farther side of the lane, and gleaming from a niche in the wall was a rosy Calvary light, which shone more brightly as evening fell.

I was about to close the casement when I observed through the branches of the chestnut tree that obscured my view to the west certain pricks of light in the gathering dusk. They were nearly a mile away. Perhaps they were torches, perhaps lanterns, some still, some moving, yet all growing slowly in numbers. A faint glow came up from the spot, strange, mysterious, indefinably pious, with the same consoling appeal as the Calvary light.

At that moment there was a step in the lane. An old peasant, arrayed in his clumsy best, came trudging along towards the distant lights. As he passed the lamp in the wall he bowed slightly and bared his head, and in a moment was lost to view. But as he turned I saw something that glimmered in his hand. It was a lantern.

Being young, curious and a stranger to life in the Rhineland, I decided to go and see what might possibly turn out to be a torchlight procession in the village. I hastily put on my coat, hurried down the staircase and in the hall met Herr Engels, a bluff old farmer and owner of the house, who looked at me keenly under his bushy brows. I seem to see him now, alert, erect, with the sun and wind of seventy years fresh in his vigorously lined face and defiantly outstanding beard.

At his feet was a candle lantern, and, as he stooped to pick it up, he turned to me and asked if I was going out. 'Yes. Should I take a lantern?' I asked, thinking of the cobbled street and the deeply rutted lanes.

A voice came from the landing. Frau Klebert, Herr Engels's daughter who helped to keep house for him, was leaning on the rail. 'No, Father's lantern is for mother's grave,' she said simply.

There was dead silence for a moment. I felt I was on delicate ground. I had blundered into another world of deep and silent traditions and was about to murmur apologies, but Herr Engels reassured me. 'Perhaps, where you come from, they do it tomorrow on All Souls, as is only right and proper. But here we do it on All Saints.'

'And tomorrow as well, of course,' added Frau Klebert. 'But go along with father. He will be glad of your company, and if you want to know anything of the Rhineland here nobody knows more about the lore and traditions of these parts.'

'I should be only too glad, but ...' I hesitated, because I still felt like an intruder. Fortunately, my old host cut all reflection short.

'Well, come along then. Perhaps you would like to carry the wreath.'

I had not noticed it before in the twilight shadows of the hall. On an old chest by the door was a heavy circular evergreen wreath, which Frau Klebert must have made from fronds in the garden – fir and holly for the most part, variegated here and there with a spray of bright red berries and with a few dark brown cones. Reverently I picked it up and followed Herr Engels into the street.

There were few people about. A little lower down on the opposite side was a small barber's shop, which seemed to serve as a meeting place for the young men of the village. Two or three were standing outside, including Matthias the barber. They all greeted us respectfully, and gazed steadily after us as we stumbled over the cobbles or picked our way among the pools.

'Quite a nice lad, Matthias,' said Herr Engels. 'Keeps himself respectable and supports his father and mother. And a good Catholic too, despite the hot politics that are debated in the shop.'

'I shall try him tomorrow,' I said, thinking my host's remarks were a kind of recommendation.

3

'Think twice before you do. If you are content with a rustic crop, all right. He simply harrows it off. But if it's a city trim you are after you are likely to leave his shop with a head like a load of hay. But look out!'

I had to skip over a pool. Such a bumpy street it was, with a strange wriggle of houses on either side. Some jutted forward, their doors and windows flush with the road; others stood back in a courtyard, screened from view by a carriage gate. Here a cottage was cramped between two lofty gabled neighbours, there a modern shop window suddenly abutted on a venerable garden wall that looked half forgotten beneath its fringe of creeper.

No one met us on the way, though my companion must have touched his hat and greeted a dozen times. I kept looking to right and left, a little puzzled. But finally, as he doffed his hat yet again I saw a curtain moving to the right. I understood.

'These villagers don't miss much,' I observed.

'Not much. It's like a whispering gallery here. What you mutter at one end of the village is loudly echoed at the other. The more you hide, the less you conceal.'

'Then I suppose they'll know me well by now?'

'Back into the third and fourth generation. But please don't take it amiss. It is the simplest and happiest pastime in the village. And what else have the people of Blankheim got beyond their weekly trip to Cologne? So let them have their peep into the street, their glimpse of life as it hustles by. Imagine, Mr Arnold, what speculations they have on even the most trifling things!'

Yes, a most innocent pastime, but a time was soon to come when I never went into that village street without feeling in a blind uncanny way that I was being observed. I suddenly became aware of a look, of eyes, of a peeping furtive face which, with the tremble of a curtain, was gone. I felt it even at night when the shutters were closed and the whole street was lost in darkness. Year by year it grew until finally it haunted me more than the frankest gaze of the Gestapo.

And then the stare of Matthias and his friends – but I anticipate. I am still in the carefree days of 1932 when a look meant nothing more than friendly interest. One had but to see a face to read the thought behind it; thoughts were still free.

A few steps up the lane we passed a villager, a strapping young fellow with a strangely frustrated air. He looked like a tramp to me with his dusty boots, his workaday things, his lack of a collar and tie. All Saints Day meant nothing to him, I thought, or perhaps he had nothing better to wear.

'Good day, Hans.'

'Good day, Herr Engels,' and he passed us with the merest touch of his cap. But a moment later he turned and called.

'Oh, Herr Engels, is the lorry going to Cologne tomorrow?'

'Why, have you got some baskets ready?'

4

'Yes, if you don't mind?' He had a haggard, colourless face, pale grey eyes and thin lips. He seemed harried and underfed to me, and there was embarrassment in every word he spoke.

'Certainly. Give them to Fritz. You want them delivered to the Haymarket?'

'Yes, and thanks very much.'

'Don't mention it.' And we passed on.

'That's Hans Zimmermann,' said Herr Engels after a moment's pause. 'Poor unfortunate fellow, married with three children. Joined the Communist Party and lost the sympathy of the village. Then lost his job at the factory for trying to organise a strike. And now he lives – well, you have seen him. Lives anyhow. Does odd jobs, catches moles, fishes in the Rhine, while his wife, poor thing, washes, weaves baskets, goes cleaning, anything to earn a copper.'

'So he's the black sheep of the village?'

'No, no, I should never say that. He is just a man who has lost his way in life.' Here my old friend stopped and, pointing with the stem of his pipe to the church, which loomed up darkly near the bank of the Rhine, he dropped his voice to a whisper.

'And the secret is, he is a man who has lost God. Yes, Mr Arnold, he is a man who has lost God. And having lost him, he has taken to clutching at straws, living from hand to mouth and from minute to minute, never knowing what the next will bring.'

'And yet he is not a wastrel?'

'By no means, but because the straight way offers no hope he is dreaming of crooked ones. He talks of revolution, of bloody revolution. Yes, his only hope is in a national crash. For in the general scramble for property and power such men rise to the top. But let us go on.'

My friend was a supporter of the old order, and judging from his earnest words he had his foreboding of things to come. But he felt no bitterness on that account, just a sense that the old traditions were passing and with them all that he had loved. Suddenly, as we reached a clump of trees, he stopped and turned round. Screened by the shadows he gazed at Hans's retreating figure and spoke as though to himself.

'Yes, Mr Arnold, in a general ferment such men rise to the top. And a bad servant makes a worse master.'

'But I don't understand you, Herr Engels? What's the trouble? There's surely no danger from a man like Hans.'

'Maybe not. But his type is multiplying. Men in a hurry, you know. Men who cannot wait. Men who, if they got the power, would try to gallop the ploughing horse. And Hans is such a man; a simple man in a rush; a man who thinks you can hatch an egg by boldly cracking the shell. But come on. It's getting late.'

It was dusk, and the road before us was solemnly still. Ahead was the little cemetery which, with its dark hedge and blur of trees, stood out in vague shadow against the twilight grey of the fields. But what drew my interest most was the strangely luminous haze from the many lantern lights that lent a spectral tone to the hallowed spot.

A few minutes later we had entered the rustic gate, to see the long rows of lanterns burning dimly on the graves as a symbol of home and comfort to those who would know them no more. Some of the peasants were kneeling. I had never felt so deeply the solace of prayers until then.

The grave we sought was near the gate, beneath an overhanging tree. I laid the wreath on the stone, and I tactfully turned away up the cemetery path.

Looking back, I saw the grave in deep shadow, the old man kneeling by the glimmering light, and the vague forms of peasants as they moved in the dusky gleam of the lanterns or knelt in silent prayer by the graves. Perhaps later thoughts have enhanced the scene, deepened the gloom of the trees and tombs, and lent a ghostly glow to those simple candle gleams. It may be so. There was a touch of eternity about it, about the willows, the graves, the peasants and the fitful flame of the lamps. There was a hope beyond despair even in these flickers over the grave. But more and more in my memory of the scene is the sense of something gone and of a past that would never know again the grace of a coming spring.

Germany seemed to me then a land of simple piety, far from the loudness of life and the tramplings of modernity.

I walked back. Herr Engels was standing by the gate talking to someone in the shadows. It was Rektor Barth, a tall elderly priest from a village on the Mosel.

'Beautiful custom,' I said, as we shook hands.

'Yes,' he agreed, 'and a comfort to us all.'

We set off for the village with Rektor Barth between us chatting like an old friend.

'Do you know why the spot was chosen?' he asked.

'No.'

'Well that's a story for Herr Engels. He's our authority for all the folklore here.'

Herr Engels was quietly lighting his pipe. 'Do you see that clump of trees over there?' he said. 'There was a cross on that spot, erected centuries ago in memory of a peasant struck by lightning as he was ploughing his little field. It was there when the Russians came in the winter of 1813. They were quartered in the villages for weeks.'

'Your grandfather actually saw them,' interjected the Rektor.

'Yes, he was a boy at the time and fled with the women and children to the woods. But the Russians were poor and ignorant fellows and did no one any harm. It was lucky that the people had fled, though, because typhus broke out among the troops and they died off in scores. A deep trench was dug near the cross, and there they lie buried, about a hundred or more, just tipped in from a cart, so my grandfather said. Trees were planted near the spot and it was later made into a cemetery.'

We stood for a few moments while the old man poured out these memories. There was history in every word he said and, standing there on the lonely road, with the village, fields and river enshrouded in the gathering darkness, I felt I was listening to the very echoes of the drums of the Grand Army.

He had another reminiscence that night. We turned off through some woodland down to the bank of the Rhine where the path led back to the village, past the rectory and the church. Out on the silent river lay the sombre shadows of the barges, their lanterns and cabin lights sending dim rippling streamers over the waters. We passed a solitary bargeman standing on the bank, and his long low whistle for the boatman to take him back to the barge seemed to linger on in the gloom. We went on, and his dark figure was lost in the night as an answering whistle came from the barge. Suddenly my companions stopped.

'Here is the spot. Just lend me your stick, Mr Arnold.'

Herr Engels pushed the brushwood aside and revealed with the aid of the Rektor's torch a fallen stone. It might have been a cross, but the upper part had gone. But no. A flash of the torch revealed it lying two or three feet away. There was a simple inscription:

> Sacred to the memory of Marcel Rollet
> of Nancy
> Murdered here while doing his duty, 1812
> R I P

'Heavens,' I recoiled, 'murdered?'

'Yes, another tragedy of those terrible years. This French soldier Rollet was one of a military escort taking a young deserter back to barracks. The deserter was a youth from Blankheim who had been recruited by Napoleon's armies, and when he got near the woodland here he made a desperate effort to escape. He suddenly turned on Rollet, threw him to his death in the icy river, grappled with the other escort for a moment or two and then escaped into the wood.'

'But who erected the cross here?'

'The villagers, I suppose,' said Herr Engels, 'perhaps of their own accord, perhaps at the instance of the authorities. You see, we belonged to France at that time. But the villagers, I think, would have set up a cross here in any case, even though the poor victim was a Frenchman. Nationality here in the Rhineland is forgotten in the grave. After all, the man had a father and a mother. He was a Catholic, too, and shared in the sacrament of Christ. God rest his soul.'

The old man took off his hat and crossed himself in silent prayer. The priest followed his example.

'We ought to set it up again, Herr Rektor,' he added after a pause, 'and renew the inscription, I think.'

'Yes, I shall see to the matter. I shall speak to Heinrich about it. He'll restore the stone just for the love of doing it. If there are any expenses we shall pass the hat round at the next club meeting.'

But Herr Engels said, 'Just leave the expense to me. These memorials must be preserved.'

And without a further word we moved off home. In any other time and place this concern for the soul of a stranger who had died over a century ago would have seemed to me most strange. But somehow on that night I was deeply aware, as never before, that it was the eve of All Souls.

The custom of remembering the dead was wholly in keeping with the mediaeval glamour of the Rhine, which was silently glinting along in occasional gleams from the barges, with the misty gloom of the path flanked here and there by gaunt and skeleton willows. Ahead was the homely spill of light from the inn as we trudged up the village street, and beyond that the tinted windows of the ancient church were aglow to the glory of All Saints. It was all so much in keeping that, like my companions, I doffed my hat as we passed on our way home.

That night I was to learn just how much in keeping it was. I joined my hosts after supper. Herr Engels had lit his pipe, and there was a strange air of long ago in that old and intimate room.

A friend or two had slipped in for a chat and perhaps for a hand of cards: Lambert, the local solicitor, a gaunt problematic man with heavy spectacles and peering gaze; Frenzel, a prosperous land agent, auctioneer and valuer; and Joseph Engels, the eldest son, who was a jeweller in Cologne. Klara, Frau Klebert to me, was settling down to some knitting.

I fell at once into talk with her, giving my impressions of the walk. She was keenly interested in what I said, above all in my reactions to the beautiful custom of All Souls. We spoke in undertones for a time, for the gentlemen were talking politics, at first in a general, impersonal way and then, as the dispute sharpened, in louder and louder tones.

Joseph, a passionate Centre man with strong nationalist leanings, was declaiming his opinions with great gusto, while Frenzel, in a cheery and humorous way, was supporting more moderate views. According to Joseph, Hitler's Nazis were preferable to the Communists, but Frenzel was wishing a plague on both their houses.

At times, Herr Engels intervened with a shrewd and decisive remark, but Lambert – the quizzical man with the glasses – just listened and said nothing. He did not even blink when Joseph, in the heat of the discussion, rose and thumped the table. He simply gazed and kept his peace. But Herr Engels had finally had enough with the complimentary mention of Hitler.

He rang the bell and the maid entered.

'Bring a bottle or two of Rudesheimer.'

8

The maid set the mats and glasses, and laid a pack of cards on the table. When she came again with the bottles the discussion had flared up again. But Herr Engels subdued it once more.

'Beware of false gods,' he warned. 'It is not the rosy skin that makes the apple. It's what lies unseen beneath. In judging things that are new, just wait until they lose their newness.'

Joseph interrupted, but his father silenced him with a gesture and told him to deal the cards.

The gentlemen were soon intent on their game and, having no taste for cards, I retired upstairs to my own thoughts.

Chapter 2

The Germans and the Jews

Blankheim had traditions, long haunting traditions that went back to the Middle Ages. It had an ancient church, the mossy wall of a former castle, and here and there in quiet corners a crumbling memorial. But that traditional part was not obvious as I looked from my bedroom window and allowed my eye to wander along that crooked trail of houses that marked the village street.

Perhaps the word village is a little out of place. It was not a village in the true sense; it had no unity of interest, no harmony of character, no even tenor of custom, life and thought. A second look told me why. To my left, at the end of the street, on the side that bordered the Rhine, was a dark, formless, sinister mass – a chemical factory as I later heard – and this touch of industry had laid its earthly mark on every house. Almost every building in the village was born of that brick and mortar heap, and the people, excellent in their way, were all in keeping with their homes. Villagers they never were – just an overdrift from the Ruhr, as ordinary and nondescript as the people of any town. And yet, in some ways, they were really countrified, as addicted to the village stare as any Farmer Giles.

I became addicted to the stare myself. At odd moments I used to stroll to the window and study the comings and goings of the people in the street: Hans Zimmermann with his fishing tackle strolling to the Rhine; Johann Zech, the postman, who came every day to the house and brought my copy of *The Times*; Rektor Barth, the priest, swinging along in his long black garb; and perhaps an occasional farmer pulling up at the Golden Hind. And I was not the only spectator. Matthias was always there, or seemed to be always there, gazing in his strangely abstract way at the children going to school or nodding to the factory hands as they crowded to and from work.

But what struck me most in those early days was the long procession of beggars. They were not the shabby professional type, but groups of unemployed who sang their way from village to village or played popular airs on fiddles, flutes and mandolins, and even danced to the music while one went round with the hat. There were in Germany in those days 6 million unemployed, and never had the streets resounded with such music, song and dance. Not even on the village fair days was there so much festive sound.

I saw much of them, and many a German song I learned by just standing at the window and throwing down a copper or two. They always stopped at the house, but they were really after bigger game. Right opposite was the house of the sisters Wolff, two Jewish ladies who had grown rich on a millinery business they ran on the ground floor.

Their fine old house, with its sedate stone front and grand oak door, its three tall storeys and lofty attic windows, commanded the whole village street, and I wondered how it had been bought from the copper takings of the modest parlour shop below. Whence were those priceless lace curtains and the genuine period furniture that an open casement occasionally revealed? And then the ladies themselves. Whence were those brilliant diamond rings, those strings of pearls and rubies, the rustle of rich silk as they stepped into some luxurious car when off to the theatre in Cologne?

But the shop was an innocent blind. The sisters had invested their money wisely within the village, providing mortgages and the like, and had bought houses and fields until their influence controlled the village. Wealthy they were, but won great respect in Blankheim by giving freely to every cause, and particularly to the Catholic Church, where they were almost held in reverence – that is, until the Nazis came.

After that they ranked as vampires, and every penny they received in rent and every farthing they gained in interest was branded as blood-sucking theft.

But that was later. All I saw at first was a dignified house of dark stone, which assumed a stately air between the mere dwellings on either side. It might have passed for the house of the local squire, but for the humble glimpse of millinery in the parlour window below. And it looked secluded, too, aloof and over-private. The door was rarely opened, and many a time I used to see people knocking and ringing without reply while the villagers at a respectful distance silently gazed and waited.

Those who knew the sisters well used to tap at the window on the other side, a code-like tap, so rumour went, whereupon a slide in the pane was drawn and a servant then conferred through the narrow slit. I witnessed this little domestic drama many times while people at doors and windows stolidly stared and ruminated. Perhaps my memory is playing me false, perhaps thoughts of the Gestapo have intensified the scene, but it seemed to me at such times that the street went strangely still. The very houses seemed to conspire in the dormant stare of Matthias.

It was here the beggars used to stop and make their most concerted effort with instruments and song. As a rule, a coin was thrown from one of the upper casements, sometimes copper, sometimes silver when women and children came along, and this, I am sad to say, was too often the case. No curtain was drawn back. No face appeared at the window. One saw just the flick of a hand, perhaps the servant's, perhaps one of the Miss Wolffs', and the casement closed again without a further sign.

11

At first it seemed mysterious to me, but in fact there was little mystery about the two Miss Wolffs. They kept their distance, of course, and they also kept their counsel, and to strangers they were non-existent. But to well-known beggars of the village access was easy. They just knocked at the lower pane and waited. Five minutes, ten minutes passed, when the lower casement was opened and the waiting beggar received not money but food.

I well remember the day when I first saw this happen. I was standing at the window with Tilde, the maid, who was talking to me of life in Blankheim and pointing out the people as they passed up and down. As we chatted, three children came out of a house and sauntered up the street. All three were neatly but shabbily dressed – to my mind very scantily, for a November nip was in the air – and their faces were pinched.

'Hans Zimmermann's children,' said Tilde. 'How cold those boys must be in their shirts and short pants!'

'Yes, the kind of rig the Bavarians wear in summer.'

'That's it. And they seem to be hungry as well. I'll wager they'll stop at the Wolffs.'

Sure enough, the three stopped opposite the house and stood for a time undecided. The youngest, a girl about nine, nudged and urged her older brothers who were not more than ten or eleven. Presently the eldest made up his mind and knocked at the window pane. It must have been a great decision, for all three turned away quickly and began to loiter about the road as though they had not knocked. Except the little girl. Every now and then she cast a longing glance at the pane.

'Well no one in the house heard that knock.'

'You can bet your life they did,' said Tilde. 'You know what Herr Engels says? The Miss Wolffs are like cats in a dark corner. They know to a tee what's going on, and hear and see every mortal thing. You wait.'

I waited, an age it seemed to me. And then the pane was opened. A hand appeared and three double slices were handed out. The elder brother who received them offered the first to the little girl. She lifted the upper slice and peered between. How her face beamed. I saw the motion of her lips.

'Cheese!' and as she began to eat she moved about with nervous joy, her blond curls falling over her cheeks as she bent her pale face to bite her sandwich. Her little frame was all of a quiver, impatient perhaps from hunger, perhaps from joy, or was she shivering in the bitter wind? And so they moved on up the street, all three munching away, busy, silent, absorbed, while Matthias and one of his friends at the door gazed without comment.

I might have lost myself in the same intense brown study, wondering why all our culture had not yet learned after countless years to still the hunger of a child, but for a quick step which sounded below. It was a boy, a dark-haired boy, well dressed and with a Jewish look, who walked straight up to the great oak door, which opened at once under the influence of his

12

coming and closed as subtly behind him. He appeared to come and go in the space of my hasty glance.

'Well I never,' I exclaimed, 'that beats the Arabian Nights. You've no need to say Open Sesame or even to rub a lamp. Your simple shadow is enough.'

'Yes, I told you,' laughed Tilde. 'That's Dr Cohen's boy. But there's Heinrich with his cart. He's going to set up the new memorial stone near the river.'

'To the Frenchman?'

'Yes, but I must be off to the kitchen.' And away she went, trilling some popular ballad while I studied Heinrich, the sexton of the church and a mason by trade, who was trundling his handcart up the street. So the Rektor had kept his word. I caught a glimpse of the dark stone together with a pick and shovel.

I had met Heinrich casually before, a slight man, somewhat bent in the shoulders, with a shaggy moustache and a rather fawning smile. One who could be all things to all men, or at least so I thought. He kept on stopping his cart to exchange words with all he met, and seemed to be nodding emphatic approval to everything he heard. He halted his cart at the Golden Hind and slipped in, perhaps to have a drink.

An hour later, after going to the post, I thought I would stroll up the Rhine and see the new stone in position. It was a blowy day with dark heavy rain clouds scudding over from the west. Out on the towpath the gusts were stronger, whistling through the sorrel and the faded weeds, and curling the swirling waters into instant wisps of foam. But apart from an occasional seagull swaying aloft in the wintry wind the scene was dead. Lines of barges lay idly in the river or floated like hulks at their moorings with the winter's sleep in every beam. Not a bargeman to be seen. Not a wisp of smoke from a single funnel. Not even the ferryboat was plying across the river. It lay moored to the landing stage, lazily swaying in the lapping waters. On that bitter November day desolation brooded heavily over the once so busy Rhine.

I stood for a while by some skeleton willows, listening to the dismal whistle of the wind and looking in a forlorn way at the path by which I had come. It was deserted. I was alone on all that length of river with no other company than my own depressing thoughts. I turned and continued my way to the copse which concealed the further reaches from my view.

Here the path curved off by the trees, the course of the wind was broken and, to my surprise, a long line of anglers came into view. They had all sought the shelter afforded by the woodland, and they stood, huddled in their coats, as glum and as silent as any queue of unemployed. For unemployed they were. Save for the scanty dole, they had no other resource in life than their fishing rods and lines. They seemed even more desolate than the rows of idle barges lower down the river.

13

Some yards further on was the cart, with Heinrich and two others tending to the stone. It was already in position and Heinrich was busy cementing the supporting stones at the base. He turned as I came up and greeted me in his usual effusive way.

'Good day, good day, Mr Arnold, good day. Bitterly cold, isn't it? Bitter.' And without waiting for an answer he went on, 'I shall be glad when I've got the stone up and am back in the village, I can tell you.' And he smiled and nodded vigorously.

'So the memorial's up once more,' I said, looking carefully at the stone and the new inscription, 'thanks to Herr Engels.'

'Herr Engels?' Heinrich looked puzzled. 'Herr Engels? It's the Miss Wolffs who are paying for this. You know? The Miss Wolffs. Just a word to the ladies from the Rektor, a casual word, he wasn't speculating you know, but mentioned it just by the way, and well there it was, a couple of hundred marks. Very decent of the ladies don't you think?'

'Yes, very decent.'

'Ach, what are you talking about!' One of the anglers was speaking, Alex Brechner, as I afterwards learned, a hard blue-eyed plumber who had been slowly elbowed out of the trade by the arrival in Blankheim of a modern sanitary engineer who had opened up a shop in the Hauptstrasse. The newcomer, Friedrich Kemp, by his skill and business enterprise, had gained every one of the contracts for the large extension of Blankheim that was rising beyond the railway. He was now a prosperous man and even had a job to spare for his unfortunate rival. But Brechner, who refused to be an assistant where he had been so long a master, was now left out in the cold.

'Decent, do you call them! Giving a couple of hundred after swindling a couple of million! Do you really call it decent to eat the fatted calf themselves and then fling us a couple of bones? I'll tell you this,' and here he waxed vehement, 'if those two blasted harpies were dumped now into the river everyone in the village would be a damned sight better off.'

I was taken aback by the outburst and by the angry flush on the man's face. Surely he must be suffering from some deep personal wrong, some grievance that was souring his whole soul and warping his judgement. What story might this man unfold? Some tragedy perhaps? Or just some feud of long years' standing by which, with every air of peace, village life is often riven? I stared at the man with interest.

'Better off?' I echoed, 'How do you make that out?'

'Why, they own the whole damned village. If both were emptied out our homes would be our own.'

'Yes, yes,' said Heinrich, 'our homes would be our own, mine would be mine, and his would be his, yes, yes.' And he nodded his vigorous approval.

'So it's a crime to own the village?'

14

'For Jews to own it, yes. We go out to fight for Germany. For four long years we battle and bleed in the hell of Verdun and the Somme, and when we come back to this homeland of ours we find it in the hands of Jews. You'd think we'd been fighting for Jerusalem.'

'Yes,' said Heinrich, 'you're right there.'

'Well, you've no complaint,' I said to Heinrich, 'they've given you a job at least.'

'No, in a sense I can't complain, no, I can't complain.'

'Rot!' interrupted Brechner. 'Think of it! Two hundred marks for a useless stone. Two hundred marks for a foreign soldier who died over a hundred years ago. Do you see any sense in it? I ask you. And we poor fellows are starving here and angling for beggarly fish.'

'No,' said Heinrich, 'there's not much sense in it really.'

'Not much! There's none at all!' Brechner's voice rose to a shout. He flared up against the 'Moses Brigade', and for a few storming moments I had my first glimpse of the anti-Jewish fury that was to sweep the whole of Germany. In such a form it was new to me. I had known of a dislike for Jews, of suspicion, of passive contempt and the like; and then the great figures of literature, Shylock, Fagin, Isaac of York, had helped to colour my rather neutral views. But hatred of the Jews, fierce and fanatic hatred, was a distant theme to me. There was something unreal about it, mediaeval.

I turned away to look at the stone now standing by the woodland edge of the path, a cross of black basalt which bore the old inscription to the soldier of Napoleon's army. It would look quite picturesque, I thought, when time had weathered the edges and when the weeds and wild flowers had clustered round the base once more and added the glows of nature to the sombre hues of the stone. But Brechner was not to be silenced. He kept on storming at the Jews in a most outrageous way.

'Well anyway,' I replied, 'the children have a friend in the ladies. I actually saw some getting a meal today.'

'Ach! Mere bread and butter, what's that?'

'What's that! It's bread and butter. Yes, it's bread and butter. And it's certainly better than no bread at all.'

'Nonsense! All the bread they give is a crumb to what they could offer. Just look at Hans here. They give his children bread, but they never let a penny off his rent and never will. They collect it to the uttermost farthing, don't they, Hans?'

'Yes, they collect the rent,' said Heinrich, 'every week, without fail.'

I turned to look at the other man who had been standing by without saying a word. It was Hans Zimmermann, the Communist, muffled up in his coat and scarf. I had not recognised him at first, but the half defiant look that lurked in his strange grey eyes and pale frustrated face was not to be mistaken. It was just a glance, however, and in the next instant he had turned away to attend to his fishing line. He had a bite and for the next few minutes the interest of the company was bent on catching the fish. I took

15

advantage of the break to walk off through the trees and to return to Blankheim down the lane.

I felt very out of humour. After all that I had heard I was happy to have no society but the wind and the occasional rain. I first went up to the bluff that lay beyond the woodland and looked back over the river to the distant deep blue line of hills on the far horizon. The Rhine! I have but to breathe the name and the thoughts that I pondered then, and which I fondly cherish still, return in a surging flood to my mind.

There is something in every glimpse of this historic river, something of legend and high romance, something of the long story of human nature and human destiny that has its silent poetry and mute appeal. Fragments of forgotten ages evoke it at every step, here a feudal ruin with its veiling cover of wild vine, there a tumbled cross with its hint of a tale half-told, the crumble of an abbey, the grass-grown scene of an old tradition, some echo of ancient song, an inscription, a name, and the fancy seems to vibrate with the pulse of a thousand years.

There is a touch of eternity in every passing wave, as well as a breath of our fleeting destiny in the everlasting hills.

I looked over to those distant Rhenish hills and felt myself in the presence not only of a land but of a people, a really human people, a people wholly at one with a great tradition. There was solace in the thought, and it helped me to forget many things that gave it the lie.

In fact, later on that very day, it saved me from graver doubts. I had gone to Bonn in the afternoon to get some books I had applied for at the library. The books were ready for me and I packed them into my bag – all but one. Its weight and size embarrassed me. It was a very ponderous volume, published in 1612, and entitled *Chronicles of the Free Imperial City of Speyer*. What a fine old folio it was, such a tome as the scholars of long ago were pleased to write and designed as a lasting challenge both to time and posterity. The librarian smiled grimly as he lumbered it over. I smiled grimly, too. There was no help for it, however. Packing it under my arm, I made for the station.

I was hardly past the Minster, however, and was hurrying down one of the cuts that led to the station, when a heavy shower drove me into a restaurant for shelter. Without the precious volume I might have hastened on, for the waiting train was only some three or four minutes away. But the risk of spoiling the tome was too great. And the lights and glow of the restaurant were certainly very attractive after days of quiet in the dim and humdrum village. So I entered.

It was just a little too early for the usual evening crowd and I was able to choose a corner spot where I could watch through the window the progress of the storm. It was clearly no passing shower, for the rain was pelting down on the dark and glittering pavements, which were now strangely deserted save for a hastening passer-by. An occasional motor swished past, seeming to leave the rain in more silent possession of the street. Night was rapidly setting in and the bright restaurant, with its glittering mirrors and spotless table linen, looked more and more attractive. I turned to the menu card, and after a long study decided for an evening meal. I should have time, so I reflected, for a long exploring peep into the ancient tome beside me. I looked up. The waiter, with his ready serviette on his arm, was eyeing me intently.

'You would like a suggestion, sir?' Willi was a great psychologist and, as I later discovered, could size up strangers to a tee.

'I should be obliged.'

His suggestions involved me in a long session, which became even longer when two young men I knew came in. They were both from the university and, spotting me at once, doffed their dripping hats and coats, and joined me. I knew them as men on the university staff aspiring to professorships, but having no salary other than their meagre college fees. Such men might wait for years before a vacancy came along, and until that time they earned a living by writing, tutoring, lecturing or filling temporary posts when the regular men fell ill. Bürger lectured on economics and Hillesheim on philosophy. However, though very able men, their circle of students was small. In view of their poor prospects, both were toying with the idea of a post in the USA, and that is how I came to know them. I had helped to translate their applications into English.

Bürger simply nodded his orders to Willi and settled down at once. Hillesheim preferred to study the menu card at leisure.

'We sent them off today,' said Bürger, referring to their applications. He was a man of ready speech and won much respect by his decisive air. He shrewdly concealed his youth with a dark and well-trimmed beard, and the mature expression it gave him helped to maintain his standing with the students. Hillesheim was clean shaven. He was golden haired, and a blond beard impresses no one.

'So you've lost all hope of a post in Germany?'

'Oh, not exactly all. There's a chance, but it is rather remote at the moment. Unless, of course, a timely bereavement ...' He broke off and smiled grimly.

'Some ill-wind that brings the windfall,' added Hillesheim.

Bürger laughed. 'Some gale you mean, to clear all the tangle of deadwood and leave light and air for the younger shoots. And I'm not speaking merely of the University of Bonn. Really, Mr Arnold, the cumber and lumber of old age lies like a deadening weight on the youth of Germany today. You see, the world is growing older and we, the dwindling youth, are bearing it all on our shoulders.'

'Only too true,' said Hillesheim. 'We lost the cream of our youth in the war and we, who have been left, are rather overshadowed. You can't expect a vigorous policy from those who are now in power. Old age is very conservative, and the older Germany grows, the deeper in the rut we shall get. As you can see for yourself, everything here is at a standstill, industry, commerce, farming, everything, and only a storm will get us going. I verily believe that a tornado, a thorough-going tornado, would do more good than harm.'

'A revolution, you mean?'

'A downright revolution.'

I nodded my head in a sceptical way, but Hillesheim was serious. He touched my arm in an intimate way.

'No, I'm not talking wildly, Mr Arnold. Technically speaking, I'm no friend of revolutions, and I've no desire to see the mere mob in control. But a revolution might, as in Italy, take place in an orderly way. By a sudden political coup, and with scarcely a tremor in the country. But it would have to be a revolution. For in politics, economics, finance, and even in philosophy, science and art we have reached a really dead end. Yes, a big upheaval in Germany would be better than staying in the rut. I say that as a philosopher.'

'And I say the same as an economist,' continued Bürger, who proceeded to describe the plight of Germany. It was a clear account of the crisis, ably and forcibly told and with a wealth of illustration, but it left me unconvinced. I felt it was Bürger's crisis, not Germany's. Had he been a professor and in receipt of an ample salary I should have heard a different tale. Even Hillesheim's comments, witty though they were, did not alter my impression in the least.

Willi came along with a *Hausplatte* for Bürger, a speciality of the restaurant. It was an ample assortment of meats and vegetables, which looked most impressive on the glittering silver plate. Hillesheim eyed it intently as he toyed with the menu card.

'And you, Herr Doktor?' asked Willi.

'I'll take a Hausplatte, too.'

'I knew you would. So I put in an order for two.' He turned and called to the apprentice underwaiter.

'Heinrich, bring the *Hausplatte*.'

'You really took the risk?' asked Hillesheim with a doubtful look.

'The rule is invariable. The gentleman who hesitates always decides for his companion's choice. Especially if the choice is a good one.' And off he went.

'First class waiter,' was Bürger's only comment.

'And a first class restaurant, too,' said Hillesheim with a critical glance at the tablecloths, the cutlery and the glittering appointments.

'Yes, Bonn's an excellent place in every way. Just look at this.' Bürger indicated the dish and, tucking in his serviette, settled down to his meal with every sign of satisfaction. He was obviously fond of life in the Rhineland. I sympathised with him.

'And there's really no chance of your settling down in Bonn?'

'Bonn! Phew!' Bürger was most decisive. 'You might as well wait for the consolation of Israel.'

Hillesheim tried to suppress a smile. 'You mean the traditional consolation as mentioned in St Luke?'

'Of course. The coming of the Messiah, you know, and the return of the long lost tribes to their home in Judaea.'

'To the lasting consolation of the Gentiles.' Hillesheim was smiling to himself and Bürger seemed to enjoy the reference. He laid down his knife and smiled his approval broadly.

'No,' he said at last, resuming his attack on the meal. 'It's a vain hope and a lost prayer. What interest have they now in returning to Judaea? The consolations they enjoy here are far more attractive than that. Just look again at this.' He indicated the meal. 'The fleshpots of the Rhineland are infinitely superior to the mouldy forgotten fleshpots of 3,000 years ago. They realise that too well. When you have a fillet of veal like this and a Munich beer to wash it down you lose all taste for manna and quails. What do you say, Mr Arnold?'

I hardly knew what to say, but Bürger did not wait for an answer. He was now at the top of his bent and well seconded by Hillesheim. He continued his fire of ironic comment when suddenly, with a low whistle, he pulled up dead. The door had opened, and a gentleman, an obvious Jew, had entered. He appeared to know my friends. We bowed.

'Good evening.'

As the stranger hung up his hat and coat Bürger gave me a meaning glance.

'Rosenbaum,' he whispered.

'Professor of economics,' said Hillesheim.

The professor stood for a moment, and gazed in our direction, but my companions made no further sign. Rosenbaum was immaculately dressed, with his faultless silk tie, his freshly ironed suit, which clipped him without a crease, and above all his aggressive cuffs, which stood out in dazzling whiteness. He gazed in our direction, but turned to sit elsewhere.

'You don't like Jews,' I observed.

'Rosenbaum is a Catholic,' said Bürger evasively, 'and a very able man.'

It was the answer of professional etiquette and I felt compelled to respect it. I was about to drop the subject when I suddenly changed my mind. After all the gibes I had heard against the Jews I decided to press the question. So I related the events of the morning with my reactions as an Englishman.

Bürger looked reflective.

'It's a ticklish question.'

'Yes, but you are assured of my discretion.'

'Well, as an Englishman, you say you have no animus against the Jews. I do not doubt it. England is an international power and a purely commercial power. You have no room for an animus of any kind. And then there's a second point. The Jews that land in England have already been laundered by *us*.'

19

'Laundered? What do you mean?'

'Laundered!' said Bürger decisively. 'Soaped, washed, ironed and laundered. You see, we get these people from the east, from the primitive depths of Poland where hygiene is wholly unknown. And so they wander into Germany, fetid, squalid, louse-ridden, with the filth of a lifetime on their –'

'Come on! Come on!' I could not suppress a laugh.

'But it's true –'

'Of a few odd cases.'

'Of more than you would think. I come, as you know, from East Prussia, and I have seen them crossing the border, carrying a tray of knick-knacks for sale as they go along. And in less than a year they are trading, in less than two they are dealing in cattle, in three they are lending money ad lib, and in four they are speculating in land, elbowing into mortgages and playing the country squire. There is not a village in the whole of Germany that is not in the hands of Jews. And when they are settled, they study law. And if you want to put my word to the test just go to the university. Go to the lecture rooms and have a look in. Do they study the arts? Not they! Medicine? A fair number. But go to the lectures on land law. You would think you were in Jerusalem.'

'Oh, come on!'

'But it's true!'

I thought the picture overdrawn and wondered how such an able man, reflective, sceptical, keen-witted, could lend himself to what I felt was an unreasonable racial hatred. I failed to understand the set intent of both my friends to see the worst side. For this they chose the worst example, some verminous intruder from the slummy depths of Poland, and displayed him as the typical Jew. Of the Jewish hold on the countryside and of their strangling effect on rural life I naturally could not speak. Save for the possible case in Blankheim, the charge was new to me. Yet there might be something in it. Or again it might be inflated talk. So I decided to press my questions.

'But supposing a Jew has been laundered. Supposing he has no interest in land and is no menace to rural society, what then? Take Rosenbaum for example. As far as laundering goes he can, to judge from appearances, give ample points to me and you. His interests are purely academic and he is, on your own admission, a scholar of the first water. Now what of him? You can't lump him with the backwash of the bucket shops of Poland. You can't condemn him and the rest, good, bad or indifferent, without one glance at the nobler side.'

'And yet I do.'

It was Hillesheim who spoke, the precise philosopher Hillesheim, with the reflective grey eyes of Schleswig-Holstein and with the tempered studious expression that one so often meets there. I was surprised. What

Hillesheim said, he meant, above all when he fell into a grave tone. He was echoing no idle talk.

'And that I say without reservations. Consider.'

Suddenly Bürger gave a low whistle and Hillesheim stopped abruptly. I looked up.

'Good evening.'

A young doctor, house surgeon in one of the hospitals, whom I had met some days before, had joined us. Heinrich Boden, like Hillesheim and Bürger, was a young and able man without immediate prospects and likely, for many years to come, to be dangling low in the waiting list for inclusion in the official roll. *Numerus clausus*, they called it, namely the restricted number or quota of members allowed in any profession, and young men used to mention it as the theologians of long ago used to mention the elect – not merely with wistful longing, of course, for passions were brewing steadily.

Envy, jealousy and bad blood had never been so rife as in those days of the slump, a really active envy that lent itself to blackmail. This was a sinister feature, especially in the younger men. With older men it was different. They were more resigned in misfortune, and sank without much protest into indifference and despair. But not the youth. They idealised their envy into a vigorous claim for rights.

It was so with Heinrich Boden. He was a heavy, plain, German type with a bullet head and a fresh complexion, and with a character in keeping with his looks. Stolid, conventional, strictly Catholic, an active Centre Party man, he was always thinking what the many were thinking, saying what the many were saying, and doing what the many did. In brief, a very very ordinary man, with a very very ordinary mind. And yet he was a bustler with it, loud, dogmatic, aggressive, as though each commonplace he uttered was news of prime importance.

He prized his niche in university circles, paraded his professional know-ledge, and in normal times he would have made it his one obsession. But the crisis gave him another one. Position, prosperity, pay had become the pivot of all his talk. His mind seemed to grovel in the things of earth. And he was not alone in this. In those days of the slump there was a definite lowering of tone and this seemed to ease the way for the brutalities that were to come. But I knew little about that then. To me Heinrich Boden was just another German, not a symbol of the worsening times.

There was clatter and commotion as he joined us. A table was shunted up to ours to accommodate the newcomer and in a trice our private circle was turned into a public meeting, with loud orders for this and that and a broad joke with Willi. I was keen on hearing Hillesheim, who doubtless had something to say, but Boden charged into the conversation and brought it to his own level. There was the beer, then the meal, and the conversation finally came round to the subject of a girl, Johanna, whom Boden was toying with the idea of marrying. She was the daughter of a noted professor, but ugly as the night, so Boden assured us. To marry her meant professional success, for appointments to high academic posts went, so they said, by family favour. And that was Boden's dilemma.

I felt it was time to go as the storm had blown over. Hillesheim raised his finger.

'I owe you an explanation. I shall not forget.'

'Thanks, when next we meet.'

'Good, I shall send you a note.'

And so I went back home. As I walked along the stillness of the Blankheim street, with its dark silent glimpse of the Rhine, I stopped for a moment to sense more fully the quiet of the night. The village was asleep, though there was a spill of light from the Golden Hind, and here and there a gleam from some window was reflected in the placid pools left by the rain. Politics seemed a far-off thing, revolution even further, and as for racial hatred – it seemed a fume of the city to me.

So unruffled was the whole scene, so restful the shadows under the starlit sky, that before I entered the house I lingered at the door for an instant and took a farewell glance along the street. But even as I did so there was a flick of light from the opposite house. A curtain was moved, just the thinnest rift, and then all was darkness again. A mere nothing one might think, a simple furtive peep, but it left a deep impression and seemed to follow me into my dreams.

Chapter 3

The Toy Nativity

Though during the week my home was as still as an abbey retreat, it had its livelier times. Every Saturday afternoon the children returned for the weekend, and the moment they entered the door they wakened every echo in the house. The two, Paul and Else Klebert, went to school in Cologne, and to save a journey every morning – a heavy strain for children since the school opened at eight – they stayed with their uncle, a jeweller who lived in the heart of the city. They loved their uncle and they loved Cologne, but they were glad to get back home to their simple village of Blankheim, to indulge their rural freedom to the full, and to relieve the pent-up feelings of five and a half long days at school. What a joy it was to both of them to roam in the woods and fields again, to visit their secret haunts in the empty barns and stables, or to gaze with an ever-welling interest at the tugs and lines of barges on the Rhine.

Else was about fifteen and Paul a year or so younger. I have never known closer companions than these two, for Else was cleverer than any boy in every rural pursuit – angling, trapping moles and squirrels, decoying birds with a whistle, paddling her little canoe or scampering on her pony along the towpath. She was light haired and fresh cheeked, the image of her brother, but though boyish, playful, roguish and always trembling on the edge of a laugh, she was as serious and reflective as old Herr Engels himself.

Christmas was not far off, and when they next came home there was something unusual about them, some air of pent-up mystery that showed itself in a host of hush-hush ways. There were nods, knowing glances, stealthy comings and goings, and both would strangely vanish for hours and then reappear without a word of explanation. I soon found out why.

It is a Christmas custom in Germany for every member of the family to have some present for the rest. Whatever form the present takes, it must come as a full surprise and remain a deep unwhispered secret until the solemn moment on Christmas Eve when father or mother rings the bell and all who have been waiting in the outer rooms throng in the tensest expectation around the festive tree. A carol is sung and then, in the cosy glow of the candle lights, each gives and receives his surprise. The surprise is always absolute. Each one not only admires but lo-and-beholds his gift.

But there is a pious and pleasing fraud about the whole of this pretty drama. Secrets are, of course, impossible in the family; they are secretly shared by all, especially if the presents from mother and the girls are knitted or embroidery work which requires long hours of preparation. You loyally look the other way or feign a deep oblivion of what anyone with half an eye would never fail to observe. You never ask what others are doing for fear of provoking a blush and an all-too-obvious fib. And then you never intrude. You halt even at open doors and give a discreet cough or wait in the outer darkness until the sudden rustle of concealment within has wholly died away. And finally when you enter the room you do it with the most unseeing eye, wholly blind to the fluster of others and rapt in personal thoughts.

But I, as a thorough outsider, was let into the deepest of secrets. Naturally, the deepest of all was that of Paul and Else, though Tilde, the maid, could hardly help knowing it, seeing she had charge of the rooms. The cook, too, was sure to be in the know, being Tilde's dearest friend, and the children's mother would certainly know all about it since she could read their innermost thoughts. And as for their grandfather, he was gifted with second sight. But they were all too loyal to let on.

The whole weight of the secret therefore rested on me, and I staggered under the gravity of all the oaths I had to swear neither by look, sign, word nor gesture to reveal what the children had in mind. They were building a new Nativity for Christmas, a new Bethlehem scene to replace the old one made by the family many years before. A really brand new scene, with a fresh consignment of figures, the Holy Family, the wise men, the shepherds, with flocks and herds and the eternal donkey, and angels hovering over all, and Herod gnashing his teeth in the distance and a glorious star of Bethlehem shining in the sky.

So one Saturday afternoon I was stealthily led by Else to their room in the far wing of the house. We might have been bent on murder so furtive were our steps. After a hush-hush knock at the door and the whisper of a password through the keyhole Paul unlocked the door and let us in. In a trice it was locked behind us and a cap hung on the key.

It was a typical children's room with a cupboard of books, a broad table and two or three wooden chests against the walls. There were shelves lumbered up with playthings, racks for whips and fishing rods, traps and sporting tackle, and the floor was cumbered with stuff from the chests. But what struck me most at first was the thing I had come to see, the Nativity set out on the table. It was a big thing, rather dusty and knocked about.

'So that's what you've been making on the quiet?'

Else rippled with laughter.

'No, that's the old one of course, made by father and mother when we were very young.'

'Yes, a most interesting bit of work, so why do you want to replace it?'

'We want something of our own,' said Paul. 'We are tired of seeing this, though I still do like it.'

'I like it too,' said Else, 'but just look at the figures.'

They certainly looked the worse for wear. I peeped into the central cavern, which was flushed with the gleams of a ruby lamp. There lay the Holy Child, rather battered from the tossings of years in the toy-box, and standing behind in rapt meditation were Mary, some tailless cows, St Joseph and a crippled donkey, while the shepherds with a flock of three and a half sheep and a goat balanced on some matchsticks were approaching in ecstasy from the fields. Simple as the scene was, it had an indefinable charm. As I looked at each figure I observed that the children were looking too, silently and wistfully, their eyes glowing with tenderness for what they had loved in toddler days.

'Poor thing,' said Else with comic pathos as she took up the holy child. 'A case for the child defence society, don't you think, Mr. Arnold?'

'I do. He has suffered a lot for his age.'

Paul picked up the figure and looked at it intently.'It's beyond redemption,' he said at last, whereat Else broke out into another peal of laughter.

'Paul, Paul! How can you say such things of the holy child?'

'But it's true, and further paint won't help him either,' said Paul in all innocence. 'We had endless trouble with him last year. Almost as much as with the three kings. There they are.'

Yes, there they were, the whole cavalcade; at first the negroes in eastern dress and bearing presents in their arms, and riding behind in elevated state were the three wise men themselves, one on a headless camel and another on a trunkless elephant, but splendid still, and bearing the blows of fortune and the rough and tumble of the toy-box with the sublimest unconcern.

'So, are you going to make the new one here?'

'No,' said Paul, who just smiled in his own quiet way, 'we are making it in Klassen's shed down the road. Herr Klassen is the headmaster of the elementary school. His boy, Ludwig, is making a Nativity for himself.'

'It was Ludwig who gave us the idea,' interrupted Else.

'Yes, and we are getting it ready with his help. Just the scene, the setting, you know.'

'But not the figures.'

'No, we've made those already in Cologne. And we are having a proper stable, with beams across the roof, and a loft and cows in the stalls and racks on the walls for rakes and forks and the like.'

'He has made it all by himself,' broke in Else, 'a wonderful stable, just like real ...'

'I shall show you,' said Paul.

Pushing the old Nativity aside, Paul rapidly set to work. He pulled the parts out of the paper wrappings in which they were concealed and began to construct his stable. Walls, roof, mangers, cornbins and racks were soon in position and the roof fitted on. Realistic little bundles of straw were stacked up in the loft, hay stuffed into the racks, and the cattle were fastened into the pens. Paul was a country boy, well versed in life on a farm and he had seemingly forgotten nothing, not even a dovecot on the roof. And then there were other things. There was the Holy Family to think of. What about them?

Oh yes, what about them? The afterthought about them came on me like a shock. I had been so fascinated by the realism of Paul's stable that I had forgotten the original purpose of the work. The stable was so lifelike, so true in its rural touches as to leave no room for idylls or romance. The pen on the extreme right had been reserved for the Holy Family, but they were as wholly out of place there as a herd of cows in a drawing room. Where was the magic of that wondrous night, with its mystic star, angelic song, and vision of a great light in the world of darkness? Where the spiritual mystery in the open face of day? I turned to look at the ladder which led up to the loft and at the cat alertly crouched on a bale of straw. How familiar it all was, how homely the little swallow that was nesting under the eaves! But I was looking at a German stable, at a typical stable of the Rhineland, and here in one of the pens was a strange intrusion from Judaea. What a truly alien thought! It surprised me like a burst of mocking laughter in an hour of silent prayer.

Else sensed there was something wrong.

'You don't like it?'

'I do.'

'But you are halting about something. You went quiet all of a sudden.'

'It's a really excellent stable, but ... ' Words failed me for a moment as Paul looked quite crestfallen.

'But what?'

'It's the most lifelike model stable I've ever seen, but it's not a Nativity.'

Both the children went quiet so I went on to explain.

'You see, the Nativity is just a sideline in your model, and a very disturbing sideline. The main interest here is the stable. It's a truly modern German one, but it ought to be an ancient glimpse from an almost legendary Judaea. The stable is better without it. But if this glimpse from old Judaea is really what you are after, the modern German stable must go.'

'So you think the old Nativity better?'

'For the purpose of a Nativity, yes. Every feature in the scene fits the simple wondrous story better; the gloomy rocks, the bare, dark, mysterious cave, the Holy Child in the manger, are more in line with traditional Nativities. You see, by disturbing tradition you disturb a great deal more. It is well to beware of novelty in things of this kind. Bring in something new and you are forced to cast out something old – the whole Christian story, in fact.'

I felt quite sorry for Paul, he looked so downcast.

26

'And there is nothing we can do about it?' he asked.

'We shall have to think about it.'

Then Else had an idea. She leaned over the table and turned the stable round so that its open side faced the front. The manger was now in the centre of the scene with nothing to disturb its full effect, while the ruby lamp, brought more to the front, left the rest in a shadow.

'Perfect!' was my judgement. 'It couldn't be better.' All that was German and modern was lost, and Joseph, Mary and the rest, who had looked so strangely out of place in their flowing, eastern robes, were now fully in keeping with their simple rustic setting. All was traditional, biblical, Hebraic, the real mediaeval vision, and the more I looked, the more I forgot the irony of it, that troubling problem of Jew and Gentile.

'But what about the background now?' asked Else.

We decided to go down the road to Klassen's house and see what was to be done. The sacking was there, the glue when we wanted it, together with the new setting which young Ludwig Klassen had modelled for himself. It was in the shed at the back, hardening out, so Paul said, and waiting to be tinted into the natural tones of a rocky hill. But Ludwig had left a hollow at the base in which to place the manger scene. This was the traditional cave which he intended to fit out as a stable.

Klassen's house was on the other side half way to the Golden Hind. We could have knocked at the front door or even tapped at the window, which was flush with the street, but Paul pushed open the wicket in the great carriage gateway and we stepped into the yard. A quaintly cobbled yard it was, such as one sees in rural parts far away from the bustle of the towns. I hardly knew which took me most, the dainty deep-set windows of the house, the benches on either side of the door for use on summer days, the balcony that ran right round and formed a sort of open arcade beneath the projecting eaves, the pious inscriptions on the timbers, or the carvings.

These and other features made their special appeal. How lovely these old half-timbered houses are! And yet from the street there was no hint of the charm of this one. We stepped from the humdrum street into the revelations of another age.

As we entered Ludwig came out, a sharp-featured boy with a pale face and dark hair, perhaps as young as Paul, but taller and with more commanding ways. He was the son of the village schoolmaster and showed the signs of discipline. He had the makings of a martinet, I thought.

'Ah, Else, Paul!' he said curtly. He stopped and made a stiff bow to me. 'Good day, sir.'

'We've brought Mr. Arnold along to see the work we are doing,' said Else, and she proceeded to explain. Ludwig made another bow.

'Ludwig Klassen,' he said by way of introduction. 'I'm pleased to meet you.'

He led us into the shed on the left and switched on the light for it was getting dusky. It was a tool shed and workshop, and on the bench by the window was a dark mass, a structure of glue-stiffened sacking, the setting of a Nativity. Just like the old one at home, a steep rocky hill, flattened at the top where Herod's castle was to be built and having a cave beneath, though this was squarely modelled and designed for a stable with cattle and pens. It was hard and dry and ready for the paint.

'You couldn't do better than this with all your fancy stables,' said Ludwig in his curt way. 'The cave, you see, is quite square and I can make it just as real as yours with only a thousandth of the work.'

Paul was silent.

'Just make one like this,' went on Ludwig. 'There's your sacking, there's the glue, and I can help you to make it if you like. Just soak the sacking and put it on a frame of boxes and things and there you are. Making the cave square is the trickiest job, but you leave that to me. You'd only make a mess of it if you tackled it yourselves.'

'No, we are sticking to our plan, Ludwig, thanks, but ...'

'But you can't make it fit. This and your fancy stable just won't go together. That's flat. If the stable idea had been better I should have made one myself. You trust me for that.'

Paul and Else looked most undecided. They gazed a little blankly at the sacking in the corner, the untidy bucket with the hardened trickles of glue down the side, the heap of sticky trimmings on the flags which had still to be cleared of the debris. Otherwise the shed was a model of neatness, the walls being thoroughly limewashed and reflecting the light in a brilliant way. Every tool and utensil was in its proper place, the boxes and tins well arrayed on the shelves, while the derelict parts of apparatus such as machines, cycles, clocks and wireless parts were arranged as in a shop. The hand of the school director was seen in every detail, save where Ludwig had been. The bucket and sacking looked very dismal, while the stains on the floor with the debris promised plenty of sloppy work ahead. Else turned rather blankly to me.

'What do you think, Mr. Arnold?'

I was given no time for reply. A footstep sounded outside, and in came Ludwig's father, sharp featured as Ludwig, with a cutting expression and looking no end of a martinet with his closely cropped moustache and short pointed beard. He greeted us with routine correctness, then flashed a glance at the mess on the floor. 'So you left it like that last night?'

Ludwig flushed and stammered apologies.

'I expected to continue with Paul's crib and ...'

'Discuss the matter later with me.'

Ludwig, aghast, addressed a breathless 'Excuse me' to us and then left in nervous haste. We three felt a little embarrassed, but Herr Klassen looked wholly unmoved. He was clearly a man for discipline and exacted obedience at the sword's point, but he was well informed, quite affable and understood our problem. He discussed it for a few minutes and finally made a remark which gave us a clue.

28

'You see, Paul, your stable seems to me like a scene from a puppet theatre. It does not strike me as a real Nativity. I confess I am a man for the old traditions, and a foe to all newfangled ideas and modern theories of this and that. What Ludwig is making is conventional, I admit, but it is none the worse for that. It is what we knew in our childhood and it appeals. But you have no need to consider my taste in the matter. If you want to have a stable, have one. But what about your grandfather? Have you considered his reactions to it?'

'No.' Paul's reply was a mere whisper.

'Well, like myself, he has no love for the modern craze of letting the youth take full control, reorganising this and that, altering customs and old beliefs. He might perhaps be very displeased. No, get back to the old crib, I say.'

'We shall think about it,' said Else quickly and she turned to the door to go. Then suddenly turning back she faced Herr Klassen in her most winning way.

'You must forgive Ludwig, of course. You see, we should have come last night in order to make our crib and he put everything off in the thought that we would come. He wasn't really neglectful. And so he mustn't be punished. We have your promise, Herr Klassen.'

She put it in such a decisive way that, though Herr Klassen was taken aback, he couldn't suppress a smile. He gazed open-eyed at her pretty insolence and simply gasped out, 'Oh!'

'Yes, I know you will be nice about it, and thanks for your kind advice. Well, good night, Herr Klassen!'

He gasped out another 'Oh!' and showed us out by the wicket gate. But as soon as we stepped into the open street Else joyfully clutched Paul's hand.

'Paul, Paul, I have got the clue. Just the very idea we wanted. Can you guess?'

'No!'

'No? Why, he gave us the hint.'

'What hint?'

'The puppet theatre of course! We shall paint a scenic background with the inn and the village and the hill. We shall have an arching heaven and the Bethlehem star and the angels either painted or tacked on.'

'On the ...'

'On the canopy above stretching over like the roof of heaven. It's all far better than a cave. And the inn, the houses, the barns need not all be painted of course. We shall tack on the wooden fronts to the scenery and Miss Logau, our drawing mistress, can paint in the side perspectives as she did in our old puppet theatre.'

'Of course!' said Paul, 'A grand idea! We've no need for the glue or the sacking.'

'No. Three-ply or cardboard will do.'

Paul stood still in wonderment. Even in the dimness of the village street it was easy to see how pleased he was. He was standing spellbound, for one of his earliest delights was a puppet theatre with its little luminous vision of a world in the bigger world of a dark room, and with a sense of Christmas in the scene and of the wondrous tree hard by and the inner glow of home. How often had he told me of it, this great revelation of his toddler days, and here was the old idea again in a far grander setting and on a truly magic stage.

'Oh, yes,' he kept on saying to himself, and turned off in a muse. We followed him, while Else talked and planned until in the space of a few minutes we were almost persuaded the thing was done and we had only to return home to see it fixed and arrayed in all its glory beside the Christmas tree.

Chapter 4

The Kevelaar Club

What a power Christmas still exercised in the heart of Europe in those days. It touched the drab December days with a strange radiance, lending a festive glint to the winter storms, and kindling in the darkness the deepening glows of hearth and home. For in the gloomiest phase of the year the soul, by virtue of Christmas, has its season of light and joy. Indeed the gloom is a welcome setting to this greatest of all celebrations, the coming of God, the gospel of peace, the promise of life eternal. Thus the sleet, the frost and the snow, which in a wholly natural world would spell the end of hope and happiness, assume in the lengthening shadows of the year an almost mystic lustre, and give an accent to inner gladness that summer, with all its glories, and even the grace of spring, could never evoke. For the delights of summer are given, but those of winter are earned, and being earned is a thing of the spirit.

I never felt it so much as then, in 1932, when Christmas was drawing near. For life in the Rhineland, from the heart of the busy city to the loneliness of woods and hills, is wholly within the tremor of the church bells. In whatever sphere you moved there was some response to the chime, some echo of the great tradition, some accent that everywhere lurked in the language, subtly controlling speech and thought, and giving even to the vilest curses a strict canonical form. And this was true not merely of festival days when the whole province was afoot, the streets gay with bunting and the buildings quivering with the clangour and swell of the great Cathedral chimes; but also of those humdrum days, when everyone was on business bent and thoughts of God were thronged from the mind. Even then, there was still the deep undertone that attuned all life to the one key. Neither the anti-clerics nor the ungodly escaped it. Even in the lowest tavern brawl we heard the voice of the church. Even in the fumes of pipe and can there was still some presence of God.

I fell to its influence myself. How could I withstand it, living in the fold as it were, breathing the air of the faith and complying out of courtesy to the countless little customs so natural in a Catholic land? And how could I refuse it when I saw the faces of the Klebert children, so tense and so expectant at every thought of Christmas, so brimming with their little plan that I found myself in the same brimming mood, and almost babbled the secret?

It was early on the Monday morning and the children were leaving for Cologne. Frau Klebert outside was seeing to the satchels and Herr Engels was turning from the breakfast table to fill his great Dutch pipe. I had come down later than the rest and was waiting to be served.

'Not a syllable,' whispered Paul as he bade me goodbye.

'Sh,' muttered Else with her finger to her lips. 'But you have not read your note.'

I had not noticed it before, a little tinted envelope under the saucer. The children bustled out and when the turmoil of parting had died away I picked it up and read it, an invitation from the Miss Wolffs. I am afraid I drew a breath. Strange how, in a month or two, I had become over-sensitive to Jews. The obsession of others had subtly become my own, having stolen on me day by day without a move on my part, but solely by the silent response of mind to mind. The obsession was in the air, and just as I was inhaling beliefs I was no less absorbing bias. The reflection took me aback.

'Of course you will accept?' Herr Engels was eyeing me steadily. He drew a similar envelope from his pocket. 'I suggest next Sunday evening.'

'Good. Next Sunday evening. I shall let them know.'

'You can leave it to me, but you seem rather hesitant. Perhaps it's not convenient?'

'Oh, it's all right. I should be glad to go.' An awkward moment followed, and I tried to end it by adding, 'I want to know as many people as possible while I am here. I'm really glad to go.'

I shouldn't have said 'really'. It seemed to give me the lie, and my old friend sought at once to reassure me.

'You'll be pleased to meet them, Mr. Arnold. The Miss Wolffs are excellent people, well bred, well travelled, well educated. An evening with them is an evening well spent. And they are highly respected in the village, despite all the rumours the other way.'

'Yes, I have heard some.'

'But not a syllable of proof.'

'No.'

'Nor ever will. Dross every one of them, Mr. Arnold. You know, rumours are like bad coins that everyone will pass and none will ever own. I have tried to track these rumours down. I have put the bluntest of questions, who and when and where and what. I might as well have looked for a lost drop in a rainstorm.'

'I suppose envy of their wealth is the real source?'

'Well, that's one source. But another is that they are not of the village, neither country people nor countrified. They have the tone and manners of the great city, the aloofness of an upper class. They never gossip. They are as tight on themselves as the lock on the door. And that is the main reason. Rumour is rifest where least is known. If your tongue does not wag in a village, the village will wag it for you.'

At that moment Tilde came in with my breakfast and Herr Engels lapsed into silence. But Tilde had heard the last sentence and joined in the talk. She was young and fresh, and her prattle was a joyous offset to the sententious speech of the old man.

'Wag is the right word, Herr Engels. The village will wag it for you. My word, they wagged it for me. I hadn't been here a week before I heard that I was engaged to a man I didn't even know. To a man I'd never seen. And they'd have fixed me up at the altar if they hadn't engaged me to another.'

'And then the Miss Wolffs. What awful stories. They don't even stop at murder. Think of it, Mr. Arnold, murder!'

Tilde was now in her stride, and I confess that my interest was fully in step. I was ready for the lowest scandal.

'Murder!' I echoed, and waited with bated breath for a revelation. But Herr Engels cut it short. He had no ear for scandal.

'Rumours don't stop at murder, but good manners do. I shouldn't like these walls to hear such stuff, for this rumour would intrude its evil note into all we say and hear. This has been my home for nearly eighty years, and there's something of myself in every atom here, something of my father, my mother and my family, and it's something that will live here when I'm gone. Let us keep the spirits of the house unflecked, let us keep their voices pure.'

'Lord!' broke in Tilde, 'What a wondrous man you are, Herr Engels. You don't really think I believe such stuff. Of course it is very bad, but, to tell you the truth, Herr Engels, personally I like hearing the worst.' And she broke into a peal of laughter. 'It's so interesting, and when you've heard it, well, you've heard it. They can't say anything worse than that, and when they've said the worst, bless us, you know where you stand. Really, I think I enjoy it.' And she broke into laughter again.

'I suppose you do,' said the old man with a quiet laugh. 'It goes well with the clatter of pots and pans.'

'And it goes well with the clink of glasses, too,' laughed Tilde. 'We women are not the only ones who gossip about other people. And what is said in the kitchen is nothing to what is said in the Golden Hind. They talk the very dregs there.'

'Yes, when they have muddled to the bottom of the barrel. But as I say to the members of the club when we have our monthly meeting there, "Every word after the first bottle is strictly out of order". And the rule is enforced with rigour, I can tell you.'

'Well, of course, Herr Engels, I wasn't thinking of you. And I wasn't thinking of the members of the club, who are the best gentlemen in the village, but men of the other sort go there, and they belch up some terrible stuff.'

'Which is no reason for belching it back.'

'What is this club, Herr Engels?' I asked, eager to turn the conversation. At that moment, however, Frau Klebert came in and Tilde discreetly withdrew. Not that Frau Klebert was aloof or dominating, but she kept the maids' talk to the kitchen whereas the old man encouraged the feeling of freedom. It led to openness, honesty, straight conduct. As he shrewdly said to me once, at home every whisper is overheard.

'It's the Kevelaar Club,' said Frau Klebert, settling down to her breakfast. 'Kevelaar's a place of pilgrimage near the Dutch frontier. It's a popular custom to go there and the people go in company. Most of the gentlemen have been together, perhaps more for pleasure than spiritual benefit. Hence the club. They meet at the Golden Hind and discuss old times and times to come in bottles and bottles of Rhenish wine.'

'Come on! We have a more serious purpose than that.'

'You, perhaps, and one or two others. For the rest, it is a mere blind.'

'But the purpose is always there, presiding at the meeting, pervading it like a spirit. We always have some charitable business, and there's a prayer before and after when the Rektor comes along, so it is not just an aimless drinking bout, as my daughter would have you believe.'

Frau Klebert smiled impishly as she sipped her steaming coffee. She was usually very serious but she could look as mischievous as Else when she liked.

'Perhaps not, but it's a grand escape from the apron strings, and Kevelaar's an excellent pretext. It is like the old indulgences, Mr Arnold. Be a pilgrim once to Kevelaar and you've the right to be a pilgrim for ever more to the village inn.'

'Come on! Believe me, Mr Arnold, we all return as we went, without a stagger. We should be a graceless lot if we babbled our farewell prayer from the bottom of the barrel. Come with me, Mr Arnold, next Saturday and see for yourself, and meet the worthies of the village. It will be an experience for you, a glimpse into our life on the Rhine.'

I accepted gladly, and so it was that the next Saturday evening I went along with my friend to the Golden Hind. There was an unusual stir in the street, the windows were aglow, the few shops bright and busy, the villagers standing about to share the last sensations of the day. Matthias and his friends were there to ponder about us as we passed, and I am sure they kept on pondering until we were lost to view. How it all comes back to me now, that strangely tense scene in the village street.

In the distance there was a muffled roar of voices, far-off singing and cheers that grew louder and louder with occasional calls like a war-whoop. Herr Engels noticed it, too, and looked back once or twice, but did not speak. He was too busy picking his way among the cobbles and greeting the people on the way. Then we reached the Golden Hind with its glowing sign and spread of light on the road. Herr Kiel, the proprietor, a short, stout, elderly man with a heavy white moustache, was standing at the door. He greeted us in a familiar way.

'It will be a problem if they pull up here,' he said, with a nod towards the source of the noise.

'Who?'

'The people from the rally, the big rally at Cologne, the Nazis, you know. Ah, here they come.'

As he spoke a heavy lorry appeared, slowly rumbling up the bumpy street. It was packed with cheering figures who were leaning out and shouting to the people as they passed. In a minute or two they had reached us, and I can still see them now, those young, wild-faced, brown-shirted, Nazi fanatics who sang and shrieked and waved their arms and then swept on into the darkness. What a dead silence they left behind in that simple village street. Like the brawl of a storm, they had come and gone, though I could still hear their shouts away in the distance, faintly echoed by others from the road to Cologne. We stared for a while into the darkness, then turned and went into the inn.

The bar room was crowded, but we went down the corridor to a quiet little room on the right. There was a general greeting as we went in and I soon saw that I was no stranger, but on fairly familiar ground. There was Lambert, the solicitor, with his gleaming glasses and lustreless eyes; Frenzel, the land agent, more cheery and florid than ever; Kemp, the sanitary engineer, young, dark and clean-shaven, who had elbowed Brechner out of business and was now prosperous enough to take his seat among the worthies; Klassen, the schoolmaster, and a number of others whom I knew by sight.

The strangest figure to me, however, was Dr Cohen, the Jew, a heavy, ashen-featured man, who looked much older than he was. He, a Jew, in the Kevelaar Club! I could not help but wonder. Yet there he sat at the long table in full fellowship with the rest of the company looking at the Christmas tree, which stood decorated in the corner.

'Excellent tree,' he suddenly exclaimed, nodding to Kiel, who had followed us in.

'Yes, from Otto, you know, the best he had.'

Cohen nodded and kept gazing into the corner. A Jew in the Kevelaar Club with an interest in Christmas trees! What human people these Rhenish men were. What a mysterious lot, the Jews. I thought of Rosenbaum, and remembered the many Jews I had met in my native land. How sociable they seemed to be, but how really aloof; at home in any and every clime, yet with the air of Israel round them and with the soil of Zion in their shoes. I kept on looking at Cohen, wondering to my own amazement how Jew-conscious I had become. I tried to turn my thoughts. Cohen was perhaps converted. He was a Catholic like Rosenbaum, though in looks and character a Jew.

But the business had begun. The Rektor was away, so Herr Engels took the chair and it was grand to see the old man at the head of that long heavy table, holding the company by the spell of his character, though sitting half-turned to the stove and speaking away into his own thoughts, as was his wont at home. But every now and again he would flash a look into the

35

company as though to challenge an answer. It was certainly a grave beginning, but a change to a lighter vein was imminent.

'A moment, Herr Engels,' said Cohen, 'let us settle the question of refreshment. What say the gentlemen? Each for himself? Or shall we all drink together?'

'A Rudesheimer all round,' called out Friedrich Müller, a hale and hefty farmer from over the river. 'After all it is Christmas.'

'A Rudesheimer,' echoed the rest with few exceptions.

'You hear, Herr Kiel,' said Engels, 'no nameless swill from the Ahr, this time. A Rudesheimer, if you can give it.'

Herr Kiel was standing gravely by the stove looking, with his heavy hanging moustache, like some remnant of the old Prussian Guard. He was a member of the Kevelaar Club himself, but he knew the dues and distances. He never sat down at the table. He never spoke, unless addressed. He stood to attention at the stove and awaited the company's pleasure.

'A Rudesheimer? Yes, 1921 vintage.'

'Excellent.'

'And an excellent price too,' objected Klassen in a curt way.

'Yes, it ensures sobriety,' said Engels.

'And have it on my invitation,' said Cohen.

The business proceeded. The question of a gift for poor families was raised. Cohen, who was the local doctor and very well informed on the domestic affairs of the villagers, suggested the Porten and Zimmermann families, whose children needed the most help. He spoke in a dry, expressionless way as though all emotion was dead within him, but it was only his scientific way. Although without illusions he had a deep sympathy for the poor and the aged, and he showed by many a remark how keen his observation was. He closed his report with an appeal for sponsors. Herr Engels called for names.

'The Zimmermann family?'

'I'll take them,' said Müller, 'although I detest their politics.'

'And I'll take the Portens,' said Hempel, another farmer.

'And I'll put old Margaret's house in order,' said Wessel, the building contractor, 'and see that she is right for coal and things.'

And so it went on, each offering himself for a duty in accordance with Cohen's report. I was surprised to see that Blankheim, a place whose former parochial charm had been lost in the drabness of town life, had still the soul of a village, the intimate nearness of one to another we find in rural parts. There was human fellowship here after all. And yet, how perilous in the years to come this one-time fellowship proved to be.

The wine came, and, after a toast was drunk to some worthy who was too unwell to attend, tongues were freer, and even Cohen's face, dryly sober though it was, lit up with a friendly smile.

The company was now in excellent humour and there were calls to Kiel for more wine. I found myself talking to Cohen, half attracted and half

36

repelled by his impervious self-possession. How well-informed he was, how soberly void of all romance. Was this the trait, I thought, this dry-eyed objectivity of economists and calculators, that had so enraged for ages the oppressors of the Jews? Had pogroms so reduced the race, so lopped all poetry and impulse from them, so trampled in a never-ending battle the forward, valiant and passionate spirits, that none were left but a commercial rump, a canny non-committal remnant who knew the runs of earth and won by their very earthiness? Where, I wondered, are the former prophets and visionaries of Zion? And yet I could not help but think how unworthy such reflections were at that particular hour, how unfair I was to harbour them when speaking to a truly selfless man whose life was a work well done.

I was so absorbed in my chat with Cohen that I failed to hear the rising hubbub in the other parts of the house. But as Kiel came in with further wine a gust of brawling voices from the public room, and the blowing of a horn, stilled our little company into silence.

'Strangers?' asked Herr Engels.

'Yes. There's been a breakdown on the main road. One of the charabancs. They have come here to wait until the motor's repaired.'

'They?'

'Nazis.' Kiel's voice had dropped. As an innkeeper he had to be discreet. Political brawls were frequent even before the Nazis took control, and it was wise to be neutral. With his finger to his lips, Kiel retired to the stove where he took his silent stand and meekly awaited his customers' pleasure.

'That blackguard crush!' exclaimed Klassen. 'They are as bad as the Reds.'

'Not a pin to choose between them,' said Wessel.

'Stronger measures ought to be taken against both.'

Kemp was checked by a loud 'Sh!' from Kiel, and the company nodded approval.

'Gentlemen,' said Cohen quietly, 'we are on neutral ground here, at least for the moment.'

He stood up, but just at that moment the door was flung open and a voice cried, 'So, here's a room!' A young Nazi burst in followed by another. He was dressed in the usual brown shirt and breeches and wore his cap at a dare-devil angle. His face was flushed with excitement, perhaps from drink, perhaps from incessant shouting. His eye fell on Cohen and I shall never forget the glance they exchanged, so gloomily impassive on Cohen's part, so contemptuous on that of the Nazi's.

'Juda verrecke!' And he burst into a sneering laugh.

'Verrecke!' hissed the other.

We all rose and the Nazis shot out. We could hear their voices as they shouted to their comrades, and we expected a full invasion. At a sign from Kiel, Cohen moved swiftly to the far door where he vanished under Kiel's guidance to a place of safety.

'What now?' exclaimed Klassen in an aggressive way.

'Nothing,' said Herr Engels quietly. 'Just let us take our seats and carry on. No words or provocation of any kind. There are no honours in a tavern brawl. In a contest of rudeness and brutality we should only be the losers.'

We all felt the wisdom of this remark and resumed our seats as though nothing had happened. There were twenty of us and the burly forms of the farmers, Müller, Hempel and the rest, promised that in any possible brawl we should play no feeble part. I felt rather anxious for Cohen, exposed to attack from hooligans who might be all the more reckless under cover of darkness in a strange village. Where had he gone, I wondered? Perhaps home by the silent path along the Rhine.

Then the door burst open again and some Nazis thronged round the entrance. One or two had glasses in their hands. They were clearly in a roisterous mood.

'Where is he?' asked one.

'Gone!' said another.

They gazed round, but Müller's patience was exhausted. He stood up and strode to the door where his hefty figure towered over the intruders.

'This is a private meeting,' he said quietly. 'You had better go.' And he ushered them out. But just as he was doing so we heard a further din from the street, shouts, singing and the sound of a horn. Another charabanc was coming. Attracted by the uproar, the Nazis streamed from the inn to cheer their comrades as they passed. We all stood up as the clamour grew, but just as we were crowding to the door there were two sharp reports that rang out in the street like a cannon.

'Tyre bursts!' said Klassen.

'No, shots!' said Herr Engels.

There was dead silence for a moment or two, an unnatural hush after the preceding din. We stood and looked at each other. I am certain we all were making a panic guess.

'Keep inside,' said Herr Engels, 'until they pass.'

The charabanc lumbered by and a loud outcry from its passengers was answered by louder cheers from the inn. All were streaming out, and we hurried along the corridor to the open street. The whole village was out with lights shining from every doorway. All were hastening to a gathering crowd which had assembled near one of the houses. It was Klassen's. Frau Klassen was looking out of the window and talking to the people outside. I could see that the casement windows were broken. The people were peering in.

At that moment, Ludwig came out of the wicket gate accompanied by another boy. I at once accosted him.

'What's the matter, Ludwig?'

'I really don't know. As the charabanc passed, two shots were fired. One went right through the crib, just where we were working.'

'Right through the manger,' added the other boy. 'An inch or two nearer, I should have been hit. The figure Jesus was smashed to bits.'

'But why did they fire at you?'

'I don't think they fired at me,' he laughed. 'I think they were shooting at random. They must have been very drunk.'

He was a dark-haired cultured boy with expressive jet-black eyes, and there was a softness in his voice quite different from the tone of the village. A thoroughly likeable boy, I thought. I asked his name.

'David Cohen.'

'Son of Dr Cohen?'

'The very same.' And he smiled in a most pleasing way.

I felt a sudden pang. But there was no time for further enquiries. As the crowd gathered round Ludwig, David politely took his leave and hastened home up the street. I looked after him as he went, and kept on watching until his form was lost in the darkness. I see his vanishing figure even now. And then that night returns once more with the gathering crowd and the tumult of voices and Frau Klassen's face at the window as she told her story again and again.

'These Nazi brigands!' Herr Klassen kept on saying in a half distracted way.

'Perhaps they meant it for Hans Zimmermann,' said Herr Engels. 'Let us go back and finish our wine.'

The members of the club trooped back and spent the evening in long talk on the gravity of the times. What had happened was just one shot in the growing war of Browns and Reds. There had been shooting affrays elsewhere, street fights and great damage, and we were lucky to have escaped with just that stray shot. Was it meant for Hans Zimmermann? Or perhaps for Dr Cohen, because his son was known to be in the house?

The mystery was never cleared up. The lorry was stopped near Bonn, and every passenger searched and sharply questioned. Nothing came to light, however, and the incident was soon forgotten in the flood of bigger and worse things.

Chapter 5

Nationalism and the Jews

In accordance with their invitation I was due to meet the Wolff sisters next day at seven o'clock. A mere visit, one might think, a mere forgettable trifle in the crowded run of everyday, yet the thought of it dominated my mind. There was now something tense in my views of Jews, something ominous and impending, as though in merely meeting them I was crossing a forbidden parallel and setting foot in an alien world. I tried to efface the impression, but in vain.

At 6.30, while I was idly reading that ponderous tome, *The Chronicles of the Free Imperial City of Speyer*, visitors were announced. Tilde ushered them in, Bürger and Hillesheim, Bürger sardonic and dark as ever, Hillesheim fresh, spruce and serious, and with a light coat that went wondrously well with his fair complexion and light hair. They had been to a conference in Cologne, and had suddenly thought on their way back of looking me up in my village home and taking me on to Bonn. Or perhaps – it was quite on the cards – they meant to test my hospitality.

'So this is your den?' said Bürger, and both gazed round with interest at my quaint little study with its low oak beams and parquetted floor, at its bookshelves and at the imposing tome on the table with my sheaf of closely written notes.

'A true scholar's retreat.' And Hillesheim lifted his hand and touched the beams.

'Far from all worldly distractions,' added Bürger. He turned to warm his hands at the great Dutch stove in the corner, while Hillesheim drew back the hangings of one of the casements and peered into the darkness beyond. It had begun to rain, and we could hear the gusts of wind and the rain plashing on the windows. I looked at them both with some dismay.

'I'm truly sorry, but you have come at a most unfortunate time.'

'So we've heard,' said Bürger cheerily.

'The old gentleman told us,' added Hillesheim, 'that you have an invitation to the ladies over the way. The Jewesses, I suppose, of whom you spoke?'

'Yes. It's a pity you couldn't be included. But that doesn't rest with me. I should have liked to entertain you here; I am usually free at this time.'

'Oh, that's all right,' said Hillesheim, 'you just carry on with your visit. An invitation is an invitation. We'll catch the next train to Bonn, wind and weather permitting. There's one in about half an hour.'

He turned to the window again. It was now raining in torrents, yet there was nothing else I could do. I should have liked them to meet the ladies and to share my impressions of the evening. I had heard so much good of the two worthy sisters that I was eager to see my two friends in their company and to triumph in a tempering of their views. I even said so.

'Impossible,' blurted Bürger.

'It would be almost indecent,' said Hillesheim. 'How can we take favours from those about whom we hold unfriendly views or sit for the whole of the evening, talking one thing and thinking another? Giving the ladies our open blessing while keeping a curse in reserve? It would be unfair to ourselves and to them.'

'Quite,' said Bürger.

'You see,' continued Hillesheim, 'I have a strong antipathy in principle.'

'And I a strong antipathy in person,' interrupted Bürger. 'You may think me a crank, Mr Arnold, but a Jew calls up before me all the vilest scenes of the east. I instantly think of the ghettos, of the overwhelming whiff of them, of those suppurating kosher dens, fetid, foul, leprous, with swarms of spawning bluebottles and the maggots crashing through the beefsteaks.'

I burst out laughing, no less than Hillesheim who was enjoying the grossness of Bürger's attack. 'Most succulent visions, Bürger, especially before my evening meal,' I said. 'But let us distinguish. Let us sunder two cultured ladies from the slummy and scummy swill-overs from Poland. Let us remember that ...'

There was a knock at the door and we all went dumb, but it was only Tilde with a note. I opened it and gasped. The Miss Wolffs had heard of my unexpected visitors and heartily invited them over. They were all the more willing to do this, since two of their other guests had telegraphed regrets. I made up my mind at once. Without a word I went outside and scribbled an acceptance. It was a bold step, but an impish spirit was in my blood.

'Many, many thanks,' I called out to Tilde as she hurried down the stairs. 'The two gentlemen are delighted.'

The last was meant for my two friends, who looked at me in a puzzled way. I quietly locked the door.

'Delighted with what?' Bürger asked.

'With the kind invitation of the Miss Wolffs.'

'What?'

'Now kindly sit down. You can flee in horror later if you wish. But you must help me now. I appreciate your visit and should like to honour it with an excellent supper. But that, alas, I cannot do. And now, like a *deus ex machina*, the two Miss Wolffs have come to my aid. It will be an excellent dinner. For all such invitations the ladies engage a chef and his wife from Cologne, a blond, blue-eyed Rhenish chef who has full control of the kitchen and who knows nothing of Kosher meat or rabbinical taboos, and would not apply them if he did. You see, the ladies are very sensitive and respect the feelings of others.'

41

'But you are not respecting ours.'

And so it went on. Perhaps I should not have persuaded them, even despite the fury of the storm, if Herr Engels had not come to my aid. He peeped in and realised that my friends were still undecided. I introduced them.

'I should be glad of your company, Herr Hillesheim, Herr Bürger.' He spoke as though their company was assured. Despite his kindly character and mellowness of view, Herr Engels had a lion-like way with him, above all an imperative glance that seemed to draw more force from his thrustful brows and beard. He was indeed so thorough a realist, so vigorous a creation of the natural powers, of the wind, the rain and the light of God's heaven, that bogies quailed before him. Even the cultured Hillesheim seemed to wither to a schoolboy in his presence.

'Well, let us go.'

'But, but,' stammered Bürger.

'But! Grace before meat and the buts after,' said Herr Engels, and he ushered us out. The street was dark and swept with rain and I thought that my two friends might try to slip off in the wintry gloom, but no. Herr Engels held them in thrall. Speeding across the street we were suddenly trapped in the brilliant telltale light of the opening door and in we went. No knock, no ring of the bell, no word of greeting until we were right inside the house. The door seemed to close of its silent self behind us.

The ladies with Frau Klebert were ensconced in the sitting room, which looked far too spacious for the house. The partition of the dining room was drawn and we could see right through to the windows that faced the garden and the Rhine. The table was set for dinner and the dazzle of the fresh linen and the glitter of the glass and silver under the sparkling candelabra were enhanced by the dark oak setting of the room.

To me this was all as it should be and I was frankly grateful to the ladies for the compliment of offering the best they could afford and for the grace with which they gave it. But to Bürger, as I learned later, it was all too obvious, forced and offensive, the flashy vanity of wealth ill-earned, the plausible flaunt of those who hoped to blind us to the darker side. In all this excess of correctness was some conscious reaction to the kosher den. And Hillesheim in a subdued way also shared this view.

I gathered all this from veiled observation later, for neither made a direct reference. After being invited to dinner how could they? I myself was pleasingly impressed and realised at once how it was that the two Miss Wolffs were the awe and envy of the whole village. Everything in their sanctum, the Persian carpet, the tapestried hangings, the gilt-framed paintings of Rhenish scenes, the genuine observatory clock ticking solemnly in an alcove, an ebony escritoire inlaid with mother of pearl, all were museum pieces that revealed not only the expensive but also, in their harmony, the expert taste of the sisters. These were clearly their jealously preserved inheritance and I was pleased to look upon them as emblems of filial piety and as testimony of a long tradition.

To Bürger and even to Hillesheim they told a different tale. Here was the obvious proof of booty, the forfeitures, pledges and pickings from the auctioned wreckage of countless homes, the priceless inheritance of others, distrained for rent and other dues, and callously included here in the select ransackings of a province. Was my friends' view too warped to be true? Perhaps those who lived through the great inflation and saw hosts of noble German homes crumbling away under the stunning hammer of some bilking auctioneer might understand the view.

The ladies, I thought, were attractive, not too obviously Jewish, but cultured, considerate and of modest opinions, most modestly intimated. Rebecca, the elder, was perhaps the harder of the two, with the more calculating, keener glance, less impulsive, less enthusiastic, less romantic than her sister and clearly given to second thoughts. Slow, deliberate, decisive, she was able to attune her ideas to the company and was always ready to agree, though one felt by reservation. Like her sister, she had large dark eyes and lustrously black hair.

Rachel, the younger, was most attractive and never have I seen a face more prettily transformed by a smile than hers. A light would come into every feature and lend it such an exquisite glint of radiant good nature that I felt that just one glance of hers was a sufficient favour for many days. And then the light would die away and a troubled look would come, half fear and half appeal, almost shrinking in its courtesy with a trembling anxiety to please as though she were still some slighted child or a poor serf dependent on our lordly humour. But soon the smile would come again, luminous, brimming, delightful, so that for long, long intervals I forgot myself, the company, the conversation, wondering what deep shadow must have haunted all her days and driven her, years and years ago, to this dull and humdrum spot on the Rhine, where all her charm was lost. Then I thought of the village rumours and reproached myself for the foul breath of them and, in trying to forget them, remembered them all the more.

After some minutes of introductory talk, we adjourned to the dining room. Here the sisters looked to even better advantage, their dark dresses and lustrous black hair contrasting most pleasingly with the dazzling white of the linen cloth. I wondered what my friends were thinking. There was nothing to remind them of the kosher den and extremely little of Jewry. Tilde had come to help with the service and she, with Frau Nauheim, the cook's wife, were such sunnily blond Nordics as to ban all sense of Judaea from the kitchen.

Opposite Bürger at table was Frau Klebert, almost fairer and more Nordic than Hillesheim himself, who sat between her and me. Rebecca, at the head of the table, was to my right with Herr Engels opposite and Rachel between him and Bürger. I was thus able to study to my heart's content those swift fluctuations of expression that animated Rachel's face and which seemed all the more mysterious in contrast with the set and bearded features of her thoroughly masculine neighbours, the resolute Herr Engels and the decisive, sardonic Bürger. I was more than fascinated. I had come to think of the Jews as a hard, calculating type, by nature egoist and materialist and thus affected in the long run with a certain blurring of the moral sense, a certain hardening of the arteries of the soul. Yet here was Rachel Wolff. Here was the impossible she, a daughter of Zion yet feminine to the last fibre, delicate, sensitive, with the vibration of poetry in every feature and without the least inner-manoeuvre or privily deliberate shuffle which, by ever blunting the first impulse, must finally numb the heart.

I could not help a comparison with her sister. Rebecca, though quick-witted, seemed rather cautious. Although always ready with an instant reply, she would pause for a perceptible moment when a dry, dull look would come to her eyes, as though she were playing for safety. Then the shadow would swiftly vanish and at once she was speaking freely in a perhaps too gracious way.

This hint of an undertone disturbed me, this play of an afterthought, this mistrust in the sphere of friendship, this anxiety for dry powder. However, with one glance at her sister I felt I was unjust, and when I saw Bürger sampling the wine with every sign of approval and giving a gracious word and smile to Rachel, his neighbour, my misgivings faded away.

The invitation to my friends was soon explained. The ladies had been expecting Professor Rosenbaum and his wife, but the latter had sent regrets at the last moment. I cast a cryptic look at Bürger, who returned a look more cryptic still.

'In Dr Bürger,' I suggested to Miss Rebecca, not without a certain malice, which Bürger seemed to enjoy, 'you have chosen a worthy successor to Professor Rosenbaum.'

'Ah yes,' she said. And then after a pause, 'I hear that his views on economics are attracting wide attention.' Bürger bowed his acknowledgement.

'No less than his views on ethnology,' I added.

'Oh!' Miss Rebecca looked surprised, Hillesheim gave me a nudge and Bürger, deposing his knife and fork, surveyed me in a tart way. I had certainly gone too far, but Hillesheim came to our rescue.

'Mr Arnold is still wincing under some hefty attacks on the English.'

'That's it.' I seized the excuse. 'Apparently in the present crisis we English are the villains of the piece.'

It was surprising how the conversation turned. All were quite emphatic that the villain of the piece was France. Had I forgotten the brutal attempt to seize and exploit the Ruhr? The separatist movement to detach the Rhineland from Germany? The shame of the occupation when Moroccans, negroes and Cochin-Chinese were let loose upon the Rhine?

I was taken aback by this outburst of national resentment, which I thought had been allayed at Locarno many years before. Only Rachel took a more gracious line. She pitied the poor colonial troops so far from their homes and people, and recalled the pathetic funerals as they moved through the streets of Bonn, a mere coffin on a cart, a squad of troops and a nameless grave in some cemetery beyond the town. She felt distressed for their relatives far away and, as she told the story, I felt that her look of pity was as charming as her smile.

To Bürger all this was just more fuel to his flagrant remarks on the French, and he might have taken a more scorching line but for the excellence of the meal and the wine. He was ready to make concessions, however. He proved an excellent neighbour to Rachel, anticipating her minor needs and sending her into peals of laughter with his curt and sardonic comments. Both he and Hillesheim were behaving extremely well, but perhaps I was a little unjust in ascribing their social correctness to the exquisite nature of the meal, gourmets though I knew them to be.

I was surprised how France seemed to obsess the little company. At dinner, talk is apt to trail away into trifling comment on the tric-trac of everyday. Questions of cooking, the choice of wine, the decorative flowers on the table, even the china are by-the-way points that grow into absorbing topics that fritter away the most serious themes. And though all these points were touched upon and tastes in this and that expressed, the subject of France returned in one of its manifold forms, not as an affair of politics in which ladies show little concern, but as a deep social factor from which the German mind could not escape. Once or twice there were tense moments when every knife and fork was still, when everything else was forgotten, the meal, the setting, the hosts, the hour, everything but the voice of the speaker. Even Tilde and Frau Nauheim, both with laden trays in their hands, stood silently waiting to serve us, yet listening as intently as the company itself.

That scene came back to me in the troubled years that followed, as a glimpse of the lost civilities that Europe once knew. And yet there was murk in the glimpse, a dimming of the highlights and a stealthy deepening of the shadows, but murk for all that; an unnoticed omen for the spate of racial passion that was to swamp us all.

I thought to change the subject, when we had finally risen from dinner, by speaking of the Rhine itself and of the host of romantic ruins along its banks. I could not have revived the subject of France in a more vivid and topical form.

'I suppose there is no ruin in the Rhineland,' said Bürger, who had settled down in an easy chair and was toying with a cigar Rebecca had just offered him, 'that does not reveal in some way the ravaging hand of the French.'

All the company agreed, none more emphatically than Rebecca, who instanced many cases of devastation. We had all settled down in the sitting room, in that distinctive little sanctum into which so few from the village had ever peeped. I no longer wondered at the secluded character of my hosts. As Herr Engels once expressed it, envy is the worst neighbour in any village. But I was awakened from these reflections by Rebecca herself, and I wondered at her strongly nationalistic views.

'In large measure the greatness of France has been built on the ruins of Germany.'

'Well, that's the general view,' interrupted Herr Engels, 'and one most useful for inflaming the German mind, but it is by no means exact. For every ruin due to the French I could name two of which they were innocent.' And he cast round one of his decisive looks before lighting his cigar.

'You amaze me.' Rebecca halted in her round as hostess and gazed at Herr Engels with an incredulous air.

'And me too,' added Hillesheim. 'I graduated at Heidelberg, where the ruins of the picturesque castle were a constant reminder of past humiliations. Why, when the French devastated the Palatinate in 1689 such towns as Worms, Speyer and the like were simply reduced to ashes. There is not an ancient memorial left.'

'Admitted,' said Herr Engels, 'but the baleful influence of the French began in the Thirty Years War. Not before. Most of the famous ruins which stand so grandly against the sky, the Godesburg, the Drachenfels, Rolandseck, were already ruined by then. Many were demolished in the Peasant War, and what were left were unfit for residence. As they became a haunt for brigands we dismantled them ourselves.'

'Of course,' interjected Hillesheim, 'you are speaking of extant ruins, not of the buildings that have wholly disappeared?'

'Yes. Only of extant and obvious ruins. And these in popular opinion are due to the French.'

'Even then the scars left by the French are very considerable.'

'Very. Above all when one includes such buildings as stand wholly preserved.'

We all looked puzzled by this remark from Herr Engels.

'You said, "stand wholly preserved". Not a slip of the tongue, I suppose?' asked Bürger.

'No.' Herr Engels was decisive. 'Such buildings as the episcopal palace at Bonn, now the university, the nunnery at Nonnenwerth, the palaces at Coblence and Mannheim, buildings wholly French in character and aping the palace at Versailles are not in the German tradition and have crossed the whole artistic development of the Rhineland.'

'Steamrollered it!' interjected Hillesheim.

'And left us,' added Bürger, 'in that one sense at least, still a dominion of France.'

'An artistic colony, in fact,' put in Rebecca.

Did she believe this last phrase? She said it with such conviction that I felt some ominous import in the word. I was right. It quivered through the whole company and evoked all those extreme statements that I was

46

doomed to hear with ever-growing weariness for the next few fateful years. Even Frau Klebert, who was bending over some needlework and who usually kept her thoughts in reserve, added her caustic drop to the flowing tide.

Herr Engels I forgive. After all he was the grandson of a man who, when the Rhineland was annexed in 1794, became perforce a Frenchman, a colonist of France. He had been born and bred in his grandfather's faith and traditions.

But Rebecca was a lady of alien race and nurture, born on the Polish border and within the contending shadows of Russian and Prussian oppression. Was she sincere in all this? Even after all these years I seem to see her now, a dark, intelligent, Medusa figure sitting forward in her easy chair and smiling effusive approval of every onslaught by the headlong Bürger, the while turning her diamond rings and scattering sparks and glitters against the blackness of her dress. Was she merely seeking to please or was she a masked and calculating figure with a sense of her own superior cunning and with some inner smile of contempt at our simplicity? Of Rachel I say nothing. She was but the echo of her sister, agreeable at any price and a lady always.

Perhaps I was unjust. Why should Jews not be loyal to the land of their birth, so at one with its speech and culture as to share to the full its joy and grief and see its destiny as their own? Save for religion, which is private to Jew and Gentile alike, they have everything in common with their neighbours and see all as a common heritage from which no justice can exclude them. They have their same feelings for their homeland, for its scenery, customs and institutions as the purest blooded native and may with the same right or reason adopt the current political views.

I knew all this; I know it now; and still the doubt remains. I still see Rebecca Wolff playing to the prejudice of my friends, still see her sitting near me with her shrewd looks lurking quietly behind an over-conscious smile, and still wonder whether she rang the bell just to draw the company on. But draw it on she did in the fullest measure, and even to extreme opinions she seemed, while yielding a cautious assent, to give her fulsome approval.

'Of course, if we had only been united,' she said, with her perfect flair for striking a common chord, 'how happy Germany's history would have been.'

Perhaps I was the only one who started at the word 'we', for the response was so immediate, so definite and so unanimous that all sense of incongruity was lost.

'You see,' said Herr Engels, turning to me as though I above all people had to be persuaded, 'right from the earliest times we have been only the shatter and scatter of a nation. The German tribes were never united even under Charlemagne, and the Holy Roman Empire, which ought to have held us together, was a mere dream and a name. Just think of the Robber

47

Knight period, when the land was split into hundreds of separate states and every man's hand was against his neighbour. Just think of the Burgundian War. And then, when unity seemed in sight and peace a possibility, came the great religious split of the Reformation and the long religious wars that turned Germany into a desert.

'We became the cockpit of Europe. Every war that followed was ruthlessly fought out in Germany's front parlour; the Thirty Years War, the Robber Wars of Louis, the War of the Spanish Succession, the two Seven Years Wars and the wars of the Revolution and of Napoleon. It is a wonder that any one brick is standing on another. What a tragedy our national story is! When shall we drop our party strife, think as Germans, Christians, fellowmen and live in security and peace?'

His voice rang through the room and I thought the final word had been spoken, but Hillesheim and Bürger took up the story, and theirs was the voice of nationalism. To them, the first step to unity, and thus to safety from the foreign invader, was nationalist feeling, which the German people had never possessed. Look at the frontier peoples who had fallen away from the Reich and who ought to be standing now with their brothers on the Rhine – the Austrians, the German Swiss, the Dutch and the men of Alsace-Lorraine. Germany was like a tree lopped of its fairest branches, a bare trunk defrauded of leafage and fruit.

'We ought to be standing together,' said Bürger, and again I started at the word 'we'. 'We' meant all those of German speech and blood, not merely those confined within the temporary frontiers of Bismarck. I saw how it was. Before 1870, Germany was a far vaguer and broader term than now, and a German, reading history, would naturally think in terms of race since the limits we know today did not exist. And this racial sense of 'we', which is common to all Germans, stood at daggers drawn with the national sense of 'we' on Rebecca's lips. What right had she a Jewess to speak of 'we'?

'It is a tragic irony of our times,' said Bürger, and here he assumed a lecturing tone, 'that just when, under Bismarck's guidance, a nationalist feeling had arisen that united Germany and made her strong, comes the theory of internationalism. This, with its gospel of disarmament, threatens to undo all Bismarck's work and land us again in the gulf from which we have just emerged.'

Bürger was now in full swing and the talk took on a scorching note. The theme of Bismarck's ruthless campaign against the internationalist forces of Catholicism, socialism and Jewry threatened to be more disturbing than courtesy would allow. I thought of intervening and mellowing the dispute with a few soft words, but Rebecca turned the edge of it in a most disarming way.

'You are quite right, Herr Doktor,' she said, with just that over-effusiveness that made me doubt its truth, 'Nothing could be more galling to a German to hear nationalism so misunderstood, after centuries of civil war and foreign invasion have shown how necessary it is. Even in architecture, art and music, internationalism is likely to steamroller all personality away and to pancake it out to the one impersonal pattern, but in politics it is pure folly. It is playing into the hands of the international powers with their vast colonial empires, England and France, not to speak of the huge continental power of Russia, which is an independent world for itself.'

'Hear, hear,' interjected Bürger and Hillesheim.

'And it must be all the more galling to a German after the tragic humiliations of over a thousand years to find internationalism set up in his land by a man of foreign race. Oh yes, I admit it and regret it as a Jewess, for I and my people have had to suffer for the fact that socialism with its pacifist and international doctrines is the work of Karl Marx, a Jew. He has put all Jewry in a false position and made us look like conspirators in the land of our birth.'

I shall never forget the momentary stillness that fell upon the company after the last few striking words. The dispute was over, the venom gone, the pent-up feelings that might have exploded simply vapoured away. Rachel was turning round anxiously studying the effect in our faces, while Bürger sat blankly opposite slowly nodding his head without venturing a further word.

Hillesheim was breathing assent through every pore, and Herr Engels, with a meditative look, made curls of smoke from his cigar. What a subtle Medusa Rebecca was. I sat in wonder, a very embarrassed wonder until, to ease my feelings, I smiled at Rachel who relaxed and smiled in return.

'It is a pity,' she said.

'Yes, a great pity,' rejoined Herr Engels. 'A pity that the thought of Catholic and Jew may embitter our land once more. And the rift is there of course, ready to widen at a moment's notice and leave us once again divided against ourselves. And be assured, when the split comes, it will come in the name of unity.'

He resumed his cigar and in the pin-drop hush that followed I could hear the embarrassing tick of the clock. We were hovering on the brink of a deep dispute, and none was prepared to go further. Rebecca kept looking at Bürger with her evasively seeing and non-seeing eye, looking right at him and past him, with a glance to spare for Hillesheim while waiting for a peep of something she knew would never come. What a plausible fencer she was and subtle double-tracker! I sympathised with Bürger. He was sitting in a mental fumble with nothing to do but to play the echo and nothing to face but a blank, as though he were playing chess and observing in the moment of triumph that the board had been turned round.

There was a sharp tap on the window outside, and we all started up with a sense of relief. The sisters exchanged a silent glance, but made no other sign.

'Did someone knock?' I asked.

49

The sisters nodded, and a few moments later the caller was ushered in. It was Rektor Barth, who stood at the door for a moment, hat in hand, and greeted us all. He had been to call on Herr Engels, so had been referred to the Miss Wolffs' house. He apologised for intruding, but the sisters welcomed him and we were all glad for the interruption.

'Council meeting for tomorrow?' asked Herr Engels.

'No, it's about the old memorial to the French soldier that we re-erected some time ago.'

Herr Engels looked surprised, and the sisters started.

'Yes. I was coming back from a sick visit, old Ursula, you know ...'

'Is she any better?' interrupted Rachel.

'Worse, if anything. Most distressing case. Anyway, I needed quiet and a breath of air, so I walked back by the river path. I had just emerged from the woodland when I heard noises ahead. I was surprised, because it is usually deserted at this time of night. I stopped and listened, and I could hear the sound of tools and two or three voices. I approached slowly and then, right by the old memorial, I saw two or three men working. I wondered what they could be doing. I moved on quietly, and then realised what was going on. They were knocking the memorial down. Then one of them paused and lit a cigarette, and I could see it was Alex Brechner. I was almost on them before they saw me and made off with their tools.

'"Alex Brechner," I called out, "you've no need to run away", but I got no reply. I could see that the ground around had been dug up and the memorial loosened, so I came on here.'

'What do you suggest we do?' asked Herr Engels.

'Settle it quietly with Brechner,' the Rektor suggested. 'I don't think we should involve the police or make a story of it. We should ask him to repair the damage.'

'You are right. It would be unwise to make an example of him. We might provoke all the other elements who would delight in pulling it down again,' said Herr Engels. 'There's a gang on the towpath now. Can you hear them?'

We listened. We could just hear a distant hubbub, doubtless from some rowdies outside the Boatman's Inn on the riverside. Rachel looked anxious, but the Rektor said they were probably Blankheim people and not likely to get out of hand, even if there were a few bargemen among them.

Rebecca stood up and, pushing back the partition, went through the dining room.

'Let's go and see,' she said, so we all got up and went out through the large French window into the garden. There was a high fence at the bottom that overlooked a cliff-like descent to the towpath and the Rhine. The river was dark save where the cabin and safety lights of one or two anchored barges sent long rippling streamers over the swiftly flowing waters. The Boatman's Inn lay to the right about 100 yards away, together with the stage and ferry, standing out in a luminous blur in the misty darkness.

50

A number of men were streaming out to join a further party that was moving up the towpath in our direction. We could just make out their forms in the shadow. All were singing lustily some popular song.

'Communists!' said Bürger.

'Why, is that their song?' asked the Rektor.

'One of them at least. It is the Masuren song, you know, but with a communist text.'

The singers below on the path were passing us, bawling at the top of their voices, and I turned back to the house, for it was cold. Frau Klebert and Rachel were ahead of me and I could see there was something wrong. The latter was obviously unwell and had to be supported. I caught them up and saw how white and anxious she was.

'Oh, it's nothing,' she said in answer to my enquiry. 'The sudden change from the warm to the chilly air has made me dizzy. I shall be all right in a moment or two.'

Was it the chilly air? I thought of the Nazi youths careering down the village street, the insulting songs, the shot through Klassen's window and then the thousand and one rumours of violence and bloodshed. Those singers on the towpath were innocent enough, and yet in their wanton way they were a symptom of the times, of a crisis when bands of armed men were marching and counter-marching in every town of note, and threats and counter-threats were driving tempers to extremes. The foam of mob politics was surging over the land, and reason was fast submerging in a flood of hearsay, slogans and scapegoat accusations where only the biggest and emptiest voice could survive. Here was ample room for anxiety, above all for a sensitive lady who might be the innocent victim of a pogrom any moment.

The company broke up soon after, and my friends sped off to the station to catch the coming train. I should have liked them to stay for an hour or so and to have heard their reactions to the visit. But off they went with many thanks, and I was left looking after their swiftly retreating figures while Herr Engels was waiting at the open door for Frau Klebert to come across.

'Two able men,' I suggested.

'Yes, very able, though a little too swayed perhaps by the prevailing wind.'

'You think so?'

'Yes, I think so. After all, they are young and in times such as these it is the most headlong policy that appeals.'

51

Chapter 6

A Marriage of Convenience

A few days later I passed the memorial cross to the French soldier. It was standing firm and erect on a broad cemented base without the least trace of having been disturbed. Falling leaves and wayside grasses would soon drift over the spot, moss and lichen would cling to the stone and add those natural touches that lend the grace of forgetfulness to a long forgotten grave. I even took some woodland litter, pine needles and leaf mould, and strewed them over the too obvious cement to tone away the unlovely break with the surrounding turf. While so engaged I wondered why no more had been said about the incident.

I had asked Herr Engels and later the Rektor, but both had shrugged their shoulders and quietly changed the subject. And Frau Klebert was equally silent. A policy of deep reticence had apparently been approved. No further word was heard about it, not the faintest whisper of Brechner's name or of the Rektor's discovery on that night. The wrong was silently righted, the memorial repaired with no one the worse or wiser. I was impressed by this policy of reserve, so opposed as it was to Brechner's brawling ways and to the ways of those whose voices were now loudest in the land. Would such courtesy be lost on him, I wondered.

I was still studying the spot when I was roused by an approaching rider along the towpath. It was Else on her pony, her hair floating in the wind, her cheeks flushed, her whip waving in recognition.

'I knew I should find you here,' she said, reining in and looking attentively at the cross.

'Why, were you looking for me?'

'Of course. You must come and look at the crib which Paul has just finished. I think it is splendid and far better than the old clumsy rock-cave, but I don't know what Grandpa will think. You must come now.'

'But there's no hurry, surely?'

'There is!' She looked almost alarmed. 'Father's coming back today and we don't want him to see it before Christmas Eve. And then the others are coming too, Aunt Maria and Aunt Gertrud and Grandmother. They might arrive any minute.'

These were the relatives of her father, lonely souls who shared the family festival on Christmas Eve. I had heard that such family festivals are very closely reserved and that strangers are rarely admitted, but as Captain

Klebert's relatives lived in isolation and as the Captain himself was rarely at home the three were always invited. In fact, I had decided to put my rooms at their disposal and to spend my festive days elsewhere. My hosts had asked me to remain, but I felt it was more considerate to move away for a day or two.

So I returned, while Else scampered off to stable her pony and to change her riding dress in expectation of the visitors. On reaching the bend of the river she waved and then was lost to view. It was a cold blowy day with snowflakes drifting off from the low and sullen clouds and floating idly in the bitter wind. The towpath was deserted and the Rhine itself was lifeless, save where occasional gusts were edging the swirling waters with a fringe of wintry grey. What a forlorn day it was, and how stark and gaunt the trees appeared, rigid, stripped and stricken as though frozen mute in the gloomy air. I thought of Brechner and the anglers all standing equally stiff and mute along the river bank and wondered as I plodded home what the promise of Christmas meant to them. Perhaps very little, but enough to inflame their spirits against an old memorial stone.

There was the usual crowd outside the barber's shop as I passed by. Brechner, more insolent than ever, was in the centre of the group, and with his hands in his pockets gave me a careless nod when I greeted him. The rest just murmured 'Tag!' and held me almost numb in their still immutable gaze. The street went strangely dead. Every step I took seemed to sound out loudly on the cobbles and to summon a peering eye to every window. I could feel the stares behind me, pointed, palpable, prodding stares, until someone emerged from a door on the right and at once the tension passed.

It was the village solicitor, Lambert, who had called on the Miss Wolffs. What a gaunt and goggled man he was, bloodless, pale and inscrutable as a roll of forgotten parchment! He looked straight at me and beyond me without a tremor of recognition, and went on his silent way. I thought of the high finances of Blankheim, of the stealthy traffic of credit and debt, of dues and rents and mortgages, and wondered whether in his cryptic way he was a match for Rebecca Wolff. And when I reached my door I could not help but turn round and watch his retreating figure up the street. The group were watching too, mutely, steadily, intently, as though they all intended to impale him with their gaze.

It was a problem to get to the children's room without catching someone's eye or provoking some enquiry. But at last, after many feints and just as many fibs, I succeeded. I knocked three times at the door, this being the agreed signal, and I was answered by a painfully audible silence. There was then some whispering, a shuffle or two, the rustle of some dress at the door and at last Else spoke.

'Is that you, Mr Arnold?'

'Yes. Open quickly. Tilde's about.'

The door was opened, just enough to let me through, then it was swiftly closed and locked again. The curtain had been drawn and the electric light was on, revealing Paul's Nativity on the table. In view of the coming visit, both Paul and Else were dressed in their best, and both were in great suspense. As I entered they looked at me in a breathless, expectant way and I decided, whatever my inward thoughts, not to disappoint them.

The work was very pretty. It was just like a puppet theatre, under the dome of a starry sky, and representing in a vivid way a glimpse of the village square. To the right was an inn, no more than a wooden facade affixed to a painted background, with dimly glowing windows and an open door, and the promise of hospitality within. To the left was a temple in the same style, built in imitation dark stone, and shedding a religious radiance from its embrasures.

In the centre was the holy stable let into the pasteboard wall at the back. It was just as I had seen it before, a full length view of the stable, but now with the holy family filling the middle pen and the adjoining pens screened from the light that gleamed above the manger. This alone was bright and clear, a luminous centre of interest, and it stood out amid the dimmer beyonds of the stable where the forms of the cattle, the racks and the corn bins peered softly out of the shadows. There was here a pleasing blend of eastern and western lore, of mystery and modernity, of the night lights and daylight shadows of the soul. I was delighted, and said so. Paul and Else glowed with pleasure.

'You see,' said Paul, 'we talked to Miss Logau, Else's drawing teacher, about it. She agreed with what you said about the mixing of ancient and modern things. To get over it she put the Nativity scene into the middle pen and then suggested this shaded light so that the pens to the left and right would be more or less dimmed off.'

'Left in mysterious shadow, was the phrase she used,' said Else, mimicking with comic effect the momentous drawing mistress. I had to laugh and Paul smiled, but only faintly for, despite all modern usage, he was no friend of irreverence to his elders.

'Yes,' he continued, 'the centre light must be so bright as to keep the eye on the middle point.'

'So bright,' interrupted Else in the most pompous tone she could muster, 'as to control the focus of the beholder and determine the centre of vision.' She glanced at me in a grown-up way, but with a laugh lurking in every feature.

Paul observed, however, in his own unruffled way, 'Yes, but this centre light must not be so bright as to leave the rest unseen.'

'Quite,' I said. 'The other details must not be too obscured.'

'No,' said Else, pursing her lips again, 'Their presence, however homely, must be more than dimly suspected.'

She uttered this quotation in such a measured and decisive tone, and so suggestive of the oracle of the art class, that my gravity gave way. I had to laugh, and Else found it very hard to suppress her pent-up titters.

'Really, Else, I think you are wicked,' said Paul in his quiet way, 'after all the help she gave us.'

'Yes, I am a little, but the demon will out.' And in a trice she was as serious as Paul himself. 'I think your work is excellent, Paul, and Grandpa is sure to be pleased. Don't you think so, Mr Arnold?'

I thought the work was superb. Everything was in keeping, the Nativity scene with the stable, the stable with the setting, and the other figures with all three, the light being so controlled that all disturbing items had been subdued or brought into line. Even the shepherds who were hastening past the inn and the three wise men on camels emerging from the shadows by the temple were wholly at one with the scene. I gave Paul my hand with congratulations.

But a step in the passage outside made us start. We paused for a time until the danger was over. Then Paul quickly dismantled his puppet scene and placed the separate parts in the chest. He then put the old Nativity on the table once more and again reset the figures so that anyone coming in might not suspect his plans. What a quaint Nativity it was! How true to the old tradition! What deep ideas of long ago were here being cast away!

I had congratulated Paul, yet I left the room with some misgiving. Reform is very easy, and youth has no light hand with what is worn and old. This seems to be only just. How superior was Paul's stable to the crude cave that it displaced, how superior in every way, in form, plan and fascination, in the spirit of modernity, enlightenment and progress, in brief in every factor – save that first and vital one to which religion owes its being!

From the very earliest times, caves have been the favoured sphere of man's approach to the unseen, of magic, mysticism, revelation, perhaps from the ancient view that the great sun god went down to the gloomy cave of night from which he rose in the morning. Or perhaps it was because, in the darkness of caves, removed from the symbols of sight and sound and more in touch with his own inner vision, early man became aware of the ghostly world within.

This was the great discovery, the one that gave us the human mind and the sense for abstract things. For just as the gloom of night reveals a myriad of worlds beyond the moon so the gloom of caves, by playing on the feelings of hope and fear and appealing to the inner view, has revealed the mightier domains of thought. Hence the cave paintings of palaeolithic man, the rock temples of Mithra, the oracular caverns of Delphi and Cumae, the crypts and catacombs of the Christian Church. And finally, like a farewell tremor of the thought, is the cave in the toy Nativities of a German Christmas Eve.

It was weird to think of Paul, the innocent unassuming Paul, as a symbol of the headlong times, yet in a certain sense he was. Unwittingly, of course. How little we know of the whence and whither of even our greatest deeds. How unaware we are of our elder selves who, by obvious though un-suspected ways, appear at last so alien from the hopes and visions of our early years. For every step we take involves some slight release from the past, and this may involve far larger releases, an ever-increasing move-ment in spheres beyond our own, until a flux of things is under way, gathering weight and pace as it goes and finally plunging blindly into some future God knows where. How far was the first step ours? Who knows? We involve and are involved. We move in seeming freedom, yet all our movement is a drift in the weighty sway of other things. And so of Paul. He had done a noble piece of work, but how in keeping it was with Brechner's view of the old memorial, how in line with that general trampling on the past which, when the Nazis came to power, was to turn every backward glimpse of ours into a far-off vision of long ago.

I apologised to myself for bracketing our innocent Paul with Brechner, but fate would have it so. As I stepped out into the village street, Brechner was still standing with the self-same idle crowd outside the barber's shop. At once I met the full broadside of their united gazes, but the stare was not for long. Someone had just emerged from the Miss Wolffs' over the way. It was Friedrich Kemp, the able sanitary engineer who had supplanted Brechner in the business and was now one of the prosperous worthies of the village. We greeted and went down the street together in the full blast of inspection. But what did Kemp care for the withering stare of Brechner? With a cheery good-day, he forged ahead in the full confidence of his own power and position, accepting the respect of others as a right and returning as an equal the nods of the best. He was a tall, spare athletic figure and there was a glint of superiority in his dark eyes.

'Somehow I don't think we passed muster with that lot,' I ventured to say.

'With what? What do you mean?' Kemp looked puzzled, then suddenly tumbled to what I meant. 'Oh, that lot!'

'It's a pity they have nothing better to do,' he went on.

'Unemployed?' I suggested.

'For the most part, they make little effort to get a job. The trouble is that every one of them has a grievance. It wasn't so years ago. A man was glad to have a job and did a good day's work for his pay. But now he blames the employer for every setback he endures. The cause of all the evil is the profit the employer makes. That's the theory and it's all wrong.'

'I suppose that's Brechner's theory?'

'Right to the hilt. Everything is wrong but himself. He could have had a job at my place, but he refused. And now I wouldn't have him at any price.'

'Why not?'

'Sabotage. His whole attitude is to do as little as possible for the highest possible wage; to go slow and do things by halves; to do nothing when my back is turned. I can't, when I employ him, employ a policeman as well. Apparently I am a criminal, because I make a profit and he is determined by sabotage to reduce that profit to nothing, in a word, to ruin me and thereby ruin himself.'

Kemp had a decisive way, and he said all this in sharp bursts of speech as he picked his forward way along the cobbled street or sent his cheery greetings right and left to the villagers.

'He seems to have a grievance against the Miss Wolffs,' I said.

'He would. Just look!'

Coming in our direction was a boy of about 13. Despite the bitter cold he was clad in Nazi garb, short pants and brown shirt, and was apparently on some errand for his mother for he turned into a baker's shop. But I at once recognised him from his sharp hard face and steely blue eyes.

'Brechner's boy?' I suggested.

'That's right, and a dangerous lot they'll be if they get the upper hand. But I think we Germans have got too much sense for that. Still ...' Here he broke off and shook his head.

'Still what?'

'These Nazis, you know, are making the biggest promises; wild fantastic promises that will never be fulfilled. But it is the type of stuff that Brechner and his like want to hear. They are all waiting for some political party to make a big revolution and a change.'

'From which they will benefit, of course?'

'Hardly. The only change that will benefit us all will come from hard and honest work, and that is what the modern man is not prepared to give.'

And off he went, forging down the village street with purpose in every stride. I glanced back as I turned the corner. Brechner and his friends were still standing where we had left them, gazing idly after us in a mute and stubborn way. I felt that when I returned they would still be clumped in the same spot, blankly facing the problem of life and waiting for someone's solution. How little did they realise what the solution was to be.

An hour later I was in Cologne in the presence of the great Cathedral, and the little feuds of Blankheim seemed far away. What an influence lies in a great Cathedral! It wields a formative power in the spirit of a city, symbolising the thoughts, ideas and emotions of thousands of years. Everywhere in the city is a sense of its light and shadow, an acceptance of its art, a confession of its achievement.

I felt it deeply that day as I went up from the river and glanced at those lofty spires that soar up, not just from the Cathedral, but from all Cologne. In one glance I forgot the drab despairs of Blankheim, and lost myself in wonder at the appeal and fascination of those cloud-piercing towers.

They bear lofty witness to the spirit, to the faith in which the plan was born, to the long unflagging effort of countless cooperative hands by which it was completed. Here was the plain proof that with effort, purpose and faith no task is beyond our powers. And who will not feel as I did that in such a precept was a haven from the shiftless drift of the times, a pause in the breathless chase of vain evanescent things?

Cologne is a city of spires. A step or two from every thronging highway, almost back to back with the clamour, glint and gaiety of a thousand palaces of pleasure, is some still retreat from the turmoil of life, some shrine with its mellowed lights, restful shadows and unwhispered hint of the eternities. I could never resist peeping into such refuges after a weary day in the city, into Saint Martins by the market place, Saint Marien im Kapitol, Saint Gereons, Saint Ursula, and the rest, wondering at the set devotion of faces which, only a moment before, were facets of the pleasurable bustle in the busy street beyond. People of the city, peasants from round about, even children, would slip in to pray. So I used to study them as they knelt in adoration while life outside went flying by.

I had to ask myself how much of this was piety, and how much was formalism. How much was personal faith and how much pure habit that might allow some opposing fashion to steal upon the soul?

But what forebodings could I have, a young man and a stranger? I made my way amid the good-humoured crowds of the Hohestrasse, studied the elegant displays in the glittering shop windows or bought simple presents for my friends in Blankheim.

It is so easy to pass the time in Cologne. Everyone is ready with a friendly word and even with a friendly hand should the slightest need arise. If ever I should fall on evil days and be, God forbid, without a home, a relative or a friend, then Cologne, of all the places on earth, is the one where I should wish to be.

My last call was at a bookshop. It was of the sedate and scientific type, less crowded than the others, more subdued among the sober bindings of the books. I was glancing along the shelves when an assistant came up.

'Good day, Mr Arnold.'

It was Hans Reimar, a student I had often met at lectures and the like, and who had now secured a seasonal job to help his funds for the coming term. He was a pale, thin and nervous fellow on whom hard study and scant living had left a distressing mark. He blinked incessantly and cast a restless glance from side to side. I say restless, not shifty, for Reimar was an honest and conscientious student who was fighting an uphill battle against heavy odds.

He soon found the book I wanted and we fell into a chat on the unhappy plight of students, on the lack of any prospects for them in Germany and on the chances of getting abroad, anywhere abroad on any terms. To get some ready cash Reimar was prepared to accept even the lowest form of labour.

'This brings in very little.' He waved his hand towards the books and to the small number of customers who were idly inspecting the stock. 'But at least it is better than nothing.'

I glanced down the shop and saw among the customers someone I knew. It was Heinrich Boden of the medical faculty, whom I had not met for some time. He looked as fresh and stolid as ever and, with his bullet head and bulky shoulders, he afforded a striking contrast to the pale and lanky Reimar. But still more striking was the contrast between Boden and his lady companion. She was frail, dark and of Jewish cast, with thin bloodless cheeks and prominent teeth. Her swift nervous movements, her flashing glance, as well as her parade of furs and jewellery, at once attracted notice. Such a difference in face, form and bearing between her and the fair and blockish Boden held my eye for a moment, and though my glance was a discreet one it was certainly long enough to provoke a comment from Reimar.

'You know them, I suppose?'

'Dr Boden and the lady there?'

'Yes, and his wife to be.'

'His wife!'

'Yes. Geheimrat Levy's daughter. Didn't you know?'

'That they were engaged?'

'Yes.'

'By popular rumour, I suppose.'

'No, officially. It was in the paper some weeks ago.'

'You amaze me.'

I looked again and recalled Boden's words of some six or seven weeks before. Was this the lady, ugly as the night, so Boden had assured us, but whose alliance meant plenty of cash as well as professional success? As far as I could remember he had represented such an alliance as a desperate and absurd proposition, a theme for pothouse laughter, unthinkable outside sheer farce. Had I mistaken his drift in the murk of German idiom, I wondered.

'She's not a Helen of Troy,' said Reimar, 'but she's a very good proposition from Boden's point of view. With her father's bankbook and influence, Boden's a made man.'

'How do you know him?' I asked in an attempt to avoid all personal comment.

'He's a house surgeon in the clinic, and I have been under him for my chest. That's how I know him. And as for the lady, well, there's been a lot of gossip in the town about her.'

'Stuff better left unheard,' I suggested.

'Not altogether. It is not just a mésalliance with the plea of love in its favour. The wedding is a sheer deal. To us Catholics marriage is a sacrament, hence the acid comment. But I don't blame either, myself. She has got the man she wants and he has won the needful cash. And if he and she are satisfied, what right have we to interfere?'

'None at all.'

'No. And I don't mind telling you, Mr Arnold, the dilemma is almost my own.'

'You don't say!'

'I do say.'

At this moment Boden and his lady left the shop. I was looking intently at Reimar to avoid any possible meeting, but Boden made no sign. He went out with a forward stare while she, with an obvious rustle, swept out in proud possession. The shop looked almost deserted. Reimar glanced round, but there was no call for his service at the moment. His voice dropped.

'Yes, it's my dilemma, too.'

'How's that?'

Reimar halted. He was wondering, perhaps, whether he should confide in me after all.

'You know my friend, Krieger?'

I shook my head.

'You surely know. Dark, sturdy fellow. Librarian in the historical seminary. I have seen him serving you with books.'

'Oh yes,' I answered, though my recollection was of a very doubtful kind.

'Well, he's married now, though he has still his practical year to do. Of course, a purely civil marriage until he gets a permanent post. He was as badly off as I am, and was thinking of jacking it in. But he got a room in a peasant's house, just beyond Kessenich, you know. He became engaged to one of the daughters, and on that understanding the father-in-law kept him until he passed his exam.'

'And he does not love the girl?'

'Well, it is difficult to say. She is a very good honest sort and will make an excellent housewife, but she has no education. You see, he wouldn't have married her in normal conditions, but he will certainly do what is right by her and make the best of it. She, in her opinion, has a better husband then an ordinary peasant, and he has got his career.'

'So you think he has made a bargain?'

'Putting it brutally, yes.'

'And you are going to follow suit?'

'Well, through him I know the girl's sister. She is a very good girl indeed, homely, capable in the house, not bad looking, but ... '

'Wholly uneducated,' I suggested.

'That's it. And not a trace of grammar in any phrase she utters.'

'A great drawback.'

'For me it certainly is. But better that, than to continue as I am, to have a breakdown perhaps and to give up my career altogether.'

'So you are feeling the pinch?'

'I am. There are times when I could sell my soul for a square meal.'

At that moment some customers came in and I had to bid him goodbye. I came out into the evening glitter of the streets where the busy shops, the ample displays in the windows, and the throngs with their burden of Christmas parcels dispelled all dreary thoughts. I mingled with the crowd. The Hohestrasse was festive on that pleasant December evening, even the poor street minstrels were well dressed. Here at least was a happy mood, such an expression of well-being that I did not seek to explain it.

I have often wondered why I was so blind. Did the absence of all squalor deceive me? The neatness of the children? The practical domestic air of the women? The high standard of personal appearance in every walk of life? It may be so. Poverty in Germany had not the same drab face as in England, where slums and all that slums imply, ignorance, overcrowding, grime and drink, were plain for all folks to see. These were the flaws of freedom, the evils of laissez-faire. It was otherwise in a country where discipline was the rule.

Perhaps, and I believed Reimar's situation was an exception, Blankheim was a casual spot on the map, and the gloomy air of crisis but a passing phase. And yet Boden's shameless act of barter rankled in my mind.

I saw them a moment later slowly making their way through the surging crowd. Boden moved stolidly forward without swaying an inch to right or left, while she, still clinging to his arm, was swept like a fluttering butterfly, to and fro and backwards and forwards as she yielded to those going past. At times she was on the pavement, at times she was off it, and once she was so delayed and separated from Boden that she was obliged to scurry into the roadway and catch him up with running steps. But Boden went blockishly on without so much as turning an eye, wholly indifferent to her and the crowd, his hands stuck in his overcoat pockets, his head bolt upright, his hat as stiffly erect as on a Prussian parade. No wonder she was jostled about. In her right hand she was carrying a parcel or two and these, however much she tried, often came into conflict with the people passing by. By chance when nearing the Cathedral Square she was suddenly brushed off the pavement and collided with a little girl who at once burst into tears. The child had been knocked in the eye by one of the parcels. Miss Levy was full of apologies and softened both mother and child by quickly producing her purse and offering to the girl a large silver coin with the best of wishes for Christmas Eve. Even after all these years I can still see the tear-brimming eyes of the child as she took the wondrous gift, the pained and sympathetic look of Miss Levy as she stooped to apologise, still hear the soothing words of the mother and her farewell thanks as she went away.

Meanwhile Boden had gone ahead and I soon lost sight of Miss Levy as she sped away over the Cathedral Square into the shadows beyond. I looked across into the darkness and wondered. What a poor flick of a thing she was, the merest flittermouse that went its dim and aimless way by the gloomy and looming immensity of the great Cathedral. It seemed to tower up as vast as night itself.

There was something ominous in it, something of nemesis, some dire frown of the avenging gods of long ago who might, when any offender passed, bring down the whole mountainous mass in a crash about his ears.

As I looked I suddenly felt aware of my own obscurity. But there was something worse. Boden might pass, I might pass, thousands might enter the portals or even approach the holy of holies without one answering tremor from that dead indifferent heap of stone. That was it. That was the thought that made me shudder. Cologne Cathedral, that emblem of communion with God and symbol of all that is best in life, was dead, and Boden, still alive, was walking past it.

A moment later I was walking past it myself, walking with a sense of its shadow, which now pervaded all my thoughts, above all with a fear, a superstitious fear perhaps, of its monumental dumbness. It was as though the living and quivering appeal of a myriad of pleading tongues and supplicating hands had been stiffened to insensate stone. I thought of the long generations of men who had lavished their lives on the building, vesting every pier and arch with something of their inner selves, distilling their very souls into it, and casting faith, hope, ambition, every ideal they had, into the lofty aspiring form of a great cathedral. Yet this colossal quintessence of the human soul was dead.

I went down to the river to catch the train back to Blankheim. Is there some strange imp in the human mind who never fails to play a prank on all our deepest reflections? It seems so. I arrived at the riverside station just as the express was leaving for Bonn. In the lights of the last carriage I thought I caught a glimpse of Boden. Of course. Boden had hurried to the station, not from indifference to Miss Levy, but just to catch that train and thus keep some appointment at home. How was I to know? And who was I to judge him? I decided to forget his gibes at Miss Levy and to consider that in the interval he had nobly changed his mind. I felt, after all, that the watchful imp in my own mind was ready to enforce this view.

I had taken my seat in the slow train when someone called my name. I turned. The Miss Wolffs were sitting behind me, both well muffled up and wearing those round fur caps that one associates with Russia. They, too, had been shopping in Cologne, and had seen me in the Hohestrasse sauntering along with the crowd. They had waved to me but had failed to attract my attention.

'You passed us by,' said Rachel with a smile that was all good nature.

'Your pardon. How could I? But I know so few people here that I walk about with eyes closed.' I mentioned the shops, the things I had bought and, knowing the Miss Wolffs to be omniscient, I casually mentioned Boden's name. They knew him perhaps?

Yes, they knew him.

I mentioned his lady companion. Perhaps they knew her as well?

Yes, they knew her.

'Daughter of some notable professor in Bonn, so I hear?'

'Yes, of Geheimrat Levy.'

Very close and laconic were the sisters. But I could see that a long story was trembling on Rachel's lips and I would have heard some interesting things but for Rebecca. At the first mention of Boden's name she had gripped her sister's hand and every attempt at gossip was stopped by the pressure of her thumb. I persevered, however, and related the story of the accident to the little girl.

'Just like Johanna,' blurted out Rachel, who could contain herself no longer.

'Yes, Miss Levy's a very amiable girl,' put in Rebecca at once, but the familiarity of the name 'Johanna' had not escaped me.

'And very clever too,' added Rachel with a sudden wince, for the relentless thumb was at work.

'You see,' said Rebecca, taking control, 'Miss Levy runs a home for crippled soldiers in Bonn. It is a noble and arduous undertaking. She has not studied medicine herself, but Dr Boden supplies what the home has lacked hitherto, first class medical direction.'

It all sounded so honourable and splendid that I wondered where the mystery came in, or shall I say the mystification? But Rebecca switched the talk to other things and I discreetly fell in with her whim. After all, Bürger and Hillesheim were surely in the know and I could count on the reverse picture. Moreover, I was disturbed by the dry doubtful look in Rebecca's eye, that canny strategic glance that made such a crying contrast to the confiding glance of her sister. At first I tried to face it, but my eye kept wandering off and finally took refuge in Rachel's pleasant expression. She was ready to speak, I could see, trembling to say something agreeable, yet afraid of saying the first word for fear she said too much. She was waiting for her sister. Finally, however, the word came.

'Where are you spending Christmas, Mr Arnold?'

She stopped and looked at Rebecca, and I saw her arm stiffen under her sister's sudden grip.

'We are there,' said Rebecca, standing up.

'Blankheim!' the guard called out, and slowly the train drew up at the dimly lit station, which lay some distance from the old village. I took charge of the parcels, and soon we were walking up the dark road that led towards the Rhine. I talked of my plans for Christmas, and how I intended to leave my rooms for a week or so until the visitors left. I should go to some hotel in Bonn or perhaps to the Seven Hills. I was undecided.

'But you would be cut off from all your books and friends,' exclaimed Rachel. We had reached the dimmest and loneliest part of the road and suddenly Rachel stopped. 'You'll be stranded.'

'Well, it can't be helped.'

'It can. We have a suggestion.'

'Let us talk about that when we get home,' said Rebecca.

We went on in silence because, instead of going by the road, Rebecca turned up a narrow path that ran between some gardens. As the path was enclosed and dark we had to look to our steps and walk in single file. Clearly Rebecca refused to discuss suggestions anywhere in public, however private that public spot might seem to be. I began to wonder what the suggestion was. It was not until we had reached the house and I was seated in an armchair in the sanctum that I was told. Would I accept their hospitality and take two rooms on the second floor while they were away?

I was taken aback. The sisters were known in Blankheim as the two most secretive people in the village. According to Tilde, who voiced the common rumour in Blankheim that nobody entered the sanctum until every door in the house had been securely locked. In fact, if you listened intently after ringing the front door bell, you could hear the click of the keys. And then the whispers, deathly pauses and hurried tip-toe footsteps made a breathless drama.

This was heightened for the waiting caller by the knowledge that, from every window, door, crack or loophole in the neighbourhood, a fusillade of gazes were blazing into his back. But that was just the itching envy of the village. The sisters had the aloofness of superior wealth and culture, but those who had access to the sanctum, the Rektor, the solicitor, Herr Engels, all spoke of the friendly character of the sisters while admitting a certain reserve. Reservations, however, have never disturbed me. I have too many myself.

I accepted the kind offer, above all when I learned that I should oblige them by so doing. The servant, a somewhat cryptic figure in Blankheim and the silent butt of much curious gossip, would be away for a day or two, and before she returned they would be going away themselves. It would ease their minds to have some trusted person in the house to keep watch in their absence. There were certain strict injunctions that I, as a quiet academic spirit, would surely not find irksome. They were certainly essential, for the times were very disturbed and the feeling against the Jews rising with every hour.

Chapter 7

Rosenbaum and Hitler

So I was settled over the way for a week or more, and on Christmas Eve I found myself alone in the house. I suppose, to a stranger in Germany, there is no more lonely time than Christmas Eve. Everyone hastens home to celebrate in the family circle this festival of festivals, the most intimate and the most reverent of the whole year. The occasion, though a religious one, now serves a further purpose, reassembling the family, perhaps reuniting those estranged, and renewing the happy memories and innocent wonder of childhood days. The light of candles in the dark fronds of the fir tree and the glow in the cave of a toy nativity revives the fairyland vista of a world in its glorious morning. But it is all in the word *Weihnachten*, a word of mystic and solemn meaning, recalling as Christmas never can the grace that came in darkness, the pure light that glows from within and makes us the lanterns of God's spirit in a blind and sombre world.

Admittedly, I felt little of it that day, absorbed as I was in study and more used from English custom to celebrate on Christmas Day. I kept going to the window and gazing, as the afternoon wore on, at the unwonted bustle in the street below where everyone seemed to be in feverish haste. Of course the idlers round Matthias's shop had disappeared. But I saw them all in the course of the day, Brechner, Zimmermann, Heinrich and the rest, either working for some local trader or scurrying to make a last purchase, or even helping Johann Zech with the heavy parcel post. There was more purpose in their movements than I had seen for many a week.

The few little shops that had drowsed throughout the year were unusually busy, above all the tobacconist. It was owned by Dorlich, a new man from the Ruhr who, so I heard from Tilde, had an excellent display of pipes. I could not see the pipes from my window, but an ever-renewing group of people, who were studying his wares, clearly showed the success of his appeal.

However, by late afternoon the street went very quiet. The shops were shut, the lights put out, and the click of closing shutters or the hasty step of some late arrival clearly indicated that the festival had begun. Only Dorlich's shop remained open like a dazzle in the gloom. Once or twice he came out and peered up and down the street. Half an hour later there was no other light in the village than the street lamps.

I looked across the road. My home over the way looked very dark and deserted. I had met the visitors in the morning, the aunts, the grandmother and Captain Klebert. The latter was a very genial soul, a fine man to look at with light hair and regular features. Like many naval officers in Germany he spoke fluent English with little trace of accent. Short though our meeting was, I was impressed by his frank personality and ready practical ability, but there was something missing that disturbed me.

Then I realised what it was. He had a most unsubtle look in his eyes, the look of a simple man who takes the world as he finds it and puts no probing questions. Perhaps I am too used to academic society, too little aware of the daylight world of men and things, to appreciate what appeared to me but a fallow, unfurrowed mind.

About seven o'clock I took my evening meal in the Golden Hind. I was alone in the public room, tensely aware of the strange stillness that prevailed there, as though all the revellers had vanished unawares and their voices hushed for evermore. Herr Kiel in person served me. He had a very reserved way as befits a perfect waiter, never intruding on the privacy of the guest and never venturing an opinion save by a nod of submissive agreement. He looked more like a Prussian guardsman than ever, short and stout though he was, for the downward ends of his white moustache had been trimmed to a point and this gave his face a most stiff and erect expression. He went in and out like a speechless automaton, and only when he opened the door did I hear from a distant part of the house a subdued murmur of celebration. I have never known such a lull, not even once when alone at night on a breathless peak in the Alps. But the deserted air of the inn was nothing to the deserted air outside. I stepped into silence, and the sound of the bolts as Herr Kiel locked the door behind me seemed to make me the sole tenant of the outer world.

Now I have always been a scholar and a solitaire, pleased with my own society and never missing the company of friends, but there was something unnerving in all this, in the echoing sound of my footsteps home, in the darkness of the house as I entered it and in the sense of absolute solitude as I closed the door behind me. I remembered the urgent words of the sisters and my faithful promise to keep watch and ward.

Perhaps someone had entered in my absence and was even now lurking in those secretive rooms. But how was I to know? Every door but my own and the kitchen was locked, and if a fire broke out in the night the house would be utterly lost. I halted on the staircase and reflected before going up to my room. Then, dismissing these idle thoughts, I went up to my study and was soon absorbed in my books.

It might have been an hour later when I heard a loud knock at the street door. My orders were to admit no strangers and to answer no night calls. Still, it might be a message from over the way and as the knocking continued I thought I should look out. No light could be seen from my window as the shutters were closed and the curtains drawn. So I put out the light, drew the curtains aside and was about to open the window when I heard retreating steps along the street. I opened the window, released the shutter and looked out into the night. Passing the street lamp was a man, perhaps a bargeman, perhaps a beggar, whose form and gait though not familiar aroused a recollection. I opened the shutter wide, but he did not look back and was soon lost to view in the darkness. So I closed the shutters again.

The unwonted stillness, however, had made me sensitive, and a little later on I found myself trying to catch a sound. I listened intently. It was a gnawing sound, perhaps near at hand, perhaps from afar beyond the river, a low regular grate that came and went and aroused a host of suggestions in my mind. I thought of the barges straining on their anchors, moored not far from the bank. Or the sound might be coming from the tugs at the quayside with their cables grating on the capstans or the gangways creaking as the river went swaying by. But the sound was less natural, more abrupt and more deliberate. It was rather like the sound of a rat, numbers of which came with the shipping and sought refuge in the houses hard by. And the more I listened the more I felt my guess was right, for the sound was one of gnawing and was coming from somewhere in the house. I thought I would try to locate it.

The sound was clearer on the landing and certainly coming from below. I tiptoed down in the darkness, but the noise had ceased. It must be a rat, I thought. I remained a minute or so in the hall, but save for the tick of a clock somewhere and the far-off sound of a carol all was quiet. And then the sound came again, quite clearly from outside, but ceased almost at once. I pressed my ear against the kitchen door and heard something or somebody moving. I could not go out to see, as all the doors were locked and I had no access to the garden.

So I crept upstairs again, resolved to open my bedroom window and look below. I had not drawn the blind or closed the shutters, so all I had to do was release the catch gently and peep out. With all the caution I could muster I peered below. True enough. There was something or somebody there with a kind of glow or masked light, and again I heard the grating sound, quite clearly this time as though of a saw or file. And then came a wrenching sound. Should I call and give the alarm? Or should I steal off to the police? There was a telephone in the house, but the room it was in was locked. What was I to do?

I feel certain now that had my presence in the house been suspected no attempt would have been made to break in. The house was believed to be empty and the knock at the front door had been made to make sure. I realise now that I should have gone and warned the neighbours, who would have called the police. But I was unwilling to leave the house. So without any further reflection I seized the bedroom pail, filled it from the tap in the landing just outside my room and then crept back to the window. The sound had recommenced and this had helped to mask my doings as I poised the pail on the sill to get a firmer hold. I had intended just to tip the water, but something slipped and down it went, pail and all, with a sickening thud on those below.

There was a cry, a groan, an exclamation 'There's somebody in!' and an instant later two figures moved down the garden, one supporting the other, while I called for help from the window. One of the men was hurt and could have been caught if anyone had gone after him.

There was no response to my calls and my voice was lost in the wide expanse of the river. The men got over the wall and vanished on the far side down the steep slope.

I closed the window and hastened over the road and bumped into Captain Klebert, to whom I told my breathless story. He treated the affair lightly, laughed heartily at my dropping the pail and rejoiced at my hitting the target. Would I come in for a glass of wine? Festivities were in full swing and I should certainly not be intruding. But I declined, and pressed him to phone the police.

'They won't thank you for disturbing them,' he said with a laugh. 'Even a policeman must have his Christmas Eve.' He went to the phone, however, and rang again and again without a reply. Eventually, Tilde came by with a steaming dish and I heard the gush of talk and laughter as she opened the dining room door.

'I shall be back in a moment,' she said.

An instant later she had returned and had grasped the situation at once.

'Try Herr Kollass, two doors down. He is the agent for the lock-up company, the one that goes and tries the doors at night. The Miss Wolffs are clients of his.'

So off I went. Herr Kollass himself came to the door and gazed at me silently as I told my story. It apparently meant nothing to him. He looked up and down the street, then nodded his head.

'I suppose I shall have to come over, but let me change these first.'

He pointed to his slippers, closed the door and left me standing in the dark street. One minute, two minutes, three minutes passed when a cyclist came slowly by on the opposite side of the road, his lamplight playing up and down the houses as he passed. It was Dancker, the policeman. I stopped him and told him my story. He took particulars.

'I've got to go to the station. I shall be back in a moment.'

A few minutes later, with Kollass and Dancker, I went down the gully to the Rhine bank and then clambered up the slope to the garden wall. This rose up a sheer six feet from the grassy slope. Dancker went up first and hauled us up. Then by the light of their lanterns we approached the house.

The pail, an enamelled one, showed up quite white in the light. But Dancker's lantern was first flashed on the large French window which opened on to the garden. The lofty shutter had been tampered with, a piece having been sawn out by the catch.

'Clumsy bit of work, that!' said Dancker half to himself.

'Like some outrage of wanton lads,' suggested Kollass.

'Shouldn't be surprised.' And Dancker peered through the hole into the window.

'But the culprits were men,' I intervened.

'Perhaps,' muttered Kollass, 'but they weren't professional burglars.'

'By no means,' added Dancker. 'Anyway, they would not have got through. There is a steel lattice behind that window.'

I peeped through. Sure enough there was a steel lattice as though the place were a bank or prison. Dancker turned his lantern away and surveyed the ground.

'Those Jew women take no chances,' he laughed grimly, 'but what is that?'

Kollass had picked up a heavy wine bottle which he uncorked. He smelt at it and offered it to Dancker.

'Good God! Paraffin!'

And they stared at each other. So it was not a case of theft but arson. The steel lattice was useless against that. The culprits had only to break the window, pour in the paraffin and apply a match. The preoccupations of Christmas Eve would have favoured their design. The house would have been engulfed before help could have arrived. And I should have been trapped and lost on the upper floor. I shuddered at my near escape.

As we were discussing the matter someone climbed over the wall. It was Fischer, the superintendent. He strolled up and heard the report without a comment. He then questioned me and asked for the present address of the Miss Wolffs. All the time he was studying the ground by the light of his lantern.

I looked at the pail, which was badly chipped, while the others continued to make a systematic search. The superintendent, who had evidently his own thoughts on the subject, studied the wall and the bushes. And sure enough he found the kit of tools behind some shrubs.

'I thought so,' said he. 'He could not carry his comrade and this as well. We had better study these at the office.'

So the party broke up. Kollass went off home up the gully while the policemen carefully wheeled their bikes down the slope towards the Boatman's Inn. I followed them, but they exchanged no further word with me. Both were from East Germany, close reserved types who had very little touch with the people of the village. No doubt they were very conscientious, save on the subject of Jews, for whom they would do what was essential but no more. Dancker I knew quite well, and we stood on friendly terms, but Fischer was a stranger to me. His manner was one of studied, icy indifference and I could explain this only by his thinking that I had some link with the Jews. He would have denied it, of course, but the prejudice was there, inborn and inbred. I am certain that he did not realise how contemptuously curt he had been.

I did not return to the house. I walked up and down the riverbank, partly to calm down, partly to see if the miscreants would return to retrieve their tools. But I waited in vain. The Boatman's Inn was in darkness and the towpath so deserted that the only sound I heard was the melancholy swirl of the waters past the barges near the bank.

I am never happier than when alone. Even after all these years I still recall the delight of that lonely hour on the bank of the Rhine, with no other society than the cool wind on my cheek, the dim lantern light from the barges and the wistful lap of the waters in the dark river below. The night seemed to weigh like a deep sleep over the scene, a sleep which easily effaced the evil event of an hour before and revealed as in some dream the pure presence of natural things. I lost myself to it, and to all those slight touches of scene on which the mind is wont to linger, to the dim outline of the shadows on the path, to the whisper of the wind in the reeds, to the dark and rippled reflection of the barges in the waters.

And so I idled on until midnight when, without my knowing why, a subtle change came over the land, something like a far-off murmur with the seeming sound of bells, with the breath of approaching voices and the stir of some awakening. I stopped and listened. More and more distinctly I heard it as though dawn were at hand and the world afoot. Yes, it was the call to midnight mass. A moment or two later a peal rang out from Blankheim Church.

I returned to the village street where, amid the light from opening doors and windows, people were trooping along to attend the service. As I approached the house I was surprised to see someone at the door. Was it again one of the culprits? No, it was Herr Gerster, the editor of the *Landwirt* or *Farmer*, a publication that was very popular in the Rhineland. He turned round as I approached.

'You come as though called,' he said. 'I didn't care to ring or knock at this time of the night, but I wanted to hear first-hand what has happened. I am, if you have not heard, one of the founders of the lock-up company that functions in these parts. I've just been talking to Kollass.'

I related the whole affair while Gerster listened intently. He was a keen-eyed elderly man with a vigorous moustache and beard and the forceful gestures of a boy. He had played a manful part in his day, being once a leader of the Agrarian party, founder of the beekeeper's association, organiser of the farmer's cooperative society and general champion of the rural community, which gratefully subscribed to the *Landwirt*. He had an office in Cologne, but all the printing was done in his own place at Blankheim. While I was speaking, he pulled out his pad and took some shorthand notes.

'An item for the news column of the *Landwirt*,' he explained. He thanked me, asked me to call round and see him some time after Christmas, then hurried off to the church. I might have gone to the church myself, but the thought of the house restrained me, and at that very moment Herr Engels's door was opened and Tilde looked out.

'Mr Arnold,' she called. 'So there you are at last. Where have you been?'

I explained.

'You should have come across. We knocked and rang at your door about half a dozen times. Many thanks for the lovely present!' She took my hand and shook it heartily. 'And so unexpected, too. Many, many thanks. And the others were delighted too with what you gave them. Come over and see the tree.'

I went into the sitting room, Herr Engels's sanctum, and very quiet it looked after the festivity, for everyone had gone to church. The dark oak panelling looked sedater than usual, the pewter on the sideboard more antique and the portrait of Uncle Joseph on his prancing steed had assumed a graver tone. The tree was in the corner, a finely shaped fir that glittered with silver filigree and coloured candles, and beside it on a small gift-table were some remaining presents that had not yet been removed. In the far corner, embowered in dense fronds of pine and evergreen was Paul's pretty Nativity, which looked wonderfully mysterious in its green and bushy setting. I could not hide my pleasure and surprise.

'Very pretty indeed,' I exclaimed.

'Yes, very pretty,' Tilde replied, 'but it was touch and go, you know. We all felt sure that Herr Engels would be displeased. He likes his old things, of course, and when they go a bit of himself goes with them. It's only natural. This new thing looked too bare and modern and – well, you know, not like Christmas Eve. At last I got the idea of packing the evergreen round it.'

'Grand idea!'

'Yes, it worked like a charm. Frau Klebert was pleased and so were the others. We wreathed the whole stand as you see with greenery and packed the pine fronds round all this bare three-ply. It sets it off, doesn't it?'

'Splendidly! The Nativity is very pretty, but without the greenery it is nothing. Really, Tilde, what a god-sent girl you are!'

And she rubbed her hands for joy.

'But let us light up the tree!'

She was hastening out when down the stairs came a scurry of slippered feet. It was Paul and Else in their dressing gowns, and barely had they entered when I was stormed with a host of questions. Where, what, when, how, why? They had been waiting for me for hours and hours, and there were my presents on the gift-table, a bookstand specially made by Paul, a tea-cosy knitted by Else and a book from Herr Engels. And then ever so many thanks for my presents to them. And so they went on, bubbling over with excellent spirits and youthful excitement. And the Nativity? Paul, after darkening the room, switched on the light of the stable as Tilde came in with a taper.

'Let me light up,' cried Else, snatching the taper from Tilde's hand and darting up to the tree. She lit the candles in turn, beginning with the one for Herr Engels on top. I stood entranced. How delightful it all was in the cosy gleam of the candles and with the soft wavering shadows playing on the old oak beams. The Nativity glowed like a revelation in the dark setting of the greenery and the religious dimness of the room.

'And now for yours, Mr Arnold,' said Else, as she lit a wine-coloured candle on one of the lower fronds. 'I chose both the colour and the position,' she added graciously.

I thanked them effusively. The one whose candle went out last would win a prize of 20 marks. 'You have the least draughty place, Mr Arnold. You are sure to win a prize.'

'It was I who won first prize last year,' said Tilde. 'I was on one of the lower branches, which are really the best place. They do not waste so quickly there.'

We had quite a long chat, then Tilde chased the children off to bed. I promised to come on Christmas morning and receive my presents from the family. I stood talking to Tilde for a moment before I went across the street. People were coming back from church, and Tilde greeted one or two, particularly a man who passed by and called out something I didn't catch.

'What did he say?'

Tilde shrugged her shoulders.

'It's Peter Hamann. He used to be in Herr Gerster's office, the man who edits the *Landwirt* you know. He was sacked. Now he's a Nazi, and as far as I can see he means no good to anyone.'

I looked after him and I seemed to recognise in his gait the man who had knocked at the door. But perhaps I was playing with fancies, so I bade goodbye to Tilde and went across the road. Still, the fancies remained, and as I entered the lonely house which might by now have been a smouldering, empty shell with my bones in the smoking ruins, I shuddered. I was prepared to pass a sleepless night when a car drew up at the door. It was the Miss Wolffs, who had been phoned up by the police. The driver was no other than Professor Rosenbaum. He had been attending the same reunion as the ladies, and, as a taxi was not available, he had gallantly offered to drive them back to Blankheim.

'Ah, Mr Arnold, God be praised,' said Rachel, who was clearly distressed. Her glance seemed to apologise for any anxiety I might have suffered.

'Fancy having our holiday spoiled like this,' pouted Rebecca, and swept past me to examine the damage.

Rosenbaum locked his car and came inside. He greeted me in a very friendly way while the sisters opened the dining room door and made for the garden window. We followed. The steel lattice was thrown back, the French window opened, the shutters outside unbarred. We all inspected the damage.

'How is it that you did not hear them at once?' asked Rebecca. I thought there was some reproach in her tone. So I explained.

'Perhaps,' I concluded, 'it was just as well that I did not hear at first. We now know the worst. Had they been seen at once, before unpacking the paraffin bottle, they might have returned at a later date and burned the house down with you in it.'

Rachel clutched my arm!

'What an escape! Yes, as you say, we now know the worst. To think you might have been trapped in the flames, alone in the house! We should never have forgiven ourselves.'

She cast an apologetic look while Rebecca was engaged in studying the damage and weighing the pros and cons of a simple repair or a new shutter.

'An iron one,' suggested Rosenbaum.

'Yes, an iron one,' said Rebecca decisively, and after a further look round we went in. While the ladies prepared coffee I had a talk with Rosenbaum. He was affable, perhaps too affable, with the over-friendly, over-genial way of Jews who suspect an enemy in every stranger and seek to disarm opposition. Still he was a kindly, tolerant man, extremely well informed, and I forgot his over-effusiveness in his revealing comments on the state of Germany and in his forecast of future events.

Although he was anxious about the growing hooliganism of Communist and Nazi gangs he was not at all alarmed about a possible change of government. Hitler evoked no terrors in him. Indeed, he seemed to think that to give Hitler power would bring him to reason. A political party was one thing, a government another. Responsibility was the great soberer, the great brake on party passion, the weight that would slow down the flights of Nazi rhetoric. In fact Hitler's biggest problem was his own fanatical party, and to bring that lot to heel would provoke a mighty crisis if ever he got to power.

To my surprise, he rather favoured the rise of Hitler to power, a sentiment I later learned that was shared by many Jews. Hitler had pledged to abolish unemployment, and this could be achieved by British and American loans, which would not be afforded to a mere vulgarian government.

This dependence on foreign help was thus a further safeguard against extreme measures. In fact, the greatest evil of the times was not Nazi excess but Socialist policy, the wasteful policy of something for nothing, of bonuses, doles and crippling taxation, and this was ruining the state as well as the moral fibre of the workers. Hitler, who was supported by many big industrial interests, would put a stop to this. He would make the right to live dependent on the will to work, and this was as it should be. To effect this revolution, however, he would require the support of the masses as well as the best brains of the nation, and here was a third safeguard against a Nazi abuse of power.

This all seemed right to me and, as Rosenbaum sat there in the reclining comfort of an easy chair, slowly rubbing his hands and warming his feet by the electric fire, I wondered at all these rumours of a crisis. He looked so happy, assured and confident, and the glint of his gold-rimmed glasses added a further pleasant glint to his smiling eyes.

If Rosenbaum saw no crisis why should I? Yet even as he sat there, so serene and hopeful and with the lamplight beaming on his brow, a shadow of suspicion crossed my mind. An unworthy suspicion, admittedly, engendered by thoughts of Bürger, Brechner and the rest and without one dot of evidence to support it, but plausible nevertheless. Was all this made up for me, a screen for very different views, part of a policy of personal safety which made me a witness for Rosenbaum's pro-Nazi views should the Nazis come to power? In view of the possible threat of mob rule and mass murder such dissimulation was certainly wise policy. Was Rosenbaum so worldly wise, such a shifty, slick illusionist in casual talk with a stranger? It was certainly possible and it proved how far I had been drifting along the Brechner-Bürger road.

The ladies came in with the coffee and we drew up to the electric fire and discussed the attack on the house, the unrest in the village and the hopeful comments the professor had just made.

'Is that what you really think?' asked Rachel, with a half smiling, half despairing look at Rosenbaum.

'I most certainly do.' And he summed up his points again, even suggesting that a Hitler regime with economy, work and discipline as its first and foremost principles would do Germany a world of good.

'It's my opinion too,' said Rebecca. 'What is needed now is the old discipline of the Kaiser's days when everyone worked and worked hard, and there was order in the land and mutual trust and, above all, the stability that is now wholly lacking in the business world. Business was possible in those days, you know. You should hear what the business people and the shopkeepers say. They are sighing for the good old days when the Kaiser was in power.'

'That's it,' said Rosenbaum. 'And when Hitler comes to power he will have to rely on the army, and the general staff is loyal to the Kaiser tradition. After all, the old army will rule and I shall not fear very much.'

Rachel looked very doubtful. All these clear and excellent reasons were lost on her truly feminine mind.

'I dread Hitler and all his works.'

'Yes, we all do,' responded Rosenbaum, 'but he is only a figurehead, the puppet of mightier powers. He was the lackey of Ludendorff to begin with, and if he gets to power he will be a true servant of the general staff. They are the true spirits of Bismarck and Moltke. They, not an ignorant plasterer, will be the real rulers of Germany.'

'So you favour a military despotism?' I said.

'In these circumstances, yes. I am a democrat, but the choice is between two evils, despotism or mob law. And I prefer a despotism that keeps order in the land and allows me to sleep securely in my bed.'

Rebecca heartily agreed; she, too, was a democrat. I looked at her as she sipped her coffee. The events of the night had not disturbed her one jot. She sat there, calm, hard, inaccessible, poising her cup without a tremor while her sister, flushed with inner fear, looked round with a half-smile as if begging for consolation.

I have often recalled the scene and pondered that strange talk. I have often thought of Rosenbaum, and can still see him as he sat there, so placid, so unsuspecting, so sure of the normal run of the world that he did not sense one shadow of the doom to come. And, when he rose to go, he smiled so spaciously and beamed his assurances in so easy and certain a tone that all my misgivings faded away. I say all, but there was a lost look in Rachel's eyes that came and went, and left me with a vague fear that no reason, however perfect, could dispel.

I went up to my room and thought over what Rosenbaum had said. Was Rosenbaum an exception, some very plausible hybrid, something both right and left, both Catholic and Jew? Most Jews in Germany at that time were socialist or communist. Indeed so many were communist that the two names were bundled together as the hallmark of all that was worst in international views. But it is also true that many Jewish businessmen were longing for the return of those palmy imperial days when German trade was outstripping all its rivals. The revival of the German army, the domination of Europe and the winning back of the colonial empire with fresh markets at the sword's point, all these offered a prospect that dazzled even democratic Jews. They felt that anti-semitism, excellent as propaganda for an extreme nationalist party, would silently be dropped when the party came to power. The Jews might suffer a little. They might be excluded from public office, from the schools and universities, but the business world would remain open and offer abundant scope for advancement.

It was playing with fire of course. I thought of the famous scene in the Athenian assembly when Kleon, a wordy demagogue, boasted that, given the command of the army at Pylos, he would capture the Spartan force in thirty days. His boast was received with cheers and he was offered the command. With a fervent God-speed he was hastened on his way, because the alternatives were so attractive to the assembly. He would either capture the Spartans or, better still, they would be rid of Kleon.

Could Germany afford to do the same? Could a great and civilised people afford to stake their destiny on the blind pitch and toss of a Nazi boast? Could they dare to say, 'Yes, take full control, for if you succeed we shall be rid of the crisis, and if you fail we shall be rid of you!' No, the cases were not parallel. In the first place, Kleon was out of the country and if he failed he would never return. Athens would certainly be rid of Kleon. And be rid at a very small price. But not so with Germany and the Nazis. Here the stake was not a small expedition hundreds of miles away. Here the stake was the nation. Failure meant national failure and the downfall of the state.

As I could not sleep I tried to forget my anxieties by delving into that grand old book, *Chronicles of the Free Imperial City of Speyer*, a book long forgotten now for it was published in 1612 and the leaves were brown and stained with age. There were more than a thousand pages and they were all so closely printed that after a while my eyes swam and the old words, with their wondrous spelling and grotesque letters, assumed human form, and I saw the characters behind them, the whole ghostly company, the emperors, princes, counts and margraves, spirit up from the ancient pages. I even strained my ear to catch some sound of the passing cavalcade and wondered at the silence of the house and at the breathless hush in the street beyond. I stole to the window and looked out. The whole village was dark and still, so I returned to my reading and lost myself again in visions of the past.

For an hour I idled along in the fullness of these illusions, half thinking, half dreaming when a simple sentence struck my eye. Not much more than a dozen words, yet every one so steeped in vision that scenes arose before me as vivid as life itself.

'1353. In this year the Jews were driven from the city, their cemetery dug over and sown with corn.'

Nothing more.

In vain I scanned the following pages or turned back in the haunting hope that some word or hint had escaped me. That simple full stop had fallen like eternal night on the scene and all I descried was a trail of fugitives on the far-off hills, some broken headstones by the wayside, and a spot, once shadowed by willows and the cypress, now glowing with the gold of the harvest.

Did any return to that poor little spot, by night perhaps, and indulge their bitterness? Did even one pang disturb the reapers and trouble their later dreams? And did any when he thought of his own dead brethren start up and refuse the bread of affliction that came from so cursed a grain? But why enquire? It is all gone and forgotten, and of the whole sad scene we know only this, that in 1353 the Jews of Speyer were driven from the city, their cemetery dug over and sown with corn.

Chapter 8

The Coming of the Nazis

Sown with corn! There is a fatalist sound in the phrase, an air of what is now no more, a sense of the end of something which, unlike the leaves of the forest or the flowers of the field, knows no returning spring. Perhaps the effect is due to the phrase itself, perhaps in part to the great break of 1933. For the break came, utter and final. Not that I felt it at once, for it took the Nazis time to show their hand, but, as month after month went by and the Nazi power grew, I began to close my eyes to what the day or the morrow might bring. But it quickened my sense of the past and gave me the utter sense of loss in even present things. Yes, I say in present things. Have you ever in some silent hour heard a door being closed at night, and then listened to the lonely echoes as they died away in the rooms beyond? Or to an old clock just ceasing to chime and the sounds still seem to tremble on, sinking slowly yet swiftly away into the mute deeps of the night?

At such moments silence is absolute, the past more poignantly past than when years have come between, the sense most profoundly felt that all the life we have lived has now passed into the dust and shadow, and so of my memories then. They are still as living as ever, though as dead as the men whose burial spot was dug over and sown with corn.

To me the government was just a new government with rather decided views. They took power without a tremor, or at least any that was reported, the socialists and communists simply sinking from view without a blow in self-defence. The foreign press spoke of terrorism, of secret arrests, brutal assaults and seizures of property, but at first I saw little of the ruthless power so swiftly and silently wielded. There were many flamboyant speeches, of course, threats of an iron and heavy hand and much wild talk of a new order that would involve the whole of Europe. Yes, I heard very much of the new era, reflected that a new broom sweeps clean and concluded in youthful innocence that the bigger the word the smaller the deed.

However, one thing disturbed me. How was it that a great nation, a great and disciplined nation such as Germany undoubtedly was, with its feudal tradition and caste distinctions, with its passionate zest for education and high regard for culture, so readily bowed to Hitler, an almost illiterate plasterer, and silently let him bellow his gross and vulgar ungrammar in Germany's name?

Perhaps Rosenbaum was right. Perhaps the crisis was such that the only remedy was a despotism followed as it would be by the saving intervention of the army. But then again there was a great fear. It is easy to be brave in a land where justice is maintained and where a sense of right and wrong restrains the ruling hand. And it is easy to be brave when one stands in the public eye and can rely on public support. But it needs a saint to be brave in the dark. It needs a saint to stand firm where the only and final appeal is to God.

I remember the day when I first realised that something evil was under way. I was standing at the window looking into the street below and wondering why young Brechner, who was pacing up and down, had nothing better to do. Though still a boy he was now the complete Nazi with his high boots and breeches, his brown shirt and swastika armlet and long-peaked cap. When anyone passed him by, his arm shot out in the approved style and his rapped-out 'Heil Hitler!' seemed to demand a like reply. Indeed, his lips remained parted and his hand upraised until the expected answer came. But when a mere nod was returned or even a courteous good-day his look of ire and contempt would have done credit to a stage villain. And so it went on, the slow parade up and down, the stand-and-deliver greeting, the appearance of waiting for something to happen with the certainty that nothing would. I wondered why.

Then Tilde entered in her free and familiar way, and laughed as she saw what I was watching.

'Oh, young Brechner, what do you think of him?'

'Why, what's he doing?'

'Picketing the Miss Wolffs'.'

'What?'

'Picketing the house; seeing that no one goes in and buys in their shop or delivers any orders or, you know, has any dealings with the Jews. Mad idea, don't you think? You know I'd like to go out and smack his ...' Her eyes gleamed as she swung her arm down to chastise the place in question. 'Shouldn't I just! Whack! Whack! Whack!' And she lashed out with joyous vigour as though she had him across her knee. How I laughed! And there was young Brechner outside, parading in dead earnest, and all unaware of his blubbering fate beneath Tilde's flailing hand.

'My word, here's another,' I said as a further Brownshirt appeared.

'Yes, Hans Zimmerman, in his new brown rig-out!'

'What? Hans Zimmerman!' I could hardly believe my eyes. 'But he was the village communist!'

'Of course he was. But he slipped over just in time. Like the rest of them, of course, or at least a good many. In the village I come from we had a communist even more red-hot than Hans, one of the fire-breathing sort, you know. You should have heard him tub-thumping and bawling and blathering for Moscow. Lord, you had to stop your ears. And now! Strolling round as large as life with the brownest shirt in the village. Good thing for him, of course. You know what they say our way?' She seized my arm and shrieked with laughter. 'Before he donned that shirt he had the brownest pants in the Rhineland.' And she shrieked again.

'Sheer fear?'

'Sheer fear.'

'But such men are no use to the Nazis.'

'No use?' Tilde went suddenly grave. 'That's where you are quite wrong. These new converts, you know, are worse than the genuine thing. You see, they have to prove themselves. And then they are so ashamed of themselves, they feel forced to vent it on others. They think people are mocking them or talking behind their backs. You see, they can't trust you and you can't trust them. Give me a true-born Nazi any day.'

Hans Zimmerman, after a word or two with young Brechner, had shot out his arm by way of goodbye. The solemnity with which Brechner returned the salute and the wondering look of Matthias who had just peeped out of his shop to survey this impressive and formal farewell made me laugh outright.

'God!' cried Tilde. 'You would think they were going over the ocean. And all as solemn and serious as the regimental last post. Gee, I wish it were, for both of them.' And she laughed herself to tears.

At that moment Herr Engels entered, attracted by our laughter.

'May I share your joy?' he asked, in his grave and happy way.

'Oh it's only about these Nazis, Brechner, Zimmermann and the rest,' said Tilde. 'My word, Herr Engels, it was a true word of yours – when things begin to boil, the scum comes to the top.'

Herr Engels looked grave.

'Yes, but I am not aware that I ever referred to my fellow men as scum.'

'But that's what you said, Herr Engels.'

'Then I am sorry. In a general sense it is true, of course. The worst in men appears in such a crisis as this. Yes, the scum does come to the top.'

'But how shall we get rid of it?' I asked.

'Get rid of it? Well if you can't ladle it off, it will have to boil over.'

'Which means that things will get worse before they get better?'

'I think so.'

'Well, the sooner it boils over the better,' said Tilde.

'Yes,' said Herr Engels, 'but when it boils over, as it certainly will, it will make a nice mess of the hearth. The proverb says – better an end with terror than terror without end. But I am looking forward to neither prospect.'

'Nor am I,' said Tilde, and off she went to a call from below. And so we parted, Herr Engels to some business appointment and I to Bonn, which, owing to a cold, I had not seen for a week or two.

I was certainly not keeping pace with events. I had scanned the newspapers, of course, heard the drum and trumpet speeches, and caught some echo of the grand tam-tam that was going on at the big street corners; but to me all this was wind and weather, something that came and went with a bluster, like March winds and April showers before the settled approach of spring. And yet I was wrong. I was looking at affairs in too English a way, and not reacting as a German would who was less concerned with general principles than with his own personal role in the drama that had begun. That we were in for a military despotism was clear. But no one shrank from that. Even Rosenbaum, a Jew, a pariah dog in the land of his birth, could hail such an event as desirable and accept it with a sigh of relief. As for the rest of the Germans, to them the Prussian military system, whatever its obvious evils, was the most successful reaction to a thousand years of foreign invasion, pillage and devastation. Herr Engels, Bürger and Hillesheim had explained that flagrant fact when we were dining at the Wolffs'. But it was left to Rebecca Wolff, of all the people in the world, to show that, to the German people, internationalism was a national evil and that the one obvious lesson of their long disastrous history was the need of a mighty army. So much I knew. But why this fear? Why this mute acquiescence in an outbreak of brutality planned and carried out by a vulgar man of the street?

Bonn was very quiet, not at all like a town in the throes of a revolution. I recalled my historical reading, thought of Paris in 1789, of the excitement, the popular fever, the daily drama at every corner, when parades, speeches, uproar and arrests brought everyone into the streets. No, the revolution here was different, not a mass movement of the people from below but a swift *coup d'état* from above that had passed without a tremor. Then again, Bonn was a Catholic town, residential, conservative, distinctly academic, one of the most reticent spots in the Rhineland. Like me, it was untouched by events. There were a few more swastikas hanging from the windows, a few more Brownshirts parading the streets and a little more Nazi saluting than before. The office of the socialist paper had been closed and looked very dreary with the shutters up. Naturally, all the Weimar flags had vanished. Otherwise, to my neutral eye, there was little reaction in Bonn to the new state of affairs.

I usually entered the university by one of the side doors, but as I had strolled through the town to see what was going on I now entered by the front. Leading to the quadrangle from the street was a broad open porch which served as a memorial hall to those who had fallen in the war. The names were engraved on either side. Ever since their inscription one had walked through without ceremony, very few stopping to glance at the long roll of honour, though not from disrespect, for the Rhineland is a Catholic country which remembers every day the dead in prayer.

Now, I was struck by a curious scene. A butcher's boy had just ridden up. Leaving his cycle at the gate, he hurried into the porch with his basket of meat and made for the caretaker's quarters. He had gone but five or six paces when he was suddenly seized by a jack booted Nazi guard and roundly clouted, the basket of meat sent flying with the contents scattering into the street. But why? What was the matter?

I might have protested, but for a fresh hubbub ahead. An elderly professor, doubtless hastening to deliver a lecture, was brutally attacked by another guard who sent the old man's hat whirling into the square with a swinging blow. Such a sedate old man, so quiet, so academic, almost like a retired cleric with his white hair welling from beneath his black round hat. He seemed to huddle up, so thunderstruck by the criminal assault that, in fear for his life, he cried out loudly for help. I might have proved a third victim, but for the timely appearance of Bürger. He cleverly and tactfully interposed, and the danger passed.

'You take your hat off or give the salute when you pass through here,' shouted the guard.

'Sheer vulgarity,' was my comment.

'Sh!'

'But it is, and you must admit it.'

'Sh! until we are out of earshot. Yes, that's what Rosenbaum said this morning when he was heftily clouted and I thoroughly agree with him.' There was a touch of malice in Bürger's tone that seemed to belie his words.

'Of course you would agree with him. This surely is not your new order?' And I pointed back to the porch where a loudly protesting gentleman was picking up his hat.

'By no means,' said Bürger, as we walked up and down the quadrangle. 'All these wanton youths are acting on their own account or else on local instructions. These, you may rest assured, have no warrant from the central power. The government has not yet settled down, but just wait for a month or two. Discipline will come, a tight discipline, a discipline for the whole of Germany. What we have needed all this time is a strong and iron hand and that, take my word for it, we shall get.'

'But this is mob law.'

'For a short transition period, yes. What can you expect? This is a fundamental revolution, quite the equal of the great French upheaval of 1789. That is, in its social and political scope, but unlike the French Revolution ours is almost bloodless. There'll be no excesses here, no bloodbaths, no devastation of Europe, but a national revival through hard work and discipline. To bring this about there must be an iron hand.'

'You mean a military despotism!'

'Yes. It cannot be avoided.'

'Why not?'

'You see, Germany has been brought to ruin by the Socialist policy of something for nothing. Millions are on the dole, simply standing in idleness and getting a salary for it. What with free this and free that, bonuses, grants and what-not, we are transforming the whole state into a charity

81

institution. It's thoroughly wrong. Widows with children, yes, old people, yes, they deserve consideration. But a healthy man who can work is no object for pity or charity. No, he is a subject for work, and work he will get, if need be at the sword's point. Of course many will not like it. The trade unions will not like it. The millions of idlers now on the dole will not like it either, because they will have to be directed to jobs. Without military despotism we are ruined.'

'Ruined? I think there's a leap in the logic there, Bürger.'

'Not a bit of it. Just think. Since the advent of socialism politics have ceased to be politics in the true sense of the word. They have become a vast bribe to the electorate. There's no hope in any party that relies on the vote. This rush to social ruin, with all the national wealth squandered in charity schemes, can be checked only by a sheer iron despotism. What is all this welfare stuff but a bribe to the simple man in the street?'

'Not merely the simple man in the street. Surely the whole nation benefits?'

'That's just it. It doesn't. It's the ne'er-do-wells who profit. The thrifty, diligent working man, the man who is a blessing to society, never comes down on the parish. It is he who has to pay. The hard-earned money that should go to his family goes instead to the idlers, louts and soakers, the scum of the nation.'

'But how will you deal with this scum?'

'There'll be a law for sterilisation.'

'Good God!'

'Oh, don't raise your brows. The Spartans had a more drastic way and they kept their race pure both from inner rot and outer pollution. But there's the bell! Heil Hitler!' And off he went.

I managed to catch the professor I wanted to see, discussed my work with him, received further directions and references to further sources and was thus able to fill up some library forms and drop them into the box. I might have gone straight home, but I thought I would step in and hear Rosenbaum who was lecturing at 11.15. It would be a compliment to the man I thought, and might stand in lieu of a formal call. So, when the time approached, I strolled along the crowded corridors to where he was to lecture. On my way I saw some groups of SA men on guard at certain doors, barring entry to the students. So I was expecting something of the kind with Professor Rosenbaum. To my surprise the way was open and a fair number of students had already taken their seats. So I took mine. Presently a lady student moved up next to me. It was Fräulein Metzenauer, whose brother I knew very well.

'Good day, Mr Arnold, you've not taken to economics surely?'

'No, I have just come along to hear the lecture.'

'Or to see the fun, which?'

'Is there likely to be any?'

'I don't know, perhaps, perhaps not.' She looked a little distressed. 'I really wish something would happen and then I should know one way or the other.'

'Why, what's the matter?' She was usually so vivacious and full of good spirits that I wondered what had wrought so great a change. Her dark eyes were moist and her once ruddy cheeks with their truly piquant dimples now looked drawn and pale.

'Well, I'm a student of his, you see,' and she nodded towards the platform as though to Rosenbaum. 'And I've swotted up all his theories and know his books text and verse. The whole of my thesis, and I've been at it for more than two years, is Rosenbaum from end to end and squared up exactly to all his pet views. And now!' She broke off with almost a sob.

'Won't anybody else take it?'

'There's not a professor in the whole of Germany would look at it now. Particularly now that Rosenbaum and all that he has stood for is completely out of fashion. He certainly would not pass it himself.'

'But he would. He's a gentleman, surely?'

She bent towards me and whispered in my ear, 'It's a case now of self first and the devil take the hindmost. Anyway, listen to him; here he is.'

It was Rosenbaum. The students trampled applause as he entered and he moved like a stately procession to the desk where he leisurely opened his satchel, extracted his sheaf of notes and smoothed them out before him. He had a pompous way in all these things and was highly conscious of his dignity as a professor. Despite the events of the morning, he seemed quite cool and collected, correct as ever to his fingertips. As he stood there, polished, immaculate, glinting, I tried to picture him going through the porch and getting a 'hefty clouting'. It must have been a strange spectacle.

He bowed to us all, and began. I must say that the very first sentence gave me a decisive shock. He cited 'our beloved Führer', quoted a text from *Mein Kampf* and proceeded to make it the *leitmotiv* of a most impassioned lecture. Nothing that Bürger had ever said was so hefty and headlong as this. It was a paean to the new order. As phrase after phrase pealed out, each a learned emphasis of the tub-thumping views of the Party and all a flat denial of what the world had come to know as the Rosenbaum school of thought, I fell into a strange wonder.

Did I despise or pity Rosenbaum? Was all this trumpery outburst reaction to the hefty clouting he had received that very morning, or a trembling premonition of the still more hefty cloutings that were to come? Or was it a proof – yes, I mean it – of true personal bravery, a casting adrift of every scruple, of every shred of private honour in order to win a title for loyalty and thus to gain some respite for his persecuted fellow Jews? I don't know. I forgot the lecture after a time and found myself dreamily gazing through the window over the lonely stretch of the Hofgarten where the rows of gaunt chestnut trees were straining in the wind. It was the end of February, the end of term and, to me at least, the end of many other things.

A student in front of me turned round with a wearied snigger. It was Otto Klein, whom I had met on several occasions.

'There's been a hot sale of *Mein Kampf* among the profs here.'

'Oh!'

'Why, haven't you heard them?'

'No, I've been away.'

'God, you ought to go round. They all begin now with a text for the day as though it were a bible meeting. The Führer ranks as a prophet now, even in geology and physics.' He gave a suppressed laugh.

I felt a touch on my arm. It was Fräulein Metzenauer who was preparing to leave.

'I can't stand this any longer. I must go.'

'Good. I shall come with you.'

We gathered our things and left. We went silently down the staircase and hardly exchanged a word until we got to the open street. It was freer and fresher there and a cool wind was blowing. I felt a great relief at being outside, and as I looked at the open sky I wished I were far away in the distant woods and hills beyond the Rhine. My companion stopped and faced me. Her face was flushed, perhaps from anger, perhaps from shame, perhaps from sheer confusion. And there was a gleam in her tearful eyes.

'Have you words for it?'

'Frankly, I haven't. But I don't know all the facts. And I know little of the fears under which he is working. After all, he is a pariah dog now. Perhaps, when all's said and done, the man's to be pitied.'

'Pitied?' She had too sweet a feature for hate, but she certainly looked daggers at me.

'Yes, pitied. The man is really talking with a noose round his neck. Perhaps, if that were all, he might be more heroic. But there's a noose round the neck of all his family as well. In fact, from what I hear, the whole Jewish race will soon be swinging.'

'Well, after that, I think they ought to be,' she said decisively. There were some placards at the other side of the road. We went over and looked at them. They were all political, largely of the *Stürmer*, Streicher's anti-semitic paper, with its vulgar and scurrilous lampoons on the Jews. It was stuff to make one blush and my companion turned away.

'Let's go on,' she said.

'Of course. But all that stuff, you must admit, is sheer incitement to a pogrom, unworthy of a cultured nation. Rosenbaum can't help but see it. And then you've heard of the clouting he got this morning?'

'Yes, I've heard, and I condemn it as much as you do. But that does not excuse him. He could resign his post and go abroad.'

'I'm afraid it's what you'll have to do, Miss Metzenauer.'

'What do you mean?'

We were passing the great bookshops opposite the university. Being students, we had halted, quite instinctively, and looked aimlessly at the display in the windows where, instead of the learned titles, there was a flood of political stuff from the Nazi press, portraits of the Nazi leaders and even a swastika. I could see from Miss Metzenauer's looks and mien that she was gazing into nothingness, so obsessed by her own troubles as to have no eye for anything else. She seemed to have forgotten her own question and was evidently deaf to my reply. So we drifted on into the square ahead with the great Minster rising before us and with the distant memorial of Beethoven to remind us of other things. We stopped outside the old church.

'I really must go in here and unburden my heart,' she said. So in we went. She knelt in the shadow of one of the arches and for a full ten minutes was lost in silent prayer. I sat down not far away in the stillness of the old Minster and wondered, amid my troubled thoughts, at the permanent peace of the spot, at the lasting solace of the aisles and the arches, at the indulgent light of the chancel so aloof and so unruffled by the pelting storms and brawls of hundreds of years.

I was roused from my reflections by my friend. She was standing beside me, wondering at my abstracted look.

'I have had it out,' she said, as we stepped into the street.

'And you have forgiven him?'

'Yes,' she smiled bitterly, 'but it will be a struggle to forget. You see, I don't know what to do.' She looked so forlorn that I felt I must help.

'Let us talk about it over lunch.'

She looked grateful. So off we went down the Poststrasse, forgetful of the Nazis and all their works, when a great hubbub behind us made us turn. Descending the street was a great concourse seemingly of the Hitler Youth, not in serried array, but simply crowding down and shouting the anti-Jewish song,

'The times for us then
Will be ever so much better,
When Jewish blood is spurting
From our knives!'

They commanded the whole roadway, halting the traffic, thrusting all and sundry aside, and striding on in full career as though to a military triumph. On they came, shouting, singing and flourishing their placards and slogans, and challenging by their brawling behaviour some brawling response from the passers-by. But even in the rising uproar I was somehow keenly aware of the stony silence of the street, which revealed no other reaction than the forced halt of the traffic and the half-wondering and half-affronted gaze of all lookers-on. Just a wild demonstration, I thought, of wanton headstrong youths, and I was about to turn away when I caught sight of the slogans, one of them anti-Jewish, but the rest against the Separatists who, during the occupation that followed the world war, had favoured an independent Rhineland and a break with Berlin. And the

Separatists were there in the column. A whole line of them in Indian file, distinguished men of the town, all hatless, manacled and roped together.

They were being hounded along at the crack of the whip like felons to the galleys. Each had a traitor's placard on his breast and it was painful to see these men, able and eminent men of Bonn, as they stumbled blindly along with eyes closed and downcast looks and wholly at the mercy of these turbulent and brutal youths. I felt a wild urge to rush forward and protest, cost what it may, when something froze my resolution. It was a policeman hard by who, in answer to some 'Heil Hitler', raised his hand in salute and then held up his other hand to halt an oncoming car. He had clearly received instructions to let them carry on. And so they surged past and soon were lost to view in the Bahnhofstrasse beyond. I looked at my companion who was standing with tears in her eyes.

'Terrible,' was all she said.

'But the police are in collusion. The man not only saluted the gang, but waved them on. Did you see?'

She said nothing until we reached a side street and then, looking round she said in a quiet voice, 'Yes, they are all in the swim. The government openly forbids these things but privately tells the police to close an eye. In this way it can terrorise people while disclaiming responsibility.'

'But that's lynch law!'

'It's what they call "folk justice".'

'So any wild act of a Brownshirt is a case of folk justice and above the law?'

'Yes, that's why the people are so quiet. It's really jungle law. I knew it already, in a way, but I didn't realise it until now. It has opened my eyes.'

It was tactful to drop the subject, so we went by tram up the Rhine and there, in the stillness of an inn by the river, we lunched with a full view of the Seven Hills. How pleasant it was to be far from all the political brawls of Bonn, to watch the barges plying up the river or to see the ruins of the Drachenfels standing up so gaunt against the slowly drifting clouds.

Over our coffee, we discussed the thesis and its chances of acceptance abroad, in Austria or Switzerland or perhaps in France. How to get abroad she did not know, having few funds of her own and no chance of a permit from the government to take such funds elsewhere. But at least she could write to some foreign professor, one of the Rosenbaum school of thought, explain to him her predicament and ask him to consider her work. But here was a further hitch. In face of the growing censorship, dare she write such a letter abroad? If such a letter were opened and read, it might prevent her getting a passport and ruin her career. Slight though the danger was, it was big enough to give us pause. I offered to post the letter myself or get it posted for her just over the border in Holland or Belgium where I could collect the reply. She agreed.

In such talk we passed the afternoon and, after further coffee, returned to Bonn by nightfall. My companion was now quite cheerful, resolute and ready to seek ways and means of continuing her studies, and to take any work abroad in order to pay her way. She was hopeful of a loan from the Catholic academic fund which was open to students in need, and with this and part-time earnings her way was clear. In the light of this new plan, all her shadows seemed to fade away. And when I mentioned Rosenbaum she waved her hand in deprecation and laughed with all her wonted sparkle and golden good nature.

'Forgotten and forgiven. RIP to his memory!'

And so we parted. I went home that day in a state of deep dejection, pervaded by an ominous sense of something I felt but could hardly define. Was it the new swastika flag I saw in the Meckenheimerstrasse hanging from a window in the convent school? Was it the look of an old professor who glanced away as I greeted him and who, despite his blushing face, his sudden halt and momentary confusion, tried to seem unconcerned? Or was it the bold 'Heil Hitler!' of a certain medical student who once within my hearing had roundly denounced the Nazis and called for their suppression? It may have been each or all these things, but suddenly I felt myself on unknown ground. I wondered. Had it all happened in a night, or was it that my eyes were opened and that a host of things I had overlooked were now becoming clear? Or in reading of suppressions, atrocities and despotism, had I read but the surface facts and failed to see the dread implications beneath?

Now that I was in the mood, I seemed to see changes in Blankheim itself, subtle and sinister changes which revealed the unseen shift below. I had reached the High Street, which was dimly lit by the occasional street lamps and with the gleams from the few shop windows. Nearly opposite the Golden Hind, which threw its own length of light across the road, was the untidy little shop of Johann Fenger. He sold tobacco and a jumble of other things.

Fenger himself, in slovenly pants and a battered cap, was standing at the door, a mere lump of a man with a labourer's hands and features who had drifted into petty trade for want of something better. Being a non-smoker, I knew him only by sight and used to pass him by without so much as a nod. However, as I approached that evening, he fixed his eyes upon me with such a penetrating stare that I stumbled over the cobbles in sheer embarrassment. Suddenly his arm shot forward and he cried out 'Heil Hitler!' with that interrogative lift of voice that calls for a reply. I looked at him in mute surprise as I went on my way, wondering with a strange misgiving whether this dull village drifter had been vested by the party with any oppressive powers. This groundling, this cast-away, was now a member of the ruling caste, a privileged figure in the scramble for positions and one who stood, like the youths of Bonn, above the law. He and his kind decided what folk-justice was. I had but to ignore his salute or buy from his trade rival and I might be made to feel his power.

His slovenly pants and battered hat seemed to follow me up the street.

I entered the house and went up to my little study with a strange relief, as though I were closing the door on an evil outside world. I sank into my chair and pondered the events of the day, slight events in themselves, yet filled with a strange foreboding. I thought of Hans Zimmermann and his prestissimo conversion, of young Brechner and his jackboot arrogance as he paced up and down the street, of the hefty clouting scene and Bürger's defence of the mailed fist, of the problematic Rosenbaum and of the brutal parading of the Separatists with the impartial salute of the policeman standing by. And then, to balance it all, was that gracious, god-sent girl, Rosa Metzenauer, her distress, her bravery, her spiritual battle in the Minster. That, and our glimpse of the hills and the spacious purity of cloud and sky as we sat beside the Rhine, were more than a solace for the anxieties I had felt. Despite the sinister show, I was still in the old Germany that I loved so well.

Chapter 9

The Disruption of Family Trust

Some days later I was taking breakfast in my room and pondering Tilde's strange behaviour. She, the carefree, happy Tilde, who always had a smile and a merry word, had entered with the merest murmur of a greeting, had placed my coffee on the table and then retired in such a mournful silence and with such a clouded look on her face that I wondered what had happened. Bickering was a thing unknown in the Engels household, and, though Frau Klebert was distinctly the mistress and Tilde distinctly the maid, the relation between them was a truly family one. The girl was definitely at home. As for Herr Engels, he treated Tilde in his fine patriarchal way almost like a grandchild. And Tilde, who was a very good girl indeed, was worthy of this high regard.

The case was exceptional. In Germany, class distinctions are stronger than in England, being at times so feudal in character and so mindful of the higher and lower orders as to shock an English mind. But Herr Engels showed no trace of them. Moreover, in disputes he allowed no time for rankling thoughts, but settled everything there and then in the resolute spirit of forget and forgive. So there could be no dispute, nothing to leave a wound. It must be only a passing cloud, perhaps bad news from her home on the Ahr where her father was a struggling peasant.

I did not have to wait long to hear the reason for her gloom. Frau Klebert came in to clear the things, and she looked as gloomy as Tilde herself, and very ill at ease. Now I had always liked Frau Klebert. It was impossible not to like her, because her sterling virtues were reflected in every feature, all of them so crystal clear, so free from reservation, that she always left me with the effect of a vision where shadows are dazzled away.

She had come to explain what was amiss, and I could see how much a struggle it was to put her plea in the best light. It concerned not merely Tilde but us all.

'I have asked father, and now I am asking you, and I hope you will understand. In the first place we must all be more reserved with Tilde. She is a very good girl and a very nice girl and I could not have a better maid, but the village now has ears. Up to now she has had the freedom of the house, in fact the freedom of the family. We have concealed nothing from her, neither family affairs nor political opinions, so anything we say might leak out into the street. Not deliberately, of course, but by chance and in all innocence, and this will be carried further and the family might be ruined. Herr Gerster was arrested last night, simply taken from his bed and ...'

Here her voice broke and she shrugged her shoulders.

'The editor of the *Landwirt*?'

'Yes. I am upset, because he was a good friend of ours.'

'And why was he arrested?'

'Oh, he condemned the government in the latest edition of the *Landwirt*. He ought to have been more discreet. But there it is. The threat is over us all. Hence my warning about Tilde. I have given her strict instructions to limit her talk with us to mere affairs of the household. You see Karl, my husband, is in the navy. He has sworn an oath to the new regime and naturally my loyalty goes with his. I have hated the Nazis and all they stand for, but now I must bring myself into line for the sake of the family.'

'So we must all begin lying!'

I murmured this just to myself, but I have never seen a woman so blush to her hair roots as Frau Klebert did then. It may have been indignation, but I really think it was shame for she had consented to wear a mask and was asking me to do the same. Now my remark, I swear it, was not meant as a reproach. It was my instant comment on Nazi rule, which had subtly invaded the house and planted its cloven hoof on our souls. I could see on what a slippery edge we stood and, having taken a first step down, how could we ever control the second, or the downward slither of the third and fourth? And if we dissembled to Tilde then why not to Herr Engels, an honest, straightforward man who, in all his conversation, said clearly what he meant?

'Now don't say that, Mr Arnold.'

She rested her face in her hands and stared at the table as she spoke.

'Lying is as odious to me as to you. But do you realise what these Nazis are? Do you think they would respect an honest enemy or even an honest neutral? Do you think that a stand against them, a private stand by you and me, would end in any other place than the gutter? Their methods are the methods of the jungle. And therefore I shall deal with them as I deal with all beings who are wholly outside the moral law. I want to have as little to do with them as I possibly can, and this I can best achieve by a pretence of submission. Is it lying to adopt such a policy towards those who have no respect for truth?'

'You must excuse me, Frau Klebert, but my comment was meant for the government, not for you. I see your predicament. Perhaps it will soon be mine. But about Tilde's position, may I say a word. Nothing would loosen her tongue more freely in the village than to tie it up at home. If she is denied society here she will find society outside, and heaven knows with whom. Better friendly prattle here than unfriendly prattle outside. Don't you think so?'

Frau Klebert looked distressedly silent, so I went on.

'No, I think our best plan is to drop all talk of politics in the house and to be discreetly neutral outside. In this way we could keep our private honour intact and preserve the peace of the home.'

'Yes, but my . . .!'

Here she broke off in confusion. Her husband had doubtless asked her, in view of his naval position, to stand up more in the open for the new ideas and the new regime, a task quite easy to those who take no interest in political affairs, but rather difficult to a Catholic who clearly stood in the opposite camp. And then the children? Had he suggested to his wife to let them join the Hitler Youth? His own position required it and, having no qualms himself, he suspected no qualms in others.

This must have lacerated Frau Klebert, the daughter of Johann Engels, to find herself aligned against all she held most dear. She would certainly have resisted but for her deep conviction that the sanest way to meet the Nazis was to hide her hand. A clash with the Nazis would not be a battle of principle with the vast powers of evil and oppression, but only an obscure brawl with the Brechner-Zimmermann gang, in which not the slightest honour was to be gained. And in a political sense she was right.

'Well, I promise you, Frau Klebert, to say nothing and do nothing that would compromise you or your husband. Being an Englishman I am naturally neutral and, whatever my personal feelings are, I shall refrain from expressing them to others. But of course I shall do no dissembling either to Tilde or to your father and yourself. I shall not condemn the government, but I shall certainly not praise it, and mislead others and belie myself and disgrace the great example which you yourself and your excellent father have always set me here.'

'No,' she said, in a dull and toneless way. But still her dilemma remained. At that moment her father came in and I repeated my promise to him, with my views on our policy to Tilde. He heartily agreed.

'There is naturally no harm in discretion, but to go beyond and play a part is certainly evil. You are right, Mr Arnold. There's no need for us to call on Barabbas. And as for our dear little Tilde, she's a daughter of the house and a daughter she'll remain as long as this roof is my own. And why should we close our hearts against her? To be shut out of the fold is to be cast to the wolves and that I shall never allow.'

'But, Father, she prattles so much.'

'Let her prattle. When she empties her heart we know what's in it. Better a wagging tongue than a whispering one. Let us have no skulking secrets in the house, unsuspected cobwebs and skeletons in unscrubbed corners. There is enough darkness in our own shadows without adding shadows to the soul.'

'But think,' cried out Frau Klebert, 'what has happened to your old friend, Gerster! Suddenly arrested, dragged from his bed and taken to goodness knows where! It could easily happen to you, for you are not loved by the Brechner crowd. We must be careful, Father, careful, for your own sake and for the sake of Karl who insists on our being square to the government. We must give no cause for even the slightest complaint.'

'My dear Klara, when the devil's strong enough he does not wait for causes. Nor is he likely to relent at our sham change of face. It's too late now to go back on the past, too late to unsay and undo what I've been saying and doing for nearly eighty years. To change now means that all my life has been misspent, all my faith misplaced. I don't believe it. I am as I am. The less time I have to live, the more precious are the moments remaining. And I feel responsible now for every single one of them. Let us hold fast to the end. For as the tree falls so shall it lie.'

He filled his pipe and strolled to the window while his daughter sat there with downcast eyes, struggling for words and finding none. I felt sorry. We had left her no alternative than to face the full shame of her position. A little compliance on our part, a keener sense of the impending danger and a true appreciation of Nazi brutality might have eased her embarrassment and revealed her change of front for what it was, just feminine tact. As I had guessed, the thought of her children, their entry into the Hitler Youth and their possible estrangement from the family and the church were weighing like a nightmare on her mind. Her husband's orders were imperative. In fact he had written to the children and, as I heard later, had given precise instructions. He had not troubled in the slightest about the reactions of his wife. Apparently, to him, there was nothing to react about.

'What's the matter over there?'

Herr Engels was speaking. I went to the window and looked over the deserted farmyard, which lay quite dead with its cover of faded weeds. Two old peasant women were standing in the lane beyond, talking and pointing and nodding their heads, and even when they moved away they kept on looking back. As far as I could see they were discussing the little shrine built in the wall, and though their faces were indistinct their attitude was serious enough.

'They are talking about the shrine, it seems to me.'

'Yes, I see that.'

Two men were coming up, Hans Zimmermann in his Nazi garb and another whom I did not know.

'Peter Hamann,' said Frau Klebert who had come up to see. The two men stopped for a moment and I heard their laugh as they made a gesture towards the house before they passed on. Suddenly Frau Klebert put her hands to her face.

'Oh, father, it has been desecrated! The figure has gone. The frame has been taken away.'

I could see it now, the dark blank niche in the wall where the figure had been. As I looked I felt something of the shock that my hosts were feeling at the desecration of the old memorial. I had come to love that little shrine, not from any motives of faith or leanings to the mystical, but just for the simple appeal of it, for its pleasing and happy humanity, for the pure avowal of fellowship that shone with a rosy glow into the silence and solitude of the night. I had often looked out of the window, when the whole village was fast asleep and all the fields beyond it lay in deep and misty darkness, and seen that little glint on the far side of the lane.

I had come to love it, and now it was gone, broken and trampled under foot, nothing left but the memory of it and the dead insensate stare of the bare wall. I could only stare back in return. Why, I thought.

'Yes, why?' asked Herr Engels, and at once I realised that I must have spoken aloud. 'Never in the history of Blankheim has that happened before. You know the date, I suppose, and the inscription?'

He gave me a searching look, and his bushy brows and aggressive beard seemed to bristle up in the shock of his emotion. Something had happened that staggered his understanding.

'It was set up in 1689, the year Bonn was besieged and devastated. It was set up by an ancestor of mine, his name is on the inscription, in grateful memory of his escape from mortal danger. He was returning home with his horses and carts when he landed between the fighting troops, a raiding company of French soldiers and the advancing Brandenburgers. All the horses and three of the labourers were killed. He alone escaped. He erected that shrine the same year and there it has remained. And now it has been disturbed after 250 years. And as you say, why? Tilde lit it last night, I suppose.'

'Yes, just after seven o'clock,' said Frau Klebert. 'Let's go and see.'

We went over the yard and out by the far gate into the lane which divided the straggle of Blankheim from the rural beyonds of the village. It was a typical Blankheim lane, neither this nor that, for it trailed its haphazard way between a sequence of fences, walls and hedges from one main road to another. But the view to the north-west was pleasantly open, and extended from the haze of Cologne to the distant foothills of the Eifel.

I could not help but glance across at the wide prospect to the far horizon, at the wistful trend of the fields and fallows and at the heavily drifting clouds, but it was only a glance. Right in front of us was the empty niche, with the frame wrenched away and scattered over the road amid bits of the red glass that had held the oil and the light. The image had gone, a mere primitive piece of carving but endeared by time and association to the older inhabitants of the village. Herr Engels removed his pipe and looked with wonderment at the wreckage.

'So it is gone!'

Just that one simple reflection and then he was silent. I wondered what he was thinking as he stood there in the lane, his look fixed on the empty niche. Certainly not of the culprits, nor of their arrest and punishment, but just of the dustbin destiny of everything on earth. Even that innocent memorial, with its happy appeal to God and man and assurance of final mercy, had not, for all its hundreds of years, been spared that levelling hand. Herr Engels turned away, speaking more to himself than to us,

'And if that goes, what can escape?'

I caught the words as we went through the gate.

Frau Klebert examined the niche and the fragments. 'Sheer vandalism,' she kept on saying, her face flushed with indignation. Yet I wondered what she was thinking and whether her views were altered by this wanton hooligan act. Surely she could not think of aligning herself with this? So I waited. Presently she came to where I stood, then looked cautiously round.

'So there!' she said with great decision. 'These are the kind of people we have to deal with. And I refuse to deal with them. Do you see my point now? It is not the leaders or the government or even the general public we have to settle accounts with but the riff-raff of Blankheim, and they are free by the official wink to do just what they please. But I shall report the matter to the police. Not that anything will come of it, but I shall just test them out and see where we stand.'

'Would it be better if I went?'

'If you like,' she said after a pause, 'but you had better not mention us. Go, if you like, on your own initiative and see how the police respond.'

So off I went to the police. I was rather pleased with the errand as it gave me a glimpse into things. I might even ask the superintendent, whom I had not seen since Christmas Eve, whether anything further had been heard about the outrage on the Wolffs' house. Or would they be annoyed by any reference to the Jews?

I entered the police office, and took my stand at the counter. Fischer was there at his desk, absorbed in clerical work, and his assistant was looking through some files.

'Good morning,' I said, but there was no reply, not so much as a glance in answer to my greeting. I waited one minute, two minutes, until the silence grew oppressive. The clock ticked on and on, and neither Fischer nor his assistant showed any sign of getting up. Their work was hardly urgent, for they were glancing in a leisurely way through some papers and exchanging a word from time to time. I should make another attempt, I thought.

At that moment the door opened and in came Heinrich, the fawning factotum of the church. Perhaps I had been studying too long the rigid close-cropped officials in front of me, but never have I seen such a crumbling-looking tramp of a man as Heinrich appeared to be then. With his slanting eyes, hooked nose, furrowed cheeks and drooping moustache he seemed to be sagging into the earth.

'Heil Hitler!' he called out, and then repeated the greeting to me.

'Heil Hitler!' replied the assistant who instantly stood up and attended to Heinrich at once. As I gathered from their talk, Heinrich had come to notify some lodger's change of address.

While the entries were being made Heinrich turned to me. 'Heil Hitler, Herr Arnold! A sad thing about that memorial shrine. After hundreds of years, think of it, after hundreds of years. Herr Engels will be upset when he sees it.'

'Sheer hooliganism,' I said. 'That's why I've come here, to report it to the police.'

'Quite right, sheer hooliganism, Herr Arnold. You've done right to come to the police.' The assistant finished the entries and then turned back to his desk without so much as glancing at me.

'Excuse me,' I called out. 'Would you kindly attend to me. I've been standing here for more than five minutes. Apparently you can serve people when you choose.' The assistant glanced back with a blank and almost defiant air.

'Attend to him,' said Fischer without one upward glance.

'Well?' The assistant approached and leaned his hands on the table, waiting for my request. I explained, while Heinrich stood by and echoed any salient remarks.

'Yes,' drawled the assistant, 'but we can't be chasing all the wanton boys of the village. Our work would never be done.'

'Quite right,' said Heinrich, 'you can't chase wanton lads all the time. The police have something more important to do.'

'It's not due to wanton lads,' I declared. 'It's the work of certain hooligans who are taking advantage of the crisis to vent their private spite.'

'Oh,' said the assistant, and waited passively for more.

'There seem to be a number in the village, to judge from the attack on the Wolffs' house and on the Rhine memorial.'

'Perhaps you know their names?'

'No, that's your business, surely?'

'And yours?'

'Well,' I answered, with just a touch of irony, 'believing you were interested in law and order, I came along to report the affair.'

'Take his deposition,' said Fischer, without even raising his head.

So I gave it and went, and I have no doubt that the notice was lost and forgotten in the files. I got rid of Heinrich at the door lest I should betray myself into quotable remarks, and then went home by a roundabout way, wondering at my own indiscretion yet wondering still more how I ever could have avoided it. 'Heil Hitler' was an essential preface to any talk with those in power, and clearly there was no place for private protest and still less for ironical remarks. Without violating my promise to Frau Klebert, I had certainly frayed it a little.

I frayed it a deal more before the day was over.

I had almost reached home when I met Miss Rebecca walking along the street. She was looking ahead and seemed to miss me, but this was mere discretion, and she answered my greeting with much warmth. Two or three of the villagers, one of them in uniform, were standing outside the barber's shop, but they were staring towards the Golden Hind where there was a small crowd. They did not glance back until I was at the Wolffs' house. The door opened as if by magic.

'Do come in,' Rebecca said, and I went inside without delay. There was a call outside as the door closed, but I paid no further attention. It occurred to me only later that I had slipped past a Nazi guard at the door. As for my promise to Frau Klebert, that came also as a second thought, and also very much later.

So I was once more in the sanctum, which, in its uncanny quietness, was as far beyond the village as the lonely fields outside. The tapestries and carpets helped to subdue all sound, but there was something else, an air of remoteness from the street, a sense, above all in the wistful pictures, of a lost culture. It was so easy to forget the present there, the over-loudness of demonstrations, the clamours of the gutter, yet could I envy the sisters? They must have felt their loneliness the more.

Miss Rachel came in, paler and more anxious than usual, and approached me with the same misgiving as she would any envoy of the Nazis. But my manner reassured her and we sat down closely at the table and talked in almost breathless whispers lest anyone in the street should hear. Any shadow that passed the window made her glance up and pause. But soon her sister came in with some coffee and we talked in more confident tones.

'You must help us,' said Miss Rebecca.

'Gladly.'

'You see, we are unable to buy anything in Blankheim, though the villagers would be happy to serve us, and no one can bring anything in. What we order is not delivered. It is held up at the door, and even, so we have heard, at the station. What are we to do? I have just been to Cologne where the people are reasonable and I have bought some provisions, just as much as I can carry. But we cannot go on like this. And our old servant has left us and we find it difficult to get another, not one that would suit us.'

'Or rather one that would suit them,' I said, turning my thumb to the street.

'Exactly. Of course, these conditions won't last for long.' She shook her head vigorously. 'There will be a return to normal, I feel certain.'

Miss Rebecca really believed this, and she spoke with a confident air, but poor Miss Rachel looked helpless. She smiled from time to time and nodded at her sister's hopeful remarks, but every smile and every nod was more an appeal for sympathy than a proof of courageous views. She kept glancing up from time to time to see the ever-returning shadow of the Nazi guard outside. And the more I saw her hunted look, the more resolute I was to help. What a nightmare that sentinel had become. Even I, who was in no danger, felt something of the stress and strain. That slowly patrolling silhouette was getting on my nerves.

My task was a simple one. They would send me a note from time to time and I should do their shopping. Orders could be sent to me and I could bring them across at night when the guard had gone or at any other convenient time. Or I could meet them by chance and leave a parcel in their hands. Nothing easier. So I took their first order and enough marks to cover orders for a month or more, assuring the sisters of my sympathy. It was only then that I thought of my promise to Frau Klebert.

There was no help for it now. My first crisis of conscience and truth was approaching. I had given two conflicting promises, and I asked myself what my promise was worth. What was my hope of either being fulfilled if I had to leave the Engels's house and Blankheim? Even worse was the question of concealment. How could I return home and in answer to plain questions give evasive, misleading and even lying replies? The Engels family would have to know what I was doing, for I could not act in a secretive way without being secretive to them as well. And once I started shuffling where would the shuffling end? Only in gross untruth.

I took my leave. The sisters pressed me to go out by the garden, slipping over the low wall to evade the guard. But I refused. In for a penny, in for a pound. I should take the plain, straightforward way and shamble round no corners. Out I went into the street and ran straight into young Brechner, who was so taken aback as to forget his Hitler greeting.

'Good day, Kurt,' I said.

'Good day,' he replied. Then a shout of laughter from the crowd brought him to his senses.

'Heil Hitler!' he shouted after me, at which there was a further burst of laughter. I was halfway across the street, but I turned and smiled my acknowledgement to the crowd. They had seen and heard the whole passage and thought it very funny. Alas, ridicule is a dangerous weapon, above all when turned on those in power. A blow is finally forgotten, but a gibe rankles for ever.

Tilde opened the door and gave me a doubtful look, but I reassured her. I took and shook her hand.

'Ah, Tilde, we must hold our tongues in future, above all on certain topics, but be assured we are the best of friends.'

'Thank you, thank you,' she said, and it was a delight to see her sunny face again and to see the murk of misunderstanding disperse like a cloud shadow on a blowy day.

'What's the matter with *him*?' she asked, nodding over to Brechner, who stood there in confusion struggling to say a thousand things and unable to utter one. As she closed the door I told her. She laughed, then checked herself, holding her breath and suddenly looking round.

'Pardon,' she said.

'My fault,' I replied. I put my finger to my lips, gave her a significant nod and went off to Herr Engels.

He was sitting in his chair by the window, pensively smoking his long Dutch pipe and studying the morning paper. He cast a glance as I entered.

'Ah, back at last. What did they say?'

I told him. He showed no surprise at the ways of the police and heard everything in his still judicious way.

'They are officials,' was his only comment.

'That does not excuse their lack of courtesy.'

'Yes and no. You see, they work to a strict code and, believe me, Superintendent Fischer could quote chapter and verse for every word he utters. Everything he does is squared up to the regulations, to paragraph this, subsection that, to some special departmental instruction. No, it's the new order. We can rely on no protection now. And we can count on no redress.'

Frau Klebert came in and heard the last few words. I did not look round, but I could feel her presence in the room. She herself was gravely ill at ease, at least that was my impression. At once I asked myself if I should temporise, if I should play for time and, while awaiting a favourable moment, carry on in a secret way, disclosing only what I must. But I had taken my resolution, so I told them all that had happened at the Wolffs'.

'Quite right,' said Herr Engels. 'We've no option but to give them a helping hand.'

'But it's not quite right, Father. We have got to be on our guard, and nothing should be done without the greatest precautions. I feel I must have a say in this. You should have consulted me, Mr Arnold, before giving a second promise.'

'Yes, I should. What I promised to Miss Wolff hardly squares with what I promised to you. I apologise, Frau Klebert. But when she asked me to help them what could I have said?'

'I don't know,' she said in a helpless way, 'but we ought to do nothing without the greatest circumspection. Above all ...'

There was a ring at the door and we all went quiet as Tilde passed by to answer it. The front door opened, there were voices and footsteps, someone came in, and the door was closed gently. Tilde knocked and entered.

'It's Frau Gerster to see Herr Engels.'

'Show her in,' said Herr Engels, standing up and laying his pipe aside.

'Oh!' Frau Klebert started, caught her breath and then recovered herself. She went to the door and offered her hand.

'Frau Gerster, welcome.'

A frail, distracted lady entered. She cast a tearful and anxious look around as though some lurking enemy might start up beside her. She was very upset. She had really nowhere to go and had come to the Engels for sympathy and advice. We helped her to take off her hat and coat. It was distressing to see how she trembled.

'I don't know what to do,' she said in a broken way, and sat down.

'Never mind, Gertrud,' said Herr Engels in his most encouraging way, 'it will be only for a day or two. Karl will have to be more careful, that's all.'

'I think it's more than that . . .' Her voice trailed away into a sob. 'They've commandeered the . . .' Her voice broke again.

'The what?'

'The office and the press. Peter Hamann is in control.'

'What?'

'How do you mean?'

'He has taken charge of the paper and they say he'll run it. Karl left a note saying so. So I went to the office at two o'clock this morning and . . .'

Suddenly she checked herself and looked round at me. I felt I had better go and let her tell her story in secret. Frau Klebert gave me a nod, so I went.

Though burning to hear the story, I was glad to go if only to save Frau Klebert from embarrassment. Her dilemma was deeper than ever. Her heart was wholly with Frau Gerster and I knew she would gladly help the Wolffs. In fact, if she had been single and without ties to her home and husband she would have faced anything to help them. I was sure she was not afraid of danger, of oppression or military power, but she certainly shrank from what had happened to Frau Gerster. A Peter Hamann in her home, some vulgar fellow who would step into the old inheritance and trample on all that was dear to her.

I went up to my room, but before the day was over I had heard the whole story. The Gersters had been knocked up before dawn. Herr Gerster went to the bedroom window and, recognising the police and guessing what they had come for, scribbled a hasty note and whispered some directions to his wife. He was not a moment too soon, for the police were getting impatient, ringing and hammering at the door.

Then he went down to let them in and, after deliberately handing over the wrong bunch of office keys, was allowed just time to dress before being hurried away. He was particularly anxious about the great safe in the office where he kept some papers and letters he wanted to make safe.

Frau Gerster herself was but a frail and trembling creature, but in obedience to her husband's wish she stole out by the back way, having just a coat over her nightdress, a bag to carry the papers and the right bunch of keys. With just a few seconds to spare, she entered the office, emptied the safe and was back before the police returned asking for the proper keys.

The whole street was now aroused by the throb of the police car and the imperative knocking at the door. Scores of faces at the windows and doors witnessed the scene, the waiting car with its flaring headlights, the big-booted police with their lamps, the frail lady at the door muffled up in her night attire handing over the missing keys.

But the drama was not over. There was also a safe in the house. Barely had Frau Gerster emptied it and hidden the contents, together with the papers from the office, in the hen coop at the back when the police returned and searched the house.

Frau Gerster was no heroine in the popular sense of the term, but she would never betray a trust, come what may. Such a spirit was beyond the police. It never occurred to their brute-strength minds that they might have been outwitted by that frail and fainting wisp of a woman who cowered and shivered in a corner while they ransacked the house.

It was Herr Engels who told me the story, with the permission of Frau Gerster. As I was an Englishman, a neutral, and unsuspected by the police, I could take charge of the papers, either keeping them in my room or leaving them with trusty friends until a safer place was found.

I readily assented, and offered to fetch the parcel, but Herr Engels had a better plan. Frau Gerster was very devout and attended early mass every morning. Herr Engels was also a regular attender at that early hour, so she had but to leave her parcel on the seat and Herr Engels would retrieve it. None of the few worshippers would notice the act in the dimness of the aisle, so the parcel would pass from one to other without a meeting or the exchange of a word. In the course of the next few days, three parcels were locked up in my trunk.

The incident, simple though it was, and of very little import in the setting of bigger things, revealed one sinister aspect. Frau Gerster, an honourable and innocent lady, of pious disposition and retiring ways, suddenly found herself alone in her distress. Neighbourly friendship melted away. She was left isolated, as strictly avoided as any criminal might have been, and allowed no more than a passing nod or a hasty good day.

The story as told in the village was all drawn from the Nazi clique, Hamann, Zimmermann, Brechner and the rest, who spread rumours of corrupt practices, malversation of society funds and the defrauding of countless clients by Gerster. The two empty safes were clear proof that he had something to hide. Corruption was the great word when the Nazis came to power. It filled the headlines of the press, was charged against all opponents, religious, social, and political, without discrimination, and as the press was in Nazi control there was no means of checking the accounts.

If any man stood his ground, he was arrested and shot 'while trying to escape', and if he fled over the border he was a cowardly slinker from justice, one whose flight was an admission of guilt.

I was pledged, however, to help the sisters. This might seem innocent enough. Indeed, no law forbade me to visit Jews, to do private service or to console them in distress. Even Hitler himself had declared that 'not a hair of their heads should be ruffled' and, in reply to foreign protests about oppression and brutality, great play was made of the phrase. There was high talk of German discipline, of the respect born and bred for law and order, and of the absence of mob opinion in this the most cultured and educated land in Europe. But even I was dimly aware that a proclamation of policy might be only a deliberate blind for doing the opposite thing in practice.

The Nazis stooped to any excuse. 'Communists disguised as Nazis', 'foreign Jews bent on blacking the party', these and similar formulae were trumped up to explain any outrage that might have come to public notice.

So it was with a certain misgiving that I stole out of the house one dark and rainy night with my first heavy parcel for the sisters. Like a thief, I closed the door behind me and made my way to the river. There was no one about. The barges, the Boatman's Inn, the towpath, everything was asleep. I stood for a while in the darkness, trying to make out the forms of the neighbouring shadows and straining my ear to catch the least unwonted sound. But the riverside was deserted, and even the nearest features were obscured in the night mist. Reassured, I climbed up the grassy slope and approached the garden wall. Miss Rebecca was already there. 'Thanks,' she whispered as I handed her the parcel and she put a note into my hand with details of further orders. Then she vanished up the garden. Away up the river the church clock was striking midnight.

Chapter 10

Blackmail and Booty

Although a great revolution was going on, and though the press was full of the drums and trumpets of the Hitler regime, I saw little of the great upheaval. At first I put this down to my village seclusion, to my pre-occupation with academic things, and above all to my own character, which keeps me wholly aloof from the clamours of the crowd. It was only later that I realised how the Nazi revolution was a vast hushed-up shuffle and scuffle between the haves and the have-nots, a threatening thing of evil whispers and surreptitious blackmail.

Of plain brutality there was little. One sensed the shadow of the mailed fist and, in fear of the impending blow, millions turned informer to save themselves. There was nothing open about it as in the French Revolution, nothing wildly dramatic, no storming of the Bastille. It was all a silent *sauve qui peut*, a sudden and sordid scrimmage for power and place and jobs.

There were 6 million unemployed with their clamorous demand for work and there were several millions more who were determined by hook or crook to keep the work they had. And with the worst hook and the worst crook both sides set about it. By the thousand they swarmed to the Nazi bureaux and told their spiteful stories, either to prove their loyalty to the new regime or to vent some petty grudge and thus rid themselves of a rival.

The Nazis used the stories, partly to swell the great tale of corruption and partly to terrorise the waverers into line. A dusky suspicion hung over the whole nation, darkening every walk of life and leaving its offensive murk between neighbour and neighbour, friend and friend, and even in the home itself.

Now I knew that informers were rife and that a campaign of defamation was well under way in every walk of life, in the village, in the university and in the country at large, shattering all trust and subtly setting every man against his neighbour. I knew it without really appreciating all it implied. For it is one thing to know of a fact and another to know it at first hand.

My first hint of what was on came towards the end of March. I had settled down to study one night when Tilde admitted a visitor. I wondered who it could be. Few visitors ever came to me, especially during the vacation, and Tilde had not announced a name. But the next moment the solicitor,

Lambert, was in my room. He faced me before offering his hand, his stare numbing my spirit. I motioned him to a chair, feeling very subdued. He peered slowly round before sitting down and fixing me with his gaze.

What on earth had brought him to me? To me, a mere nobody to him, whom he always passed in the street without a recognising glance? Some evil impulse, I felt sure, and I suddenly remembered Gerster and the papers in my charge, which were in the trunk in the corner.

So that was why he had come, and despite my quiet nature I felt really roused. I was pledged to keep those papers and keep them I would, come what may. I should betray nothing and no one, and with this firm resolution I addressed him.

'You have come to see me?'

'Yes,' he said with a further stare.

'About what, may I ask?'

'Oh, a trifling matter, a mere nothing, but you can help me. It won't take you very long.'

As he spoke he drew from his pocket a paper, which he unfolded and smoothed out. He then changed his spectacles, adjusted my lamp to suit himself and perused the paper carefully while I sat mutely wondering what it could be. The man himself disturbed me deeply. Behind him were my bookshelves, and the familiar backs and titles seemed to peer at me in mute surprise. Who was he to come between us? What alien being was this in our private domain? His very shadow left an infected print on everything it fell on. But presently he was finished.

'I should like you to translate this into English.'

'For what purpose?' I asked, prompted by a sudden suspicion that here was a simple trap. I had taken the paper without a glance at it, and kept on looking at him. He gazed at me in mute surprise, but seeing I made no further move he finally gave me an answer.

'It's a letter for the English press.'

I read the letter. It was written in fulsome praise of the Nazis and in denial of all the charges of oppression and brutality that had appeared in the foreign press. It stated that before the Nazis came to power Germany had been a sink of corruption, exploited by Jewry and corroded by Communism so that the only barrier to Bolshevism was in danger of collapse. From this imminent lurch into chaos we had just been saved by Hitler. And so on. There was not a tittle of truth in the whole letter. It was sheer blather and ballyhoo from beginning to end.

'Well?' he asked as I gazed in a bewildered way at all this obvious trumpery.

'I am afraid I must decline.'

'Why?'

'It's political and as a foreigner I must not abuse my position here by taking sides in your affairs. I am sorry I cannot oblige.' And I handed the paper back.

'But it is a clear defence of Germany against the slanders of the foreign press.'

'But you are repeating many slanders to do it, and I can't be a party to that.'

He was clearly taken aback by this response, but I realised I had said too much. He gazed at me in a most curdling way, so I stood up and bade him goodnight. He remained seated in dumb surprise.

'So you are against our new government?'

'You must not try to involve me in any political debate,' I replied in my most decisive tones. I moved to the door, opened it and beckoned him to leave. The man was really dangerous. He changed his glasses where he sat, placed the paper back in the case, slowly stood up and then went out of the room, gazing at me in a fixed way without one farewell word.

I had to tell Herr Engels. He heard everything in his silent way and finally nodded his head.

'So that's why he came?'

'Yes. I think he needs a little certificate to prove his loyalty to the new regime, and a letter from him to *The Times* would be excellent evidence of this.'

'I suppose it would. He has had many dealings with the Separatists and the Jews, in a purely professional way of course, and he would like the Nazis to forget this. Do the Miss Wolffs know of his change of front?'

He gave me a meaning look, and I knew what he meant. Yes, I must warn them. I wrote a note at once and enclosed it in the parcel I took a few hours later. There was no one about, so as I handed the parcel across I whispered to Miss Rebecca that I had enclosed a warning note about Lambert.

'Solicitor Lambert?'

'Yes,' and I told her briefly what had happened. I had expected some anxious comment and I was pleasantly surprised by her matter of fact tone.

'Thanks, but we have got the measure of him all right. He has dealt with us as the agent of others, but we have never employed him ourselves.'

'I am pleased to hear it. You see, I thought he might have powers of attorney in your affairs.'

'Oh la, la, la!' she said, and laughed as loudly as she dared. 'As if we would leave our affairs in the hands of any villager! But thanks for the warning, and take care he does no harm to you.'

So we parted. I had no fears for myself. How could I? And yet a disappointed man in those years of mass betrayal might do a deal of mischief. I should have to be on my guard and give him no cause to involve me or the Engels in any dispute. But was he after all a disappointed man? And had I thwarted him in his little ratting scheme?

Strange though it may sound, he was content and even pleased with the result of his visit. He had got, if not all, at least much of what he wanted. For he went straight to the Nazi headquarters, made a parade of his loyal letter, and denounced me as a hostile foreigner, as I learned a fortnight later.

I was waiting one Saturday afternoon for the train to Cologne when the one for Bonn came in. Among those who stepped out were the Miss Wolffs, and I greeted them quite openly, though they gave me the shyest reply and kept their glances strictly to themselves. I felt sorry for Miss Rachel as she struggled with her bag, while the conductor stood sullenly there and no one offered to help her. So I stepped forward and gave her a hand. Months before, most of the people there would have touched their hats or given a nod of recognition, but now there were none so poor and certainly none so bold as to do her the slightest reverence.

I was the exception. In fact, despite my quiet demeanour I was almost the clamorous exception, and in a subtle instinctive way I felt the observing presence of every member of the crowd. There was one, in fact, whose gaze was more probing than the rest. It was Brechner. So to ease the tension I bade him good day.

'Heil Hitler!' he replied and, after a few words had passed, he suddenly said, 'So you are no friend of our new government?'

'No friend?' I exclaimed in some surprise.

'Yes. No friend. You are against our revolution.'

'You mean, by greeting the Miss Wolffs?'

'No. I mean in general.'

'Excuse me, but as a foreigner and a guest in the land I have no right to express an opinion on political affairs. It is my duty as a student here and as one enjoying your hospitality to be on good terms with all Germans, irrespective of their religious or political views. In a word, I am a complete neutral.'

'Are you sure?'

'Positive.'

'Would you defend our government against slanders abroad?'

'Yes, if I knew them to be slanders and felt the call to refute them.'

'Then, why didn't you?'

'When?'

'When Lambert came with a letter to be translated.'

'Because I respect Germany and the Germans too much to help the publication of such a letter abroad. If that letter were true, then Germany is a sink of corruption and millions of Germans are embezzlers, thieves, hooligans and humbugs of the worst type. What would be the effect of such a letter? You remember the atrocity campaign that was waged against the German people during the last war?'

'Yes. Atrocious lies, the whole of it.'

'Quite. But, if that letter were published and the world were to learn on the word of a German that there were millions of skunks in this country, people would perhaps begin to think that those tales were true after all.

No, Brechner, I am not having it. I have a different and a far better opinion of the German people.'

This answer quite floored Brechner. He stammered a little, mentally groped for some rejoinder, but before he could utter a word I went on. I was thoroughly roused against Lambert and resolved to let fly.

'Doubtless Lambert has had dealings with Separatists and Jews, and he would like the world to forget it. But if you think I am going to help him to sneak his underhand way into the National Socialist Party by publishing stuff he never believed then both you and he are mistaken. You are not clamouring for such a colleague surely? A man who would blacken millions of others in order to whitewash himself!'

Perhaps I had gone too far and ought to have shown restraint, but as I let fly at Lambert a broad smile spread over Brechner's features, and as I uttered my last remark he couldn't restrain a laugh. The ice was broken. We grew quite friendly, and on the journey to Cologne we sat together, while he told me the drab story of his long unemployment days and how, thanks to Hitler, he had now got a job with prospects for the future.

I was glad to talk to Brechner and even to sit with him, but all the way to Cologne I felt deeply troubled. On a seat nearby was Frau Gerster. She looked lost and forlorn, and once, when our glances met, there was such an appealing look in her pure bewildered eyes that I was quite upset. There was I talking to Brechner, one of the prominent Nazis of the village and bosom friend of Peter Hamann, who had usurped her husband's business, while she sat in all her loneliness, left by her friends and unaware what further evils might befall her.

Save for those few moments when she had called upon Herr Engels, I had never met her before, not so much as exchanged a greeting, but seeing that her papers were now in my care I felt I could make an advance and, as far as lay in my power, reassure her. So after parting from Brechner at Cologne, I followed her for a short distance and overtook her at the end of the Hohenzollern Bridge. She was standing at the kerbside, gazing at the traffic, or rather gazing beyond it, with such a far-off look in her tearful eyes that she remained at the spot when all the traffic had passed. So I addressed her.

'Good day, Frau Gerster.'

She gave a start, and seemed far too surprised to reply to my greeting. What a look she gave me! Was it fear, suspicion or the sheer helpless stare of one who does not know which way to turn? There could be no harm in a word of sympathy and a simple offer of help.

'I know your story, Frau Gerster, and if I can help in any way I should be only too glad to oblige.'

She thanked me, but I could see she was brimming with fear or suspicion, and hardly knew what to say. Eventually she told me she wanted to make a phone call. I suggested doing it from the station, because it was clear she dared not do it from Blankheim where she was already under a shadow and sure to be dogged by the police. So I accompanied her to the station, found a vacant phone box and, feeling she wanted to be alone, I started to walk away. However, something held me back.

I looked round and watched her, a frail and elderly figure, fumbling with her address book while her tear-dimmed eyes searched for the number she could not see.

The minutes went by while I paced up and down the hall, mingled with the crowd, studied the times of the trains and wondered what urgent call she was making and whether I could help. And still she peered and peered and fumbled and fumbled until at last, in sheer despair, she gave up. She stood there in the box just gazing into nothingness. But others were gathering outside and their urgent knocks and impatient calls roused her from her daze. She groped her way out and stood bewildered amid the bustle, while the queue gazed at her with wondering eyes.

I could not help myself. I approached and spoke to her, and she seemed relieved that I had come.

'Made your call all right?'

She shook her head and it was clear that she was crying dry-eyed.

'If I can help, let me know.'

'Not here. Somewhere quiet,' she stammered.

We went into the station restaurant and found a corner table. The matter was urgent. She had just received a letter from her son who was travelling for a Cologne company in Switzerland. Letters to him must have been held up for he clearly knew nothing of his father's arrest. He had been recalled by the company and expected to be home in the next few days. Why had he been so abruptly recalled?

'It's all the government's doing,' she sobbed. 'They will arrest him when he returns, because he has always been a prominent anti-Nazi. I must warn him. I thought of appealing to the people he works for, to one of his friends, to anyone but ...'

Amid her sobs and stammers I pieced out the story. Her problem was a simple one. She must send an urgent message to her son telling him not to return. She had written a letter to that effect, but there was no one in all her circle of friends to whom she could entrust it. She knew of people who might help – that is, who might have helped – and in whom she once had confidence, but now that the crisis had come she had no faith in anyone. It was a case of self first and the devil take the hindmost in Nazi Germany now, and all the one-time loyalties of man to man, friend to friend and even brother to brother had gone by the board. Moreover, to her honour be it said, she was afraid of involving anyone else in a perilous affair.

'What can I do?' she sobbed.

'Nothing easier. You have the letter?'

'Yes, but ...' and she pulled the letter from her bag, holding it jealously in her hand. 'What are you going to do with it?'

'Post it.'

'Where?'

'Abroad.'

'Abroad? When?'

'Now. If you look at the screen over there you will see that the Hook of Holland express leaves in half an hour. I shall be in Nymegen about eight o'clock, and I shall post it there. If it will ease your mind to have it sent to-day from Holland, give it to me now.'

She looked at me in bewilderment. So I took the letter from her reluctant hand and scanned the address. Postlagernd, Bern, Schweiz. Nothing could be simpler. Crossing the frontier with no baggage might arouse suspicion, but I brushed the fear aside. I had my passport and sufficient money. The only question now was whether the message would arrive in time. Just in case I might be able to make a trunk call once over the border, I got from Frau Gerster the telephone number and address of Herr Werner, a friend of her son in Switzerland.

I wrote a note to Herr Engels to explain my absence for that night, and Frau Gerster promised to deliver it as discreetly as she could. So after buying my ticket we went off to the train.

It seemed a trifling mission to me, a big much ado about nothing. I was doing just a little service to a sweet distressed old lady, and this involved me in nothing more than a slight sense of adventure and a certain expense. Even my lack of baggage fear was removed in the first half-hour. Two English ladies with piles of luggage were in the same compartment and had been deeply touched by the lost look in poor Frau Gerster's face. They thought it was my mother grieving at my departure.

'Poor thing, she's broken hearted.'

I explained as much as I dared. I mentioned my baggage difficulty and they were at once ready to help.

'Pretend that some of ours are yours,' said one, nodding to the cases,

'We can be travelling *en famille*,' said the other with a laugh.

Despite my anxiety, the time passed very agreeably until we reached the frontier station of Emmerich. Passport, money, baggage inspection, all passed off without a hitch, but before leaving Germany I bought a paper. I did not glance at it until we were nearing Nymegen and then a little paragraph caught my eye and struck me dumb. I was harrowed. 'Karl Gerster, former editor of the *Landwirt* and awaiting trial on charges of embezzlement and corruption, was shot dead while trying to escape.'

My eyes went dim. The carriage seemed to swim and all that I saw was that poor pathetic figure as it bent over the address book and fumbled with the pages, and that drowning lost look in her eyes. I felt completely gutted. To the ladies who noticed my distress I could only point to the paragraph.

'Her husband?' gasped one, after studying the report.

'Yes.' I was too dazed to say any more. The ladies gazed at me aghast. Then one of them leaned across and whispered, 'You must warn the son at all costs, even if it means going to Switzerland. My purse is at your disposal.'

She offered her card and assured me of every help. I thanked her and said I had funds enough. At all costs I must warn Albert Gerster even if, as the lady said, I should have to go to Switzerland. So on alighting at Nymegen I went straight to a hotel, and there wrote two express letters, one to the young Gerster's address in Bern enclosing the newspaper report and the other to the address of his friend, Herr Werner, in Basel. I posted them, together with Frau Gerster's letter. Then a waiter put my trunk call through to Switzerland, where Herr Werner answered it. He expected Gerster to call before returning to Germany. In any case, he would do his best to seek him out and warn him. I breathed a sigh of relief. With the three letters posted and the call put through to Basel my mission was over.

It was Sunday evening before I reached Blankheim. There was a deserted air in the streets, a drabness in the cobbles and muddy pools, and above all a darkness in the dripping clouds that filled me with foreboding. I went out of my way to a solitary spot by the Rhine and there, in the shelter of an old tree, I debated to desperation point what I ought to do. I had bought a paper in Cologne, but search the columns as I would I had found no mention of Gerster. Perhaps the report was false, perhaps suppressed in the Rhenish papers or issued in mistake to the newspaper at Cleve. Who knows? Perhaps Frau Gerster might have heard the worst and was sitting in her lonely home, lost in desolation. And when I thought of this I felt that I must see her and offer the small solace that my success with the letters and the phone call might afford her. With my mind tossed this way and that I lingered in that lonely spot until finally, when heavy rain set in, I could linger no more. Come what may I should see her.

The house was in darkness, and such was the stillness of the street that when I rang the bell I thought the whole neighbourhood would hear its rousing clangour. I looked round with a start. To my surprise there was not a stir, not a movement at any of the neighbouring windows nor the creak of an opening door to show the call had been heard.

Then, a light footfall, Frau Gerster's, and when her face appeared I saw with the deepest pang that she did not know the worst. The moment she saw me at the door a light came to her saddened face, such a gracious smile of welcome, a golden innocent glint that has never left me.

I went in and she led me to her sitting room, which was half lounge with its easy chairs and sofa, half study with its wall of books and slowly ticking clock. It was Frau Gerster's home, the house where she and those before her were born, and something of them still remained in the heavy oak desk, a ponderous dresser that almost touched the ceiling and some old gilt-framed paintings. This was her retreat, his retreat, where he would have sat where I was now sitting, thinking, reading or taking notes or perhaps talking to his wife, who would never see him again.

My heart sank at the thought of him. I seemed to sense his presence, feel his enquiring glance, hear his earnest voice, whispering, urging, warning of something I knew not what, while his poor wife sat there before me, relieved, hopeful, almost happy, without one hint of the terrible truth.

I was harrowed, and could not bring myself to destroy the bliss of her illusion. Who was I to slay her peace of mind?

I told her then my story as far as I dared. That I had spoken to Herr Werner gave her the greatest relief and she returned to the subject again and again, asking repeated questions and assuring herself of the slightest details, even of the tone of voice in which Herr Werner spoke, whether anxious, shocked or merely surprised. And I gave her what she wanted, the most hopeful version, and assured her that her son was safe, that the Nazi terror would soon pass and that a reunion of her family was only a question of time.

Was it right, was it wrong to say these things when all my being was at death-grips with itself and every falsity I uttered seemed to swirl back like a flail and lay a long flaming weal across my soul? For in her simple trustful way she believed every word I said, esteemed me as a real friend in need, and felt so grateful for my visit that she pressed me to stay for supper, which I helped her to prepare.

It was ten before I left. I did not dare leave earlier lest some neighbour should come along and, in a blunt peasant way, break the tragic news. My mind was in turmoil at leaving her so unprepared for the worst. As she bade me goodbye at the door she seized my hands in impulsive gratitude, thanked me for the comfort I had given her and asked me to come again. I promised her most fervently I would, and, having thanked her for her kindly reception, I tore myself away.

She stood at the door until I reached the corner of the street, and when I looked back she waved her hand. A moment later I halted and in the stillness of the night heard her close and bolt the door. Pathetic sounds, that I recall even now. They haunted me all the way home and sounded so loudly in my ear as I stood before the house that I could not enter.

I went on down the street, aimlessly, in a daze, stumbling amid the pools and cobbles until I found myself not far from the Rhine in the shelter of the same old tree I had left some hours before. I felt better there in the solitude and darkness. The cool wind was on my cheek, the freshness of the rain on my heated brow and I felt grateful for a gust of drops that were swept from the dripping leaves above me. I lingered there in that still spot until the church clock struck eleven. What should I do? I was wholly at a loss.

To go home and shut the doors behind me, and feel myself locked in from the world outside was more than I could stand. And then, as the chimes ceased and the stillness of the spot grew upon me again, I thought of Rektor Barth. He was the man to confide in. Surely he was the man to take the task in hand.

The church and church house stood some distance from the road beyond a pleasing stretch of garden that had once been the village churchyard. The house itself was embowered in trees, and when I reached their shadow I could see that the Rektor had retired for the night, not a sign of movement anywhere, not a chink of light in any of the windows, the whole building, like the church itself, veiled in darkness and deep sleep. I stood in silence at the big, heavy, monastic door that once led to the monks' quarters, and wondered what I should do.

There was a knocker, a weighty fantastic knocker such as one sees in cloistered buildings, and an old-fashioned bell-pull, which at the slightest touch I knew would send long resounding clamours through the house. For a minute or more I faltered, then, pulling myself together, I gave a timid knock. There was no response. Two or three times I repeated it and then, in a surge of recklessness, I seized and rang the bell. It clanged like a fire alarm. Almost at once the window above was opened and the Rektor peeped out. I could not see his face, but I recognised his voice.

'Who's there?'

'Excuse me, Herr Rektor, but I am the Englishman who lives with Herr Engels.'

'Bless us,' he gasped, 'nothing serious, I hope?' And without waiting for a reply he shut the window and in a minute or two, just time enough to throw on his clothes, he was at the door.

'Has he called for me?'

He had thought that Herr Engels was dying and he was prepared to hasten off and minister the sacrament.

'No, it is not so serious as that, but it is something very grave indeed. May I confide in you?'

'By all means. Come inside.'

He led me into his study where he replenished the stove with a briquette or two, for the night was rather chilly and he had not fully dressed. He was not in the least annoyed that I had roused him from his sleep. In fact he seemed pleased to see me, addressing me as 'My dear Mr Arnold', with every sign of welcome and esteem. It was a delight to have his regard, for Rektor Barth was an excellent man and despite, or perhaps because of, his academic qualities, the most respected priest I have ever known. To the simple peasants he was lord and law in his own right, yet never lost that human touch without which a priest is nothing.

I told him the whole story, which he heard without comment. He was deeply moved, however. Leaning forward in his chair, he buried his face in his hands and was lost in meditation for a long time. I did not dare speak. The silence grew so intense that I heard my own pulse, while the clock ticked into the stillness like the slow taps of a hammer.

At length he spoke. 'If I go to her tonight I might cause her a great shock. She's very frail, but she's an early riser. Perhaps if I go before first mass I could break the news gently. The report, after all, is not confirmed. There has been nothing in the local press.'

He said all this as if talking to himself. Presently he stood up.

'Leave everything to me, Mr Arnold,' he said, looking me straight in the eyes, 'and absolute discretion on everything you've done. I speak not merely for yourself, but for others who might in all innocence be involved. Discretion. My hand on it!' I took his hand, and we parted.

I left the rectory and addressed myself to the truly leaden task of going home. I liked everyone in the Engels family, Frau Klebert as much as any, yet there was just that sense of tension, that touch of strain in what we said and did, which threatened, as time went on, a violent break between us. The fault, I knew, lay not with the Engels family, nor even with Frau Klebert, but with the all-intruding finger of the growing Gestapo government. Wherever I went, to another home, another town, another university, the same uneasy feeling beset me. There was no privacy now, no confidence, no trust.

Of course, when I returned the whole house was fast asleep. I tried my key, but the bolts had been set and there was no entry, front or back. Should I stay out until morning? Tilde slept in the attic, the small window of which looked out on to the street. I gathered some small stones and threw them up. In a moment she was there peering out into the street.

'I'm sorry to disturb you, Tilde.'

'Heavens,' she gasped. 'You! Just a moment.'

She was down the stairs in no time, and, after softly drawing the bolts, she slowly opened the door and looked at me in astonishment.

'Mr Arnold, where have you been?'

'Sh!' I said putting my finger to my lips. 'There's nothing to talk about.'

She set the bolts, and after helping me off with my coat, followed me upstairs to my study.

'You'll be wanting something to eat and drink.'

'No thanks, Tilde.'

'But where've you been?' She gazed at me in anxious expectation. 'We got Frau Gerster's note, you know. That is, I opened the door just as she was slipping the note into the box. She didn't say much, then went off with just a nod, but I saw from the writing that the note was from you. Then, when you did not return, from what Frau Klebert said and from what I could guess myself, I felt you had gone abroad, to Holland.'

I stood aghast. I adopted a stern tone, reminded Tilde of Frau Klebert's warning and forbade her to draw conclusions or to breathe such thoughts to anyone. Tears came to her eyes as she humbly apologised and swore that she would never betray the trust that we had placed in her.

'What makes you speak of Holland?'

'Well, you asked Herr Engels's son, Joseph, who is often in Holland, to post a letter for one of your student friends. You remember, some weeks ago. You got the reply from Switzerland, as I heard Herr Engels say.'

It was I who had been careless, Joseph Engels doubly so. I should not have asked him to take the letter for me, but should have sought the help of a stranger who would have seen the letter through in a truly anonymous way. So I took Tilde's hand and apologised in turn.

'Nothing further of this! Absolute discretion!'

This she promised and bade me goodnight. For an hour or more I sat down and pondered. In the course of the next few days everything I had done would be bellowed from the housetops and the tongue of every informer would be mobilised against me. By dint of mass denunciation even a slight offence becomes a grievous evil. And when such a man as Lambert whispers an evil tale no evil is lost in the telling. Some might think I had little to fear. But Gerster's foul murder revealed to me most clearly that the Nazis would stop at nothing. Blackmail, theft and murder were all the same to them. Having absolute power, and with neither press nor opposition to call them to account, they could take the shortest cut to any goal. All was fair on the surface, all was in order in the fresh clear light of day, but underneath, underground, in silence and in secret the dirtiest possible work was going on. And though few knew what, or where, or when, we all of us guessed and feared.

And this fear made for the worst suspicions. One felt that not Gerster himself, but his press and property were the objects of attack. Booty was what they were after, booty by any and every means. For the Nazi rank and file had to be rewarded, and this was done most cheaply by pillaging every opponent. No wonder the German nation, hordes of unemployed and ravenous wolves for the most part, threw all their scruples to the winds and made a Gadarene rush to join the Nazi Party. It was the one and only way to favour, jobs and loot. And if Frau Gerster and her son, who should rightly inherit the dead man's estate, stood in the way, then woe to her and him.

I was not surprised that the Cologne firm, acting on the imperative word of some nameless one in power, had recalled the son to Germany, and I did not doubt his fate if he returned. I thought of Dr Cohen, of the Miss Wolffs, but no less of Herr Engels who, as the owner of broad estates and of the finest home in Blankheim, was a man marked out for plunder.

He could join the party, of course, and, to avoid being wholly stripped, lay himself under tribute. But, if he stood aside, what would a noble life, a good character and a high reputation avail against secret arrest, a trumped-up charge of bad faith, a renegade's death that silenced every answer and then, as the vultures gathered for the spoils, a public confiscation?

I was so lost in these thoughts that I had failed to notice a letter on the table. It was from Rosa Metzenauer, whose letters had been passed on by Joseph Engels. A professor in Zurich had promised to see her work and to accept her as his student if she enrolled at the university there. Her letter was brimming with spirits, and, though her funds were low and hopes of a year in Switzerland were at the moment rather slender, she did not doubt that a way would be found.

Chapter 11

The Case Against Christianity

It was a strange meeting at breakfast next morning. I took my seat at the table as though nothing had happened. Herr Engels glanced across and Frau Klebert shot an enquiring look, but, remembering my promise of absolute discretion, I simply said good day. Herr Engels disliked comment, and, Frau Klebert being too proud to take the first step, we lapsed into silence, the most tense and exacting silence I have ever endured. Tilde too, who was serving, had lost all her natural frankness, and stealthily eyed us each in turn as though expecting, or rather fearing, some distressing revelation that might involve her in its grievous effects.

But there was something else. The children were there, about to return to Cologne. Else, I am sad to say, was in the dress of the BDM, the Nazi League of German Girls, and Paul in that of the Hitler Youth. Of all the children in the world, Else and Paul! Both smiled shyly across at me, and though I returned their smiles I struggled in vain to say a pleasant word. To see those two dear children arrayed in the garb of those who had done Herr Gerster to death, masking with innocence and purity the low-down gutter acts of the footpad and the assassin, numbed me in body and soul. Perhaps to an outsider, now that these events are so long passed, such a mere thing as Nazi dress might appear of no account. But under stress as I was at that time, I winced at every affinity with the crime.

Nevertheless, I felt it my duty to ease the situation. So happening to catch Frau Klebert's eye when the children's faces were turned away, I put my finger to my lips. She understood and rewarded me with a smile, which showed me most clearly that I had not lost her regard. Herr Engels had caught the gesture and nodded in approval.

We ate on in silence, though my mind was in turmoil, for I knew that my discretion, promised so faithfully to Frau Gerster and the Rektor, was to be cast to the winds. However excellent Herr Engels was, however upright his daughter, they would be partners in something that should have been left secret. So when the children went I clasped their hands most warmly, promised to see them in Cologne and to bring them each a present. Then, with Tilde carrying the bag, they went off to the station.

I returned to the breakfast room, followed by Frau Klebert who carefully closed the door behind her. It was clear from the way she sat down that she expected the full story.

'I may disappoint you, Herr Engels, Frau Klebert, but I am under a strict promise of absolute discretion, so I shall not tell you the story. Then, if you are asked any questions, you know nothing. I just acted on impulse and helped a poor old soul who was in distress; that's all. And for your own ease of mind, that's enough.'

'Excellent,' said Herr Engels. 'I respect your decision. We are living in treacherous times. It is well to keep one's counsel and the closer you keep it, the better.'

'We were thinking . . .' said Frau Klebert when I interrupted her.

'I'm afraid you thought too much and I'm afraid you thought too loudly.'

'How?' She flushed and gazed at me in sheer surprise for she was clearly groping about, not knowing what to say or think.

'Well,' I said after an embarrassing pause, 'Tilde was also thinking and doubtless thinking the same thing. When I entered the house last night she suggested not only where I had been, but also what I had been doing. They were suggestions that I chose to ignore, but I feel certain they were yours.'

The words were barely off my lips when I realised the mistake I had made. Where was *my* discretion? Where was my loyalty to Tilde, whose regrets I had accepted and whose natural gossip I had promised to forget?

Fortunately, Herr Engels broke in with a laugh. 'It's the old, old story. You can't control gossip. What's whispered in the cellar, Herr Arnold, will in time be bellowed from the roof. Above all in a village like this. For hearsay, wild surmise and rumour are too attractive to be left at home. And in this we are all alike, master and man, mistress and maid.'

The last phrase was accompanied by the slyest and faintest of winks. He then filled up his pipe while Frau Klebert gazed ahead in sheer confusion. I was sorry for both the quip and the wink, since his daughter looked thoroughly ashamed. Perhaps the effect was heightened by her white blouse and light hair for, whenever she flushed up, her cheeks seemed to tingle. She was also too straightforward to take refuge in denials. Her blush was always a conscious confession.

'Yes, my fault,' she said at last, 'but it all confirms what I have said.'

'Perhaps so,' I rejoined, 'but say nothing now to Tilde. She regretted her comment last night and I forgave her. It was my mistake to mention it now.'

Frau Klebert was too good a Catholic to rake up things that were forgiven, but she repeated her demand for the strictest neutrality in all disputes on the government and even for approval where this could be honestly given.

'As far as politics go,' she said, 'we all ought to lie low and say nothing.'

'Well, we can't be too careful,' said Herr Engels, 'even in secret things. What's done by day is merely seen, what's done by night is watched. Believe me, Herr Arnold, if you want to prick up a person's ear, just whisper.'

'Quite. But now there's something else.'

I said this in such a low grave tone that both looked up in surprise. I realised they knew nothing of the tragedy.

'Herr Gerster has been murdered.'

Both started and stared at me aghast.

'What?' Herr Engels had not quite grasped it.

'Herr Gerster has been murdered. Or, as the report puts it: "Karl Gerster, former editor of the *Landwirt*, and awaiting trial on charges of embezzlement and corruption, was shot dead while trying to escape." I suppose that now he has been done to death they will go after his property.'

I said these things in a slow, subdued tone. There was a tense silence for a few moments, then Herr Engels, whose face took on an ashy grey, staggered up. I had never seen him before in such a state. He was always so calm, so reflective, so resigned, as though nothing on earth could touch him further. For him the inner battle was won and thus he always struck me as a man who had made his final peace with God. But my news had unnerved him. Misfortune, his own murder, he could have faced without a tremor, but not this. Without a word he struggled to the door.

'Where are you going?' asked Frau Klebert, rushing after him.

'To Gertrud. I must see her.'

'Not just yet. You are upset. Wait a moment until you are calm.'

He gave her a stony non-understanding look. He had only one thought; to see the wife of his old friend and stand by her, heart and soul, come what may. 'Poor Gertrud,' he kept on saying, 'she'll never stand it, she'll never stand it.' And at the thought of the poor old lady Frau Klebert burst into tears. I thought it better to intervene, for if in his excited state he met anyone in the village he might be tempted to vent his feelings and say things we should regret.

'Herr Engels, didn't you see the Rektor at early mass?'

'The Rektor?' He looked at me, puzzled. 'No. He wasn't there. The curate took the mass. We all wondered why.' He pulled himself together and gave me a keen look. 'Why do you ask?'

I was afraid of saying too much and the Rektor's word 'discretion' trembled in my ear. I hesitated a moment.

'Why?' he repeated.

'Well, I thought it would be better if he made the first call. I think it would be wise to wait a while before you go to her, because if you met anyone in the street in your present state you might be tempted to speak your mind.'

'I shall go whether anyone meets me or not, and shall say, so God pleases, whatever comes straight to my lips.'

Frau Klebert shot me a panic look, and seized her father's arms.

'Wait a moment. Wait until Tilde comes back. Then I'll go with you.'

I thought it best to withdraw, but I knew I could not study that day, neither in Blankheim nor in Bonn. I needed to get away from the stress of the times, to seek solace in a roam over the distant hills and lose all evil thoughts in the pure plenitude of cloud and sky that ranged so spaciously beyond the Rhine. It would be a deliverance to repose wholly alone on some lonely mountain top, resting, dreaming, forgetting, with only the slowly drifting clouds as my companions, or the flight of some solitary bird or the soft rush of the wind in the bending grasses.

So I took my hat and stick and, after a word with Frau Klebert, set off to the train. As soon as I stepped outside I knew that the murder was no secret. Matthias knew, the village knew, the whole street was a-rumouring with the crime. Not that anyone spoke or looked very alarmed or even gathered in ominous crowds as one might have expected. But here and there, at doors and windows, or standing idly in the street or lingering near the main shops, people were cautiously looking and listening, avoiding talk.

There was Frenzel, the land agent, standing with Hempel, the farmer; just standing, not talking nor even exchanging nods, but standing in the blankest way not far from the Golden Hind as though in want of a sub-ject. They played the stranger as I passed and, in a flatly indifferent way, failed to return my greeting. And so with Wessel, the contractor. Surely the florid, round-faced Wessel, the cheery member of the Kevelaar, the frequent guest of Herr Engels and renovator of his house, surely he would not fail to recognise me. But he did. He looked most frigid when I passed him, staring right past and beyond me, as though we had never met before. As for Johann Fenger, the lubberly tramp-like owner of the tobacco shop, he eyed me like some dog on a chain and kept on glaring at me as I strode on. Everyone, man, woman and child, was tremblingly afraid to speak, yet tremblingly ready to overhear. And then there was something else, the force of which I learned in time.

My innocent 'good day' and avoidance of 'Heil Hitler!' was a perilous trap for me and for them. I was a man to be avoided, a pariah, a leper of the village. Do not blame them. Blackmail, theft and murder, when wielded boldly by the state with all the force of the press and with all the bellow of public opinion bawling out its sanction, are powerful persuaders. Let only those who have faced them be a witness.

On turning the corner, I saw Tilde coming back from the station. As she approached I saw that she looked disturbed and that the tears were standing in her eyes. And well they might, for Tilde was a favourite of Frau Gerster who referred to her always as the 'golden girl' and invited her on many an evening to learn the finer points of needlework. Frau Gerster knew Tilde's people and had spent many a holiday at their cottage in the Eifel.

'So you've heard?' I said.

'Yes, dreadful.' And the tears ran down her cheeks.

'I suppose Frau Gerster will also know by now?'

'Frau Gerster?' Tilde gave me a blank look.

'Yes. I suppose someone will have broken the news.'

Tilde stared and then, with a sudden glance round, seized my arm and spoke in a hissing whisper.

'It was the police, the police! She was arrested, last night for interrogation. They took her away in the middle of the night. Just fancy, the poor old lady. They say she's in hospital now, with shock. In Bonn.'

'But ... but why arrest the old lady?' I could only just stammer out my astonishment. Tilde glanced round again and there, coming out of the police office, was Peter Hamann. A flash of wildcat anger came into Tilde's eyes, her fists clenched and, more to herself than to me, she hissed: 'I'd like to drag that swine by the hair all round Blankheim, and then string him up. Wouldn't I just!' And she shook her fist.

I restrained her from any further outburst, and after a few more words she went off home.

To get to the railway station I had to pass Hamann. He was a hefty fellow with a slight stoop and with his forearms so poised as to give him the air of a boxer or of someone emerging from a tavern brawl. To me he was the double of Hitler, even to the falling forelock and the stubby short moustache.

I had convinced myself that he was the man who had knocked at the Wolffs' door on Christmas Eve, and I believe he sensed my suspicions. He glowered at me as I approached, and I shrank from his over-light grey eyes. He was exchanging a word with Fischer at the door of the police office. Should I greet him or not? This question of greeting had become an embarrassing one, though I was too distressed at the moment to bother much. So I passed on with a muttered good morning, to which there was no reply.

Poor Frau Gerster. And then I thought of the Miss Wolffs, and imagined them cowering in some corner at home in fear of being led away. This was the uppermost thought in my mind as I hurried to the station and bumped into them on the platform. They were calm, cheerful, almost happy, and in their array of expensive furs struck a great contrast with the modest village women who were also waiting for the train. A little indiscreet, I thought, and almost asking for comment and attack.

'Dreadful news,' I said in a half whisper.

'Yes.' Both nodded their heads, Rachel with a grave arching of the brows and Rebecca with a curt glance round. She moved away from the people standing about, then resumed the talk in normal tones.

'Yes, but I think the position is easing a little,' said Rebecca. 'In fact we are able now to manage about supplies.'

'You see,' added Rachel, 'we can get deliveries now without interference from anyone.'

'Good, but when you need my help again, let me know.'

'Yes, we are very grateful.'

'Very,' added Rebecca. 'How is Herr Engels?'

Perhaps it was wise of Rebecca to avoid compromising talk in such a public place. Yet her nonchalance offended me, her freezing indifference to any fate but her own. She ought to have been afraid, visibly afraid. A tremor of pity for others would have made her tremble for herself. But hers was the bravery of sheer hardness of heart, perhaps of downright calculation. For she was living under no illusions, no fool's paradise of hope and expectation, but in a cold-blooded Nazi world, knowing what the Nazis were, hearing daily their racial theories, and studying their ruthless deeds.

Surely, if anyone in Blankheim had been marked out as a prime victim, it would have been Rebecca Wolff. But there she was standing in the obvious open in all her blatant finery, cool and unblinking. However, she was no fool, and, if she appeared unmoved, she must have every reason to be so.

Frankly puzzled, even more by the unconcern of the more sensitive Rachel, I left for Bonn.

The town was more beflagged than ever and a very large swastika was hanging from the convent school in the Hegenheimerstrasse. Brownshirts, too, were more numerous, and in some of the shops there were notices, 'Only Aryans served here'. The Nazi revolution was well under way with plenty of din from the press and wireless, but with little open violence. I went over to the Hansaeck, the terminus of the Bonn-Honnef electric railway, where I was hailed by two men, both in walking kit and prepared for a stroll in the hills. One was Waldemar Sanders, the lecturer in Protestant theology, the other his old school friend, Otto Wagner, a lawyer.

Wagner was an open character, friendly, talkative, without a trace of guile in his pure nordic features. I was soon chatting about this and that with him, while Sanders stood attentively by with his half-sly smile, eyeing us both critically and throwing in a caustic word now and again. Presently the tram came in, and when they heard I was going for a ramble in the hills they asked me to join them. They were going to the Westerwald and had ample food in their knapsacks. Despite my longing to be wholly alone, I joined them, journeying first to Beuel and then by the state railway to Linz.

I had intended when setting out to lose all thoughts of Blankheim and yet, charming though our ramble was, I was destined to retain those thoughts in an even deeper form. On reaching Linz, I found that one of my bootlaces had snapped and we went into a shop to buy a new pair. The owner was an obvious Jew and, after serving me, he pulled out a tray and offered to sell us a buttonhole Nazi flag. He had quite a large assortment and, without a blush or stammered apology or even an ironic smile, he pressed these things upon us. Sanders thanked him and asked him in the gravest way if he had any copies of the *Stürmer*, the Nazi-supporting newspaper. But the Jew was unabashed. Brimming with business politeness, he directed us to the newsagent over the way.

119

Wagner laughed outright when we finally got outside, while Sanders indulged the most sardonic grin. 'Good God! If that fellow were sentenced to death he'd try to sell a rope to the hangman.'

And so it went on. Sanders and Wagner were anything but Nazis, yet their talk was soon as cynical as that of Bürger and Hillesheim. Their gibes, I admit, had some excuse, for the Jew had shown no conscience either to his own race or ours. And though I hated to take an anti-Jewish position, I had to agree.

'Conscience?' said Sanders. 'When had a merchant conscience? Money, not morals, is the aim of business. After all, to get money even legally is a problem, to get it morally is an absolute miracle. If a merchant bothered about morals he'd never make a profit.'

'Come on, come on,' I said, 'there's such a thing as ethics in business.'

'Not ethics, surely,' said Wagner. 'Legality you mean, an exact regard for the letter of the law and for the terms of a contract. Beyond those it would be folly to go. Take England, for example, the greatest mercantile power. For centuries it has monopolised the carrying trade of the world, honestly, efficiently, I admit, but not ethically. It never bothers about the nature of the stuff it carries, slaves, opium, gin and the like, or about the origin and destination of any article that is not forbidden by the law. No, it simply carries the stuff and honours the terms of the contract. If *that* is ethics, then there is ethics in business.'

'Hear, hear!' said Sanders.

'And so you see no difference between England's reputation in commerce and that of this haberdasher Jew?'

'None whatsoever,' said Wagner. 'What's the difference between a Jew selling Nazi flags and a Christian nation trucking dope?'

'None at all. But you talk as if we did nothing else but truck gin and dope. That is a blot, I admit, but it is a blot on a very clean page. And our reputation is based on that page and not on the mere blot.'

'Admitted. But it is a reputation for legal means and not for ethical ones.'

'Don't you think however ... '

'Ah, Herr Arnold,' broke in Sanders, 'you may raise your protesting eyes to heaven, but if cash could be earned in the business you'd truck us all to the devil. In fact, I firmly believe that when this life is over we shall find that you English people have again got there before us, and instead of Charon and his boat it will be you, yes you, who have seized and monopolised the carrying trade to Hell.'

'Carrying you, I suppose,' I laughed.

'Yes. As I have said before, you'd truck us all to the devil. And believe me, when we get to hell, you'll charge us to go in.'

'Well, the more fool you for paying!'

'And the less moral of you to exact the fee,' laughed Wagner who, with the caustic help of Sanders, began in combined earnest to belabour my native land.

120

I enjoyed it of course. But oh, that opium trade! I have never met a foreigner who did not at some time or other trump up the opium war and reflect on the evil means by which our empire grew. I am not a jingoist, nor even a nationalist. In fact I pride myself on being a citizen of the world. But how many times have I felt the thwack of that unhappy event? And what a salve that event has proved to the still more guilty conscience of all the other nations?

But Sanders and Wagner were not malicious and I enjoyed their pleasant gibes. They had an eye for scenery, and we indulged in some golden moments on the heights above Linz and lost ourselves in the spacious views of the Eifel and the River Ahr. What a wistful air there is in distant scenes, in the hint of a village, in the vagueness of a far-off feudal ruin, or in some half-deceptive spire faintly peering up from the veiling blue of the valley.

They have all the frailty of a failing reminiscence, all its pang and fascination, so that the more we observe them the more we see some vanished phase of past years, some form once loved and lost again, some dimming glimpse of our forgotten selves. How dreamily far away they are, those soft touches of woodland, those blurs of farm and field, that feudal crumble or that mere mote of a hamlet vaguely grouped around its wraithlike guess of a church.

We then went down to a deep glade, rutted and miry from recent rain, and on up through field and woodland into the Westerwald. The sleep of winter was still in the trees, the dark tone of the pines and the leafless grey of the beeches covering the fold of every hill. But the paths were deserted, the woods without an echo and the fields trended on in unruffled solitude up the valley. I felt the restful influence of every step of the way and even my companions, subdued by the hush of the woodland, lapsed into silence.

There was only one break, that of a little village at the head of a grassy valley leading down to the River Wied. We had passed the first cluster of cottages and had come to an open space which fronted the little school. It was the lunch break and the children were free. All but a dozen of them were members of the Hitler Youth. None was more than ten years old and they were standing stiffly at attention in a squad, awaiting the orders of a comrade who was swaggering in front. At last the order came and I stood aghast at the brutal tone of it. No vulgar sergeant major ever rasped his blasphemous throat in a viler way than that young boy. It would be hard to say what repelled me more, the blackguard voice of the one or the palsied response of the rest. Their faces were rigid with fear. Every nerve was strained into a blindly staring attention.

With another screech of an order, off they marched. I studied them for a while as they goose-stepped up the village. Then I hurried on to catch up with my friends.

On we went down the grassy valley with only the babbling stream as our companion. Here it was pleasantly cool and still, for the hills towered up on all sides, but on the slopes ahead the sunlight was playing on the sombre expanses of beech and pine. We then cut across to the right and after a steep ascent reached the summit of the Höchstel.

I shall never forget that moment. We had been toiling up the slope through the shadows of the woodland when all at once we emerged on to the open grassy summit, right into the face of heaven, with the bright sunlight about us and all below and around, as far as the eye could reach, the superb panorama of the winding Wied amid the encircling hills. Deep down below was Waldbreitbach, a pretty village that seemed to span the gorge with its steep roofs and ancient gables, and beyond to the right was a large sanatorium, which appeared to me even then as a very minor blot on a superbly dazzling page. But unlike most blots it disturbed the eye but little and its tone was so blended with the grey of the valley that we were hardly aware of its presence. After all, the page was the thing, a truly lustrous page, a vision of Germany as it was to me then, as it still is and always will be.

We sat down in a sheltered nook and shared the coffee and eatables my companions had brought. For an hour or more we lingered there watching the great cloud shadows as they stole over hill and dale or catching at sunlit moments a more revealing glimpse of the scene, a village, a lonely farmhouse, a spire or the ruinous keep of the Neuerburg that lay in a fold of the hills not far away. I was so delighted with the scene that I was surprised that any German would want to leave his native land.

'And yet I am wishing to leave it,' said Sanders, and for once he lost his cynical smile.

'Leave it?'

'Yes, for America. You must translate my application into English when you've time. There is no future for me here in Germany, neither for me nor my subject.'

'Like Bürger and Hillesheim?'

'Oh no! They have a future now, not only in Hitler's realm but in any realm that follows it. They are assured of a professorship. But I am at loggerheads with my own subject and, much as I hate the Nazis, I am in sneaking agreement with them about Christian theology.'

'So am I,' interrupted Wagner. 'But I shouldn't bring in the Nazis, Waldemar. Your view, and it's mine as well, is a thoroughly German one. In sharing that view I am thinking as a pure German, not as a Nazi. In fact it is a great pity that the Nazis have that view. By their treatment of the Jews they are bringing the view into disrepute.'

'What view is this?' I asked.

'Just freedom,' interposed Sanders. 'Freedom in the broadest sense. You saw those boys in the village? A dozen boys. A dozen delicate organisms, each a being more wondrously formed than the most wondrous machine that was ever devised, a being wholly unfathomable in the mystery of his being at all, infinite in his emotional response – but enough. It is taken like a block, chopped, lopped, hammered, planed and moulded into the insensate form of a soldier, a thing to slay and be slain, and to erase any and everyone else who is not of the same pattern. Now, Herr Arnold, we are on common ground here I think. I saw your shocked look, and you were thinking just as we were.'

'Yes, I was shocked, but how does this feeling of ours conflict with Christian theology?'

'You'll see in a moment,' said Sanders, and his cynical smile had returned. 'You see, each of those boys is no longer an individual, no longer a personality, no longer a free natural being able to develop in his own way.'

'Quite.'

'Now it is the same with your colonies. Your explorers go to Africa and find a simple native tribe, with its own native customs, its own social and religious system, its own way of tilling the ground, its own distinctive design of huts, in a word its own culture ideally suited to the local conditions as well as to the people who live there.'

'And we English destroy all this, I suppose.'

'Worse than that. After a generation or more not only has the culture gone but a degradation has set in that is a disgrace to black and white alike. The wondrous little cosmos goes, so distinctive, so unique in every way. A generation later that village, with its one-time picturesque kraals, has become a jumble of louse-ridden European shanties where the blacks in dirty cotton pants loaf round the pawn and gin shops ...'

'So we've come back to that,' I exclaimed in a burst of laughter in which Wagner heartily joined.

' ... with no other aim in life than to excel in the bad habits of the exploiting white class. And as for the black girls who had formerly lived in all their primitive innocence ... '

'Come on! You are piling it on a bit,' I exclaimed.

'Well he's doing his best,' said Wagner, with another burst of laughter.

'Yes, but where does the Protestant theology come in?'

'Patience,' said Sanders. 'I am trying to show you how one culture ruins another and does unspeakable harm. And to ruin the culture of a nation is to slaughter it body and soul. Take a simple kaffir in his primitive state, one who is touched by no influence from beyond and who lives in his own little world of native art, tribal lore and animistic hopes and fears. This simple kaffir in his kraal, who prays to his ancestral gods, who honours his taboos and orders his sowings and reapings by the aspect of the moon, by the flight of birds or by the form and path of passing clouds is a man, a MAN!' Here Sanders slapped his thigh. 'But as a fellow in cotton pants louting round in a shanty or swinking on some huge estate for European cash he is just sheer riff-raff.'

123

'Hear, hear!' cried Wagner.

'Yes,' I rejoined, 'he would be sheer riff-raff if he simply louted round. But he is not compelled to lout round either in a shanty or anywhere else.'

'But he is,' retorted Sanders. 'In his native home there are a thousand things to occupy his time; weaving, pottery, grinding corn, making weapons and the like, building and rebuilding the kraal and the countless other tasks that make for an active civilisation. But when living in a shanty he buys everything ready-made. As Gandhi has pointed out to us, his home life ceases to be. Without that round of daily tasks, without gods, a cult and a ritual appropriate to his place in life he lives in a mental void with nothing else to fill his time but dicing, dope and drink.'

'But supposing he becomes a Christian?'

'A belief, however excellent, is no substitute for the culture he has lost. Despite his Christianity, he is an infinitely poorer man. In fact he is worse because of it. When he bawls his Methodist hymns he degrades them and they degrade him. Christianity in such a mind is the vilest gin and dope.'

'So you are against Christianity?'

'As a dumping ground for converts, yes.'

'And as stuff to be dumped on others,' added Wagner.

'Now don't think me a Nazi,' said Sanders. 'I have gone a long way round just to prevent your thinking so. But Christianity is an alien culture, something suitable for Semitic tribes and the Near East, but baleful stuff for Europe. Remember that the Christians, in their persecution of others and in their drive for a universal faith, were the spiritual Nazis of long ago. And they bludgeoned all Europe into line. Think of the terrorism of it. Take the cathedrals, churches, monasteries, convents, which were ten times more numerous in the Middle Ages with a population ten times less. Every one of these buildings was a refuge, a panic retreat, a final air-raid shelter from the ire of the Almighty.

'What agonies that morbid pharisee, that pestilent fellow Paul, with his rabid rabbinical doctrines of damnation and redeeming blood, inflicted on the happy and open mind of northern Europe! What mental stress the idea of Jehovah has caused, this ruthless eastern despot with his eye for an eye and a tooth for a tooth and the hanging of his only begotten son as an essential condition for mercy!'

'You are plunging on,' I interjected.

'Perhaps I am. But don't stumble over details. Just take the broad theme. The philosophy of Christianity, the philosophy of resignation, prostration and adoration, might be all right for eastern peoples who cringe under an absolute and almost divine despot, but it is no use to the self-assertive Nordics of Europe. The mysticism of the east, ideal for Hindus and for contemplative Arabians in the centre of the desert, has wreaked havoc in our northern souls and led, as the religious wars reveal, to the devastation of Europe.'

'But how about the Christianity of today? While preserving its virtues it has surely lost its venom?'

'Yes, it has. And it has lost its venom because it is no longer a real thing. We no longer believe in it. It is a verbalism, a formula, a sentimental setting for births, marriages and deaths, as well as a very useful peg on which to hang the festivals of Easter and Christmas.'

Sanders was raising too many points for me to answer him there and then. Moreover, I was more eager to listen than to speak. His point of view was a popular one in Germany at the time and was clear of Nazi influence. It suited the Nazi book, but it was not of their invention. So Wagner, who was an anti-Nazi, was able to say amen to every word of it, and broke in with a reference to the asylum we had seen in the valley.

'To bring the argument down to a lower plane,' he said, 'I shudder every time I see that building. It is a blot on the landscape in the first place and it is a home for mental defectives in the second. But it is not these facts that repel me. What grates on me is that it is run by the Franciscan Order, and I never see these men in the village with their sandals, coarse sackcloth and rope of servitude round their waists without feeling how utterly un-German their view of this life is. Despite our illustrious past we Germans are an essentially modern people. By our industry, knowledge and skill, we can solve all the material problems of life, poverty, ignorance, disease and the like, and rise with our technique and science to the loftiest cultural heights. Yet right in our super-modern midst we see these fellows shuffling round, these lingering spooks of the darkest ages, backward, benighted, superstitious. It is a gross anachronism, an insult, a flouting of the genius of the nation.'

'Quite,' said Sanders, 'there's one of them there, walking along the river. Can you see him? Not far from the cottage.'

He pointed down into the valley. Away in the distance I could just descry the tiny form, a friar in his robe moving towards the village. 'Yes, I see, it's a friar or priest of some sort.'

'Of course,' said Wagner. 'Now what's that fellow doing here? Just look at the landscape round us, a truly German landscape with well-kept fields, a spick-and-span village and woodlands that reveal the care and skill of a twentieth-century forester. And here is that fellow in his poverty-stricken dress, a primitive intrusion from the near east, a figure you might expect to see in the slovenly bazaars of Baghdad or loafing in the desert faubourgs of Marrakesh or Timbuktu. Here he is in defiance of twenty centuries of science and culture still using the methods they applied to the conditions of the year One.'

Now Wagner was no bigot. He spoke more in pity than contempt for those who were still in thrall to obsolete ideas and to a view of life that affronted the very nature of the German people. Unlike the Nazis, however, Sanders and Wagner did not reject Christianity as something purely Jewish, thus alien and baleful in itself. They were just as decisive against the Latin influence in German culture, above all in German poetry, and its choking of all the abundant springs of native inspiration. Here, their proofs were positive and their examples clear of encroachment, but in the midst of this we broke off.

'I suggest we go down and have some coffee,' said Wagner, pointing to an inn, which stood in the picturesque square. The coffee was excellent, the sun brilliant and we had just burst into laughter when two of the friars passed.

'Heavens,' said Wagner in a low tone, 'they certainly don't look like God's own chosen people.'

I was taken aback. I had met several monks in Bonn, and excellent men they were, distinguished, ascetic and a credit to their calling. But I shrank from those two friars with their coarse insensate look. It seemed to sour and curdle all my pleasant impressions of the day.

Our way back home was a memorable one, first along the swirling Wied, then by failing light through the deep gorge of the Nonnenbach and finally, as night fell over the lofty uplands, to the Rhine. But with the splendour of all these impressions was an undertone of thought that was destined to possess my mind for a long time to come. Nazi theories were detestable but, in some respects at least, they were just a stretching and warping of very popular views, of much that was natural, reasonable, understandable. So even in their distortion they were bound to appeal to many minds.

When I recalled what my friends had said there was much I could dispute, but nothing I should detest, nothing that I should dismiss as beyond the pale of civilised debate. Their Germanism, their modernity, their national culture, their rejection of Christianity and their deep distrust of populism were all in themselves allowable views and yet how allied to the nationalist, anti-Semitic and fascist views of the Nazis. Hitler would have smiled approval of all my anti-Nazi friends had said, though they were among the most outspoken critics of the illiterate Austrian. The paradox haunts me still.

Chapter 12

The Policy of Loot

I suppose Blankheim was no exception and that all over Germany, in every village, town and city, the same smothering effect could be observed, the same growing reticence of friend to friend, the same mutual evasion and muffling of one's inner self, the same silent suspicion, so that even within the family one paused before speaking, one looked askance at the rest and either fenced all questions or confided honest answers to nods and winks and whispers.

This was the effect of the Gerster affair, an effect as plain as it was furtive and reserved. Nothing happened, nothing that usually happens when a tragedy takes place, no crowds, no talk, no airing of opinion or feeling, no meeting one with another to impart the latest rumour, not a protesting breath of the whole affair in the bar of the Golden Hind. The effect was more unobtrusive. Each ceased to know his neighbour in the open familiar way of villagers to one another. For Blankheim, though a small town, was still a village in many ways, a place where the door had always been open or only on the latch.

But after the Gerster affair the doors were closed. Blankheim was no longer a village. It was a shatter of isolated souls.

Thus days and days passed before we learned the whole of the Gerster story, or the story as edited by the police. Suspecting that the son, Albert Gerster, had returned, they went on the Sunday night to interview him. Had someone seen me enter and mistaken me for the son? I do not know. They entered soon after I had left and let slip the brutal news about her husband, whereupon Frau Gerster collapsed. A doctor was called and, by his advice, Frau Gerster was taken straight to Bonn in the police car and given specialist attention.

She never recovered from the stroke. She lingered a few days and died without uttering a word. The funeral was at Blankheim and, though it was well attended, I observed that apart from the Rektor the only men at the graveside were Herr Engels and me. The rest were women from the village who made their silent protest in a mound of lovely flowers.

I retired to my studies after that, saw no friends and confined my talk in the family to the topics of every day. Fear was in the air and, though I had no cause, I felt unsafe.

Yet one thing puzzled me. Despite an official boycott of the Jews, despite the placards of the *Stürmer*, which began to deface the village walls, the two Miss Wolffs were as free and carefree as any Nazi partisan. No one picketed the house. The tradesmen came and delivered their goods. The Brownshirts passed the door with mysterious unconcern, and when the ladies ventured forth – and they did so in all their finery – they met no protesting glances from Brechner and his friends. Were they made of braver stuff than gentiles? And as for the Nazi boast of discipline and self-restraint, what else could I do but accept the evidence of my eyes and believe that what the foreign press was reporting was untrue?

I could not help comparing the Miss Wolffs and Frau Klebert, and finding that the latter was an even greater puzzle. What had she to fear? The Miss Wolffs, alone and helpless, stood unflinching in the blizzard; Frau Klebert, on the other hand, shrank in all her safety from the few stray drops of the distant storm. Yet Frau Klebert was no craven. One saw her courage at a glance, in her decisive step, in her upright bearing, in the very way she looked one straight in the face. Perhaps she was too practical, too domestic, too ready to believe that something was better than nothing and that half a loaf was ample solace for the other half she had lost. Her sense of duty to her father had reduced her day after day to the little prison realm of pots and pans.

But for an instance. One evening about two months later I was sitting with Herr Engels in his sanctum. We were sitting there alone, lost half in story, half in reverie, when a sudden knock aroused us. Thinking it was Tilde, I called out, 'Come in.' But as I spoke the door opened and in walked the brown-shirted Peter Hamann. He came in as though by right.

'Heil Hitler, Herr Engels! I've come to see you about the *Landwirt*.'

Herr Engels stared, half surprised, half bewildered, then demanded, 'How did you get in here?'

'The front door is open.'

'Then you had better go out by that door.'

'But I want to see you about the *Landwirt*.' Hamann's shoulders stooped and his arms seemed to swing as though he expected an attack. The situation was critical. I got up, Herr Engels got up, his face tense with indignation.

'I have told you to go.'

'But how about the *Landwirt*?' Hamann shouted, and I started back at the ringing tone and the brazen cheek of the man.

'Go, you vulture,' cried Herr Engels, shaking his finger in the man's face, 'and if you darken these doors again ... '

'You'll rue this,' Hamann blurted out with a shake of his fist.

'Then I'll rue it!'

'If I am a vulture I'll see that you are carrion!'

'I don't doubt it. Having gorged one victim, you are ready for the next. '

I stepped between them. Goodness only knows what might have happened if Frau Klebert had not returned. She met Hamann as he backed out into the hall.

'Oh, it's you!' I heard her say.

'Ah! Our subscription has expired?'

'Yes.'

'Then we shall renew it.' And she ushered him out.

Every Tuesday after that the *Landwirt* was delivered and within ten seconds of delivery was flung into the kitchen bin. Herr Engels, I am certain, never knew. Behind his back the *Landwirt* was paid for and received. A sane solution, one might think, of a really perilous problem, but it was deception, one of the scores of deceptions that slowly corroded our character and thoroughly tainted the home. We were all a party to the frauds, and as time passed we lied without a blush.

Herr Engels read the *Reichszeitung*, a Catholic publication, and very popular in the west. For a time the paper held its own, but it was later shouldered out, being forced to change its title for a far more cumbersome one, to alter its policy and to winnow the staff until at last it fell into Nazi hands and helped to swell the burgeoning chorus from Berlin.

On the whole, the people stood firm, and it was only by silent blackmail that the leading Nazi paper in the Rhineland, the *Westdeutscher Beobachter*, was sold. All teachers, officials, civil servants, all professional and business men were asked to support it or – and here was the crux – to state on an enclosed form their reason for refusal. That is, you were asked to send written proof of your hostility to the party. Needless to say, all those who had anything to lose paid up.

Yes all, even the simple workman whose job was in the balance.

Yet I remember that up to the first half of 1933, in the earlier days of the Nazis, I used to pass the chemical works, which lay just up the road, and see the workers stream out at noon with the vendors of the Nazi paper standing outside the gates. They stood there quietly, those brown-shirted SA men, models of innocence, order and politeness, just calling the name of the paper and asking no one twice. Even Kurt Brechner, little braggart though he was, made no attempt to force the sale. The workers just streamed out, either touching a paper in their pockets to show they had a copy or shaking their heads and passing on.

But as time went on there was more tapping of pockets and less shaking of heads, since the best of jobs went by party favour and the dirtiest, worst and least paid jobs were left to the outsiders. There were no means of protest. All trade unions had been abolished, their funds impounded, while all societies, however unpolitical they might have been, were brought under Nazi control. The president, treasurer or secretary had to be a Nazi.

The Nazis seemed to be everywhere. So, not knowing your own neighbour and suspecting a spy in every friend, you wisely held your peace. No wonder the wholesale slump to the right was silent, subtle and surprising. A man might bravely go to the stake, but even a saint will shrink from taking his family with him.

Against such unbridled power it was folly to be brave. And how foolish Kurt Dorlich was. He was a new man to Blankheim and had opened a tobacconist's shop, a spick-and-span affair not far from the factory. The shop was a treat to see with its elegant front, framed sign and tasteful display of tobacco and pipes on the glittering glass shelves. And to go in was to enter a cabinet, a really artistic cabinet of lightly polished panel work, seen only in the high-class parts of Düsseldorf and Cologne.

The workers from the factory simply streamed into his shop and showed their appreciation of this attractive little business. And Dorlich himself was equally well liked. He was a serious, straightforward man, pleasant, affable and well-groomed, with a twinkle in his grey eyes. His shop was a goldmine, but because he had invested heavily in it he took a part-time office job in the factory to help with the repayments, leaving his wife to look after the shop.

One day as he left the factory he was stopped. The vendor was an SA man, no other than Johann Fenger, also a tobacconist of a sort, a slovenly seller of mouldy goods, who had wholly lost caste since the coming of Dorlich. Was it from malice, or jealousy or just chance that Fenger stopped his rival? Who knows? He stopped him and insisted on selling a paper. Dorlich declined, but Fenger was insistent.

'Come on, and support the new order.'

'No thanks, no,' said Dorlich with a laugh, 'I haven't used up the last one yet.'

Those who heard the remark turned round and laughed, for the words 'used up' had only one meaning in Blankheim, namely 'used for a very lowly corporal purpose'. Dorlich went on and doubtless forgot the matter in coping with the rush at the shop. He was reminded with a vengeance next day.

It was Saturday and the space before the factory was thronged with silent workers. In the roadway stood the police, Fischer, Dancker and two others, all just watching and taking no part. On the steps that led to the office was Dorlich, and on both sides were SA men who were urging him to kneel down and apologise to the party. I could not hear a word, but the gestures were clear. Dorlich flatly refused, saying he had made a simple joke without any further reflection. He appealed to the crowd. A murmur went up, perhaps of surprise, perhaps of approval, perhaps of friendly advice. I was expecting violence, when a policeman hidden in the doorway intervened. The SA men restrained themselves, for their power was not so absolute as in the ruthless times that followed. Hamann stepped up to Dorlich and, shaking his fist shouted, 'Well you'll not enter this factory again until you do as you're told.'

130

'Keep your factory,' said Dorlich, undismayed, and the two, Hamann and Dorlich, gazed daggers at each other. A silence fell on the crowd as the policeman gave a sign of dismissal. Dorlich descended the steps and was lost in the crowd, which began slowly to disperse. The SA men, thus flouted, remained upon the steps.

Perhaps Dorlich had thought that with his prosperous shop he could remain independent of the party and play a neutral role, but he was soon disillusioned. When I passed the shop ten minutes later it was picketed by Nazis, Hans Zimmermann, Brechner and others. Save for Frau Dorlich, the shop was empty. I caught a glimpse of her tear-stained face as I passed along the road. The blockade and the blackmail had begun.

Dorlich held out for a time, sold his stuff in secret, either personally or through friends who acted as his agents. They called in a whispering way on all his former customers, who responded most loyally. Even Herr Engels, who usually shopped in Cologne, became a direct customer, dealing openly with Dorlich and promising his support to the last. But the shop was dead. The pickets never tired and from early morn until late at night, day after day, they kept a strict watch, stopping all sales and turning all deliveries away and subjecting the poor family to real hardship. They bore up valiantly for weeks in the hope that justice would prevail and that the splendid little business would once again be free.

Dorlich refused to yield, but the courts to which he appealed kept on delaying and reserving judgement, finally referring the matter to the police, who declined to intervene. It was clearly a party affair, a case of 'folk justice', a matter that would settle itself by the natural triumph of the 'people's will'. Thus the last door was closed, and the day came when Dorlich, for the sake of his family, had to sell up his business and leave the village for good.

With his departure the last flicker of open resistance died away.

The triumph over Dorlich was a triumph over all Blankheim. It was a signal for a general attack and the Brownshirts, who up to now had loomed up only in the streets, began to loom up at every door. They decided to sound out every household in the village. They came to us, Brechner and Hans Zimmermann, Brechner flushed with a sense of power and Zimmermann a little uncertain in his new role of dictator. Tilde had opened the door to them, but, instead of waiting until they were announced, they pushed straight in and faced Herr Engels and me.

'Heil Hitler!'

'Who told you to come in here unannounced?' Herr Engels drew his pipe from his mouth and pointed with the stem to the door.

'We've come about the *Westdeutscher Beobachter*,' blurted out Brechner. Herr Engels stood up.

'What right have you to intrude here? Out with you!'

He strode towards them and there was a short altercation as he conducted both to the door and showed them into the street. But later on they came again. Herr Engels met them in the hall, and refused to subscribe to the Nazi paper.

'Would you mind filling in this form and saying why?'

'Not in the least.'

Pen and ink were brought and Herr Engels there and then wrote boldly on the slip that he took the *Reichszeitung* and had no intention of dropping it.

'You are against our paper,' said Brechner in an effort to draw Herr Engels into a compromising discussion.

'I know nothing about your paper.'

'Then why not try it?'

'Why not try every new craze? Because, my dear Brechner, I'm too old for things too new. It is easy to shift a seedling, but it is madness to root up the old oak and try to plant it elsewhere. Your common sense ought to tell you that.'

'A stick-in-the-mud attitude, don't you think?'

'Yes, very. But life is a choice of one mud or another, one mud deep enough but the other very much deeper. So just leave me stuck where I am.' And with that he ushered them out.

It was not the only rebuff the local Nazis received. Though open resistance had died away there was still much opposition, a deliberate deafness to all appeals and a heavy weight of inertia, which defied all efforts to move it. Appearances were deceptive. One would think from the swelling display of flags, the growing host of Brownshirts and the frequency, even among women, of the 'Heil Hitler' salutation that the village was wholly Nazi and that all opposition opinion had been finally forsworn. Those not Nazi from conviction were Nazi from convenience, and in the general flaunt of the swastika there was no telling friend from foe. And yet there was a distinction, sharp and well-defined, which showed up on occasions and startled me into a realisation of the double game we were all playing. This was clear from the Dorlich case, which took a strange turn after he had gone.

Many felt that Dorlich had been ruined, not by his political opinions, but by jealousy of his success. He, a stranger to Blankheim, comes and opens a little shop not far from the big factory and by the best business methods secures the whole tobacconist trade of the town. It was something that the hucksters of Blankheim could neither forget nor forgive. They quivered with envy. Not only the peddlers of cigarettes, but the whole trumpery company of grocers, butchers, bakers and the like felt ashamed and aggrieved. For he had done what no one in Blankheim had ever done before. He had actually secured the trade that normally went to Cologne. For that is where the village purse was drawn. In Cologne was a wider choice of better and fresher goods, so every Saturday afternoon the villagers streamed to the big city and bought in supplies for a week.

Dorlich was gone, but the shop remained and there was a jealous scramble for its possession. Frenzel, the estate agent, who had to dispose of the shop, was besieged by every trader in the town, and there were scores of offers from other parts. It was like an informal auction. Some unknown client of Frenzel's kept topping the highest bids until the rumour rose that Frenzel had a puppet bidder to boost the soaring price. But Frenzel disclosed the name, one of the leading business houses in Cologne. It was certainly consoling to know that Dorlich, who was penniless, would get an excellent price.

The shop was sold, not to the Cologne firm, but to solicitor Lambert who was acting for the Nazi Party. It was Lambert's own suggestion. He felt that, whatever the price, the business was worth it and would repay with a handsome profit all the money invested. But everywhere was secret disappointment, even among the party leaders who felt they had been baulked. I broached the subject with Brechner one day as I was going home.

'It's a pity we didn't get it for nothing,' he said.

'Just commandeer it, you mean?'

'Yes, blockade it until it was ours, but there might have been trouble with the police. At least Lambert said so. So we had to let it go.'

'An excellent business!'

'Yes, a positive goldmine.'

We had arrived at the crossroads and stopped for a few minutes. His eye had a faraway look and I could see by the lamplight that he was indulging a lost dream. So he had been speculating too in his poverty-stricken way, and wondering in envy or despair why the simple plums of life were never his. He spoke again but he seemed to be talking to himself.

'I'd drop my present job for a shop like that.'

'You are putting a manager in, I suppose?'

'Yes.' He shook his head gloomily, and in the long pause that followed a look came to his face. Contempt? Disappointment? Resentment? Perhaps all three. As he stood and pondered a figure passed us by. It was Lambert.

'That damned Lambert,' he muttered. 'The sneak, the renegade. We ought to have taken the place by storm and not listened to the likes of him. What business has he in the party? Thrusting us into the background who have been members all these years.'

His voice rose and I could see that much was rankling in his mind. So we parted.

What was rankling in his mind? He now had a good job in the party, his salary was higher than ever and his hopes of promotion were bright. Perhaps he resented men like Lambert, the schoolmaster Klassen and all those helter-skelter converts who by their superior training were taking control at every turn. Brechner was a man for clean sweeps and as time went on he would surely show his hand.

Some days later I did not wonder at Brechner's bitter look. I was passing Dorlich's old shop and wondering how the affair was going when to my great surprise I saw a familiar figure at the doorway. It was Johann Fenger, the slovenly failed tobacconist, who appeared to have been installed in the successful business. In his Nazi garb he certainly looked more respectable than before, but the vulgar glare was still there and his face and hands were obviously none of the cleanest.

Then I noticed something else. It was noon. The workers were streaming from the factory, not in scores but in hundreds, but no one went into the shop. I stopped, ostensibly to look at the window, and waited minute after minute as the crowd went surging by. Nazis, non-Nazis, young and old, all went by without one sidelong glance. The shop was dead.

So Blankheim had a conscience after all, the still small whisper that is louder than the loudest voice. No one entered the shop, not even those responsible for driving Dorlich out. Despots though they were, they suddenly sensed what the village felt, and none was bold enough to bear the blame himself and flout all public opinion.

Clearly, the whole incident was a party affair, an order from above, an act in which the rank and file had only the role of obedience. Publicly they might seem to be guilty, but privately, of course, they were above that kind of thing. And so like everyone else they kept away from the shop. How long would the boycott last? I made a point of passing the shop when the factory whistle had sounded. Day after day the workers went past while Fenger, with his hands in his pockets, stood idly in the doorway and glowered at the passing throng. But none returned his gaze. The boycott was so absolute that even the boldest would have feared to break it. What brazenness he would have needed to slip into that pilfered shop and peddle his pence for loot.

The Nazis made one effort to retrieve the situation. Fenger was dismissed and the Porten family placed in possession. Porten was a crippled soldier and had three children of school age. He was a ne'er-do-well himself and a burden to the parish, but his wife and three children were perhaps worthy of support. The village had been kind to them and was always ready to help, and here was an obvious way to set them on their feet.

But the village was resolute. The shop was banned for ever more and nothing the Nazis could devise could redeem it. Porten lingered for a month, canvassed the village for support, took to hawking tobacco from door to door and to opening a stall at the factory gate. There was no response.

I was glad Dorlich had made so valiant a stand, that the village still had a conscience and that, despite all pressure, spying and temptation, the people had refused to aid and abet the culprits. I was glad, Tilde was glad, Herr Engels was glad and said so. Coming home one afternoon and meeting Fenger at the door hawking a tray of tobacco, he boldly moved him on, telling him, in tones that rang over to the listening group outside the barber's shop, to reap only where he had sown and to sow only on land that was his. Herr Engels was quite frank about his views. But how about Frau Klebert?

I remember coming home one day after seeing the crowd walk past the shop and exclaiming to Herr Engels as he sat talking to her, 'I have just seen the factory men go by. My word, they are not to be tempted, not even by Porten and his three children, who were standing outside the shop. They were not moved a bit.'

'I am glad,' said Herr Engels.

'Sh!' Frau Klebert put her finger to her lips and gave a warning nod towards the door. 'Tilde!'

'She's in the garden. And even if she heard us, what of it? What a pity she isn't in the room to hear the whole story!'

'Father, be reasonable! I propose we drop the subject.'

'I don't see why we should. It is surely one of the most cheering that we have heard for a long time.' Frau Klebert shrugged her shoulders and did not reply. So I replied for her.

'I think it is most cheering. The village is showing a splendid spirit. You must agree, Frau Klebert.'

'I don't. The village is going too far.'

'How?'

'How? What grievance has the village against Porten and his family? A man we have always helped? And who has now been put into a position to keep himself and his family? Surely to boycott him is to show enmity for enmity's sake, and to fight on when the war is over. I am all for peace and harmony.'

'So am I,' rejoined Herr Engels, 'but it must be peace with God, not peace with the devil, least of all when he brings stolen fruit for repentance.'

'Stolen fruit! If you mean that Dorlich's shop was stolen you are not rightly stating the case. Dorlich got an excellent price for his shop, far better than he expected.'

'Yes, for the shop. But it was a poor price for his career. Where would he get another chance like that? Let us be frank about it. Both his shop and career were filched. And the village is passing judgement on the culprits.'

'Well that's a matter of opinion.'

'And of fact.'

'And the fact is that Dorlich got an excellent price. I admit that when Fenger was put in control it looked as though the party had exploited the affair for private advantage. But now that Fenger has gone the case has another aspect. Whatever Porten himself may be, his wife and children have been given an excellent chance in life and I think we ought to help them.'

'Yes, as fellow men but not as decoy ducks of the Nazi Party. Let them trade on their own account and I shall support them. As it is, the shop is a

Nazi shop, sold by Nazi compulsion, bought by Nazi money and run for Nazi ends.'

Was Frau Klebert convinced or, having taken a stand, was she determined, come what may, to maintain it? She must have sympathised with Dorlich, she must have condemned the Nazi ban on the shop; and she certainly detested Fenger and resented his appointment. Yet when Porten received the post she was reconciled at once, saw the best side of this very bad case and denied her better self in its defence. Yet how many millions in Germany were in the same ignoble plight, saying one thing and thinking another. Time and time again I met them, people who had lost their bearings, people who for safety's sake fenced and fibbed and counterfeited until all their inner selves were blurred, their previous faith forsworn, their life such a pretence that the false became the real thing.

But, despite the private panic and backsliding lurch of so many friends and neighbours, the two Miss Wolffs looked most serene. I had expected Miss Rachel to look haggard and worn, but she seemed to bloom up happier than ever, with rounder cheeks, brighter eyes and a more elastic step. She revealed not the slightest fear or fret or even the merest awareness of what was going on. And as for Miss Rebecca, she looked and talked and walked about as though the vast Nazi upheaval was an idle fiction of the press or no more than a passing bluster before the ensuing calm.

And yet, in reality, they were on their guard. I stood one night at my window watching the occasional passers-by and studying the silent street before drawing the shutters and going to bed when I observed a move at the opposing window. It was the merest drawing of the curtain, the flash of a torchlight and then darkness. It was a signal for me to go across. We had agreed on it months before, but this was the first time that they had given it. So I went over.

They received me in their sanctum, and quiet it was at that time of night with the village mostly asleep and the clock ticking clearly in the stillness. We took seats at the small round table and were thus able to talk in subdued tones. Would I do them a favour? Of course I would. Their friends in Bonn had all had a call from the police and they were expecting one themselves at any moment. Would I take a parcel, hide it in my room, lock it up in my bags and preserve it until the danger was past? It was a parcel of documents, of no great value in themselves but awkward if read by the police. Miss Rebecca had concealed them in the conservatory, and, while she went to get them, I stood with Miss Rachel by the glass door leading to the garden and passed a comment on affairs in the village.

'You've followed the Dorlich case?' I asked in a whisper. Rachel just nodded, but the nod was such a knowing one as to hint of deeper insight than I could claim myself.

'Grand the way Frenzel beat up the price.' She again nodded and a sly smile lit up her features and gave them that transfigured look which had so delighted me when first I met her.

'He managed it superbly,' I added.

'Yes, she did it with . . .' She broke off in confusion as her sister returned and I was left with a wild surmise. Was the 'she' just a slip of the tongue evoked by her sister's return, or was Rebecca herself the unknown bidder and champion of the pillaged Dorlich? As the question flashed across my mind the parcel was placed in my hands and I moved stealthily out through the garden and so back home. As I crossed the street a car drew up by the Wolffs' house. It was the police.

The throb of that moment seems to vibrate in me now. What perils had the sisters just escaped? And what new perils lay before them? And then again, what was my own embarrassing role? Bearing away the very things of which the detectives were in search, I let myself in quietly and hurried upstairs to my study. Where should I put the parcel? In my bags where the police could find it? Under my books or amid my linen where its alien presence would betray me? And what of Frau Gerster's papers? They were still in my room and likely to remain there for some time. I cast a hurried look around while a mill race of suggestions went swirling through my mind. There was no safe spot in the room. Better throw them both into the yard and pick them up early in the morning. I opened the window, threw back the shutters and looked out. Thank goodness, there was the chestnut tree blocking the view from the road. Why not hang the two on the branches until early morning?

I seized the two parcels and was about to lay hold of a branch when I thought of the staples on which the shutters clicked when thrown back to the wall. They were difficult to reach with the shutter in the way, but I managed it and hung up the parcels. Then I hastened to my bedroom and looked out into the street.

The car was still there. It remained there for nearly an hour, so I took my chair to the window, sat down and watched. The whole house seemed in darkness save for the fanlight down below, but through the chinks here and there in the shutters of the upper rooms I saw a gleam or two.

I expected any moment that the police would come across, discover all and leave me with the bitter thought of having failed my friends. But finally the door opened, the police stepped out and after a word or two at the door drove away. The sisters were left in peace. As I learned later, the police had gone through all their papers, secured a statement of their means and income, and removed a sheaf of accounts for further enquiry. But Rebecca had expected them and made her dispositions. I suppose there are very cool people in the world but, believe me, Rebecca was cooler.

My shock came next day at nine o'clock. Tilde came into my study and announced the police who, without a moment's hesitation, entered. The parcels, which I had unhooked, were lying on the couch plain for both men to see. I was so taken aback that I could not utter a word. They were very correct, however. They politely asked for my passport, checked my student's card and asked me one or two questions about my studies. They

137

then looked at my typewriter, noted the number and the model and asked me for a specimen script in English and German. They insisted on my typing it there and then. And when that was done they left. I sank back limp in my chair and wondered at the ways of mice and men until the rest of the family entered to hear my story. They all looked reassured, especially Tilde, who beamed in the doorway.

'I don't fear the police,' said Frau Klebert.

'Nor I,' said Herr Engels, 'so long as they pursue the guilty.'

How far was I one of the guilty? The question faced me all the time I was packing for the summer vacation. It was the question that faced my mind when I returned.

Chapter 13

How They Got the Stranglehold

While I was in England I was faced by all I met with the simple question: Why? Why had Hitler triumphed? Why had the Germans so tamely submitted? Why without even the semblance of resistance had Germany gone wholly brown? Here was a great nation, the most highly cultured in Europe, with a reputation for discipline unequalled since the days of Rome, not only yielding to a party of thugs but, in a fit of mass hysteria, bellowing its approval of the biggest thug of them all. Why, they asked.

They could think of only two answers. Brutality on the one hand and cowardice on the other. It was a gross misreading of the facts. For the moment the Nazis came to power the battleground was shifted. It was no longer a case of the Nazis versus the rest, but of each man against his neighbour and the devil take the loser. As the political battle died away, a social one succeeded, a silent deadly duel between those with jobs and those without, an underhand stampede for safety, a belch of internecine blackmail, which spared neither friend nor foe. The whole nation was riven, not into rulers and ruled, but into a helpless shatter of one and one where each sensed in everyone else the furtive and fell presence of the informer and the spy.

Despite a big show of the mailed fist, the Nazis worked in a subtler way than that described in the foreign press. It was very silent, too, like the pressure of an octopus, and all the more effective since the victims themselves supplied the stranglehold. How? Were those Nazis really so super-sly or had they stumbled blindly, unsuspectingly, into simple, subtle plans which the wit of no exchequer had ever before devised? Personally, I feel they were headlong, arrogant, vulgar and crude, and that fortune, the devil's own fortune, led them by the hand. But an example.

After months of absence in England, I had returned to Blankheim and entered the house just as Herr Engels was going out. He took my hand and greeted me, rather curtly I thought, but a lost and troubled look in his honest old grey eyes showed me that something was amiss. There was a bustle in the house, the sound of voices and visitors, and as I stepped into the hall Tilde came whisking past and stopped only for a moment to welcome me. Frau Klebert, a few steps behind, was whispering a hurried order.

139

'Rudesheimer, Tilde, two bottles, in the bottom far corner rack. And a box of Havana cigars. Middle shelf in the cupboard. Oh, welcome, Mr Arnold. And, Tilde, a bottle of Asbach Uralt. You know. Oh, welcome, Mr Arnold. See you later. Or better still, come down and join us.' And away she went.

'Rudesheimer! Asbach Uralt,' I kept murmuring to myself. The best wine and the best brandy in the Rhineland. Some favoured visitors had come. I peeped over the banister to see if I could recognise the hats and coats on the stand. They lay in shadow, however, and I could hear Tilde coming up the cellar steps, so into my room I went and pondered the curt reception.

I did a little unpacking and then went down into the sanctum. The men stood up to greet me. One was Herr Engels's son, Joseph, the jeweller from Cologne. To my surprise, the other two were Herr Klassen, the village schoolmaster, and Alex Brechner. Both were in Nazi rig, sprucer than ever I had seen them before, and with a look of self-possession and command, which took me aback. Alex Brechner of all men. But there he was, former down-and-outer, seated in Herr Engels's chair as though by right, enjoying the old man's finest cigars and sipping his choicest wine.

'And what do the English people think of our revolution?'

It was the stock question in those days and I answered as emolliently as I could. But that wasn't good enough for Klassen. 'Quite wrong, quite wrong,' he protested in his high-pitched, staccato voice. 'You English don't seem to realise that Germany was on the brink of ruin. With 6 million unemployed, with a burden of war debt impossible to pay off, and riddled with corruption. We would have slumped into Bolshevism but for the resolute action of the Führer. The two great pests of the modem world are communism and Jewry ...'

'And militarism, of course,' I interposed.

'Yes, militarism,' exclaimed Brechner, in his mob voice. 'But the Führer is no militarist. He is a working man. He was a common soldier. He would never dream of hounding millions of his fellow comrades to the slaughter and hell of the trenches, as the Kaiser did. That game is over, for once and for all.'

'But why these military organisations?' I asked in an almost apologetic tone.

'To have discipline in the land,' rejoined Brechner, 'and to put the stranglehold on conspirators and saboteurs. And Germany must be restored. We must regain our lost provinces, our colonies and trade. And it's not right that we should be encircled by unfriendly countries. The German people must be put on their feet. Look at the misery in the land, the hunger, the unemployment. That's one of the reasons why you see us here.'

As he spoke he struck some papers on the table, a list of names and a receipt book.

'Collecting?' I asked.

'Yes, there's no private charity now, you know,' said Brechner in a tone of triumph. 'That's all dead and done with.'

'Yes, dead and done with,' echoed Klassen. 'We've stopped that source of corruption. The money now goes to where it was intended.'

'But the Caritas of the Catholic Church? The Kevelaar Club?'

'Gone with the rest,' cried Brechner. 'They all just tinkered with the problem. But now that we are facing every German with the problem, as you see by this list, we are bringing the responsibilities of everyone in the village to his own doorstep. And it works far better than the old way, doesn't it, Frau Klebert?'

'Yes, they are bringing it home to us all.' Frau Klebert was really trying to be decisive. 'The Nazis are certainly ...'

'The National Socialists,' corrected Brechner.

'Pardon, the National Socialists are certainly making a success of these voluntary contributions. There'll be no want in the village after this.'

I asked to see the list. It was a long array of names and, as I realised at the first glance, included all the prominent names of Blankheim. So Brechner and Klassen were going round and dunning the whole village, openly and brazenly with a public list. The contributions of each were plainly to be seen, and the remarkable fact about them was that each sum was greater than the one just before it. That is, each man in the village was going one better than his neighbour. Frau Klebert's gift was flagrantly more than the last, namely that of Alfred Wessel, the building contractor, who lived just a few doors away. Two hundred marks! A hundred for Herr Engels and a hundred for herself. At a glance I realised that this was sheer bribery to buy off something worse.

'And then the homeless,' added Brechner. 'They'll have to be quartered somewhere, even if we have to commandeer rooms. Look at the Porten family, look at ... ' And he proceeded to name the drunken down-and-outs of the village. As he finished the sinister list his hand went to the brandy.

'If I may, Frau Klebert?'

'By all means, fill your glass. It's a glorious brand, Herr Brechner, mellow, warm ...'

'By God it is!'

'I'm glad you enjoy it. Try one, Herr Klassen.'

'No thanks, I'll keep to the wine,' said Klassen. 'It's a splendid vintage.'

He, the sharp-faced, precise martinet was looking a little flushed. He was clearly seeking to keep control and doubtless the wine before him was not the first that night. As for Brechner, he was reckless. He, the former down-and-out, who for many a dreary year had shivered and starved on the dole, sat there like some nabob, draining that priceless brandy like beer and indulging with every gulp his swelling lust for wealth and power. He thumped the papers again.

'And those who refuse to do their bit ... ' Here he halted and flashed upon the company a defiant look of his hard blue eyes.

141

'Will have their bit thrust upon them,' added Klassen.

'And quite right too,' broke in Joseph. 'Quite right too. As the Führer said, we must all bear one another's burdens.'

'And well said, too,' cried Brechner. 'It's high time the burden was taken from our shoulders and put on those that can bear it. We have borne the burden long enough.'

'Very true, very true,' said Joseph.

'Especially as you yourself, Herr Brechner, have had such a hard time,' interposed Frau Klebert.

'My God, yes.'

'And your poor wife too. I wonder how she has had the courage to stand up to it all. Here! How about giving her a bottle of Asbach Uralt? It will pull her round. Where's Tilde?'

She rang, and in her eagerness went out to meet the girl, who presently returned with a bottle of the exquisite vintage.

They went at last. Brechner was most effusive, taking Frau Klebert's hand in both his own and praising her most highly on her gallant stand for the party. To me, he was equally effusive and prophesied the time when England and Germany, shoulder to shoulder, would rule the world in justice and right.

They went, and not until their steps had died away did anyone venture a word. We were all standing in the hall, silent, embarrassed, perhaps a little ashamed. Then Frau Klebert bridled up, and, with her eyes fixed on the door as though she expected Brechner's return, she blurted out, 'Have you words for it?'

'Words for what?' I stammered, bewildered.

'For what? You saw the list.'

'Yes.' I wondered what she was driving at.

'And you saw Alfred Wessel's contribution?'

'Yes, 100 marks. I thought it rather high.'

'High! A shameless sum to offer. Just to go one better than Frenzel and land him in the cart. And all without a thought for the others who come after. Twenty was more than enough. And now he has set the pace for the whole village.'

'Yes, but Frenzel's was double that of the man before him, Wegener.'

'And Wegener's was higher than Frankau's. The five marks that Kiel gave looks a very poor sum indeed.'

'Say what you like, Mr Arnold,' she insisted, 'to my mind the gifts were all in order until Wessel came to pay. He's a man without a conscience, a turncoat. Since the Nazis came to power he has never been to see us, and only the other day he cut father in the street.'

She blurted all this out without one thought for what her own gift meant to the next man on the list. She felt no qualms about it. For she was fighting an heroic battle for her father and her home, and for that she was ready to pay any price the Nazis asked. I did not judge her. Without doubt her conscience was clear. But what distressed me most was the bad blood in the village. Everyone was cutting himself silently adrift from the rest.

Historically, tyrants relied on whips and scorpions, or guillotined hordes in the public street, but the Nazis were more subtle. They gave the people plenty of rope and left them to hang themselves.

Some time later I went out for a stroll, and was nearing the end of the village street when I saw in dark silhouette against the dim light of a street lamp our two Nazi friends studying their sinister list. It was a whispered conference with each peering at the other in mutual query. They started back as I approached in the darkness. 'Ah, it's the Englishman. Heil Hitler!'

'Good evening. And how's the collection going? Each man bidding one better than the last?'

Brechner laughed, while Klassen responded only with a wry smile. Brechner laid his hand on my shoulder. He was swaying a little and his voice was rather muffled. He had drunk rather deeply of the hospitality of the village.

'Herr Arnold, Herr Arnold,' he gasped, as he looked left and right along the dim and misty street, 'they are cutting each other's throats, cutting each other's throats.' He laughed and waved the list. 'Just look!'

He was about to show me the list when Klassen intervened and took it.

'Confidential, Herr Arnold, confidential, you know.' But Brechner went on despite all Klassen's efforts to restrain him.

'Yes, it's confidential, strictly confidential between you and me, Herr Klassen, but I'll tell you, Herr Arnold, what that damned Lambert offered us.

'We went to see him with the list and when he saw how much Frau Klebert had given do you know what he offered us? The mean calculating skunk, guess how much? Guess.' Brechner's voice rose to a drunken shout and we had to hush him up.

'Well, just guess.'

He did not wait for a reply, but after spitting on the ground to express his disgust, hissed: '210! Just ten more! Skunk enough to go ten better, but not skunk enough to go any more.'

It was a rigmarole of a story, but the two rogues had made it clear to Lambert that unless he was more generous they would arrange for him to contribute in some less pleasant way. They reminded him that he was a single man, with a large house and no family. So he could spare a flat for the Portens or some family still worse off, some drunken brawling ne'er-do-wells who would make his private life a hell.

'Well, he stared at us and stared at us and finally signed for 300.'

When I got back from my stroll Herr Engels had returned. I could hear his voice and Frau Klebert's voice in high altercation, in a tone that jarred the whole house and shattered its serenity. Tilde stood in the dark far corner of the hall and looked at me aghast. She laid her finger on her lips. I could see that she was crying.

143

'If those fellows come here again,' thundered the old man, 'you'll keep them on the outer step or, if business is to be done, keep them standing in the outer hall. I'll have my front door locked between me and the public street. I'll have it barred and bolted between me and the public gutter. Understand!'

'Understand!' cried Frau Klebert. 'Understand! Do you? If we don't let them in they'll break in, whether the doors are locked or not. And if we cross them we might have to share our home with such riff-raff as they choose to thrust upon us, the Portens or worse, the Heidecamps or other drunks of the village. This house is yours or theirs, and I'm doing my best to keep it yours.'

'And mine it will remain, or I'll blaze it up in smoke,' he thundered in return. 'If the worst comes to the worst this house will share my earthly fate of ashes to ashes and dust to dust even though my flesh and bones must reek and smoulder with it.'

I hurried out of earshot. I slipped up to my study, closed my door and sank into my chair by the stove. I had returned after many weeks to my tranquil haunt on the Rhine only to find it my tranquil haunt no more. But worst of all, the brawling spirit of the Nazis had involved not only the house but the family as well, and opened up a grievous breach for evil feeling and bad blood.

One question pestered me. Should I tell Frau Klebert what Brechner had related and inflame her still further against Lambert, one of her former friends? Should I remain silent even to the dubious edge of deceit and play a double part? I was saved any further thought by a quiet knock at the door. It was Frau Klebert herself. She sat down and faced me. Was it the mote in my own eye or the possible beam in hers that made me feel so ill at ease?

In her plain straightforward way she came to the point. Could I help her? Could I use my influence with her father, my knowledge of the times and my plain unbiased views to bring him to some reason? He was living in a bygone age when right was right and law was law and when the social forms, which centuries had established, had been implicit in every phase of public life. Now, whatever the provocation, he must shut an eye, hold his tongue and not play himself and all he had into the hands of the devil.

'I shall try,' I answered quietly, 'but ...' I halted and wondered at my own blundering thoughts.

'But what?'

'I'm afraid your father is too good and honest to play a double part.'

As she flushed up I realised my blunder.

'No reflection on you, Frau Klebert, no reflection on you, but for an honest man it is a great dilemma. Not for your grand old father of course, who would never go trucking with half truths, but certainly for me. Yes, trucking with half-truths. I'm wearing a mask this very moment, even to you.'

'To me?'

'To you. I saw Brechner an hour ago and he told me something I should like to conceal.'

'But why conceal it?'

'Well, I heard what you said of Alfred Wessel.'

'And?'

'I didn't want to inflame you against another friend, if friend you like to call him.'

'What happened at Lambert's house?'

She shot the question so directly that I felt she knew much more than she wanted to confess. Then I realised that she must have seen that Lambert's name was the next one on the list. So I told her the whole story, and her eyes flashed in triumph as I quoted Brechner's judgement, 'skunk enough to go ten better, but too much of a skunk to go any more'.

'The devil!' she kept on saying to herself. 'He betrayed you about refusing to write that letter he wanted you to write for him, he has betrayed us and he has betrayed the Miss Wolffs. What is more, I hear he is worming out all their money transactions and dunning others to break faith and reveal their business secrets.'

Amid all this underhand intrigue, what else was going on?

I began to make some guesses. Unable to sleep that night, I slipped out of the house for a stroll along the Rhine. The church clock was striking twelve and a dark murk lay over the river, obscuring the lantern reflections from the barges and blurring the Boatman's Inn, which lay like a misty shadow ahead. I halted for a moment to glance up the steep bank where the Wolffs' house overlooked the river. Even at that distance I descried some movement. Something white was moving on the wall. Was it Miss Rebecca taking a glimpse of the river and was that the white wimple she often wore at her household tasks? I was too much in the shadow for her to see me. Should I call and climb the bank?

In that moment of hesitation I observed some further movements. Something dark was slipping over the wall. In the tense silence of the night I could hear steps descending the bank. Two men. I slipped back into the darkness and observed the two as they emerged into view. They had not seen me. They passed within four or five yards of me as I crouched in the shadow of the wall. Alex Brechner and Hans Zimmermann.

What had they been doing in the Jews' house, a burglary or carrying out a search?

I looked up the bank again. The white wimple was still there, two white wimples, both the ladies. And both were calmly standing there, engaged so it seemed in simple talk and pointing to some spot beyond the river. I cautiously mounted the bank in the shadow of the wall. Yes, it was the two sisters and I heard Miss Rebecca laugh. And then the two went up the garden and I heard them close the shutters. So I went on my way in bewilderment, but before I got home I had made a shrewd guess.

Chapter 14

The Writing on the Wall

I thought, and perhaps Frau Klebert thought, that she had bought a long lease of peace. Brechner was now the local group leader, and, though his voice was only one among many, it carried weight with the rank and file. Unlike Lambert and Klassen, he was one of the original crew, a Nazi when Nazis were little known and Hitler a mere street-corner ranter. It was a great thing to be well in with Brechner. And then there was something else. As Brechner was an original Nazi he expected others to have different views and to offer opposition. Indeed he suspected and even hated an all-too-ready agreement. No, it was not Brechner we feared. It was the rats and renegades from the anti-Nazi parties, the Lamberts and Klassens who had a past to forget and a future to ensure, men who would stop at nothing to save their cringing skins. They were the ones we had to dread. And there they moved in every walk of life, at your elbow, behind your back or intent at the nearest keyhole, burning to prove by some betrayal their loyalty to the new regime.

A few days after my return from England it was the night of the plebiscite. There were few signs in the village that anything was afoot and Frau Klebert, who had gone in the morning to record her vote for the new regime, told us that, save for the receiving officers, the polling station was empty.

'I signed my slip at the table and handed it over to Klassen.'

Herr Engels gave her a quizzical look.

'You gave an open vote?'

'Of course; one has no option. And I'm not going to play into the hands of such men as Zimmermann and Klassen. For it was they who received the votes. Just guess what Klassen said the moment I went in.'

'What?'

'He called out to Zimmermann, "Well, you've nothing to conceal, Frau Klebert?" And I replied that I certainly hadn't. So I boldly signed for the new regime. I hope he was disappointed.' And she gave a triumphant smile.

'A sort of mutual cheat,' observed Herr Engels as he slowly puffed at his pipe.

'Yes, a mutual cheat. They won a vote, but lost a victim. I think I gained the trick, don't you?'

'Well, if life's a gamble with the devil perhaps you didn't. For what you staked he has won. Personally, I think you've raised a voice for Barabbas. I hope you haven't been helping to howl the saviour down.'

It was all said very quietly, but Frau Klebert flushed and, with some show of indignation, faced up to her father.

'Father!' she exclaimed and then without a further word went out of the room.

'She means well,' said the old man after a long and dead pause, 'but to go halves with the devil is to go hand in hand. And his hand, believe me, is a grip. Where he leads, you follow. For you are bound to him hand and foot.'

I silently agreed. But was Frau Klebert wholly in the wrong? There are many times in life when wisdom is at a loss, when truth insists on one course and tact suggests another.

It came to the test that night. I had been sitting in the sanctum with Frau Klebert and her father when a loud and insistent ring roused us to a sense of the outer world. We all started up and a panic thought of the Gestapo came suddenly to my mind.

'Is it the police, I wonder?'

'The police!' gasped Herr Engels.

'Sit down, father. I shall attend to it.' Frau Klebert cast her sewing on the table and hurried to the door. At the same moment it was opened and Tilde peeped in.

'It's about the voting,' she said.

As she uttered the words she was thrust into the room by two men behind her, Hamann and Fenger. Hamann looking grim and aggressive with his falling Hitler quiff and boxer stoop, and Fenger, flabby-faced, as brutish as ever.

'Heil Hitler!'

Hamann called out his greeting as though he were in the open street, but meeting no response he called again in still louder tones, 'Heil Hitler!'

Herr Engels for a moment was speechless. He gazed at the intruder with tense indignation and finally asked, 'Who authorised you to come in here?'

'I have come about the voting.'

'Who authorised you to come in here?' thundered Herr Engels in return. 'Leave this house at once.'

'When you come with me,' Hamann thundered back. 'You've not recorded your vote yet and we have come to escort you to the poll.'

'By force?' cried Herr Engels.

'It will be at your peril if you don't,' shouted Hamann.

I flung myself between them.

'You've no business here,' I told him. 'It's not by the order of the Führer that anyone be dragged to the poll. And if you attempt to drag him, you'll drag me, and believe me you'll get no change from the deal.'

147

Our voices rose in high dispute and Hamann was losing control when Frau Klebert, who had slipped out for a moment, returned. Making for Hamann she thrust him back. My word, how she blazed! Of the slightest fear, not a trace.

'You'll get out of here,' she cried, thrusting him through the door, 'or I'll have you thrown out, neck and crop.'

'He'll come with us,' shouted Hamann, raising his fist, but in the nick of time I caught his wrist.

'What? You coward. You'll strike me, a member of the party and an officer's wife. I've just sent for the police, but I've a mind to throw you out myself.'

She rushed at him, but I restrained her.

'The police will be here in a moment,' I said, 'let us leave the matter to them.'

'Oh,' blustered Hamann, 'I don't care a rap for the police.' And he tried to thrust me back. 'They dare not touch the uniform of the Führer.'

'But I shall,' cried Frau Klebert.

Heaven knows what might have happened but for a movement outside. There was a rush into the hall and a Nazi suddenly entered and forced his way past Hamann. It was Alex Brechner, whom Tilde had met in the street.

'What's the meaning of this, Hamann? You've no business here, forcing your way into people's houses and bringing the party into disrepute. Get out! And you, Fenger, beat it!'

'But he hasn't recorded his vote.'

'What of it? He's an old man with old-fashioned ideas. You can't change those in a night. And we don't want the votes of turncoats. The man knows where he stands and he has the courage to say so. Come on. Get out.'

'But the maid hasn't voted either. We'll take her, whatever you say.'

'You take her,' said Frau Klebert to me. 'I won't have her paraded through the streets. Mr Arnold will take her, Herr Brechner.'

The intruders left and soon after that Tilde and I were gingerly picking our way along the dark and stumbly street to the schoolhouse. There were few people about and we passed without one word of greeting until we reached the schoolhouse door. One of the rooms, the polling booth, cast its light on the school yard and a gust of voices came from the open door. We entered and everything went still as all eyes were turned upon us. It looked like a gathering of party men, for nearly all were dressed in Nazi garb and the smoke from their pipes was suffocating. But their faces were familiar.

'Heil Hitler!'

'Good evening,' I replied and a burst of laughter greeted my reply. It was not ironically meant. From the lips of a German the greeting 'Good evening' would have implied defiance, but from me, well – they laughed outright.

'England has come to vote for the Führer,' someone shouted and they all laughed again.

'No, he has brought back those colonies he pinched,' said another, and so the chaff went on. Behind a long table sat Klassen and Hans Zimmermann, a rather humourless pair who kept very sober faces. Tilde received her slip. There was a little partition by the table where one could vote in private. Tilde moved towards it.

'So you've got something to conceal, pretty miss.'

'Something what?' retorted Tilde, halting in confusion.

'Something to conceal,' they called out in chorus.

Tilde halted. Despite her happy nature she could be extremely resolute. Her cheeks were flushed, but not in mere embarrassment. She was very annoyed and showed it.

'You mean, if I vote behind the partition I'm voting against the party?'

'You've said it!' The whole room rocked with laughter and a smile flickered over Klassen's face.

I had always liked Tilde, but I had never liked her so much as then. She stood there and faced them. She seemed to set her teeth and clench her fists so that the slip lay crumpled in her hand. She darted a look at Klassen and Zimmermann and caught something of their mocking smile.

'So that's your secret vote,' she said, and, snatching a pencil from Klassen's hand, she slashed a cross on the slip. 'Well, there! Against! Against! Against!' And she flung the slip in Klassen's face.

'Bravo, Tilde,' I said, and as she was all of a tremble I took her hand and led her out.

There had been a dramatic silence, but the moment I said 'Bravo' there was a murmur, not of anger but of applause.

'Yes, bravo,' said one. 'Plucky girl.'

'Yes, plucky girl,' they muttered.

There was a tense air in the house when we returned. Herr Engels, in a trembling way, was puffing vainly at his pipe, while Frau Klebert with a stony look was trying to sew. Words had passed between them, plain outspoken words which had deepened the dilemma and left the rift between them more gaping than before. Both had proved their point, but neither, of course, to the satisfaction of the other. I seemed to enter unnoticed. For some moments there was a dead pause.

'Well?' said Frau Klebert at last. She was expecting a word about Tilde and I was determined to evade the issue, even by a little flattery.

'What a lucky stroke of yours,' I said, 'to get Brechner on our side.'

'Hear, hear! Are you listening, Father?' She spoke in a low triumphant tone as though she relished every word I said.

'Without his help we should have been in a pretty pickle tonight. We certainly would; men like Hamann and Fenger have no scruples whatsoever.'

'No, they haven't,' said Herr Engels, 'and they are the villains whom we are putting into power; men who on their own saying don't care a rap for the police, and whose violence, theft and blackguardism are done under

149

cover of the law. Their uniform is sacrosanct. Apparently it's a passport through the whole moral code. And I'm to bow and do it reverence? Never! I shall never degrade myself by kissing the hem of Hitler's shirt.'

It was a drastic picture. So drastic that I laughed outright. It saved the situation and as Frau Klebert laughed as well the old man's anger softened into a smile. We agreed to drop the subject, to forget the ugly incident that had shaken the house badly and to discuss the new topic that was interesting the village.

Professor Rosenbaum had lost his post at Bonn and had taken a flat at the Miss Wolffs until he found a post abroad. I saw him from my window next morning as he drew back the curtains and looked down into the street. He caught sight of me and bowed, smiling in his effusive way and rubbing his jewelled hands. In his meticulously ironed and immaculate attire he looked strangely out of place in the dingy setting of Blankheim. I tried in vain to picture him in all his city finery tripping along that deeply rutted and clumsily cobbled street, and running the drab gauntlet of Blankheim's bucolic gaze.

How would Hamann and Fenger react to this new influx from Jewry? And Brechner? But I thought of that strange scene when he and Hans Zimmermann came slinking over the garden wall after a meeting with Rebecca Wolff. Perhaps Frau Klebert was not the only one who had played for Brechner's support.

For Frau Klebert's sake and to keep well in with Brechner, who was now a power in the village, I had taken to avoiding all my Jewish friends, either affecting not to see them or turning aside in good time when I saw them coming along. So imagine my embarrassment when, two or three days later, as I was walking along the street, a car drew up beside me and Professor Rosenbaum with his glinting and effusive smile asked me to step inside.

'To Bonn?' he asked, assuming I was on my way to the university and beaming with assurance as he released the door to let me in. Taken completely unawares, I stepped inside. I was all the more embarrassed as Hamann came ambling past and I felt his scowling look and heard his 'Judah verrecke!' as I closed the car door. I realised my mistake. I ought to have said I was going to Cologne, but no help for it now as I sat in Rosenbaum's car, the butt of every village glance as we drove slowly and carefully along that deeply rutted street into the countryside beyond.

When well out of earshot of the whole village Rosenbaum grew quite expansive. I was an Englishman, therefore a friend; a friend, he assumed, of all oppressed peoples, a man of sympathy and understanding, a Christian. He said how much pleasure it was to be able to speak so freely and to have in so close a neighbour a man who knew no racial hate. He took it as read that I would help him and that any letters or applications he had to address abroad, to England, America or the dominions, I would be willing to translate. And then he had some articles he intended to publish in London and for which he would need my assistance.

All of this I heard with steadily growing dismay. I should have liked to oblige him, had time and my studies permitted, but my position in Blankheim would become a little clouded, indeed a little too clouded, if Rosenbaum, as he indicated, should call upon me in my rooms. And then with regard to his car. We had plenty of parking space in the disused yard at the back of the house and even empty sheds. Would Herr Engels be willing to rent him one for a garage? Not for long of course. Just for the time being until he got a post abroad.

But even as I promised Rosenbaum to do my best to help him I felt that my assurance was merely an empty phrase. I decided to let it sleep. I was afraid to tell Frau Klebert of my ride with him to Bonn or to ask Herr Engels about the yard for fear he would consent. Alas for my dissimulation, Rosenbaum called a day or two later and found Herr Engels alone at home.

According to Tilde, who heard snatches of the conversation when she brought in the wine and cigars, Rosenbaum argued persuasively that Hitler was not so bad, Goebbels was eloquent, Göring thoroughgoing, but their policy had been spoiled by the counsels of the vicious few. The Germans were a noble nation. He, Rosenbaum, was a German, of German culture, feeling, speech, and he was glad to think that the majority regretted his misfortunes and were ready almost to a man to atone for the guilt of one or two. Herr Engels was surely the man to offer a helping hand if only to save the good name of the German nation and the Christian faith.

Herr Engels consented and gave him the key of the outer gate. Tilde whispered the fact to me and revealed her own dilemma. She was very uneasy.

'I'm afraid to tell Frau Klebert and yet feel guilty if I conceal it. I hate being underhand, but if I tell her before Herr Engels does I shall seem to be a blabber.'

'I'm in the same boat,' I replied, 'but after all it's up to Herr Engels to discuss it with his daughter. You as a maid know nothing. You are not supposed to hear what's said when you drop in to serve the guests. Everything you hear is strictly confidential. You remember Frau Klebert's rule some time ago. She almost excluded you from the home.'

She went away relieved, but not for long. An hour or two later I heard voices in the yard, so I went to my study window and looked out. There at the bottom of the yard, ready to drive away in his car, was Professor Rosenbaum. In that drab and unused yard, so overrun with moss and fading weeds, the elegant Professor Rosenbaum looked more elegant than ever. His glasses, tiepin and bejewelled fingers glittered in the autumn sunlight and his face and bald head literally shone as though he had been anointed. He was standing with his hat in his hand conversing with Frau

151

Klebert, who was in her most decisive mood, and the light that shone on Rosenbaum flared through her golden hair like a fire.

'Impossible!' I heard her exclaim. 'As a member of the party I cannot have you in the house.' She raised her voice at this and I saw the reason why. People were gathering at the gate, two or three Brownshirts and a policeman, and they all gazed in silence, intent on every word. Rosenbaum looked deference itself, soothing, submissive, apologetic, and I heard him suggest, with a most disarming smile, a more private place for discussion. A moment or two later he was careering down the lane while Frau Klebert, who was closing the gate, had a word or two with the crowd.

It was Tilde of all people who had to bear the brunt. Their voices resounded in the hall as they had never resounded before. Why had she, mistress of the house, been kept so deep in the dark in this underhand way, and baffled before the village? Who was Tilde to have information denied to herself, information so important to the house that the fortunes of the family, their standing in the village, their very lives might well depend upon it. It was Tilde's duty to be open and honest and not to keep back what was not hers to withhold.

It was Tilde's turn to blaze up, but she did it with perfect restraint. She was a mere maid and not an enquiry office and whatever she may have overheard she had not the slightest right to take the words from Herr Engels's lips and to blab them to the rest of the house. She had assumed that Herr Engels in his open honest way had told Frau Klebert.

'As you said yourself, Frau Klebert, what I overhear has no business to be heard or remembered. And I have borne those words in mind. Is that not so?'

'You might have told me the Jewish professor was here. You opened the door.'

'Yes, I might have done so and perhaps, Frau Klebert, that was my mistake. But on the other hand I've no right to betray your father's confidences. You and I conceal things from him, such as taking those Nazi papers, but I would never dream of mentioning the fact for fear of betraying you. But let me tell you now that I feel most unhappy at practising such deceit.'

I was descending the staircase at this point and I saw Frau Klebert put both her hands to her face.

'You are right, Tilde,' she said at last. 'Kindly excuse my outburst.' And taking Tilde in her arms she kissed her on both cheeks.

So far, so good. But how about Herr Engels? The matter blazed up when he came back home and perhaps never before in all their lives had father and daughter such a dispute, so furious and forthright on her part, so cutting and ironical on his. The whole house seemed riven in two. Tilde, who had never known such scenes, felt so upset and alone that she quietly slipped up to my study and begged for a little refuge. So we whispered our fears to each other and wondered what the morrow would bring. But

152

finally I decided to go downstairs and try to restore peace. After all, Frau Klebert had pleaded with me and begged me to speak to her father. I felt it right to intervene.

As I entered, Frau Klebert was making a final onslaught.

'Well go and look at the yard gate and all along the barn walls. "Judah verrecke" in big chalk letters has been scrawled there right across them. So we are lumped along with Jewry, and the racial hate of the village is concentrated upon us. And all because you refuse to listen to the counsels of common sense.'

'So "Judah verrecke" has been scribbled all along our gate and walls?' His tone was loud and grim.

'Yes, and much more a deal worse.'

'And so I must order my conduct and frame my character on the scribbling riff-raff of Blankheim. Their scrawled back-alley curses are to be my future gospel, and when I finally meet my Saviour, himself a son of Judah, I'm to greet him with a "Judah verrecke"? I was asked for help and I gave it, so that the only question between us is – which loyalty comes first, loyalty to the Nazi Party or loyalty to God? I am in no doubt on the point.'

'But loyalty to God is not a thing apart.' Her voice rang in real anger. 'It's the sum of all your loyalties, of the loyalties to your family, your home and your friends. You've no right to forget your loyalty to us in order to oblige a stranger who might bring destruction on you and yours. And all for such a trifle as parking a car. Where is your sense of proportion? This Jew could park his car in Dr Cohen's yard without the slightest prejudice either to Cohen or to himself. As it is we are faced with the fury of the village.'

'Well,' and he thumped the table, 'we are faced with the fury of the village. I'm not afraid. I've done my best, so let them do their worst, if that's their only reaction. When people ask me to do them a favour I don't go and haggle the pros and cons. I don't cast up a copper account or study the profit and loss as you would have me do. Life isn't a moral deal with God on strictly cash terms.'

'In my opinion it is, and He reckons to the uttermost farthing. It's a deal in the strictly moneyed sense and it is not for you to throw it away on any trumpery occasion. And trumpery occasion this one is, and I'm determined to alter it. I shall forbid that Jewish professor to park his car in the yard.'

The fat was in the fire now. The quarrel blazed up again despite all my efforts to intervene. Herr Engels's grey eyes flashed and his bushy brows and shaggy beard stood out more defiantly than ever. His voice rang out and he enforced many a sentence with such a thump of the table that the vase of flowers rattled on the stand and threatened to shed every petal of the quivering blooms. Not that he had lost his temper, but the pent-up aggravation of months burst out into full expression. He felt that his daughter was a trimmer, playing up to both sides and doing right by neither.

But Frau Klebert was resolute. She sent a letter to Rosenbaum, asking him to return the keys and to apply elsewhere for a garage. Rosenbaum replied in person and, finding no one else at home, asked Tilde to refer to me. Before I could say yes or no he was in my room expostulating. There was surely a misunderstanding. Herr Engels had given him his kind and express permission. He had let him have the keys and had offered to stand firmly by a persecuted fellow man. How happy he was to think that he had such a noble Christian as a neighbour and a friend. Surely – and here he dropped his voice lest Tilde should overhear – Frau Klebert must be acting behind Herr Engels's back.

He waved his hands despairingly, such a look of disaster as contrasted in a spurious way with his glossy and prosperous attire. He repeated his whispered query in his suavest way and with his hands coaxingly clasped in supplication. But alas for my own soul, I said I knew nothing about it; I was a mere guest in the house, wholly absorbed in my own studies and tactfully deaf to all that I unavoidably overheard. Times were very perilous, and it was well for all outsiders to lie low and say nothing. The Nazis were firmly in power and nothing but a foreign invasion would shift them.

'Don't believe it,' said Rosenbaum with his most pooh-poohing smile, and he waved his hand in elegant contempt. Nazidom was a passing phase. It had come and it would go like the bluster of a summer storm. Commercially, industrially, socially, Germany was at a standstill and nothing but foreign capital could get it going again.

'Do you think England and America are going to finance Hitler's schemes? And bolster up his plans for war? And help him to exterminate the Catholics and the Jews? Not they. Realities will bring him to reason. Before he gets one penny from abroad he will have to alter his policy, and if he refuses to do so, well – in the space of a year or two poor Nazi Germany will be broken and bankrupt and done.'

Rosenbaum snapped his fingers and for a moment it seemed to me that the Nazi bubble had burst. It sounded plausible enough, and many Germans were lying low in this deep and happy conviction that for want of foreign capital the Nazi realm would wither away. And this thought, so consoling and also so widespread, lulled millions into submission. They had only to wait a year or two, in silence and self-effacement, and lo, without striking a blow or even raising a voice in protest, Hitler and all his myrmidons would vanish from the scene.

Our meeting was over and I escorted the hapless professor to the front door. He left with the solemn assurance that I should do my best to serve him. He bowed his profuse thanks and offered me his hand as though he were bestowing a fortune. I watched him as he tripped across the street and as he vanished through the Wolffs' door which, by some premonition, seemed to open of its own accord.

As I returned to my study I found Tilde waiting in the hall, and I knew what she had in mind. Tears came to my eyes.

'Mr Arnold,' she said.

'Yes.' I could hardly speak.

'You've just made a promise you don't intend to keep.'

'I know. I was honest until I came here.'

'You were. I made you my conscience in the difficult days we have gone through and you were the measure by which I measured my own words. And now?'

'I'm sorry. You are right. I'm fast becoming a plausible liar. And I don't know how to undo it.'

'Nor I. The Nazis are partly to blame, but when I mention them in confession the priest cuts me short. I must not accuse others in confessing my own sins. And then I must consider *him*.'

'Whom?'

'The priest. So many go to trap him and lead him to say things that might lead to his arrest. But I always had your example and now even that has gone.'

Her voice dropped and the stillness of the room went through me. I felt very sick at heart. She had also been *my* conscience, good and sterling girl as she was, no less than Herr Engels himself. Yes, there were stains on my escutcheon, a tarnish, foul fingermarks indubitably my own. For I was lying not only to others but also to myself, proving in self-discussion that I was acting for the best and even taking a pride in my tact and self-restraint. Verbal jobbery all of it, hypocrisy and lying. I felt ashamed.

'Thank you, Tilde,' I said and took her hand, 'I shall try to keep erect in the future.'

As I went up the staircase to my study and my lonely thoughts I felt her gaze behind me. Would I keep erect in future and live in all transparency to everyone I met? I realised my dilemma. How about the parcels entrusted to my care? They lay hidden in my bags, yet far more deeply hidden in my mental reservations. I should quibble? Equivocate? Boldly lie to the police to keep them safe? Yes, I realised my dilemma.

Chapter 15

The Inner Canker

Rosenbaum, to say the least, was a little indiscreet. I am ready to admit that he was in a drowning state and would clutch at straws to save his sinking skin. And who would blame him? Not I. And yet he might have been a little more self-effaced, more mute and submissive, and much more appreciative of the equal plight of others. Frau Klebert had asked for a return of the keys and in answer to her demand he had begged for a little delay. He was making an arrangement with someone else and had another place in view. But day after day went by and he continued to park his car in our yard, oblivious of the great chalk marks that scored the gate and barn walls. And then one fine morning more appeared on the front of the house itself. Not on the Jews' house of course, but ours.

It was Saturday morning, and peeping through my bedroom window I saw the usual crowd outside the barber's shop. There was Matthias, of course, with his mutely bovine gaze, a Brownshirt or two, Heinrich with his fawning smile and two or three peasant women with baskets on their arms. And right down the cobbled street was a small group of farmers outside the Golden Hind. All were standing there, gazing across in blank wonder, not at the other passers-by, but at us. I could hear Tilde's protesting voice.

Leaning out I saw she was cleaning the door and walls. An hour later I heard a gentle hubbub in the yard. There was Frau Klebert directing the village locksmith who was fitting new locks to the gate and sheds. A crowd in the lane beyond was murmuring its approval. As usual on Saturday mornings Herr Engels had gone to Cologne and the children, who were now at a state school, had classes until one o'clock.

Frau Klebert had taken matters into her own hands, even at the risk of a further row with her father. When Rosenbaum returned he would find himself locked out.

I had settled down to my tasks again when Frau Klebert knocked and entered. She sat down and faced me, her eyes defiant, her lips pressed together in silent determination. It was no slight thing to flout her father and to take him down a peg before the eyes and ears of the whole village.

'You must say nothing to Father about this.'

'It might be difficult.'

156

'Not at all. You know nothing at all about it until the affair has blown over or the Jew has found a garage. And even then, Father need never know. He rarely uses the yard.'

'So we are to keep him in the dark?'

'Absolutely.'

'Even to the length of a white lie?'

She went hot and her eyes sank for a moment.

'No, no, no, not a lie. Heaven forbid! But say nothing at all on your own initiative.'

'But supposing Rosenbaum comes round?

So I was to be discreet.

The children returned in the early afternoon, and, as they entered the house, who should enter with them but Professor Rosenbaum? Had he come just by chance or had Rebecca Wolff been quietly lying in wait ready to give the word? I do not know. He came in with the children, asking if Herr Engels were at home.

'Wait a moment,' said Tilde and she hastened to call Frau Klebert. But Rosenbaum followed the children into the hall and was talking to Herr Engels, whom he had glimpsed through the open sanctum door, before Tilde and Frau Klebert returned.

'Someone has been tampering with the locks,' he was saying, 'and I can't get into the yard.'

'Someone's been and ruined the locks?'

'Yes, so it seems.'

'It's the riff-raff, Herr Professor, the Nazis once again, believe me, worthy sir, I might have known.'

An explosion could not be avoided, even though the children were present. Frau Klebert resolved to face it.

'Sir,' she said to Rosenbaum, 'would you kindly leave the house and leave the affair of the yard to me.'

'Pardon, madam,' replied Rosenbaum, in his most accommodating way, 'but I'm sorry that I seem to have intruded. My apologies, my apologies. I wished to have just one word with Engels, your father, an affair of no more than a minute, a matter that I had to report to him and which concerns you as well as him. '

'Sir,' she repeated in a still more imperative voice, 'would you kindly leave the house. Your call is most inconvenient as the children have just come home and I've no time for discussion with you.'

'But why,' exclaimed Herr Engels, 'should a visitor to me be asked to leave the house?'

'Because I've locked the back door against him and I'm going to lock the front one as well.'

She faced her father with a resolute look, but he, no less resolute and with his arm defiantly outstretched to the door, raised his voice and exclaimed, 'My front door is open to all whom I wish to see. That door is mine, the keys are mine and I'll not have my rights to either stolen from me behind my back.'

'Nor shall I, your daughter, have this home of yours stolen from you before your face. Have you forgotten Herr Gerster? Have you forgotten his fate? Keys, lock, door, the whole house and office besides, stolen, brazenly stolen and nothing left but his dead body and the corpse of his hapless wife. Have you no better sense?'

She went flashing on in her headlong way while the children gazed on aghast and Tilde, with her face in her hands, moaned in the far corner. Why didn't Rosenbaum go?

I hurried down the staircase and motioning the children to my room made a sign to the professor and quietly asked him to retire. He seemed at first to ignore me, but recovered himself when I raised my voice a little.

'Be a gentleman and go.'

'Yes, yes, a thousand pardons.' He seemed a little ashamed, but perhaps he was in a daze and unable to grasp the situation. With a low bow, he went out and tripped across the street while Matthias and his clients gazed at him in gaping wonder without so much as a comment. Father and daughter had retired to the sanctum where I could hear their voices raised in hot discussion. As I turned to the staircase someone took my hand. It was Tilde. She had been crying.

'Come up to my room with me,' I whispered, 'and let us talk to Else and Paul.'

The children rose to meet us as we entered. They looked pale and distressed, as though some great light had gone from their young lives. Never had they lived through such a scene, and that in a home endeared to them by the untroubled memories of childhood. I took both their hands in mine and spoke a consoling word while Tilde embraced them both in silence. They were dressed in Nazi garb and both looked taller, older and more subdued, as though the glint of childhood had finally gone and some of the dust and murk of a workaday world had dimmed the one-time sheen of their souls. The shock of coming to a home riven by bitter strife had shattered them. A shadow had fallen across them and darkened their young lives. Or had their Nazi contacts added a little tarnish?

'What's all the row about?' asked Else in her eager way.

'And who is that Jew boy?' Paul asked. His voice was as gentle and cultured as ever, but I winced.

'The Jewish gentleman, you mean,' I corrected.

'Yes.'

'The Jewish gentleman,' I repeated, and understanding my look of reproach his face reddened.

'Yes, the Jewish gentleman.'

'Now don't be annoyed, Mr Arnold,' smiled Else, and all her old girlish charm returned if only for one sunny second. 'We have been lumped with all these Nazi youths and, believe me, Jew boy is the politest term they use.

Poor Paul has got used to it; I have got used to it; and somehow used worse terms without one pang of conscience. You are right, Mr Arnold. It is good to speak to you again. But do tell us. What's all this ghastly row about?'

Her smile was mingled with such contrition and such a biting of her bottom lip that I forgave her at once.

'Pardon, Mr Arnold,' said Paul, equally repentant, 'I'm also, er – not so polite as I was.'

'Not by a long chalk.'

'You must excuse me. But my talk is worse than my thoughts. Our comrades are very rough-cut and I have got into their rowdy way. And the trouble is, the more rowdy you are the better you get on. If you are polite and talk in a cultured way you are a milksop. And I'm an absolute milksop to the others. I shall never get higher than the rank and file. But who is this Jewish gentleman? And what's the row about?'

I explained. I believed both parties to be in the right, the one in trying to save the home, the other in upholding the Christian faith. Neither could be reconciled and neither would give way. It was all the evil effect of the Nazi policy of racial hate, and this policy had rent the home in two and exposed it to the brawling storms of the street. For what they were hearing now was simply the resounding echo of the stamping Nazi jackboot and Hitler's bellowing voice. But they, as children, had a duty to do all they could to appease these quarrels and restore the peace of the home.

'And you can do that,' said Tilde, 'far better than Mr Arnold and ever so much better than me.'

'Yes,' said Else gravely.

We could still hear the quarrelling voices and both children strained their ears to catch what was being said. For a moment or two we were all very silent until Tilde spoke.

'We mustn't play the eavesdropper.'

Else seemed to wake from a dream. She had been deeply reflecting on what I had said and a light had dawned upon her. She began to speak in a low tone, half to herself, half to Paul.

'Uncle Joseph,' she meant the jeweller at Cologne with whom they both lived, 'is a thoroughgoing Nazi. And he oughtn't to be, you know. And we hear him day in, day out, raving against communists and the Jews and praising the Nazis sky-high. And believe me, it's all untrue. He's thinking only of his pocket and his business.'

'That's true,' said Paul, 'but he is very good to us and treats us like his own children. I shouldn't criticise him.'

'No,' replied Else, 'but the truth is the truth. You see, Mr Arnold, now that the Jewish jewellers are being cleared out there's a free field for our uncle. Cohen over the way has gone, Julius Marx down the street, Goldstein's in the High Street, and a good many others if I could only remember the names. Uncle Joseph's business has gone up by leaps and bounds. No wonder he has become a Nazi and a member of the party.'

'Else, Else,' protested Paul. 'You are going a bit too far.'

'Not a bit.'

'Of course you are. Uncle was against the Jews before the Nazis came to power.'

'Yes, but only as business rivals. He did not hate them as a race and preach their extermination. Paul, Paul, Paul,' and shaking her finger at him she dropped her voice to a whisper, 'Uncle Joseph is like the rest of them, the furniture dealers, the clothiers, the pawnbrokers and solicitors. Besides gloating over the misfortunes of others, he's revelling in sheer loot. Not that I love the Jews, of course; I'm a bit of a Nazi in that respect, but Uncle Joseph is less a Nazi than a lover of sheer plunder.'

'For shame, Else,' protested Paul, 'I don't think you are fair to Uncle; he is very good and generous to us and thinks the world of you. What would he say if he heard you talking like this?'

'My dear, dear Else,' he would say. 'What you say is gospel truth, but for heaven's sake keep it quiet. If you go on talking like that people might even believe you. But when we've thoroughly soaked the Jerusalem gang and stripped the whole job lot of them to their bare and dirty pelts, we shall behave ourselves to the Jews once more and become good Catholics again.'

She accompanied this with such mimicry and with such a joyous display of the imp within her that we all burst out laughing. What a delicious girl she was. And yet I could not help but ask her.

'But you say you are a bit of a Nazi?'

'Yes, in a sense, but how can we help it? It's the Jews this and the Jews that, all of them vile and pilfering skunks, either a plague of locusts devouring the land or a swarm of crawling, bloodsucking lice or else a ghastly horde of garlic-chewing, stench-exuding scallywags.'

We screamed with laughter for Else was in a malicious mood, holding her nose, scratching her armpits or pretending in Nazi fashion to spit upon the floor.

'But it's true,' she continued, 'and we've been hearing this stuff for months and months until I'm ashamed to look at a Jew. Heavens, it curdles my tummy to see one. And when Uncle Joseph says these things and confirms them by a serious "By God!" I somehow begin to believe them. After all, I say to myself, there must be something in it.'

She burst into a peal of laughter into which we heartily joined. Our outburst of laughter seemed to have caught the ears of those below for the voices died away and peace began to reign once more. Tilde put her finger to her lips.

'I'd better go down and see if I'm wanted.'

'Yes, do, dear Tilde,' said Else, 'and let us know if the coast is clear.'

Tilde stole out. Else sat down and, resting her elbows on the table and supporting her chin in both hands, stared across at me.

'You are disappointed,' she said gravely.

'Yes, he's disappointed,' added Paul.

'Oh!' I rejoined evasively and wondered.

'Yes, you are disappointed. You don't love us as you used to. Does he Paul?'

'No, he doesn't,' was Paul's quiet answer.

'Now that's too strong a statement. You are different and a little stranger. I dislike the Nazi garb, of course, and you've been in rougher company than at home.'

'And we show it and we are all the worse for it?' She had a frank way of asking things that made me feel I might have been mistaken. And then the roguish smile that lurked in her eyes and dimples revealed the childlike spirit of pre-Nazi days.

'I preferred you as you were.'

'Of course you did. And so did I. But we are not worse really. The girls I have to mix with either at school or on our rambles are a very rough lot. They are rude and they talk slang and say mock grace at meals and make fun of my religion. At least some of them do. And perhaps I've got used to it. As Fräulein Wagner, our German mistress, says, "Girls, beware! Your poetic sensibility is being woefully blunted." Now that's my fate, Mr Arnold, and Paul's.'

She said this last bit in such duenna tones and with such a vivid snap-shot glimpse of the worthy Fräulein Wagner that we reeled with laughter.

'I think we had better go down,' said Paul at last.

'Yes, the storm is over,' said Else. They sprang up and bumped into Tilde as they opened the door. Off they went, all three, and I waited until the hubbub died away before I left the room. Yes, the worthy Fräulein Wagner was right. The light of childhood is easily dimmed and when the inner glint has gone, the early bloom and lyric innocence, then something of the dust and shadow of our earthly fate, something that must be finally buried, settles on the soul. I went out and almost by instinct crossed the street and knocked at the door of the Miss Wolffs. I felt I must explain our conduct and, if need be, apologise to both Rosenbaum and the ladies. Luckily, as the weather was cold, Matthias and the rest were inside the shop and the street seemed deserted, for most of the villagers had gone to Cologne to do their weekend shopping, to go to the cinema or to con-fession in one of the churches near the Cathedral.

I was admitted almost at once and ushered by Rebecca into the sanctum where all stood up to receive me, Rachel, Rosenbaum and his wife, and then Johanna Levy, now Frau Boden. I always felt some misgiving when passing from our house of true Nordics, all radiantly fair and golden, to this house of dark foreigners who even in the simplest affairs of life were silently on their guard. Save for Rachel, who took my hand and welcomed me with her truly exquisite smile, the others met me with a certain reserve in which I felt suspicion. Had Rachel not spoken I should have been embarrassed for all remained silent, and the clock began to tick and tick,

161

each tick louder than the last, and the company looked and looked at me, waiting for a word.

'It's nice of you to come,' said Rachel. 'Do sit down and tell us your news.'

'And it's nice of you to welcome me. I thought after what has passed I might have lost a little of your regard. But I've come to put matters straight and to prove there is no ill will.'

My task, I thought, would be a difficult one, but I was at once assured by Rebecca, who told me I could spare all apology as they all understood the position. They had no grudge against Frau Klebert whose policy of holding the candle to the devil was not to be wholly condemned.

'We are all in the same boat,' added Professor Rosenbaum, 'though our position is decidedly worse since we are faced with an absolute stand-and-deliver, our money and our lives. We are now being hunted from pillar to post and have really nowhere to turn. Do you wonder that we cling to straws?'

He was alluding to his unfortunate stand in the hall when awaiting the issue of the combat between Herr Engels and his daughter. Owing to his misfortunes his mind was at sixes and sevens. But he had now found a place to park his car.

'I don't know for how long, since Dr Cohen has lost his post and intends to go abroad.'

'Yes, if he gets leave to do so,' added Frau Rosenbaum. 'He can't live here and he's not to live abroad, and if he goes abroad he must leave his property here. Be reduced to beggary in fact. Ah, Mr Arnold, we are pilloried for our wealth, though I've seen little of it, but, believe me, there are none so poor as the Jews.'

Of course she meant it in the social sense, but it was a most unhappy remark. I was aware of the setting around me, the Persian carpet, the tapestries, the gilt-framed Dutch paintings and the real observatory clock, as well as the ebony escritoire inlaid with mother of pearl, all of which according to Bürger was so much auctioned loot. The thought was a most unworthy one and was soon dispelled by one of Rachel's smiles as she suggested a cup of coffee.

'Or would you like tea?' suggested Frau Boden. 'You Englishmen are so fond of tea if we can make it to your liking.'

'No, coffee will do, thanks,' I replied.

I looked at Frau Boden, the lady who, according to Boden himself, was as ugly as the night. At first glance I was inclined to agree. Her cheeks were sunken and white, her teeth protruded and her eyes were rimmed with an edge of inflammation. But the way she suggested tea, the gentle voice and the almost pathetic appeal of her frail and unhappy figure, made me forget all that was displeasing in her face and form. She got up eagerly and forestalled Rebecca.

Obviously Frau Boden had the freedom of the house. I wondered at this since I had never seen her before on a visit to the Wolffs'. However, from a chance remark of Rachel's I knew they were acquainted, intimately acquainted in fact, for Rachel had referred to her not as Miss Levy but as Johanna. I was soon to be enlightened. It was Frau Rosenbaum who spoke, with a meaning glance at the door by which Frau Boden had left.

'Another victim of the Nazis, and in a worse plight than ourselves in fact.'

The whole company nodded a silent assent, though Rebecca frowned at the talkative Frau Rosenbaum as though dreading further disclosures. I had to break the oppressive stillness that followed.

'But I thought Frau Boden was a Catholic?'

'Catholic,' sneered Frau Rosenbaum. 'What's a Catholic? Since the Concordat they are aligned with the Nazis and have deliberately closed their eyes to all persecution, even hounding down many of their own flock. For it's race that counts with the Nazis, not religion, and Johanna is by race a Jewess. She can naturally expect no help from the church.'

'But as she is the wife of Dr Boden ... '

'Was, you mean,' said Frau Rosenbaum with a brief contemptuous laugh and ignoring the stony glare of Rebecca. Frau Rosenbaum was a decisive, independent type, dapper and good-looking, and was not to be frowned down by Rebecca or anyone else.

'Was?' I echoed. 'Divorced?'

'Not yet. But he abandoned her last July when a questionnaire was sent round enquiring into one's descent as well as the descent of one's wife. It was posted to all officials, in fact to all in government employ.'

'And to all in leading positions in public life,' added Rachel with a glance at her sister.

'So she's been left?'

'Left, abandoned, tossed aside, though married by all the rites of the church.' Here Frau Rosenbaum dropped her voice to a loud stage whisper. 'He married her for money and position, of course, but he thinks he now has a better chance with the Nazi regime. He's a young man in a rush, a most unhallowed rush, be it said. Why did Johanna marry him, she so spiritual, sensitive, clever, and he such a clod?'

'Why, indeed?' said Rosenbaum in a tone of utter gloom.

'And the house she ran for the crippled soldiers in Bonn has naturally been commandeered. It put the Nazis to shame to see the wrecks of the last war cast on the charity of a mere Jewess.'

'But she still has her home in Bonn,' I pointed out.

'Oh, no. Her father sold all that beforehand to avoid a confiscation,' continued Frau Rosenbaum, in her forthright way. 'Her father is no fool, of course, and he made no settlement on Boden, so she is living here,' she added with a triumphant glitter in her eye.

'Here,' answered Rebecca curtly. 'I shall go and see how she is getting on.'

I liked Frau Rosenbaum. She was open, honest, outspoken, with none of the sleeky air of her husband. She had courage, too, and seemed to be little daunted by the crash in their affairs.

'We shall get over it in America,' she said decisively. 'I don't speak English, but I shall learn. I have already started. I shall be calling on you for help.'

I felt very embarrassed, but before I could reply Frau Boden entered with the coffee. She was very hasty and nervous in her movements, timid, apologetic, but she had all the delicate responses of Rachel and such a speed in divining one's thoughts and wishes as made her an excellent companion. My German was rather imperfect, but she helped me in a pleasing way over many points and many a construction, guessing with a weird skill what I had in mind and smoothing over every awkward pause. I quite forgot Boden's remark and concluded that she was a very gracious and very wronged lady.

'You will soon come over again, I hope,' she said.

'I should be very glad.' I said this without the slightest reservation. I had thoroughly enjoyed my visit and this joy was due to her alone.

It was dusk when I left. As I had to go to Bonn to do some reading in the library I hurried off to the station. Going along that cobbled street was always a tricky problem, and in the deceptive lights and shadows of Saturday evening I stumbled more than once. Some of the shop windows sent their gleams across the street, but most of the houses were dark since the people were still in Cologne. I was about to turn the corner when I ran into a burly figure who went stumbling off the path.

'Pardon,' I said, offering a helping hand.

'What, you!'

I stared. Yes, it was Boden who had just come up from the station.

'Ah, Dr Boden, I didn't recognise you in that winter coat and muffler.'

'No?' he drawled, and he stared in his silent querying way.

'And this street is pretty dark and tricky.'

'You've said it,' he replied. 'But you've come just in time.'

'Oh?'

'You live here, so I've been told?' And he stared at me again as though wondering who I was and what to say next. How Johanna Levy could have married so obtuse a being was a great puzzle to me. But he had golden hair and a fresh complexion, and looked every inch a man. And then of course he was a doctor.

'Yes, I live here.'

'Then would you mind taking me in this God-forsaken hole to the Rheingasse, number 8. I think that's the place. Just come over to that light.'

He drew out a letter from his pocket to confirm the address.

'Yes, that's the address.'

164

I gazed astounded.'But that's Dr Cohen's address.'

'Yes, Dr Cohen's. That's the address I want.'

'But your wife's not living there,' I corrected.

'My wife,' he muttered gruffly. 'I've no wife. But, what makes you talk about my wife?' He said this as though he had never known the lady.

I felt very embarrassed and sought refuge in evasion.

'I thought, er, I saw the lady here today.'

He stared at me in such a scathing way that I knew I was guilty of an unpardonable lapse. I decided to grasp the nettle.

'Your pardon. I thought that you had married Miss Johanna Levy, the lady you were with in Cologne. I saw her here in Blankheim today.'

'I should be obliged if you'll drop all talk of my wife. I know nothing now of the woman in question. But enough. Where is this Rheingasse 8? Dr Cohen's house? You see, I'm taking over, and I've got to discuss some matters and go through many papers.'

'As the municipal doctor of health?'

'Yes.'

I had decided to bid him goodbye and leave him to stumble his own way along that muddy and rutted street, but in view of his news I changed my mind.

'I'll take you there.'

We went along in silence, but I cannot help confessing to a certain mischievous pleasure whenever he stepped into a deep pool or stumbled over a cobble. And his blasphemous allusions to the pavement served only to spice my joy. I have no malice in my soul but – Heaven forgive me for it – the first sips of its tart delight I savoured to the full.

We reached the Rheingasse. At the corner beneath the lamplight stood Paul and Else talking to David Cohen. The latter shrank back as we approached and took refuge in the shadows while Else and Paul gave me a joyous welcome.

'I shall be with you in a moment,' I said.

I turned into the narrow street that led straight down to the Rhine and soon stood before the doctor's house. It all lay in darkness, the portal, the fanlight, the windows, for no one went to the Jew now in view of the Nazi ban. Moreover, the shutters were up, perhaps to guard against a hooligan attack on the windows. And I felt in vain for the bell. It had been removed.

'Well, here is the house,' I said.

I was about to turn away when Boden detained me.

'An extremely pretty girl, that. Who is she?'

'To whom are you referring?'

'The girl to whom you just spoke and who was talking with that Jew chap.'

'Oh, Else. What about her?'

'She's an extremely pretty girl, I say. Who is she?'

'Nothing for you,' I retorted and turned off.

165

He called after me, but I strode on. I was seething with indignation. And he was to be the local doctor of health! A leading Nazi of the district! A turncoat like Lambert! And like Lambert, so unscrupulous as to stoop to any nasty act on his way to power. I compared him with Dr Cohen and shuddered to the bone.

What a pleasure to see Else and Paul again, to listen to their eager talk and to laugh as they skipped in instant peril over the ruts and pools and cobbles. I gave up all thought of going to Bonn and decided, when the children pleaded with me, to spend the evening with them at home.

Chapter 16

Looking for Scapegoats

One day, some weeks later, on my return from Bonn I met Frau Klebert leaving the house with a basket on her arm. I guessed her mission. There was a look of festive packing about the basket, just a glimpse, between the chinks of crimped and coloured paper, of fruit and sweetmeats and wine. At least it seemed so to me in the gathering dusk. It was a heavy basket and my arrival was welcome. I took it from her arm and, without asking where she was going and leaving my satchel in the corridor where Tilde was sure to find it, I accompanied Frau Klebert down the street and past the Golden Hind. The lights were streaming across the road, but there were no voices or signs of revelry yet and the windows of the skittle alley were in darkness. We went on into the further shadows of the street towards the path that led to the Rhine. I suddenly guessed we were going to Brechner, and enquired if I was right.

'Yes, we are going to Brechner's. He is very ill.'

'Very ill? What's the matter'?

'Double pneumonia, and there might be complications.'

I felt anxious. Years of short commons, shivering days on the banks of the Rhine, feelings of defeatism with no hope or prospect of better times, had finally taken their toll. He had borne up stolidly for years, with resentment and hate as his only supports, and now when the clouds had drifted away and life seemed once more assured he had relaxed and wholly collapsed. The forces that had firmly braced him up – race hatred, bitterness and thirst for revenge – had left him quite unable to face the ease of a prosperous and better career.

The cottage stood by itself on a path that led to the Rhine, like a forlorn outcast from the village with bits of this and bits of that about it, a patched-up tool shed, a water butt, piles of logs, sheaves of sticks for the peas and beans, a crumbling dog kennel which for years had never known a dog. Sloping down to the Rhine was the kitchen garden with some beehives on the sunny side. Frau Brechner opened the door.

She received us into the living room, which was warm and heavy with the odour of ironed linen. It lay about on the sofa, table and chairs; sheets, pillowslips, pyjamas and night shirts, obviously in the main for the invalid, who had to look his best when the doctor came. Frau Brechner was very house-proud, and the cares of the cottage, small though it was, weighed heavily upon her. She received Frau Klebert with an awe that almost masked her joy.

'God bless you, Frau Klebert,' she said in her modest and humble way. 'You have come as though in answer to prayer.'

'How is he?'

'Still in danger, I think, though the doctor was hopeful this morning. He is sleeping now and is not as delirious as he was. You see ...' and she looked at us in great anxiety, 'he is afraid of losing his post after three years on the dole.'

'But his job is with the party.'

'Yes, he was one of the original members. But new ones have come in, Herr Klassen, Herr Lambert, Herr Wessel and the rest, all more educated than Alex, and all very eager to get him out.'

'Herr Lambert, you say?'

'Yes, he has been applying for admission for a long time, and they've been using his services as secretary and treasurer, but now he is a full-blown member with a big say on the committee.'

'And he doesn't like your husband?'

'No; that's it.' She lapsed into an anxious silence while Frau Klebert clenched her fists and set her teeth. She was about to let fly against Lambert, but restrained herself in the nick of time.

'Such a turncoat,' was all she said.

'Yes,' whispered Frau Brechner, 'and Alex one of the original members of the party, almost as old a member as Hitler himself.'

'Well, never mind,' replied Frau Klebert. 'I have brought something for you and Alex.'

She stooped to the basket and unpacked the contents on the table, some port and brandy for the patient, some fruit, sweetmeats and ham. It was all of the very best, such a quality as never enters a poor home, and there it stood on the table decked out with the crimped and coloured packing on the snow-white tablecloth, the fruit and ham glowing in the lamplight, and the wine bottles glinting between. Frau Brechner clasped our hands for joy. It gave the little room with its sober furniture and low-beamed ceiling a most festive and colourful look.

'I suppose he is too ill to be seen?' said Frau Klebert, looking to the little staircase which led up to the rooms above.

'I think so,' said Frau Brechner, who stole up and opened the door above. We listened in the tense silence. She was asking if he was awake. A moment later she asked us very quietly to come up. We slipped up and saw him. His fevered face looked glaringly red on the white pillowslip and by the light of the oil lamp near his bed we saw him glance up. He had recognised us. He smiled, then closed his eyes again.

We did not return directly home. Frau Klebert suggested a further walk to the dark and deserted towpath along the Rhine. I wondered at this for she had much to do at home. I soon realised why. Barely had we reached a dark spot far from earshot of the whole village when she burst out into a fierce denunciation of Lambert. She felt she must relieve her heart before she went home. Her home was no place for unbridled revilings, above all with Christmas so near, but vent her feelings she must.

'An absolute reptile,' she exclaimed, 'with no bonds of party, family or belief. He lives in this village like a prowler in the night, like a rat, a foul and verminous thing that worms its way into private affairs, raking out skeletons long forgotten, mucking into the mould of past deeds and then using the ensuing stench to blackmail friend and foe alike. He knows all my father's affairs, has reckoned to every skinflint penny what he has and what he receives and what he is ever likely to receive right down to the day he dies. And all this, which he knows in strict confidence, he will betray and sell to the highest bidder. I am a Catholic, Mr Arnold, a Catholic, but with these hands here I could throttle him to death.'

She curled her fingers like the talons of an eagle and clutched the lapels of my coat. She certainly gave me a shock for I thought from her swift movement that she was about to strangle *me*.

'Heavens! Frau Klebert.'

She had to laugh and, somewhat mollified, she declared herself ready to return. But before we had gone very far she gave me another outburst. It was all so much against Lambert and Klassen that I looked anxiously up and down the path and over the gloomily swirling river to the lantern-lit barges by the further bank. But all was silent. The scattered lights of the village looked very far off in the night. Still, there might be a lurking shadow in the nearby trees.

'And then there's that fellow, Wessel ...'

'Sh,' I interrupted, 'no names.'

'That devil, Alfred Wessel,' she exclaimed, in an even louder voice. I had to silence her and drag her along to the main road. I felt there must be something else that had wrought her to such a pitch. Some fresh act of the Nazis. Some threat to the household peace. Her husband was expected on Christmas leave and might arrive any minute and here she was on the dark towpath almost raving against these Nazis. I felt I must mention the fact.

'Yes, I know he is coming this afternoon and he might be home even now, but I can't meet him just yet. I must welcome him, Mr Arnold, with a happy smile and a happy heart and these I haven't got. I'm blazing with anger and you are the only one on whom I can blaze it away.'

'But there is something else on your mind. Out with it. Something you have not mentioned yet. Tell me. I might be able to help.'

'You are right. It is this. Father has received a note to go to the Golden Hind. He's to meet the local committee. He used to go to the Kevelaar Club at this time of the year but, since the Nazis came, the club has rarely met and then only under the presidency of some member of the Nazi Party.'

'You amaze me.'

'Well, that's the fact. How gladly Father used to go and what happy hours he spent with the worthies of the village. It used to be a meeting, you know, of the upper class, the better sort, the gentry, and they used to do some splendid work, preserving monuments, planting trees, helping the poor and so on. But now it has been captured by the Nazis and turned into a Nazi committee, a Nazi caucus, a clique, into a rendezvous for such gangsters as Lambert.'

'But what is this about your father?' I asked.

'My father?' she echoed. 'Well, he's been summoned to meet this committee. He thinks it's to bluster him to join the party, but I'm certain it's simply for loot. There's an employment drive all over the land and he might be asked to engage people to do some work on his land, to build new drains or fences or stables, anything to provide work. It's nothing but blackmail and loot, Mr. Arnold ...'

'And you think they'll dragoon him into it?'

'They'll do their very best. Whatever the outcome may be, it will cost us a pretty penny. Go with him, Mr Arnold, and give him your support. I would go myself, but they refuse to receive women at their meetings.'

I agreed. We returned along the village street and past the Golden Hind, which was now fully aglow with the cheerful lights of the evening. Hamann and Hans Zimmermann were just entering as we passed. Hamann gave us an insolent stare, but Zimmermann affected not to see us. In his new Nazi garb he looked sprucer than he did in his pre-Hitler days and his face was not so pale and sullen. Was he going to join the committee? The rump of the Kevelaar Club? The upper class? The better sort? The gentry? Was he, Hans Zimmermann, the Communist and down-and-out, about to sit in judgement on Herr Engels, his former patron?

An hour or two later Herr Engels and I were also entering the Golden Hind. The inn had been renovated and looked wonderfully spick and span with its bright paint, brilliant lights and linoleum floors. Obviously, the Golden Hind had gained by the new order and was abreast of the head-long times. The age-long gloom had gone and there was a glitter about the new glass doors that revealed a younger and fresher spirit. The whole place was agog with new faces and new voices.

'Heil Hitler, Herr Engels!'

'Good evening,' replied Herr Engels with some surprise for he did not know the stranger and had not been in the inn for months.

'I'm Stenzel, Johann Stenzel, the new proprietor. I've not had the pleasure of seeing you before in my house, so welcome. I hope to see you again here. Ah, you'll be wanting to see the committee.'

After taking our hats and coats he opened the door of the room where the Kevelaar Club used to meet. For a moment we were dazzled by the change and gazed in dismay at the scene before us. The dark old stove with the dusty chimney pipe that went along the ceiling had gone. A new electric fire glowed beneath an elegant mantelpiece which was surmounted by a gilt-edged mirror. The dingy paper had vanished from the walls, which were now frescoed with idealised Rhenish scenes. And the curtains at the windows that looked out over the Rhine added light and colour to the room. However, the table was still there, and the committee was seated along it. Familiar faces, most of them. But the brown shirts its members wore banished all thought of the Kevelaar Club. And the dead silence as we entered showed that the Kevelaar spirit had gone for good. An awkward pause followed.

'Good evening, gentlemen,' said Herr Engels, coolly taking his seat at the head of the table. 'You wanted to see me.'

I sat down on a chair against the wall and surveyed the committee. There they were, Klassen, Lambert, Wessel, Hempel, Müller and Kemp, all of the former Kevelaar Club, with Hamann, Zimmermann and two or three others, clearly the non-gentry and wholly out of sympathy with their more genteel colleagues. They sat at the further end of the table and gloomily surveyed the proceedings.

'Yes, we wanted to see you,' replied Herr Klassen. He was nervously searching for words and was obviously ill at ease. It was not easy to dictate to Herr Engels, who had been the president of the Kevelaar Club and who, wherever he sat, had the air of a president still. Klassen, as he spoke, kept gazing before him at the table, without one glance at his old friend.

'Yes, we wanted to see you. But it is not only you we want to see. You are only one of many. We are seeing all the leading men of the district, such men as you, Herr Engels. You are, if I may say so, the foremost man in Blankheim.'

'And your business?' asked Herr Engels in his quiet composed way.

'Well, we are the committee of the Nazi Party of Blankheim, and a suggestion has come from headquarters about a new, great, national effort to right the wrongs of the Weimar government, to make restitution to the victims of the old regime and to bring new hope and prosperity to the downtrodden people of Germany.'

'I see, your party programme,' said Herr Engels, slowly pulling out his pipe and carefully filling it from his pouch. 'And I'm to support that, I suppose. Well, all party programmes are very splendid, but the bigger the word, the less the deed, and doubtless in a few years time we shall be hearing the same old blurb from other and younger lips, of wrongs to be righted, victims to be compensated, hope and prosperity to be restored. The hopes of the cradle, Herr Klassen, are usually the despairs of the grave.'

'We want no sneers against the party,' shouted Hamann as he thumped the table with his fist. 'We are not here to listen to any croaking from the old Centre and Catholic Party gang.'

'Silence, Hamann,' rapped out Klassen, 'I'm chairman here and I want no interruption until I've done.'

What a martinet Klassen was, a precise pedagogue to his nervous finger-tips and with the manners of a schoolmaster even to adults. His closely cropped moustache and short pointed beard gave his sharp features an almost cutting expression.

'I'm an old member of the party,' cried Hamann in reply, 'and I'm not going to be silenced by a new arrival with a long Centre Party record.'

He might have said much more but for the joint and decisive action of Hempel and Müller, the two hefty farmers from over the river. Müller rose and leaned threateningly over the table. 'Hold your tongue when you are told.'

'There'll be a chance later for you and for us when the chairman gives the sign,' said Hempel in the same menacing way.

'We are not here to discuss politics, Herr Engels,' resumed Klassen. 'That's not why we have asked you to come.'

'I'm just here to listen and receive orders?'

'Not so much orders as suggestions.'

'Which will be orders if you don't comply,' shouted Hamann.

'Silence!' The air was tense and electric.

'And these suggestions are?' asked Herr Engels when the flare-up between the two factions had finally died away.

'The suggestions have come from headquarters, though they are not official yet. We, the committee of Blankheim, however, have decided to explore the ground. The suggestion is of a capital levy, not of course an enforced levy, but a quota from each district which may be raised by collections or free gifts, offers of work, remissions of rent, surrenders of land and houses, everyone giving according to his means and in accordance to the needs of the district.'

'I see,' said Herr Engels. 'You mean some substantial gift I shall be forced to give of my own accord?'

'I say it's a suggestion.' Herr Klassen was a little nettled by the calm commanding way of the old man. 'I say once more it's a suggestion and it's up to you to take it in the best spirit.'

'Well, that depends on whether it's being given in the best spirit. You might be a bit more precise.'

'You might offer a piece of land. You've plenty in the district and the sacrifice of some would not be felt by you in the least.'

'The choice being left to me, of course, when the quotas have been properly defined?'

'We've been thinking of that seventeen-acre plot to the west of the old cemetery.'

'And who's made that suggestion?'

'Excuse me, Herr Engels,' said Lambert in his muffled and nasal voice as he turned towards us, 'the suggestion was mine, of course. I thought,

172

knowing your affairs as I do, that such a gift would be the one that you yourself would suggest. A gift of money might embarrass your domestic routine, but a gift of that piece of land for which the rent is not due until many months have passed will hardly affect you at all.'

'So the knowledge, given you in confidence, is now being made public? A bright solicitor you are, Lambert. Well, I've only one answer. I'm quite willing to give the land when the quotas have been properly defined. That means that every man of property in Blankheim must submit to a public assessment, you, Lambert, you, Wessel, you, Hempel and Müller and the rest, and in the same proportion that I am fleeced, in that proportion may you all be stripped. I am ready, on that condition.'

'Bravo!' A shout of joyous surprise came from the lower end of the table. They slapped the tables and trampled their approval. Even Hans Zimmermann, who usually played a silent role and rarely concealed his embarrassment in the presence of the more educated, broke out into a laugh with the rest. The confusion at the Klassen end of the table was obvious and complete.

'Yes,' continued Herr Engels, 'I am willing to surrender that land for the benefit of the people of Blankheim. But there is also a second condition which will also meet the approval of some members of the committee. And I shall see that the condition is enforced.'

The whole room went still. Lambert, whose face had gone ashen-grey with rage, gaped at Herr Engels's pipe which was pointed at the committee. Hempel and Müller looked very crestfallen while Wessel sat all of a heap. But Hamann and his set gazed on in raptured interest.

'We are having no shady transactions, no mutual winks over the loot, nor are the rich men of this committee, the Lamberts, the Wessels and the rest, to get their forefeet in the trough.'

An outburst of applause from the lower end of the table held up the proceedings for a full minute. The upper end rose in a body and called out sternly for silence. The gaunt owl-like figure of Lambert rose up as the others sank to their seats. He raised his accusing finger at Herr Engels.

'What do you mean by this insinuation? What do you mean? Do you brand me a common thief?'

'He wouldn't be far wrong,' shouted Hamann.

'Sit down,' replied Herr Engels, who had preserved his calm with wonderful restraint. 'You will answer me this one question. What is the land for? To be sold at auction to the highest bidder and the proceeds to be passed on to the poor? Or is it for building? A nice building plot for ... I say, Wessel, have you a building plan for that field? Come on!'

'I should act under the orders of the committee,' said Wessel evasively.

'Building at an exorbitant profit, I suppose, with Kemp supplying the installations at a profit no less great,' came a shout from the end of the table, followed by further applause.

173

'We had better close this meeting,' said Klassen, packing his papers and rising to go. 'Some members of the committee simply don't know how to behave.'

'No,' replied Herr Engels, rising in turn and raising his voice. 'Certainly not when it comes to a capital levy and the use of confidential knowledge. I have a certain knowledge myself, equally confidential and equally public when it comes to the push. Yes, Lambert, yes. In your transactions with the Jews of the district and as a partner in their unscrupulous deals you have made a pretty pile. I'll see that you pay your share when the public assessors come round.'

The applause was so deafening from the Hamann, Zimmermann faction and the prospects of a free fight so imminent between the rival groups that I flung the door open and called for Herr Stenzel. He came rushing in followed by some of his clients and, with this break-in from outside, the committee recovered control and agreed to adjourn in peace.

'Now, come on,' said Herr Stenzel, 'stay for a drink of reconciliation. You are old friends and have no need to part in anger. It ill becomes the gentry to fall out in public.'

The former members of the old Kevelaar Club agreed to stay for a bottle of wine, but Herr Engels and I made our way through the throng of interested customers out into the open air. I could see that we were followed by the Hamann and Zimmermann faction. They looked as elated as schoolboys after a football triumph.

'Good for you, Herr Engels,' shouted one of them.

It was Kollass, the insurance agent, who was returning home with the others up the street. He was beaming with admiration.

'Bravo!' he repeated. 'You gave them a jolly good shaking up and it is just what that gang needed.'

'By God it was,' added Hamann. 'I've no time for you and your lot, Herr Engels, and you'll have to pay up when the time comes. But a thousand thanks for those slaps at Lambert and Wessel. It's all graft with them, you know.'

They went on ahead while we stumbled on behind. It ill became Hamann to speak of graft, he who was battening on the business of the hapless Gerster. Herr Engels visibly shrank from any converse with the man. He suggested a slight stroll along the Rhine, first to lose sight of them and secondly to recover his peace of mind.

So we turned back and passed the Golden Hind on our way to the riverbank. In a few minutes we were standing on the very spot where I had stood with his daughter some two or three hours earlier. The night was darker and the distant barges lost in the gloom. The wind was faintly rustling through the faded weeds on the riverbank and I could feel its cool touch on my cheek, all the more cool and refreshing after our session in the warm inn. Just the rustle of the fitful wind and the lap of the waters as they flowed past, otherwise all was silent. For a minute or so we did not speak.

174

'It's very quiet here,' said Herr Engels at last, 'the ideal place to lose the heat and burden of the day.'

'Yes, I was here three hours ago on this very spot with your daughter.'

'With Klara?'

'With Klara. And for the same reason as now.'

'And that is?'

'To relieve her burdened soul of Blankheim and all its works. You should have heard her. She blazed for a quarter of an hour against Lambert and his treacherous kind.'

Herr Engels laughed softly.

'Just like her,' he said at last, 'but what do you think of this racket? I mean what we heard at the inn?'

'I was delighted with the way you went about it. You not only thoroughly trounced them, but you revealed the rift in the party. You played off one against the other in truly heroic style.'

'Yes, they played into my hands, but I'm none too happy about it. The Hamann, Zimmermann lot are the ones we really have to fear. Ignorant, brutal, ruthless, shortsighted, they will stop at nothing and no one. And if *they* get control they will ride roughshod over friend and foe alike. They have none of the restraints which culture and religion bring.'

'But the Klassen gang is worse, I think. They'd do any wicked act to save their skins.'

'Yes, they would. But they really got on the committee to prevent the worst excesses. They went as sheep in wolves' clothing and mingled with the pack. Their renegade step had some excuse and I do believe they have saved us from many unspeakable crimes, from a repetition, for instance, of the Gerster and Dorlich affairs. But they have a devil's hoof for all that. I suppose you've seen it?'

'I have, but I couldn't define it precisely.'

'Let us walk a little further while I explain.'

We went on further into the night and stood at length in the shadow of some overhanging trees. We were beyond the view of the village lights and Herr Engels felt more at ease in venting his suspicions.

'It's quite true about the capital levy, but it is not the aim of the government to levy it in proportion. The whole nation would resent the tax. So they are picking on the wealthy few, gaining the applause of the mob. But then there is something else. Everyone is interested in dodging the tax himself and in seeing that someone else pays. And the more one man pays, the less remains to be paid by the rest. So if I could be fleeced outright Lambert and Wessel would go scot-free. Now do you see?'

It suddenly dawned on me. It was the principle of the public list which Brechner and Klassen carried round. It was a scheme that would rend the village asunder, with everyone determined to tip his neighbour into the ditch. If Herr Engels were fleeced to the skin a great sigh of relief would go all round, for in his downfall was their salvation.

175

'But do you think it's all deliberate?'

'Yes and no. For it is really the devil's suggestion. They have stumbled onto the path and he has shown them where it leads. So if I stood out for my rights I should be no martyr in a good cause. I should be fighting only my own case and letting the others down. If I win they must pay their share. I should become the pariah of the village.'

So that was the Nazi policy. Not blatant brutality as popular writers would have us believe, but universal blackmail and mutual betrayal. And though in a silent invisible way every man's hand was against his neighbour yet, to all appearances, everywhere in the land was discipline, unanimity and order. In fact so silent and so absolute was the slump into Nazi slavery that foreigners glibly ascribed it to the herd instinct of the Germans, to the blunting effects of militarism or to the blindness and hysteria of certain popular beliefs. Sheer myth for the most part.

The German is as valiant as any other man, as independent, as freedom-loving and as proof against all cant and false persuasion. But against doubt, suspicion, blackmail and betrayal he was absolutely helpless, especially in the general *sauve qui peut* for jobs, position and power. In the general stampede for safety they flung away their former faiths as fugitives their coats. It was the only hope of survival. But with the loss of all their loyalties the Germans became a drifting mob and the morality of a mob is that of the worst man in it. When one clutches at a last straw, rival clutchers must go down.

With such thoughts as these we turned for home, and had just reached the Golden Hind when we were hailed by Captain Klebert. He had come to give his support, but, finding that we had gone, he had not cared to broach the committee, the right wing of which was still sipping wine in the inn. The street was now busier with the returning shoppers from Cologne, and when the Captain loudly asked what had happened at the meeting Herr Engels bade him be silent.

'Our young friend will tell you. Discuss it with him over there.' And he pointed back in the darkness to the way we had come.

'Discuss it there?' asked the Captain, frankly puzzled. He was an open-minded man, rather vacant, I thought, with a breezy sailor's way and with a dislike of murk and darkness. Moreover, he was wholly oblivious of the underhand work of the new regime.

'Yes, down there, away from the crowd. You won't be long.'

The Captain gazed at me amazed as Herr Engels moved away. Speaking as loudly as before, he asked me what was the matter. But this time he spoke in English. There was a touch of vanity in his nature and he liked to show off his fluency in both English and French. And when I replied in English and hinted that he should be careful he agreed, though not without protest, to go along to the bank of the Rhine. On arriving in the shadow of the trees I deepened his mystification by saying he was the third I had met that night in secret conclave there.

176

'But what in heaven's name for?'

He was a man who knew and felt only the blunt and the obvious in life. I tried in vain to explain to his impregnable understanding some of the underhand doings of the village. To him it was all female gossip and he betrayed a certain annoyance that I should encourage his wife and her father to indulge in seditious talk in such a secluded spot. In vain I tried to assure him that it was their suggestion and not mine. He was one of those blinkered men who stubbornly hear their own voice and who assume that all replies are a testy interruption of the right line of thought. I had to give up the struggle. Clearly, he thought my anti-Nazi views were the cause of the whole trouble.

I mentioned the seventeen-acre field which the committee had mentioned as the temporary price of peace.

'But that field is mine, at least in prospect. It's a part of the marriage settlement and earmarked for me. What does Herr Engels mean by offering what is no longer his as a sop to the committee? Where do I come in? It's a scandal.'

'Excuse me. Herr Engels offered nothing. The field is what they choose to take. It's Lambert's suggestion.'

'In consultation with my father-in-law. A solicitor does nothing without orders, as you yourself will readily admit. But I have the deed in writing. I shall not be fleeced behind my back of what is mine.'

I tried to convince him that he was jumping to uncalled-for conclusions; that Herr Engels had been faced with an ultimatum; and that he had met the shameless demand of the committee in a bold and upright way. In vain. The Captain had drawn a conclusion and that conclusion must be right. Despite the fact that it was Christmas time and that he hated disputes at home he intended to have it out with Herr Engels and with his wife.

Seeing that I could explain nothing, I suggested going back home. As we emerged from the shadow of the trees we ran into someone strolling along the bank. At first I thought it was a bargeman, for he quickly descended the bank on to the shingle below and in a moment was lost to view. But the figure was familiar, or at least I thought it was. My preoccupation with this reminiscence made my talk with the Captain somewhat vague and disjointed, so I was glad to bid him goodnight on the outskirts of the village.

'I am going to call on Brechner,' I added by way of excuse.

Off he strode up the village. I had always known the Captain as a genial man, open, breezy and with a store of pleasant anecdotes about his life at sea. But in politics, religion and in any cultural subject, he was wholly beyond his depth. Mentally speaking, he could never see his way from one sentence to the next or from a premiss to an obvious conclusion. How he won Klara Engels was a mystery to me.

After lingering near Brechner's house, I returned to the main road home. Ahead of me was someone else, also returning to the village. As we approached the lights of the Golden Hind I saw who it was. It was Heinrich. And at once I recognised the man on the Rhine bank. But why had he avoided us? He who was usually so effusive in his greetings? I slackened off the pace until he entered the inn and then I hastened on. As I entered the house the blind of the window opposite was pulled back for just an instant. I paused at the door with a sense of being watched from all sides.

Chapter 17

The Growing Family Rift

The illusion of being watched lasted only for an instant. I halted as I closed the door. My home in Blankheim had always been a tranquil retreat, almost breathless in its aloofness from the outside world and inviolate in its reminiscent charm. But now the whole house was shattered by the storm of disputing voices, hard and loud on the Captain's part, tense, headlong and tearaway on that of his indignant wife. Frau Klebert, when her mind was set, could be as impervious to any argument as the Captain himself and I could hear her pell-mell reproaches as they careered, rough-shod and reckless over his wild expostulations, leaving him no instant to assemble his disordered thoughts. The pent-up feelings of months and years seemed to blaze up in a furious ultimatum.

Else assured me later that her parents had never quarrelled before and that in all the years they had spent together in Kiel and Wilhelmshaven she had never heard a hasty word from either. All the more shocking, therefore, was this sudden and furious outburst. Paul and Else fled to their room, Tilde in distress to the church, while I went off for another walk along the Rhine.

I kept wondering what had happened. Such fury, I felt, was of more than one day's brewing. Had Frau Klebert suddenly realised how empty her husband was, void of all deeper and second thoughts, wanting in all the elements that go to the building of a soul. He was a breezy man, doubtless a good one, and in the trifling play of life he could keep the company in broad smiles. But that was all. And she had loyally followed him, joining the Nazi Party, enrolling her children in the Hitler Youth, braving her father's opinion and also flouting her own. And all at once she compre-hends what a lickspittle part she is playing, grovelling not to a thinking man but to a being no better than a tailor's dummy, defacing herself to wear his blinkers. No wonder she blazed up in fury. No wonder she snatched her heaviest hammer and battered her god of crumbling clay.

I dined out and came back very late. The whole house was quiet and in darkness. After leaving my hat and coat in the hall I crept up to my study where the stove had been replenished for the night. I had hardly sat down in my chair, however, when a knock came and the door opened. It was Frau Klebert. She looked so tense and resolute, so quivering with inner fire that words of formal greeting failed me. She sat down opposite me just as

Else had sat some weeks before, and, planting her elbows on the table and supporting her chin on her clasped hands, she gazed at me in silence. At last she spoke.

'Mr Arnold, I want to know exactly what happened at the inn.'

'Your father hasn't told you?'

'No, he was too upset to tell me.' I told her in full detail. I described the rift in the committee, her father's masterly self-control, the hostile outbursts of the Hamann group, Klassen's suggestion about the field, her father's brilliant counter-attack, the applause of the Hamann faction with the final triumphant threat. I had no need to colour the picture. Frau Klebert's rapt attention assured me that the whole scene was vivid in her mind.

'Yes, a most successful skirmish. He not only captured the Hamann faction, but trounced and routed the rest. It was they who quitted the stricken field in most indecent haste.'

Her eyes glinted in triumph, but in a trice she was serious again.

'And that's the story you told my husband?'

'No.'

'No? How's that?'

'He would not listen. He was so beset with his own preconceptions that he had no ear whatsoever for any voice but his own. He put me down as the villain of the piece for secretly egging you on to oppose the new regime. Then he accused your father of suggesting the surrender of the land that was not really his to give.'

'That's what I wanted to ask. Who first made that suggestion?'

'Lambert, of course, as I have just mentioned. Naturally not your father.'

'Quite, quite. That's all I wanted to know, or rather, that's all I wanted to be absolutely sure of. And now there is something else. I hope you won't take it amiss, but I know I can rely on your understanding.'

'Completely.'

'It is this.' Her voice dropped and her face took on a hard expression. 'You'll have to go elsewhere for the Christmas break as you did last year. But this time it must be for two or three weeks. You see, there are stresses and strains in the family that will have to be smoothed out in private. Tilde will also be away for the same period. You see, our affairs must be our own ...'

'Not the talk of the village. I understand. I can pack up my trappings in the morning and be away in the afternoon.'

After some more talk, she went. For an hour or more I lay back in my chair and pondered the doings of the day. Perhaps I was right about her husband, perhaps I was wrong. But her case was common enough. For years people live in harmony, merely skimming the surface of life, flitting from one small topic to the next and sparing themselves the trial and tribulation of second thoughts. They are happy; their minds are serene; but it is the happiness of mere existence, the serenity of the laugh that speaks the vacant mind. And then some day a crisis comes, a Nazi revolution. Like a flash the flood is upon them. It took such a sudden flood to reveal the mental emptiness, the absolute spiritual void of Karl Klebert to his wife.

And Frau Klebert? Used as she was to the grave character of her father, she had turned at first with delight to her husband's entertaining ways. And now that the flood was upon them, there he was and there she was with a widening gulf between.

I spent the following day packing up and writing letters. There was an ominous stillness in the house, for the Captain had gone out with the children, Herr Engels had gone to Cologne and Frau Klebert had left the house without saying a word about when she would return. It all seemed to me like a lull before the storm. I thought I was alone in the house when there was a knock at my door. I started up with some premonition of danger. But it was only Tilde with coffee and biscuits, and I sent her for another cup so that she might share it with me. She had something to tell, I could see. In she came again bringing the jug of coffee, which she placed upon the stove.

'You've something to tell me, Tilde.'

'Yes, one or two things. But first for the news in Blankheim. Last night when Lambert was returning from the meeting he was waylaid by two or three men and knocked unconscious, and while he was in hospital his house was broken into and an attempt was made to open the safe. The housekeeper raised the alarm and the thieves made off.'

We discussed the matter for a time, wondering whether Lambert's injuries were fatal and what might be the effect on the village. We assumed the attack was a political one; we always did in those days, and we wondered whether the outrage was the work of the Hamann group. Such political suspicions made us feel unsafe and lent colour to the alarm that brooded over the whole village. Then we heard some voices in the little lane beyond the yard. We put the light out, crept to the window, drew the curtain and looked out. There was nobody in the yard or in the lane beyond. All was peaceful and quiet.

When we had settled down again, Tilde said 'There is something else I have to tell you. Frau Klebert wants me to go home for two or three weeks, until her husband's leave is over.'

'So I've heard.'

'And you are to go too.'

'Yes.'

'Then how about coming with me and spending your Christmas break on the Ahr? It is really Frau Klebert's suggestion. You could come as our guest, but as my people let rooms in the summer we have two rooms for holiday visitors. You could have one of them if you like. I prefer you should come as a guest, but you might feel you would like to pay your way. In any case you are welcome. And I could show you the pretty scenery of the Ahr.'

I at once agreed, because Tilde was a truly gracious girl and her people, though simple peasants, very highly respected. I insisted on payment, as was only fair to her people. So we arranged to leave together by the Tuesday morning train. But suddenly a doubt seized me. How about the parcels entrusted to my care? When in England I had left them with Hillesheim. But he would now be away in Schleswig. I mentioned my misgivings to Tilde.

'Leave them with me,' she said. 'They will be safe at my father's house or at my aunt's in Neuenahr.'

It was a little after midnight and I was still sitting in my study, brooding over some old tome I had ordered from Berlin. I was in a weirdly unsettled state, unable to go to bed, and confusing my historical reading with thoughts of Hamann and Lambert and with half-forgotten stories of night crime.

Suddenly a panic seized me. I had a premonition that someone was coming, a visit in the night, the police were going to inspect my rooms. Were they already at the door? I put my light out again, anxiously opened the window and timidly peered out into the dark yard. Nobody. Not a sound. Not a light. I had imagined it.

The breath of winter deepened the gloom and soft snow was falling, covering the whole scene with a cold ghostly grey. But the police *were* coming. I felt certain, so I had better do something about the parcels. But the moment I picked them up I realised how difficult it would be to hang them on the shutter staples. And then I did hear, quite clearly, the throb of an engine, not in the lane beyond but on the far side of the house in the main street.

In a panic I cast the parcels out, right against the far wall where some boxes and flower pots were almost wholly obscured by a thin film of snow. As they thudded down into the night the bell went.

It *was* the police. I thanked my premonitions. I waited. The seconds passed like minutes. But at last they came up.

'Heil Hitler!'

'Good evening.'

'We are sorry to disturb you, but we require you for examination. Have you any other rooms?'

I showed them into my bedroom whereupon, after searching my pockets, they led me down through the hall, past the whole family, dressed in their night attire and looking at me aghast as I passed. To my surprise, Captain Klebert was already sitting in the car, but he cast me such an indifferent look that I got in in silence. Three officers remained in the house. The driver and another took us to the station where the Captain, who seemed to be in their good books, was motioned to a private room while I was locked in a cell.

'Just a short interrogation,' I heard them say to the Captain.

It must have been some hours later when the cell door was finally opened and I was led to the private room, where the Captain had been examined. Fischer was there, rigid, close cropped and silent as ever with the exactness of a Prussian in every feature. Two other officials took down all particulars.

At first, I was a little bewildered, but a sudden light flashed upon me. Heinrich had played the informer. He had seen me in secret parley with three other people on the Rhine bank, meeting them one at a time in the darkness, and speaking above all about Lambert whose name we had uttered with every expression of contempt. Such strange behaviour marked me as an accomplice. I was an anti-Nazi and a spy. And then those parcels! Had they found them in the yard?

'Excuse me, gentlemen,' I interrupted, 'but perhaps I could clarify matters if I made a full statement. You are under a misunderstanding. You have doubtless been misled by the wild evidence of a man called Heinrich who observed us on the Rhine bank and overheard our talk.'

The officials listened impassively, but allowed me to make my statement. I made clear that none of the three with whom I had spoken had gone at my instance to the Rhine bank, that the topic discussed was wholly theirs, and that in no way had I tried to influence their views. I was a student, of moderate opinions with no more than a stranger's interest in the politics of the Reich.

The officials continued to survey me in a most objective silence, but finally one said, 'You cannot deny that you strongly dislike our National Socialist government.'

'Say "dislike" without the "strongly". I am an Englishman and, like the majority of Englishmen, I do not favour the present regime. But I am opposed only in the English sense and not in the German one, in the English sense of being a critic and not in the German sense of being a traitor and a spy.'

'Perhaps not. But we have evidence of strong dislike. First-hand evidence, in fact.'

The thought of the parcels sprang to my mind, but I reflected these officials knew nothing of my doings. And then I thought of the Captain.

'Or has Captain Klebert said anything against me?'

There was no reply, but after a full hour of further talk the examination ended. I was about to go when one of the officials called me back.

'We have searched your rooms and commandeered all your bags and papers. You will receive them back in due course.'

My heart went to my mouth. Had they found the parcels in the yard?

It was early morning when I left and it was still snowing heavily. The streets were as silent as a grave, and the shuttered windows seemed all to be shut against me. I shook the snow from me and entered the house. It was all asleep, and without flicking on the lights I took off my shoes at the door and went upstairs in my stockinged feet.

The room was pleasantly warm and I could see that Tilde had replenished the fire. My bags were missing. But I had no eyes for anything but the windows. I hurried across and, opening one, looked out. I could see nothing in the dusk and the heavily falling snow. I must wait. And with a strange misgiving I sat down near the stove and pondered over the events of the night.

But not for long. There was a knock. It was Tilde who peeped in and showed her joy at seeing me free once more. She always had a pleasant face, but I thought that despite all her anxiety and pallor she had never looked so pleasant or so kindly and pretty as then. She stole in with a finger to her lips.

'My parcels,' I gasped. 'I threw them out of the window.'

'They are safe. I have them.'

'What a god-sent girl you are, Tilde. But how did you know?'

'Oh, knowing you and all your ways, I guessed. And not a moment too soon, either. I had hidden them away when one of the policemen opened the window and looked out into the yard.'

'But didn't you open the door to them?'

'No, it was the Captain.'

She went suddenly grave. She looked round suspiciously and put her finger to her lips. There had been another row after the police had gone away. When the Captain returned from the station he actually helped the police to go through my English notes. He made no bones about saying that he had denounced my anti-Nazi views. So that was the first-hand source. Hence the furious row with his wife when the police had taken their leave.

'He who knows nothing about me. What a vile thing to do.'

'In a sense, yes,' whispered Tilde, 'and yet in another, no. He is a hail-fellow-well-met kind of man and likes to be in the centre of things. So he greeted the police in his cheery bluff way and tried to look important. He at once began to tell them what they were only too eager to hear. That's it. I don't really think he's mean. Only breezy and brainless.'

If only Frau Klebert could have heard that last remark. She nearly did, for she came in a moment later having heard me coming in. She apologised for everything, since the whole affair was none of my doing. What is more, she was amazed that the police apparently suspected her and her family of a dastardly attack on Lambert. To think that she and her father would go and bribe gangsters to do such a deed was to her the most flagrant of insults. And all for a strip of land, a bagatelle, which they would have to lose in any case.

'Still, the police must leave no stone unturned and our meetings on the Rhine bank with such stormy abuse of Lambert were not to be ignored. You must admit it,' I said.

184

'Yes, I do. But think of the scandal in the village. Think of the suspicion, which many now will entertain, that we were secretly pulling the strings. Now that mud is being thrown much of it will stick,' Frau Klebert replied.

'Well, we shall have to live it down,' she went on. 'We are honourable people, above such a suspicion, at least with the worthy people of the village. What the unworthy will think is beyond our control.'

We were talking like this in subdued voices so as not to disturb the house, when the door opened and the Captain peeped in. Now I do not think he was aware of the baleful part he was playing. He was doing nothing from resentment, nothing from antipathy to me. As Tilde said, he was a social man who liked to be the centre of things, to be the soul of the party, the one on whom the conversation turned. He was certainly not angry when he entered and his expression and tone were cheery enough.

'Well, you're a nice one to bring us into a mess like this. You can't ply your tongue here as freely as in England. Mum's the word here, you know.'

'Karl!' His wife bridled up.

'Ah, the same old tale. He wheedles round the women and gets them to share his point of view, and after that the old man is in the bag. No wonder the police are raiding the house.'

His wife flashed up like lightning, so that Tilde, who expected an outburst, swiftly and silently left the room. I understood Frau Klebert at once. That she should be lumped among women who could be wheedled round by anyone, and that her father, the staidest man in the village, should like a ninny come tumbling after, was more than she could stand.

'What! You dare to use the word "wheedling" to me! I'm a woman to be wheedled! Do you think I am one of your Reeperbahn tarts to be ...'

But, suddenly realising that I was there, she halted for a tense moment, then turned to me in complete calm, shook hands and said goodnight. Off she went without a further word, while her husband, stunned, closed the door and followed her.

There was a long silence in the house after their footsteps had died away, but soon I heard a furious outburst of voices in which her impetuous tones seemed to override all opposition. I've heard Hitler in his stormiest moments giving the shrieking cue to hordes of yelping devotees, but his stentorian shout would have withered before Frau Klebert's onslaught. She attacked, with such power and resolution, that any answer simply crumbled away. Did she feel she had said too much when she spoke of 'your Reeperbahn tarts'?

Such outbursts were shattering to all home life and were casting a murky shadow over the festive days to come. Personally, and I frankly admit it, I always liked Frau Klebert best when she flared up in a family tempest. All the honesty, directness and spiritual power I so admired in her father, showed up to the best advantage. I know I was alone in my admiration. Herr Engels was deeply distressed, Tilde prostrate, and young Else's face

185

went ashen grey. As for poor Paul, he would slink away in hiding, whether for grief or shame or sheer fear. In his mother's indignation there was nothing to be ashamed of, though I suspect, as I have mentioned before, that perhaps some self-reproach may have played a decisive part in her emotion.

To reassure the Wolffs, I wrote a note and smuggled it across the following morning. And to avoid comment in the village Frau Klebert suggested I should go by the early train and Tilde by a later one. We could meet in Bonn and then travel to the Ahr together.

Tilde placed my traps on the handcart and away we went to the station along the bumpy village street, she and I pulling together on the shaft and chatting as we went. All the gapers of Blankheim had assembled on our path. First we passed Matthias and the rest, who gazed at us with a rigid stare, seeing us as the suspects in the Lambert affair and the darkling instigators of local political crime. Groups outside the various shops, at Fenger's, Kemp's, The Golden Hind, all went suddenly still as we passed while the women nudged each other or made some whispered observation. Everywhere was a moving of curtains, the glimpse of a lurking face, and I felt the impression of a thousand stares relentlessly levelled behind me.

I felt embarrassed, but Tilde strode manfully on, her right fist clenched, her head erect, a defiant smirk about her lips, and rat-tat-tat went the handcart over the cobbles, rousing the whole street. Obviously, the villains of the piece were getting out in good time, perhaps from sheer fear, perhaps at the order of the police. In the space of a day or two I had become a public figure.

It was the same down Station Road where our parade came to an abrupt stop outside the police office. There stood the inspector who had questioned me that night, and with him were Hamann and Zimmermann, both in Nazi dress. They stared at us as we approached. Perhaps some awkward glance on my part or some swift suspicion on theirs, as they saw the cart and bags, induced them to stop us.

'Running away?' asked the inspector drily as he took a step in our direction.

'Aye, in an absolute panic,' answered Tilde in a tone of mocking contempt.

'Well, he's got the jitters all right,' added Hamann. 'It wouldn't be a bad idea to inspect those bags.'

'Yes,' retorted Tilde, 'you might find something you missed the other night, treasonable documents, time bombs, plans for murdering the Führer and so on.'

'Well, in that case, pretty miss, you had better open up,' said the inspector with a grimly humorous look.

Now, at this distance of time I believe it was just chaff on his part, but there was just that touch of gravity in the tone and manner of the inspector

186

which revealed how serious things might have been if I had been taking the parcels. So I unlocked both my bags and opened them out on the pavement while the inspector made a semblance of examining the books and papers.

'Be careful you are not blown up,' mocked Tilde. 'A bomb in the eye might spoil your good looks.'

The inspector stood up and smiled while Hamann continued the search in a much more ruthless way.

'Enough, Hamann,' said the inspector, with his most malicious smile.

When I had packed up and we were out of the crowd, Tilde halted and burst into a peal of laughter. 'Oh, Mr Arnold, did you see?' She jerked her thumb towards Hamman. 'He got the jitters all right. He got into an absolute panic as he handled your shirts and pyjamas.'

Then Tilde checked herself, picked up the shaft once more and with a look of suppressed amusement resumed her way to the station. But she was serious enough when we got there.

'When it's my turn to leave the village I had better leave those parcels of yours somewhere here in Blankheim.'

'In some safe hiding place?'

'Yes. I know one.'

'But the inspector wouldn't risk your gibes again.'

'He would. For sheer devilment.'

It's a strange fact, but he did, as Tilde told me an hour or two later when we met again in Bonn.

Chapter 18

The Jackboot on the Ahr

It was dusk when I peered out from my little casement window over the wide and snowy landscape of the Ahr. It had been a pleasant journey and now I was ensconced for a few weeks in two little toy-like rooms still gay with the fresh paint of the previous spring. The bedroom was the merest nook and seemed, with its snow-white cot, its two little peeping casements, its dainty lace curtains and pretty image of the Virgin on the truly immaculate wall, to be the primest piece of innocence I had ever seen. There was a tiny washing stand, spick and span with a glistening jug, a spotless bowl and freshly laundered towels; an equally tiny wardrobe, which might bear the lightsome burden of a summer frock or two; and a natty little chair which stood at the head of the bed. A place for fairy dreams and childlike recollections which seemed to wake up gladly as Tilde peeped in at the door.

'Ah, Tilde, a pretty little room. Once yours, I suppose?'

'Yes, once upon a time. But now ...'

She stopped and suddenly looked so sad that I had to ask her why.

'I cannot help but think of Frau Gerster to whom I owe so much. She always had this room whenever she came to stay here. This and the sitting room here.'

I looked in. It was a little larger than the first, equally trim with a green enamelled stove and a glossily painted table, dapper cupboard to hold my writing materials and a shelf to place my books. From the casement I could see the broad valley of the Ahr and beyond it the snow-covered hills of the Eifel.

'It's all very pretty,' I said.

'I'm glad you're pleased, but I knew you would be.' And she looked extremely happy. She must have thought I would be longing for my cosy rooms at Blankheim.

'Well, there's one thing. We are far from all this Nazi stuff which has made Blankheim so distasteful.'

She pursed her lips and shook her head.

'It's everywhere the same,' she said. 'And they've even spoiled the view. Look.'

We went to the bedroom again where in the distance we could see the Landskrone, the loftiest hill in that part of the Ahr Valley. On the top amid the snow we could just make out the dark form of the restaurant and above it a swastika flag. The cross itself was not discernible, but the pole with its drooping flag stood out faintly against the sky.

'And worse still, they have painted a massive swastika on the rock face right beneath the summit and ruined the pure and natural view of the hill. It was once the Landskrone, and truly the crown of the land, but now it is just an eyesore. It's the same in Neuenahr, down there in the valley. A swastika hangs from every house.'

'Well, I'm glad that Neuenahr's afar off.'

'Neuenahr! Oh, Neuenahr's not so bad. It's bigger, you see, and you're less known. But here in the village it is different. At heart they are all against it, yet you can't trust them in the least bit. We are afraid to say anything even to our best friends for fear they might blab. Over their glasses, you know, in the village inn.'

'So you have your Hamanns here?'

'Hamanns, Zimmermanns, Brechners, even a Lambert and a Klassen.'

At the name of Klassen she became more angry. 'These village school-masters! Once Catholic and Centre Party, now worst and vilest of Nazis. I could ...'

She broke off, cramped her fingers as though throttling a vicious snake, 'Die, you devil, die!' she hissed, and so tensely obsessed was she with the strangling of the village teacher that she seemed to forget my presence

'Tilde, Tilde!'

'But I could, I could!' She clenched her fists, ground her teeth and looked her very fiercest, but when I burst out into a laugh she pulled herself together.

'Let's go down,' she said.

The evening meal awaited us, but before we sat down Tilde took me to a corner of the room where a panel hung on the wall.

'That's how it is with us,' she said.

'And it's never less than fifty pfennig a time,' said her father.

'And even a mark at times,' added the mother who came in with a steaming dish.

I gazed at the panel on which were pinned a number of coloured emblems of various charities, as well as of national movements, all now under Nazi control, such as Help for the Aged, League of German Girls, Youth Hostels, Germans Abroad, Aerial Defence, Zeppelin Fund and the like. Each was a little pictorial receipt for the voluntary contribution.

'You see,' said Tilde's mother, from whom she derived her pretty looks, 'we have to give our quota now. They come round for it and it's stand and deliver. Before the Nazis came we gave to the Catholic Charity, organised of course by the church. But all that has been stopped.'

'Only they,' said Herr Weichert, and he emphasised the *they* with a significant shake of his head, 'are allowed to be charitable now. At our expense of course. And when they have raked in all they can get, they can afford to be generous.'

'And get all the credit for generosity,' added his wife.

We sat down to our evening meal and I was able to study my simple hosts. Herr Weichert was a typical Rhenish peasant, with his muscular frame, weather-tanned face and hands bony and gaunt with heavy toil. But he had a very frank expression, grey eyes free from guile and thin lips that parted in a somewhat tart smile.

Frau Weichert had Tilde's features, rather worn with care and outdoor work, but sweet and attractive still, and wonderful golden hair.

As for Tilde, now in her own domain, she looked a very princess, such a Cinderella after a touch of the wand that the whole room reflected her happy presence and assumed a glint of youth. Without her the room might well have been gloomy with its little casements now shuttered for the night, its sober oak wainscotting and darkly painted floor, all of them rendered more sombre by the subdued glow of the oil lamp which, despite the dazzling table-linen, seemed to cast less light than shade.

It was a happy family circle as, in response to a nod from his wife, Herr Weichert bent his head and said grace for all of us with a simple prayer for the departed. Even after all these years I recall the hush of those solemn moments, those faces bent in prayer and the plea for eternal peace to the family dead.

But the solemnity of the moment passed, the smiling faces rose again with happy talk of home affairs, of a coming trip to Cologne, the purchases they intended to make and the preparations for Christmas Day. It was the first Christmas for three years Tilde had spent at home and she felt so supremely happy that she babbled away for sheer joy. In fact her parents began to think she had been sipping some heady wine.

'You haven't been down in the cellar, Tilde?' Her father stared at her in amused amazement.

'And broached that last bottle of 1921?' tartly suggested his wife.

'To the last drop,' rippled Tilde. 'But I don't need wine to make me happy. I'm home, mother.'

Then there was a loud knock. Someone had entered the porch and was knocking now at the inner door. Frau Weichert sprang up to answer the knock, but the door was opened and someone peered in. A cold draught coursed round the room.

'Heil Hitler! Sorry to disturb you, Frau Weichert, but it's only for a moment.'

A bulky figure entered with snow clinging to his cap and coat and boots. A second followed, and both were Nazis, evidently on business.

'Oh, my freshly polished floor,' moaned Frau Weichert, 'do shake the snow off before you come in.'

The two halted for a moment.

'We've shaken the bulk off,' said the first, casting a careless glance at the mess he was making. 'We've called for the Help for the Aged Fund.'

'But I thought I paid that last month,' said Herr Weichert, raising his brows in astonishment and looking towards the panel.

'Yes, but there'll have to be a supplement,' said the other. 'The cold weather has meant more coal and an extra allowance for blankets and clothing. But don't let us disturb you, Frau Weichert. We can wait. It's warm here and it's cold outside.'

'By God, it is,' said the first, taking a seat in the corner. 'It is chilly work trudging round in the village. One can do with a little warming up.'

Herr Weichert understood. He went to the sideboard where he kept a small flask of schnapps, filled two glasses and handed them over.

'What is it to be this time?'

'Well here is the list. You can see what they've given.' He handed over a paper, which Herr Weichert studied and signed.

The two sat there supping their schnapps. The first, whose name was Hermann, was a bulky adventurous type, who looked fit for any enterprise, good, bad or indifferent. A scar, which had given a turn to his eye, gave him an almost reckless appearance. The other was quieter and more cultured, the village schoolmaster as I afterwards learned, Johann Zeller. He resembled Klassen with his pale sharp face and concentrated glance. He kept gazing at me in a challenging way.

'I suppose it will have to be a mark,' said Herr Weichert at last, fumbling in his pocket.

'Yes, a mark will do,' said Hermann, the adventurous one. 'By the way, where's Tilde? The word's gone round that she's come back.'

Tilde must have slipped out. I stared at her empty seat in surprise. She had even taken her plate, so that there was no question of her coming back so long as the Nazis were there. Hermann kept gazing at the chair in a questioning way.

'Yes, she is back for a few days. She has just gone upstairs to lie down,' said Herr Weichert by way of excuse. 'She's tired from the journey.'

The two eventually went after a rambling talk of events in the village. As they trudged off through the snow Frau Weichert took care to lock both the outer and the inner door.

'That will secure us from a surprise the next time,' she muttered to herself, as she went away for a mop to clear up the melted snow.

'Yes, we must keep it locked in future, or our house is no longer our own,' said Herr Weichert, turning round to me and jerking his thumb towards the street outside. 'That's the way they manage it. Plain bullying.'

'Of course they get more money,' interposed Frau Weichert, 'and in a way the poor are better off.'

'Are you sure?' It was Tilde's voice. She had suddenly returned with her plate. 'Are you sure?'

'Well, with all the money they get ... '

'They can buy swagger cars for the officials,' said Tilde, 'provide them with an up-to-date office as well as with a swagger salary.'

'Tilde, Tilde!' remonstrated Frau Weichert, who always thought the best of everyone.

'Oh, you know the old joke, mother, of the beggar who was discovered stroking a posh car outside the Adler Hotel?'

'Oh?'

'And when they asked him what he was doing he said he was only trying to get in touch with the Winter Fund.'

'Tilde, Tilde!'

'Well, all the posh trappings have got to come from somewhere. And the only place they can come from is from the innumerable funds they run.'

'I wouldn't put it past them,' said Herr Weichert, 'and certainly not past Hermann.'

'Now that's not for us to say.'

The worthy Frau Weichert was resolved to believe evil of nobody. She turned to Tilde.

'You shouldn't have left the table, Tilde. You know what Hermann is. He could easily take offence at it and make things quite unhappy for us. He is the uncrowned king of these parts and what he says is law.'

'That's why I went. I would only have snubbed him and given him real grounds for complaint. Give such a man an inch and he'll take a thousand miles.'

'A villain?' I asked.

'A villain,' echoed Herr Weichert. 'Well, if you like. He's been everything in his short life, sailor, lorry driver, poacher, farmer, vintner, bargeman, jerrybuilder, everything, but none for long.'

'Except when he was on the dole,' said Tilde. 'But now he's landed. District organiser for the Nazi Party with undefined powers.'

'Yes, with undefined powers,' Frau Weichert nodded her head vigorously. 'You see, he has not forgotten the Albert Gerster affair.'

'Son of Frau Gerster?' I asked.

'Yes, he paid us a visit once when his mother was staying here and the village youths thought he was interested in Tilde. So they waylaid him and gave him a good thrashing. We were afraid they might thrash Tilde too, so she went away in service to Blankheim. Frau Gerster got her the post and took care of her, teaching her the finer arts of sewing, and reading books with her. And Frau Engels has been equally good.'

'I think he *was* interested in me,' said Tilde with a twinkle, 'and Frau Gerster thought so too. I believe she must have thought to herself that if it's got to be Tilde Weichert I'd better make the best of her. So she took me under her wing. But I didn't care for him really.' And she fairly rippled with laughter.

'Though it would have been a splendid match.'

'Far too pedantic, mother.'

'Yes, he was a finger-rapper,' said Herr Weichert.

'You know,' said Tilde, turning to me, 'I've been spoiled by Herr Gerster, the father, and by Herr Engels. I have got used to their wise old ways and serious conversation. Whenever I get with younger folk, they are all so green and inexperienced, so utterly childish and daft that I think of turning them over and fastening their napkins afresh.'

'Tilde, Tilde!' cried her mother.

Tilde fell into a fit of laughter in which we heartily joined.

Yes, Tilde was spoiled for the youth of the village. To her they were mere yokels, with no higher style in life than hobnails and corduroy, while she to them was a very proud hussy, self-opinionated and perhaps a little contemptuous with ideas too high for her rank in life. And she certainly held herself aloof. But she was really a very gracious girl, with all her mother's delicate conscience and strictly Catholic view of life.

No wonder she shrank from the rough-cut youths of the Ahr, their uncouth conversation and horseplay type of humour. But they couldn't forgive her for it and when the Nazis came to power they found ways of harassing her.

One day, after a ramble along the Ahr, Tilde and I were returning home up the hill and had stopped for a moment to regain our breath at a picturesque bend in the road. There below us was the broad dusky valley where the lights of Neuenahr were beginning to pick out the lines of the streets and gardens. We were leaning on a wall by the wayside when suddenly Tilde whispered.

'Somebody's following us.'

'Yes, I can see him.'

A figure was just visible at a bend in the roadway and was coming up at a great pace. We had caught him staring at us at the station when we had arrived on the train. On that occasion he had turned and slunk away, only to reappear later in the street outside studying us with the same embarrassing stare. 'Let's go on,' said Tilde, 'This is a dark part of the road. There are lights along the top.'

'No, let's meet him, and hold your stick ready.'

Really we had no option. He was calling, and after a few moments was standing before us.

'Excuse me, sir,' he said with a stiff, hasty bow, 'but I should like a word with the young lady. In private.'

Tilde would have none of it.

'Stand by me, Mr Arnold! Don't move a step.'

He started back and gazed at me.

'Oh, you're Mr Arnold?'

He pulled off his thick-rimmed glasses and revealed rather close-set eyes with a tense and concentrated look in keeping with his sharp features. A short sharp-pointed beard gave him a very severe and ascetic appearance.

'Herr Gerster,' gasped Tilde.

'Yes.'

He looked hastily about him and then explained. He had come back to settle his affairs, to recover the papers secreted by his mother and to arrange for the transfer of some properties. He had no doubt that he would be detained if recognised by the police. Perhaps for life. Without trial.

'Or be shot while trying to escape,' I interposed.

He stared at me and I wondered what thoughts were rankling in his mind. His eyes glowed with hate, but he shook the emotion off and asked about the papers. We told him and suggested that the parcel should be sent poste restante to some distant town. He gave us an address. Then, hearing footsteps coming down the road, he bade us a hasty goodbye. He held both Tilde's hands in his and begged her not to forget him. Then off he went.

We both breathed a sigh of relief. The parcel would soon be off our hands, and one anxiety at least would be off our minds. A few moments later someone passed us on the road. Tilde did not know him, and as he moved off into the darkness we breathed a second sigh of relief.

A day or two later we were setting up the Christmas tree, fixing the candles, hanging the filigree and adjusting the silvered cones and glittering globes. The parents, who were seated near the stove, had left the task to us. I was working strictly under Tilde's orders for the tree was a large one and reached from floor to ceiling. We were busy with our work when a knock came to the door. The knob was tried, but this time the door was locked.

'Heil Hitler!' came a voice and with it a louder knock.

'Who's that?'

'Hermann. I must come in.'

He came in, the same bulky figure, the same sinister expression in the turned eye, the same heavy voice, gruff from the winter cold. He threw off his gloves revealing his large bony fists and sat down on the nearest chair.

'I want a word with you, Tilde.'

'With me?'

'Yes with you.'

'What about?'

'Ask your own conscience what it's about.'

'My own conscience? What are you talking about?' Tilde stood there with her hands on her hips and blazed her question at him.

'Yes, your own conscience. Who is it you have been meeting of late?'

'What's that to do with you?'

'Nothing, if it's an ordinary friend. But you've been secretly meeting a traitor. An enemy to the Reich.'

194

'I most certainly haven't.'

'You most certainly have. You've been meeting that Gerster.'

'I've – not – been – meeting – that – Gerster.'

She bent forward and hissed out each separate word while her parents looked on aghast. I said nothing, for Tilde seemed well able to defend herself.

'You deny it?' shouted Hermann.

'I deny it,' cried Tilde in return. 'If you mean that Albert Gerster met me, then Albert Gerster met me. Not one step have I taken in his direction, not one word have I uttered to encourage him to come to me.'

'Oh,' laughed Hermann ironically. 'So you admit it, do you?'

'Admit it!' cried Tilde. 'What do you mean by making these base accusations? Albert Gerster met both me and Mr Arnold on the road the other night. We didn't ask for the meeting. We didn't ask for it to be repeated. I think you are a shameless man to come and make a scene like this at Christmas time in our house.'

'I shall make a bigger scene in a moment.' He dropped his voice. 'If you've nothing on your conscience then tell me what you said and heard.'

'I shall do nothing of the kind. Who are you to ask these questions?'

'Look here, Tilde. You are in a difficult position. You've been meeting a traitor, the son of a traitor who was shot for treachery. He fled to Switzerland to avoid a trial and now he has stealthily come back and had a meeting with you. Now look here, Tilde,' and he spoke in a more mollifying tone, 'In my position I can arrange things. I think you had better come along to my place either tonight or tomorrow and explain things.'

'To your place, you rascal,' replied Tilde, 'and walk like a poor fly into your spider's web. No. I'm going the very first thing tomorrow with Mr Arnold here to the police at Neuenahr. I shall make my depositions there and tell them of your threats. Now go.'

After more shouts and threats he went. Tilde's parents were prostrate. Their Christmas Eve was ruined. Hermann with his indefinite powers and ruthless use of mob law could make things untenable for the Weicherts. There was therefore no help for it but to go to the police next day.

And go we did, first thing. But Hermann was there before us. He went there in his car. In fact, as he tore past us, I thought he actually intended to run us down. When we entered the inspector's office, Hermann was already there. He looked quite annoyed when he was asked to go outside.

The inspector we met was a young fresh-looking man, not only with a sense of humour but also with a sensitive eye for Tilde's prettiness and charm. He took her depositions in a very pleasant spirit and smiled broadly as she slated Hermann.

'Tell that fellow to mind his own business,' he said.

'But he actually asked me to go to his house to explain things.'

'The rogue! And you preferred to come to me instead?'

He said this with such a meaning wink that we all three had to laugh.

'Don't worry, lass,' he said. 'As far as I can see, this Gerster's not a wanted man, though his staying abroad for a longer time than is allotted in his passport might open him up to question. But now for a final word. Why did he come to see you?'

'An embarrassing question,' I interposed.

'Doubtless.' The inspector gazed at Tilde with undisguised amusement.

'He came for the same reason, Herr Inspektor, as Hermann came to see her. Gerster's a very amorous man and Hermann a very jealous one.'

The inspector put down his pen and laughed.

'I'm sorry I sent him out. He ought to have heard that last bit.'

So after a little talk we signed the depositions and went. Had we really triumphed? Had we really enlisted the police on our behalf? Hardly. The police were far away and far too busy with other things to have a constant eye on the Weicherts, while Hermann was close at hand, ready at a moment to use his insolent powers to bring his opponents to heel. He was a ruthless man and a jealous one and unfortunately certain awkward facts played into his ready hands. On our return to the village we noticed two or three people gaping at an elegant car which was drawn up at our gate. I recognised it at once. It was Rosenbaum's.

Now Tilde as a good Catholic had no animus against the Jews. But this elegant car at the gate and this obstinate group of village gapers, who seemed to be priming up for the breathless gossip of a fortnight, most certainly annoyed her. For Rosenbaum, though polite and correct in many ways, had not the least appreciation for the parlous plight of others under Nazi rule. Instead of making a discreet appointment by telegram, phone or letter, here he arrives in the broadest daylight in the most sumptuous car. In such a poor outlandish village everyone is apt to wonder why. I, as an Englishman, afforded ample scope for gossip. How much more a pompous Jew who went flaunting his own importance in the face of the Nazi power.

He was awaiting me in my little study, which he seemed to fill with his presence. With an expansive gesture he motioned me to a stool while he himself sank into my chair like one in full possession of the room. Naturally, I was but a student and he a proud, full-blown professor with all the spacious manners and amplitude of gesture of one who lorded over the student youth of Bonn. He smiled graciously, cordially, condescendingly, so that the gloss of his forehead, the glint of his glasses and the sparkle of his bejewelled fingers all seemed to smile in keeping with his plump and parted lips. But in a trice the smile had gone. He assumed a cautious look, raised his forefinger and gave a querying sign with his thumb towards the door. I nodded. He could speak quite freely for we had nothing to fear.

He had come for the parcel Miss Rebecca had asked me to keep safe. He said he must have it that very day. He was prepared to take me to Blankheim and then return me to the Ahr as soon as our business was finished. I had but to name the conditions and he would accept them without question.

I had to call Tilde, of course, because she had hidden the parcel for me somewhere in Blankheim. After some hesitation, she consented to go with Rosenbaum from Neuenahr to a point just outside Blankheim where she could get out unobserved and do the last few hundred yards on foot. After delivering the parcel she could return to Neuenahr by train.

Clumsy and roundabout though her conditions were, Rosenbaum accepted at once. So off they went, with all the village giving them a peeping send-off.

She came back in the late afternoon looking rather puzzled and certainly a little anxious. As she had been leaving the Engels's house with the parcel she had been accosted by the Captain.

'Are they the papers?' he whispered, tapping the parcel with his forefinger.

'What papers?'

'For Professor Rosenbaum.'

'They are not Professor Rosenbaum's,' she answered. The reply was quite honest, for she knew they were Miss Rebecca's. 'It's just a parcel I have to return.'

The captain had given a huge wink, but Tilde was alarmed, and so was I when she told me about the incident.

'I don't trust the Captain one iota,' she said. 'Not that he's dishonest, but he can't keep a secret to save his mortal life. I am surprised at Miss Rebecca; she is usually so cautious.'

I was surprised too. Surely Miss Rebecca would not blab.

The thought clouded my stay at Tilde's home, a thought strangely linked up with Hermann. It haunted all our wanderings and lurked in every dip, blur and shadow on our path so that we often halted at a bend in the roadway, or hastily looked back to surprise the vague follower we imagined holding us stealthily in view.

I felt it most intensely when lingering for a precious moment amid the ruins of the Saffenburg, a lone romantic spot, perched on a steep precipice right above the River Ahr. Far away below us, though almost lost in the twilight, was the little church of Mayschoss with its memorial to Catharina, the lovely peasant maid who had married the lord of the Saffenburg 300 years before.

Leaving me to muse over the ruins, Tilde went off to peep into the headlong deeps of the Ahr gorge while I sat on a crumbling stone amid the leafless shrubs and trailing brambles and awaited her return. How silent it was in that tumbled ruin, how mouldered away, how desolate. Minute after minute went by, though Tilde's parting footsteps still lingered in my ear, and her face and form were wondrously blended with my visions of the lovely peasant maid of long ago, when suddenly I was startled by a piercing shriek which wakened eerie echoes all along the valley. Had she fallen or been flung down by that evil shadow who we felt had dogged our steps all day?

I sprang up in a fright and found myself facing – so intense had been my musings on the romance of other days – the staring, pallid face of Catharina, a flash from the grave it seemed to me, a revenant with a message. But it was only Tilde. She was white, trembling, panting for breath. But what a deep relief to see her face again and to feel her warm responsive hand in mine.

'Tilde, Tilde, I thought you had fallen into the gorge.'

'It was an owl, an owl,' she gasped, and broke into a nervous laugh, which revealed to me how great her shock had been. 'I thought it was the man we keep . . .'

'Thought what?'

'I thought . . .'

'It was that man we keep imagining following us?'

Her laugh was so convulsive that I was afraid to press my questions. Taking her hand I led her down the hill and when at last she was able to tell me, she said she thought I had been stabbed by Hermann.

'Tilde, Tilde, what a crazy idea!'

'It was the first that came to my mind. The man haunts me. But what did *you* think?'

'I thought you had been pushed into the gorge, and when you suddenly stood before me like a ghost out of the gloom I thought you were Catharina, lovely Catharina with a message from the grave.'

'Bless us,' she said. Then smiled and clapped her hands.

'So you really, really thought I was lovely Catharina of Mayschoss?'

'Yes, I did.'

'How pretty of you to think so.'

'Yes, in a way, but it is prettier still to know that you are Tilde.'

It was thus we spent our days amid the lonely wilds of the Eifel, ideally happy days. A flush of my lost youth is in them now. I have but to hear Tilde's name again, catch a glimpse of her happy face or sense the touch of her confiding hand, and the vision is mine again, with the upland winds about me as they gust away over the Steinerberg, with the great cloud shadows racing past, the woodlands straining in the brawl of the storm and the fresh cool rain plashing over the fells that sink abruptly down to the Ahr.

It was winter then, and wreaths of snow still lingered in the shadows of the Saffenburg. Yet, despite the sunless bluster of that wild, wintry weather, a radiance still illumines this vista. There's a glitter in the dripping fronds which scatter their liquid sparkle as we pass, and a lustre in the tumbling rush of the brooks we spring so riskily across. And at the end there's an absolute splendour in the vast expanse of cloud and sky as we stand in the gathering dusk upon the Kreuzberg.

There are scenes that never leave us, some presence all the lovelier for the passing of the years, and of such she was and is and ever will be. In her society, time is at a standstill. We still roam over hill and dale, still feel the breath of the morning cool and fresh on our cheeks, and all of it so palpable, so present and so real, that a chance touch of her hand, as we once went down the Ahr, is a tremble even now.

Chapter 19

Bribery Versus Blackmail

Some two or three weeks later on my return to Blankheim I called on Miss Rebecca, braving the stares of Matthias and his comrades who stood there mute outside his shop and agape as I rang the front doorbell. I felt very uneasy that the captain, who was an avowed Nazi and something of a blab, should have shared what I thought to be a secret. There was no controlling the Captain's tongue. In company, he had to be the centre of things, the man of mark, the constant point of interest whatever the cost to plain fact or even to obvious truth. And then there was Professor Rosenbaum, who also knew more than he ought. But Miss Rebecca and I, at least, ought to have some common story ready in case the police came round.

Miss Rebecca was alone. She received me into her sanctum, sat down by the stove and eyed me in her stonily dry-eyed way. She thanked me for the services I had rendered, but summarily nodded away any breach of a mutual secret.

'The Captain knows nothing. I told Professor Rosenbaum that I had mislaid a paper on which I had made some important notes. I had used it for a time as a bookmark and then I lost it. I searched for it high and low but in vain. And then I reflected that it might be among some English papers that you had agreed to glance through. That was all. Quite harmless, you see.'

'But in case the police should ask, what were these English papers?'

'Oh, holiday brochures, if you like.'

I certainly did not like. I distrusted Rebecca. Her story was obviously false. And I was now involved in this web of lies where the police would find me easy prey. And yet there was normally no one more cautious than Rebecca.

I looked into her dark face and concluded that, whether she was cautious or not, I was only a cat's-paw in her hands. When once I had served her purpose she would ruthlessly drop me dead. As she sat there in her black satin dress that gleamed subtly in the subdued light of that richly furnished room I thought of the ironical Bürger who had likened Rebecca once to a sleekly feathered bird of prey, and her sanctum to a grisly garner of legally gotten loot. I was in the mood to believe it.

I was wondering what troubled story each precious piece in the room might tell, the tapestried chair on which she sat, the genuine observatory clock, the gilt-framed paintings of Rhenish scenes, the ebony escritoire with its inlaid mother of pearl, the Persian carpet, the figured vase. Each of them might be a lost and lamented relic of some tear-stricken family wreck, and all of them wealthy evidence of unfair and furtive profits on the inside fringe of the law.

So I believed Bürger was right, at least until Rachel came into the room with her charming and disarming smile. The light that came into her face as she saw me dispersed all my shady thoughts. I could believe no evil of Rachel Wolff. And when she sat down beside me I felt the reflection of her gracious spirit in every piece in the room.

But it was only when her sister went out that she began to speak to me freely.

'I'm so glad to see you back again,' she said.

'It's nice of you to say so.'

'No, I'm not just paying a compliment. It's a great relief to know you are back and that you live just over the way. We are alone, Mr Arnold, amid many enemies or, what is so much worse, amid hosts of Christian friends who are dying to deny their friendship. Everyone has betrayed us. So it is a blessing to know that there is at least one man in the village we may regard as a true friend.'

'I'm glad you feel like that about me. But, you are in no immediate danger are you?'

'There's the Lambert affair.' She whispered this and looked anxiously towards the door. 'My sister does not like it mentioned,' she added by way of excuse.

'And how about Lambert himself?'

'He's still in hospital. And his house has been raided and the safe rifled.'

She whispered as though her own home were marked out for the next attack.

'But I thought the thieves had been foiled.'

'The first time, yes. But they succeeded later, even though the house was sealed and under guard, so there are all sorts of rumours in the village. And ...'

Here she stopped almost in a panic casting an anxious glance at the door.

'What?'

'Just between you and me?'

'Naturally.'

'Hamann has been here.'

'To threaten you?'

'Yes. At least I think so. He saw Rebecca alone. At dead of night. And to spare me she has said nothing of what passed between them. But because she has said nothing I feel all the more afraid. And she has been graver and more anxious since, although she keeps on telling me that there is nothing to fear.'

She told me all this in such panic whispers that I grew quite alarmed for her.

'You must hope for the best,' I said in consoling tones, and added, 'I have the greatest faith in your sister. If any one can ride the storm she will.'

There was a ring at the doorbell. Rachel started. Not that she knew who was at the door. Far from it. But nothing now from outside boded any good to Rachel Wolff. A footfall on the pavement, the rumble of some passing car, the voice of someone calling over the street, a knock at the door by some errand boy, sent a streak of fear to her heart.

The front door was opened. There were voices, hostile voices, insolent and abrupt on the part of some man, hard and staccato on Rebecca's. Rachel stood up hastily.

'Let us go into the other room,' she whispered.

She had barely taken a step when the door was flung open.

'I say she's not here. It's not her voice you've heard, but my sister's.'

A man strode in and looked round. It was Boden. He stopped and gazed at me in his insolent way, his brows raised, his head thrown slightly back and his lips pursed up in contempt. Perhaps he meant no disrespect. But being something of a dullard he used to try to make up for his obvious failings by rudeness. He turned to Rebecca with the same overbearing look.

'I'm giving you a warning,' he blurted out, 'I won't have you harbouring her here, following me round and persecuting me.'

'What? It's you who are following her around and persecuting her. She was here in Blankheim before you were. You ought to be ashamed of yourself, bullying your poor wife like this. Be off with you!'

'She's no longer my wife. Just drop that word, will you?'

'Of course she's your wife, and the child, when it comes, will also be yours. And if you don't give them a shelter I shall do so.'

'Will you? You dare! If you harbour her here I shall make things worse for you.'

'Then make them worse, if you can. Do your damnedest. I shall be the next woman you have foully struck and my sister the third. But when Johanna comes out of the maternity home I shall welcome her back to Blankheim. Here in this house, here, as Mrs Boden, your wife. Do you understand?'

'Drop that term,' shouted Boden.

I admired Rebecca. She stood erect before him in all her clear superiority of soul. His face was flushed, his fists clenched and he would have struck her in the face had I not caught his hand in time.

'None of this. Out you go.' He lashed out a blow, which I easily parried as I thrust him to the front door. Rebecca brushed past and opened it and, as he turned round to strike again, I tripped him up and with the lightest of blows sent him flying into the street. There he sprawled, narrowly missed by a passing car. He picked himself up and in his blind rage was about to assail me when Hamann suddenly emerged from Matthias' shop and, followed by the other customers, stepped between.

'You English spy, you pro-Jew,' Boden roared. 'I'll make things hot for you.'

'What's the matter?' asked Hamann, casting a lowering glance in my direction.

Half to himself, half to the crowd, Boden shouted his accusations. Then, turning to Hamann, he cried: 'You are a party comrade. You will help me through with this.'

'I'll see the matter through. Leave it to me.'

Hamann was in a most sinister mood, and with his fists clenched looked ready to attack.

'Leave it to me,' he said, and the way he looked at me seemed to spell my fate in Blankheim.

I went back into the house, where Rachel was sitting by an electric fire between the garden window and a broad screen, anxiously awaiting our return. She was in tears. But what distressed me more than that were her obvious efforts to be brave and her despairing efforts to please. As if she needed to try! Was she wholly oblivious of her fascinating powers, her winsome face and her gracious ways? She was grateful for my consoling words, while her sister sat mutely by, unmoved and shaking her head at any thought of danger.

'Boden's just a passing nuisance.' This was the only comment she had to offer. And that was how I left them.

Frau Klebert had different views. She was frankly afraid of the bullock-headed Boden. Brechner, despite his braggart ways, his Nazi ideas and class hatred, was at least amenable to reason. And he had a respectable home and a pious wife. Even Hamann was not wholly blind to what was right, blackguard though he was. But Boden, a Catholic who could disown his wife, abandon her and her coming child, and renounce his Christian faith for mere position or sheer cash, was a man who would stop at nothing. He would trample over corpses to gain his ends.

A few days later I received a note from Klassen. Some charge had been preferred and I was to be arraigned, as Herr Engels had been, before the local committee. I was to appear on the Saturday evening at 7.30. So I went. The family saw me off at the door, Herr Engels, who wanted to accompany me and add his word to mine, Frau Klebert, who as a member of the party wished to have a slash at Boden, and Tilde, who actually pleaded with tears to come and speak on my behalf.

But it was better to go alone and avoid involving anyone else.

When I reached the Golden Hind, however, and was about to enter the porch I felt a hand in mine. It was Tilde's. She had slipped out at the last minute to wish me well. Her face was radiant in the golden light of the porch lamp, her cheeks flushed and her lips parted after her hasty run to the inn.

'Once more, good luck!' she panted. 'I thought I should have missed you.'

'I'm glad you didn't, Tilde,' I laughed. 'I now feel brave enough to face a dozen committees,'

She smiled, took my hand again and speeded away home.

So I was once again in the Golden Hind, facing the committee as Herr Engels had done and sitting on the self-same chair at the long table. But this time the out-and-out Nazis were seated on the left and the conservative ones on the right. Klassen, my right-hand neighbour and president of the committee was facing Hamann on my left. At the bottom of the table was Boden, clearly not a member of the committee and only there as a plaintiff.

'We have a complaint, Herr Arnold,' said Klassen, tapping some papers before him.

'And that is?'

'That you are giving aid and encouragement to the Jews and even helping them to assault a member of our party.'

'I like the charge giving aid to the Jews. My experience of them is that they are very well able to take care of themselves.'

A sardonic smile went round the table. It was difficult to say whose smile was broadest.

'As for assaulting a member of the party, I certainly did so after he had struck the first blow.'

'You intervened in my dispute with one of those Jewesses,' shouted Boden, 'when she was insulting me ...'

'Sit down and be quiet, Herr Doktor,' cried Klassen. 'Don't speak without permission.'

'But I must correct him.'

'I've told you to be quiet.'

'Quiet!' A dozen voices silenced the interrupter. I continued.

'He was about to strike Rebecca Wolff when I intervened. He then lashed out at me. I parried the blow and threw him out of the house. I see nothing reprehensible in that.'

'Perhaps you don't. But in any dispute between a Jew and a National Socialist you have to close an eye.'

'But in this case I should have to close them both, or keep them both wide open.'

'What do you mean?'

'A member of the party must be a man worthy of respect and able to inspire respect in the village.'

'What! You dare to accuse me! Who are you to say ...'

The rest of Boden's outburst was lost in the uproar. I was happy. The committee were at loggerheads and the more they were embroiled, the safer I was. I resolved to take the offensive. When order was restored I went on.

'And what respect does a Catholic inspire in this most Catholic village when for mere cash he marries a Jewess and then repudiates her to make what he thinks is a better deal? Repudiates his wife and child to become a member of the party? What will the village think of you if such a man is in your ranks? And what will the rank and file think if he becomes a member of the committee?'

I did not say all this without loud interruptions and calls for order, but finally the uproar was so great that Boden had to be removed. He protested, of course, and I thought he would make a fight of it, but Müller and Hempel combined were far too strong for him. He was frogmarched out of the room. There was a strangely tense silence when both came back and resumed their seats. They were flushed, but rather from inner than outer agitation. Hamann and Zimmermann were clearly embarrassed and stared mutely at the table while Klassen, with fists clenched and teeth set, strove to look master of the situation. Was he sincere? He began to speak abruptly as though overriding some inner restraint.

'We are not here to discuss the acts and character of Dr Boden. It is you who stand accused. It is your association with Jews that has brought you here tonight. In defiance of the policy of the National Socialist Party you are giving help and encouragement to Jews. What is your answer to that?'

'My answer is that you and other members of the committee set me a clear example. I cannot forget that as members of the Kevelaar Club you introduced me to Dr Cohen, who was a highly respected member of that society, and that you, Herr Klassen, gratefully shared a bottle of wine which you know he kindly paid for. Far be it from me to condemn *you*.'

I had expected an outburst of laughter from the party on the left, but to my no small embarrassment Hamann and Zimmermann were ominously quiet. So were the others. Klassen was flushed and Müller and Hempel looked most embarrassed. I thought I had played a trump card, but I realised at once that I had deeply offended the meeting by referring to their pre-Nazi past. I had made an unpardonable blunder, and Klassen was not going to let me get away with it.

'What happened years ago has nothing to do with the matter in hand. Dr Cohen was medical officer of health and had an official position. It was (and here he wrung for words) not our province to protest against this. Your case is different. You have openly flouted the government by helping and encouraging the Wolff sisters, Jewesses of course, and hostile to our present state. You were clearly a guest at their house.'

He rapped this out in staccato tones, feeling that he had happily shuffled out of an awkward situation. He looked triumphant and unless I made a vigorous defence I would be in a bad position. Goaded on by the hypocrisy of the man I decided to let fly.

'Of course I was a guest at the house. I was only following the example of some members of the committee who also make a practice of visiting the Miss Wolffs. If the committee sets the example why accuse me of following it?'

'What?'

Was it tactless of me to say so? A bombshell had fallen. Hamann and Zimmermann started up and gazed at me. Klassen looked as though he would spring at my throat, and Hempel and Müller and Wessel, after an accusing all-round glance, suddenly gasped out, 'Who?'

'Yes, who?' Klassen demanded.

'I shall mention no names,' I said calmly. 'That's for the committee to enquire.'

'Did the Miss Wolffs mention names?' Hamann pursued.

He stared at me with those sinister light grey eyes in which the tension of anger and fear were clearly shining.

'No. The two Miss Wolffs are too clever for that. They have never, even in an undertone, referred to anyone here. But I have eyes, and I happen to live over the way and see much from my bedroom window. And being fond of midnight strolls I see much that certain people would very much like to conceal. Now, less hypocrisy, please.'

'I demand that you mention names,' cried Klassen.

'I shall do nothing of the kind,' I replied. 'The members of the committee can rely on my absolute discretion. They can also rely on the absolute discretion of the Miss Wolffs. I am speaking not from hearsay but as an eyewitness. All I ask is that when you climb over a garden wall kindly see that the towpath is clear.'

That floored them. They clearly accepted that I was speaking the truth, but I had lied, of course. Miss Rachel had mentioned Hamann's name. However, now that I had started I intended to cast them in the worst light, cost what it may. They stared at each other in suspicion, Zimmermann and Hamann as brazenly as the rest. Kollass, the insurance agent, was blushing to the hair roots and Wessel looked embarrassed.

It was Hempel and Müller who broke the stillness.

'Well, I've climbed over no garden wall,' said Hempel.

'Nor I,' said Müller in a toneless way.

But they did not ask who had. A sudden light dawned on me. The whole lot in some way or other were involved in the financial net of Rebecca Wolff. Everywhere in the village she had some standing loan, some stake, some property or landed interest. And with the exception of Herr Engels, she had everyone of note in her relentless octopus grip. I looked at all those suspicious and highly embarrassed faces and then stood up.

'I shall leave the committee,' I said, 'to discuss this rather interesting matter in camera.'

And off I went without a word of protest from anyone in the room. My mind was in a swirl. Was I right in my conjecture? Surely if they felt themselves in the grip of Rebecca Wolff they could, as out-and-out Nazis, repudiate all obligation. Who were they to keep their faith with Jews? And what remedy had Rebecca Wolff if they snapped their fingers in her face and told her to whistle for the money? And yet? There was something I could not explain. Despite all their political power, she held every one of them in the hollow of her hand.

But in that case, why had I been summoned before them for doing what they all were doing? Were they all playing a game of bluff, and showing zeal in a common cause in order to mask their private guilt? Did they feel that they might betray themselves if they ignored Dr Boden's protests and that, by convicting me, they best acquitted themselves? Perhaps. But how about Hamann? According to Rachel, he had threatened them. As a private person or as a Nazi official? All the way home I was torn by doubt, not to speak of a big misgiving. I ought not to have mentioned the garden wall.

On my return, I was ushered into the sanctum and was met by a storm of questions. Frau Klebert was rather pale, but Tilde was trembling with excitement while Herr Engels vainly tried to stuff his pipe with his nervy and erring fingers. I told them my story, as they crowded round me, and they gasped their approval. But they gasped even more when I spoke of the garden wall. I had not mentioned the fact before and, of course, I suppressed all names although they urged and urged me to divulge them. I had made a promise of absolute discretion and that I intended to keep.

'And they actually call on the Miss Wolffs?' asked Frau Klebert in a tone of sheer disbelief.

'Yes, they have called on them. And the sisters, as far as I can judge, were quite happy about the visit.'

'Impossible!'

Then Herr Engels laughed softly.

'They all have a finger in Rebecca's pocket while she has her hand in theirs.'

'No wonder,' he went on, 'the sisters are living in peace. Still the hunger of wolves and you still their howls. It's the old, old story. To tame a beast of prey you must feed it. And it's the same with men. To catch them napping just give them a meal; when you soothe the belly you sober the brain. But I should like to see Rebecca's accounts and learn her assessment of each; of Klassen and Wessel and Hamann and Zimmermann and even Hempel and Müller, whom she helped in the past with generous loans. Every building Wessel erects stands secure on Rebecca's cash.'

'She must be paying a pretty penny to keep them all quiet,' I suggested.

'Not a bit of it, for she's paying them back in their own coin.'

So that was the answer to the great mystery that had puzzled me for many months. The sisters, though regarded as pariah dogs, were at peace with the whole village. They could parade their finery wherever they went, career to Cologne in a luxury car, visit the opera and the theatre, and carry on in the flash pre-Nazi way without one word of abuse from the most Nazi of Nazis in Blankheim. The initiative lay with Rebecca, and I did not doubt that if the worst came to the worst she would strangle the whole gang. For whether they were demanding by blackmail or accepting bribes they stood equally condemned.

Late that night when the house was still the bell rang out so defiantly that I started from my seat. Again it rang, so that I hastened to my bedroom window and looked out into the night. All was dark and deserted and, save for a lamp or two, there was no light in the whole street right up to the Golden Hind. Then I heard a voice and a sound of the closing door. Tilde, pale and anxious, opened my door as Hamman brushed past her. He eyed me defiantly as he slouched to the opposite side of the table. I turned to exchange a glance with Tilde as she slowly closed the door. He kept staring at the door until Tilde's footsteps slowly but audibly went down the stairs. Then he turned to me, not knowing that she had swiftly returned in her stockinged feet and was sitting on the stair by the door. Not that she was listening, she was too honest for that, but she was there in case of need. And I had guessed it.

'How much do you know?' He blurted out the words in such a way that I was taken aback.

'Know? About what?'

'About us and the Jews.'

He was staring at me as though he had a knife at my throat.

'Nothing more than I have said.'

'What do you know? What did she say to you?'

'She?'

'Miss Rebecca.'

'Nothing at all. She has never uttered a word. She has never mentioned a name. She has never breathed a syllable to me about her affairs. What I know, I know from these very eyes. I've guessed the rest.'

'Oh, have you? What have you seen?'

'What I told the meeting. You were there.'

'You saw me get over the garden wall?'

'Now, Hamann, no names. I told the committee that I should observe an absolute discretion. I shall preserve this discretion even against the Gestapo, employ what tortures they might. Once again, let me say that Miss Rebecca has said nothing and that I have heard nothing. I have seen what I have seen. No more.'

'You are a liar!' He rose and stemmed his hands against the table. 'You know God knows what and you're keeping it back.'

'I'm not. And if I'm a liar why do you ask me questions?'

'Come on. No sidestepping. I ask you to come clean.'

'Come clean? If I were to say more, I should certainly tell you lies. I've seen what I've told you and no more. But I've guessed a great deal.'

'What?'

'What happens to be public property throughout the length and breadth of Blankheim. Everyone on that committee has at some time or other had dealings with Rebecca Wolff. They are either tenants in her houses or farmers on her land or debtors for various loans or dependent for their business schemes on her ability to raise the funds. Do you mean to say that all this ended when the Nazis came to power? As you know, and as I know, it has all gone on in the same old way. And all of them transact with her in secret. Either over the garden wall or ...'

For some tensely long moments we stared at each other in silence. I was thinking of some alternative that would round off the sentence. As I looked at Hamann's face I thought of Frau Gerster and my meeting with her in the station restaurant at Cologne, about the last place any of the people from Blankheim would think of meeting.

'Or in a place not far from the station restaurant at Cologne.'

It was a wild guess, but Hamann went stonily grey. I learned some time later that it was in the Cosmopolitan Hotel. But my guess was near enough. It floored Hamann.

'So you do know more than you said at first.' His voice was hoarse with rage, or was it fear?

'Not a syllable more.'

'You do, of course you do.' His voice rose, and he shook his fist in my face. 'Out with it or I shall deal with you.'

'Then deal with me.'

Again we stared at each other and I could see that he was quivering.

'But I think,' I went on, 'that you must have a guilty conscience to be carrying on like this.'

'A what?' he shouted.

'A guilty conscience. What your guilt is, Heaven knows but...'

He went for me. I flung the chair in his way. He seized it and what might have happened I do not know, but at that moment the door was flung open and Tilde had seized him from behind. There was a cry, a short fierce struggle and a toppling of chairs and books, but I managed to grasp his wrists and we forced him to the floor. At that instant Frau Klebert stood before us.

'What do you mean, Hamann?' she asked.

'I've come to see the Englishman.'

'At this time of night?'

'It's something that won't bear delay.'

'You'll leave the house at once or I'll have you removed.'

She faced him boldly so that after an attempt to stare her out he turned and left the room. And then he looked back. He was struggling for words. I went up to him and offered my hand.

'Hamann, I know nothing more than I have said. Miss Rebecca has never even breathed your name to me, nor any other name. She is far too close and clever to blab her affairs to me. Here take my hand. You have my solemn word.'

Suddenly Tilde slapped my hand down.

'After what happened to Frau Gerster!'

'Frau Gerster,' he blurted out, 'I'm not responsible for what happened to Frau Gerster. What are you talking about?'

'About Frau Gerster. Why, the office ought to be pulled down over your head.'

'Tilde, Tilde,' cried Frau Klebert, 'enough of this. And you, Hamann, go!'

And so he went. But for a whole hour we discussed the affair and wondered what suspicion was troubling Hamann's mind.

Chapter 20

The First Threat of War

In the course of the next few weeks I was sounded out in private by every member of the committee. Save for Hans Zimmermann, who approached me in the street, each came alone by night. Each spoke of the suspicion I had raised against him, and each asked for what I knew about him and the rest. All with the exception of Klassen were friendly, submissive, apologetic, wholly silent about themselves, yet all pathetically anxious to allay the least suspicion and to learn in the strictest confidence what the others had said and done.

I gave the same answer to each. I knew little, but suspected much. Moreover, whatever the pressure employed by the party or the police I would preserve an absolute silence. Klassen alone was dictatorial and tried to bluster a reply from me about himself and the rest. In vain. I met all his protestations with a silent smile. I knew that I had the whip hand and that his secret, however well concealed, was crying out against him.

'I have nothing to conceal,' he said.

'I didn't say you had. But whatever charge is made against me I am ready with a counter-attack.'

'What?'

'Wait and see.'

I knew nothing, nothing at all, but I was glad to lurk in ambush and to send my shafts at a venture. Klassen's house, as I knew, once belonged to Rebecca Wolff, but now it was his own.

'I want no hush-hush,' he blurted out.

'On most things, I agree,' I answered, 'but when you've made a bargain you must try to be content with the terms.'

He gave me a piercing look, went white and clutched the table in front of him as though about to leap across it. I stood up and went to the door, but he remained stock still, rigid, cramped and at a loss to utter a word.

'There's no need to fear,' I said as I went out on to the staircase, 'I shall preserve an absolute silence.'

It was the old, old story. When the Nazis came to power the whole land resounded with reports of fraud and public plunder by those whom they had overthrown. Even the character of Adenauer, the Lord Mayor of Cologne, was blackened by such charges of corruption. He had fled, so we were told, leaving proof of peculation on every page of the city's accounts.

The new rulers, however, were men of Spartan mould, who were prepared to take office on honorary terms and to surrender it as poorer men than when they took it over.

Day after day such statements appeared in the press in monstrous type, proved, self-evident, undisputed, until it was folly to disbelieve them. And yet in this village of Blankheim, doubtless typical of the rest, double-dealing, bribery and blackmail were the prime instruments of office. Not only Rebecca Wolff, but every man in the village was paying Danegelt.

And they paid it under stress of a subtle fear. Despite all the exhilaration of the new ruthless order, the parades, the fanfares, the colourful flags, the endless beat of the drums, there was a haunting shadow in every mind, the headlong threat of war. I felt it every night when looking from my study window at the dimly illumined blur I knew to be Cologne. The Rhineland was still demilitarised. The troops did not enter officially until 1936. Yet there, sweeping the silent sky, was a searchlight over the city, one, then two, perhaps three, long white streamers that hovered and flitted over the dark clouds and probed the far-off blackness for some elusive foe. Even in this phantom form we felt the threat, a menace that seemed more imminent since it stole out mutely at night and then vanished just as silently and left no trace behind. By day we all pretended that the only aims in view were peace, fair play and full employment, but at night we mutely knew that we were all helpless pawns in some muffled, brutal plan of blood and iron.

Slowly, so it seemed, yet with swift and stealthy strides it bore upon us. In those days we used to hang out flags on every national occasion, and so often were these occasions that we rarely thought of hauling them in, leaving them hanging out, hail, rain, snow or blow, until the new call came round.

We had no swastika, of course. Nor had we the old imperial flag, nor the new republican one. We displayed the church flag, a long banner of yellow and white, which contrasted quite prettily with the other national and provincial ensigns floating from the bedroom windows all along the street. With the advent of the Nazis, however, the flag of the republic disappeared and then the Rhenish and Marien flags were one by one withdrawn. At last only the old imperial flag still maintained its place amid the spreading flaunt of the swastikas, that and the one church flag that floated from our house.

We were warned on Empire day that this would have to go. Frau Klebert ignored the warning, secure in her membership of the party and in her husband's naval rank. She shrank from the swastika and she felt that, owing to the Concordat, no action would be taken against showing the colours of the church. But as the first of May approached a further warning came, a call from Klassen and Hamann. I came in as they were going away.

'They are the church colours,' rapped out Klassen, 'not our national ones and must not be displayed.'

'And if they are displayed we shall tear them down,' cried Hamann.

Perhaps to placate them, perhaps to save her face, she bought two little swastikas and placed them against the windowpanes in front. She was technically covered and could plead to her husband that she had complied with the order, but the local Nazi group seemed to take it as defiance.

It was Hamann and Fenger this time who came along with a bundle, which they laid down in the hall.

'What is this?' demanded Frau Klebert.

'The flag,' replied Hamann with a threatening nod. 'It's rather bigger than your church flag, as is only right and proper, and it's the right flag for one who pretends to be one of the party.'

'But what right have you to dump this upon me? Away with it and away with you!'

'We are leaving it here, whether you want it or not, and there's the bill pinned on it. You'll take it or ...'

'I'll do nothing of the kind.'

'You will. Your position in the party depends upon it, and your husband's position in the navy. Those two trumpery flags in the window are a gross insult to the whole movement. Do you mean to hold us to scorn?'

'Yes, you and all those like you. Do you think I'm going to be blackmailed into buying a thing I don't want? I'll see that the flag firm takes that back with any expense to you.' And she kicked the thing out of her way.

'You will, will you?' cried Hamann. 'We are leaving it here. Send it back at your peril. You are a fine party woman to trample on the national flag.'

They brushed past me as they went out, while Tilde hastened away to the phone to tell the Cologne firm to take the flag away. They promised to do so by the morning. But late in the afternoon came a telegram from the Captain. The committee had sent him word detailing what they were going to do. So the Captain decided to submit and the flag remained.

It was left to me and Tilde to hang out the flag on the first of May. It was one of immense size. We struggled with it up to the attic, lugged it around on the dusty boards until we finally roped it to the pole. And then we unfurled it on the floor, yards and yards of the thing, while Tilde trampled across and across it. Then she spat on it, cleaned her boots and mine with it and did a swift dust-round that cumbered attic with the cleaner parts of the crumpled folds. After that she seized my hands and danced me round on the swastika cross. And then I helped her to thrust it out, handing it up from the floor while she leaned perilously out of the window and gazed into the street below.

'Heavens,' she said, 'it reaches down to the footpath.'

I took my turn to look.

'It will be a hindrance to the passers-by.'

'Well, what of it? When it's mucked and bedraggled at the bottom we shall just tear the bottom off. And I can always polish the windows with what is still hanging down.'

213

Here she burst into peals of laughter.

'Well, there it is and there it remains, and I've only just one wish about it.'

'That is?'

'That the colours are not fast and that when it rains, as to heaven I hope it will, it will hang there as a ghastly sopping rag, an eyesore to the whole street.'

And we laughed until tears came to our eyes. Then we got a call from the police, insisting that we weight the ends of the flag, fold them up and clamp them to the wall. That done, our work was over.

Call or no call from the government, festival or no festival, celebration or no celebration, that rag drooped from the dormer window, grimier and grimier with every day, limp, listless, woe-begone, like someone hanging slumped from the gallows. In time it came away from the wall and my last glimpse, years later, was a flutter of rents and tatters from which the emblem of the swastika had almost faded away.

The day of the procession came. Tilde and I went out to see it, the band, the SS and then the SA, followed by a rally of almost the whole village, mustered by factory, trade and profession, together with the Hitler Youth and the League of German Girls. And there was little Ursula Zimmermann, as sweet and neat a girl as one could wish to see, fairer than when she danced for joy at the gift of bread and cheese from the Miss Wolffs, but grave, pathetically grave, so that we were deeply touched. And the two young brothers looked very well, polite, subdued, with all the influence of a careful mother about them. But young Ludwig Klassen, the cutting son of a cutting father, looked very unpleasant indeed. Tilde thought so too.

'I'd like to drop his pants and smack his bottom,' she said with a tigerish look.

What really caught our eye was the committee, men like Lambert and Wessel in ill-fitting brown shirts, wondrous to look upon and wholly out of place. But even in the procession, which was held to demonstrate the unity of the new order, the committee was sharply divided, the lefts in one part and the rights in another, and Brechner with his fellow tradesmen far behind. He looked out of touch with the whole celebration, as though he had entered the new era through the splendid portals of hope only to find himself on the wrong side of the door.

The haunting fear of war was deepened some time later by an order from the committee to clear the attics of all inflammable stuff. A simple order, yet it added to the dread of things that were to come. Now that the war is over, after air raids became commonplace and the blazing of cities from end to end a right and proper action against the civilian foe, one wonders at our silent alarm in those early days of Nazi rule. But alarm it was, a deep uneasiness, a sense that all hope was vain and that the nightmare that had harried Europe since the outbreak of the Great War was again descending on us.

Even I, a stranger, felt it, above all on a day when Tilde, who was alone in the house apart from me, knocked at my door. Klassen and Kollass, who was the warden, had come to inspect the house, the attic in particular. Tilde asked me to help her. So up we went with the two men, who gazed at the lumber that cumbered it. Ghosts of long ago lay under the dust, a past fireside, a wrecked spinet, a crippled harp, the spokeless ruin of a spinning wheel, the reflected lights of a huge and gilt-framed mirror, lumped there in undusted unloveliness, clouded, cracked and spotted.

'The whole lot will have to be cleared,' rapped out Klassen.

'Every stick of it,' added Kollass.

'If that got ablaze in an air raid,' continued Klassen, 'the flames would engulf the whole village.'

'And guide the raiders to the factories.'

'Quite. And when the stuff is cleared, have two pails ready, one of sand and one of water to put out the flames.'

'The flames?' echoed Tilde. 'You talk as if it will be another Sodom and Gomorrah.'

'It would be if we didn't take steps to prevent it now.'

'And who's going to shift this stuff?' asked Tilde, staring with undisguised alarm at all the unwieldly derelicts. But Klassen shrugged his shoulders and left.

The attics were cleared with some outside help, and the lumber was transferred to one of the sheds in the yard or disposed of to second-hand dealers, who were doing a roaring trade at rock-bottom prices.

When, a week or two later, Herr Engels peered into the now void attic he must have sensed that something had gone from the house, some echoes of the past. He must have wondered what had happened to the years invested in the lumber. For, though it was merely lumber, when it went something more than lumber was erased from his brain.

Later on, much later now that I come to think of it, there was a sequel to this tale of the attics, namely the tale of the cellars. There was going to be a siren, a warning bell or whistle, and we were expected without exception to retreat to the cellars and to remain there until the relief was sounded. Guards would then come round and inspect the safety arrangements.

This all seemed innocent enough. There was just one proviso that made us a little uneasy. The front door had to be left ajar. However, as no one was allowed in the streets while the state of alarm was on, and as guards were patrolling up and down, the danger of surreptitious theft when one was confined to the cellar seemed to be removed. But how about the guards?

The night of the first test came and Frau Klebert, who was warden for the house, ushered us all below. There were six of us, including Else and Paul, and they seemed to rejoice in the excitement of a family rally in the cellar, though Herr Engels jibed emphatically and Tilde complained most loudly against the useless loss of time. It was very still in the cellar, for the

215

streets were now deserted, and only now and again did we hear the tramp of a guard as he patrolled on the pavement above. But at last the inspectors came.

It was only natural that Frau Klebert, as warden of the house, should go up and meet the inspectors. But judge her surprise when, despite all protests, she was ordered to go back into the cellar. There was a sharp altercation, resolute and fiery on her part, loud and threatening on the part of the guards. I rushed up the steps to help her. She was being held by Kollass and Fenger, while Hamann and Hans Zimmermann went up to the rooms above. They claimed it was just a tour of innocent inspection, justified by common safety and authorised by law, and any other inter-pretation was a scandalous suspicion. But Frau Klebert refused to be convinced.

'If you want to avoid suspicion then cease to act in a suspicious way. Who gave you the authority to go prowling round my house, breaking into rooms and prying into my private affairs? I've a right to my own house, an absolute right to keep my eye on those who choose to enter it.'

And on she went. Tilde and the children came up and the dispute became a loud hubbub. But in one of the momentary breaks we heard loud voices above and a peal of girlish laughter. It was Else. She must have slipped past us and was now surveying the intruders in the bedrooms. We heard her voice quite clearly.

'Well, I've more right than you to walk about my own home.'

There was a muffled reply, which seemed to come from my study, with a further rejoinder from Else.

'But you are not helping to fight the air raiders by fumbling in Mr Arnold's cupboards.'

There was a shout and a scurrying of steps, but eventually they came down, with Else in a titter behind them. Hamann was furious, above all with Else who, when he turned to shout some threat, shot out her tongue.

'I'll see that you don't get away with it,' he shouted.

'And I'll see you don't get away with it either, certainly nothing from Mr Arnold's cupboards.'

And she put out her tongue again. There was a furious interchange, which threatened to come to blows when Hamann shouted.

'If this house blazes up as the result of an air raid it will serve you right.'

'Well,' responded Else, 'if the office of the stolen *Landwirt* goes blazing up along with it we shan't be over-worried.'

What made Else say that? Tilde had said something like it when Hamann had paid his last visit, and he could not have forgotten it. He yelled himself into a rage, and but for the fact that I barred the staircase would have gone up and struck the girl. As it was, we nearly came to blows.

In the midst of the tumult, which now resounded loudly through the open door into the street, two men lumbered into the hall, the two hefty farmers, Müller and Hempel, who were acting as guards outside. Since the rise of the Nazi Party we had seen very little of them, but their intervention was now very welcome. Herr Engels had just come up from the cellar.

'Kurt, Friedrich,' he said quietly, 'kindly show our friends the door.'

Hamann began to storm out his protests, but Müller gently but firmly ushered him out. Hempel, in like quiet fashion, shoved Fenger and Zimmermann to the door.

'Go!' was all he said to them. And in the face of superior force they went.

As Hempel and Müller were on duty they could not stay for the glass of wine Herr Engels suggested at the door when they were leaving. So off they went and none of us spoke a word until their footsteps died away. Herr Engels turned to his daughter.

'I don't know, Klara, who is most to be feared, our future enemies or your present friends.'

The remark touched Frau Klebert to the quick. To find herself tarred with the same brush as Zimmermann, Hamann and Fenger, lumped into their society as one of them and made a party to all their misdeeds was more than she could stand. She flared up.

'My friends! My friends, do you say? Father, how dare you say such a thing? I may be a member of the party, but I am not the boon companion of the worst individuals in it. Shame on you, Father.'

'And why?' he sternly replied. 'The more I throw them out, the more you let them in. Till you joined the party they never got over the threshold. Now, with your approval, they enjoy the run of the house. My home was once a sanctuary from such riff-raff as that. Now my only refuge is the street.'

'But how can I help that? How can I run counter, not merely to the rules of the party, but to the laws of the nation? They would enter this house of yours whether I were a party member or not. But since I am a member they enter in a normal way. If you alone were in the house and tried to deny them entry, they would force their way in and annex it like Karl Gerster's office.'

'I don't doubt it. On your own showing, these friends of yours are just a pack of thugs. Annex this house? Of course, they would be like the camel in the story. You let in the head and then the neck until, when the whole camel is inside, there's no room for anything else. No, and no room for me either. This is my house, remember, mine. And I'll not have it filched from me to please some holiday-fly of a captain, whether the husband of my daughter or not.'

At once the fat was in the fire. To allude to the captain as a day-fly, and a mere holiday-fly at that, led to such a flare-up as I had never known, neither there nor anywhere else. We packed the children off, hurrying them to the play room on the other side of the house, beyond even the undertones and echoes of the storm. There they sat trembling, almost prostrate, while Tilde sought to ease their minds and smooth over the crisis in the home.

From my room, which was just above the sanctum, I heard snatches of the furious dispute in which the character of the Captain was torn and trampled to shreds. It was dreadful to hear. Frau Klebert must have guessed what a prattling tailor's dummy her husband really was, but so long as she alone knew it she could bear her cross with patience. But to have it thundered at her, by one in whose sure judgement she placed an absolute trust, lacerated her heart. All those months of self-effacement and all those harrowing efforts to attune her tingling conscience to the policy of the party had led to utter wreck. Her voice at times rose to a wail, an eerie wail at which I stopped my ears.

But silence came at last, such a deep oppressive silence as left a conscious echo in every corner of the house. In vain I tried to study and to stop my listening ear to every sound from outside. The dispute seemed to persist in a loudly inaudible key, so loud, yet so inaudible, that I kept on pricking my ears and catching whole passages which doubtless both my friends had wisely left unsaid. There was an accent of something uncanny in the home, something unspoken, unspeakable, unsuspected. It was as though the vanished lumber still spooked above in the attic, and the crippled harp and spinet still whimpered in their palsied frames.

It was good to see the children after that. They slipped up to my room, and Else's peep through the door, so eager, so girlish, so young, came like the primrose glint of spring through the mould of the departed year. She was distressed, however, as Paul was, pale, tearful, apologetic, but resolved in her buoyant way to make the best of it.

'We are coming in,' she said, 'and Tilde too.'

'By all means. It's a relief to see you.'

They slipped in as though they had some plan in mind, for they exchanged a silent glance and nod as they settled down at the table, Paul and Else in front and Tilde at my side. As she took her seat beside me, I felt the appealing pressure of her hand.

'You know why we've come?' said Else, clasping her hands to support her chin and looking at me more earnestly than ever she had done before.

'For sympathy?'

'Partly. But no. No, this is the one spot in the house that is home, home, home to us.'

Tears started to her eyes as she repeated the word home.

'You amaze me.'

'But why? Now that our home is breaking up ...'

'Surely not.' A pang went through me.

'Oh, it is. But, by the way, what did your mother call you? Your Christian name, I mean.'

'John.'

218

'Well, you are John to all of us here, to me and Paul and Tilde. We should not be at home if we spoke to you in the formal way. We have lost, lost ...'

Her voice broke and for a moment she battled with her tears. Paul, though equally tearful, came to her aid.

'You see, we took it to heart what you said to us last year. Something had gone, something was lost ...'

'And we knew it was true,' sobbed Else. 'We lost our home when we went to stay in Cologne.'

She cast me a despairing look as she struggled for a word.

'Your lovely childhood days.'

'Yes, that's it. We were so happy when father and mother loved each other and Grandpa was patient and kind. And the nativity we made, do you remember? And my pony and Paul's canoe, which we had to sell when we went away to Cologne. And it's all gone, gone, except when we are with you.'

'But, Else, it will all blow over. It's a passing crisis. Don't take it too hard.'

I could not check my tears. But then she said something that left me aghast.

'You see, father is not coming back.'

'What?'

'No,' stammered Paul. 'He's gone for good.'

So one phase of their life was over, the first and loveliest phase, the truly seraphic phase of home and infancy. For a year they had been aware of some lapse from their early days, a slide into the incivilities of life, some slump into what was worse. They had been lumped neck and crop into the Hitler Youth, cast into the society of God knows whom and exposed day after day to their blatancy of speech and brutality of idea. But were they really affected? Hardly, they thought, for there was an easy escape from all that to their beloved home on the Rhine where the graces of the spirit and the refinements of society were still preserved. And now their home had failed them. Riven by angry clamour it was no longer a haven of love and understanding. It was no longer their refuge and their strength but a thing of bricks and mortar whence the soul of home had fled. No wonder Else sobbed, that her father should have abandoned her to seek the embrace of someone else. Else sobbed for shame.

I was silent. I have always refrained from peeping into the private affairs of others, above all with the Engels family of whom I was an honoured guest. But, though I was glad to know nothing, I soon knew all that had happened. From hints, hearsay and words half-heard, as well as from the breath of rumour that breathed through the whole village, I had learned that the Captain had been unfaithful to his wife and had yielded to the Nazi view – one which later on was carried to scandalous lengths – that loyalty to a static family was disloyalty to the growing state.

The Captain's friends, by way of excuse, even spoke of political pressure, but many of us felt it was a personal lapse, an unforgivable looseness, however favoured it may have been by the prevailing philosophy of the times. In any case he had gone. Not perhaps by his own free will, for he still loved his wife and children. Frau Klebert had spoken, and I do not doubt for a moment that her furious upbraidings had blazed him from the house.

But there was a terrible self-reproach in her fury. She had wrenched her very soul to follow her husband's leading, had flouted her father, surrendered her children and even betrayed her religion to keep her faith with a man who had trampled on his own. Strange are the ways of the human heart. Even when he had gone, there was no peace for her troubled spirit. She wandered about the house, a prey to her own conflicting emotions, accusing yet excusing herself, proving that what was flatly wrong was really right after all, and frantically squaring her crooked conduct to the straightness of her character and beliefs.

She came into my room one day, perhaps to relieve her battling thoughts, perhaps to find some understanding, but I have never felt so uneasy. Was she looking at me or not? She was facing me across the table, but her eyes were out of focus and though gazing at me, seemed to be gazing right beyond me, into some elusive dream. And her words were incoherent. She did respond a little to some sympathetic thoughts of mine and thanked me for my consideration, but a moment later her eyes were wandering again and she went out in the middle of a sentence and forgot to close the door.

The breakdown came at last. She was kneeling one day at confession in Cologne, trying no doubt to admit what she was only too ready to deny. For days she had been in turmoil, her nerves racked by endless self-dissection, her conscience lacerated, her thoughts in a hopeless scrimmage. In this mood she knelt at the confessional. Heaven knows what she was mumbling, but she collapsed and was carried out amid heart-rending shrieks.

When first we heard the news we thought her reason had gone. But an hour or two later we were assured by the director of the clinic to which she had been taken that, though her nerves had broken down, psychiatric treatment would surely bring her round. In the meantime, she must remain under observation.

I thought I should find Herr Engels distressed, but he seemed to be quite happy.

'You are not worried,' I ventured to say.

'No, for the struggle has begun.'

'How's that?'

'Well, in obedience to her husband she let her soul be taken without putting up a struggle. That's what worried me. But now I am reassured. For though the devil had got a grip, the Almighty never lost His. No wonder she's nearly rent in two. No wonder her soul's in shreds. But what was broken will be repaired. What was lost will be found again. And when she is finally restored to health she will return as Klara Engels, not as some gadding captain's wife.'

Chapter 21

Scapegoats

But all that was months ago. The summer had gone and with it the night of blood when Hitler shot down friend and foe and stamped his brutal heel upon the party. For a while the nation held its breath. What uneasy days we passed, and nights too. Nights of sleepless fear when every footstep meant the police and every dubious shadow the presence of a spy. No wonder I often lay awake, or stole to the window to peer out, or studied the opposite casements for any telltale chink of light. Like the rest of the people in Germany I was waiting and waiting and waiting – for what? Some stealthy whisper behind my back? Some secret accusation? Some silent slip into a Nazi cell from which I should never emerge? Mere fancies one might think, but I had put myself outside the law and made myself an outcast.

I had done what the Nazis could never forgive. I was living with the Miss Wolffs, who had offered me hospitality until Frau Klebert should return. Herr Engels had gone to Cologne for a time and Tilde back to Neuenahr. So there I stood in no-man's-land. Admitted, I had the whip hand over the nabobs in the village, over all the committee in fact. For every one had had some truck with the Jewess, Rebecca Wolff. But here, as with Frau Klebert, I was tied by unspoken loyalties; to Rebecca herself, whose guest I was, to Brechner, who had proved himself a friend, and even to Frau Zimmermann, who would be plunged into distress again if her husband were denounced. And then there was Hamann, a man who would stop at nothing and might bring my hostess to ruin. I must lie low and say nothing.

Then, perhaps I was a hostage, too, of the shrewd Rebecca. For the word had gone round that Englishmen, whatever their rank might be, were to be treated with great respect. England had to be appeased and lulled, if possible, into approval of the Nazi revolution. Every Englishman who left the Reich was to take home glowing reports of the splendours of the Nazi regime.

Yes, Rebecca knew a thing or two. I was an excellent decoy duck for her cleverly cryptic schemes. Unless – a more gracious thought – it was Rachel who had proposed the invitation. For her sake, more than for my own, I had accepted.

My two rooms looked on to the street, while those of Frau Boden, who was now again being sheltered by the Miss Wolffs, faced the Rhine. I was therefore unable to see the garden wall or to note the cryptic comings and goings of the members of the committee. In fact, it was my own movements that were now being strictly observed. So cautious was Rebecca, so circumspect in all her doings, that she came up the staircase every night to give me a parting word. Or so it seemed. She used to cough as she knocked at the door and at first I thought it was a warning for me that she was coming in. But later on I realised, as I ought to have done before, that this cough, this knock, this creak of an opening door were signs to a secret visitor to slip out unobserved.

'Good evening, Mr Arnold. I have come to see if everything is in order.'

'Yes, thank you.'

She would look at me steadily with her piercing dark eyes, and I was bound to return her gaze. We each seemed to sense the other's hidden thought. As a rule, she brought me tea and biscuits and, in the clink of the tray and the china, the sound of distant footsteps was lost. But one night the exception happened. I had gone to bed early with a cold and was fast asleep when a creak on the stairs roused me. She was at the door. She was whispering my name. She was waiting for an answer. In my drowsiness I did not reply. Then it dawned on me that Rebecca was descending the stairs. There was a step outside in the street. Someone had stumbled on the pavement. After which came the cautious creak of a door.

I slipped to the open casement and cautiously peered out. The footsteps were echoing up the street, but I could not see who it was. Then someone crossed the road. It was a mere figure to me in the starless darkness, but something in the gait was vaguely familiar, the stiff mechanical gait of an elderly man. A thought of Lambert crossed my mind, but before I could confirm it the figure had disappeared. As an elderly man, Lambert would avoid the garden wall and the steep grassy slope to the riverbank. But Lambert and Rebecca were at daggers drawn and bent on mutual destruction. So it could not be Lambert.

As a student I was used to solitude and could spend whole days alone in the society of my own thoughts, but never had I so felt the dread of isolation, in the no-man's-land around me, the unbreathed whisper of obvious suspicion, as when I lived with my Jewish hosts at Blankheim. I was a hybrid, an untouchable, a pariah dog, the butt of long backward glances in the village. When I entered a shop there was a sudden hush, when I passed a crowd there was a mutual nudge, and when I entered the train there was a non-committal stare into sheer and obvious nothingness. Even when at home with the ladies I was also an outsider, while they lived half enshrouded in their mental reservations or obscured by the obliquities of Rebecca. There was a mark, a blur, a darkling play of mystery even in the glances of Rachel, who was always on the point of blurting out avowals that fell away in trembling silence from her lips.

222

'Without my sister, I should be lost.'

She whispered this to me one day as she was sitting near the window that led out into the garden. She looked secluded as she sat there in her armchair, fenced off from the rest of the room by a lacquered screen. The electric fire beside her cast a cosy glow on her cheeks, or was it a flush of suppressed fear that sent a tremble to her lips and fevered along her fingers as she knitted with unnatural haste? Her dark expressive eyes were glinting with anxiety.

'I don't doubt it,' I replied, 'but don't worry. I have every confidence in her ability.'

She was grateful for my remark and I was rewarded by an exquisite glance, but she still looked troubled and upset. I hastened to console her.

'She'll get the better of the best of them, Lambert, for example.'

As I mentioned Lambert she looked up and winced. She was startled, as though I had surprised some inner thought she was holding closely in reserve. So I knew after all. She did not say so, but she was far too sincere not to confess it in every look. She was almost panic-stricken.

'Don't mention him, Mr Arnold. He haunts me.'

Her voice died away to a whisper and I felt that the man I had seen in the darkness had been Lambert. Poor Rachel was mumbling. I overheard 'papers' and 'copies' and 'stolen', all of which led me to assume that Lambert had been putting pressure on Rebecca, but for what? For copies of some papers that were stolen from his safe and of which Rebecca presumably had the duplicates? For copies of transactions he had had with her? For proofs of his own Semitic deals? It made no sense to me. Half to Rachel, half to myself I blurted out: 'Well, press her as he will, he will never get them.'

'No, never, he'll never get them, but not a word to my sister about this, promise?'

I was soon to be enlightened. Rebecca brought my breakfast in one morning. With it there was a letter for me, which she laid on the table without lowering or raising her eyes from mine. Had she assumed, or did she know, from whom it was? I tried to parry her challenging gaze.

'A letter stamped in Blankheim? From whom can it be?' I wondered aloud.

'Open it and see.'

'You know, of course.' And I handed the letter back.

'Open it yourself,' I said.

She took it without shifting her glance, slit it open and only then did she take her eyes from mine.

'From Lambert. He wants to see you.'

'About what?'

'Important business, but what kind he does not say.'

'We could see him together, if you like.'

She was smiling softly. 'No, go and see him. But remember you're our guest. You know absolutely nothing.'

'No. Nothing.'

I saw him in his home. I was ushered into a gloomy apartment, half sitting room, half office with a massive oak desk and bookcase and shelves and shelves of files. I sat down in a ruinous armchair and, while trying to find some neutral spot in the havoc of springs beneath me, I wondered when the grimy ceiling, the dowdy hangings and curtains, the dingy discoloured wallpaper, as well as the defaced and stricken carpet, had last been replaced. Lambert's gaunt figure seemed cumbrously in keeping with the unlovely tumble and crumble as he took his seat at the table.

'I want you to answer my questions,' he blurted out. He gazed at me with those crystal goggles of his, like some primeval spider.

'Well, what do you want to know?'

'I want to know what you know.'

'About what?'

'About what you said in the Golden Hind.'

'I've nothing further to add.'

'You have.'

'And what may that be?'

'Look here. If you don't answer me you might have to answer the police.'

'And so might you.'

A silence ensued that strained my nerves to the highest pitch. Normally, I would have walked out, but I felt that I must hold my ground and cross-examine him. What designs had he against Rebecca? I thought with a pang of Rachel and of the haunting, hunted look in the face of Frau Boden. I decided to let fly.

'Sir, I have nothing further to add. What right have you to bully me here? What designs have you against the other members of the committee? And what plot are you weaving against the Miss Wolffs? I refuse to be involved in your sneaking underhand schemes. If this is an affair for the police, then call in the police at once. I am conscious of nothing illegal either on my part or on that of your friends. But if anything wrong has been done then I should suspect you. You and no other.'

There was another silence. Was he angry or just embarrassed? It was impossible to say in the gloom of the room. And was anyone else in the room? Anyone else in earshot? I gave a hasty glance round.

'Look here,' he blurted out. 'This is a serious matter, an affair of life and death. I have been attacked, murderously attacked, my house has been entered, my safe rifled. That safe there. All the papers have gone, private papers, valuable papers, papers which mean everything to me.'

'And which, if found, may perhaps incriminate you?'

'What! What do you mean?' He had risen from his chair and was grasping the table with both hands. For a moment I thought he meant to assault me.

224

'Now sit down, no bluster. It's for me to protest. What do you mean by trying to involve me in some act of common robbery? Me, an Englishman, an outsider, a mere student? If you have any suspicions, then voice them to the police.'

I rose to go, but he interposed.

'You live at the Wolffs',' he said.

'Well, what of it?'

'You know who goes in and out.'

'I know nothing of the kind. And even if I did, I wouldn't abuse my place as a guest to reveal such things to you. But, in any case, what have the Wolffs and their visitors got to do with your stolen papers?'

'What? Do you ...'

He broke off and his goggles seemed to glisten more silvery white in the gloom. He was between me and the door, facing the window. I could see him plainly now despite the dimness, and yet more plainly still I could sense his every emotion and reaction. His 'What?' was a blatant betrayal of his suspicions. Yes, what had the Wolffs got to do with the stolen papers? That was what he meant. Yes, what? Half to myself and half to him I blurted out the question again.

'What have the Wolffs and their visitors got to do with the stolen papers?'

We glared at each other in silence. So that was it. Over him, the rifled safe and the murderous attack at night hovered the vaguely shrouded form of Rebecca Wolff. No one in the whole village had such an interest in scotching Lambert. She had the whole lot in her octopus grip, but he, more than anyone else, to save his cringing skin was ready to bring them all to a common ruin. Brechner and Hans Zimmermann with what, I wondered. Rent-free houses? Klassen with a mysterious mortgage? Müller and Hempel with their unredeemed IOUs?

These were all mere guesses, yet nothing was plainer to me now than the moneyed understanding of Rebecca with the whole committee. But crime? Would she resort to that? The more I gazed at Lambert the more likely it seemed to be. Why should Rebecca respect a law that no longer applied to her? Or be bound by considerations her foes had cast to the winds? Unable to rely on society she must now rely on herself, and by fair means or foul she must do her enemies down. Yes, what had the Wolffs and their visitors got to do with the stolen papers? I really wanted to know. I grew reckless.

'So you really think Miss Wolff was behind that attack on your life?'

'I have never said such a thing.'

He was so agitated that the thought must have been in his mind.

'And that I was privy to it?'

'No, no, no, I've never suggested such a thing.'

'No, but you've implied it. I had better get in touch with a lawyer.'

I made for the door, but he prevented my exit by placing his hand on the knob.

225

'You have information,' he cried, 'valuable information. You understand, *valuable* information. I am increasing that reward I offered.'

'Let me go,' I interrupted. 'I have no information and I would refuse all
bribes if I had.'

'You are a student, a poor student, dependent on your parents, I
presume.'

'Let me go.'

I left. Rebecca met me on my return and, after a cautious peep into the
sanctum where Frau Boden sat with Rachel, accompanied me to my room.
Without a word she sat down at my table and calmly gave me a nod to
begin, a close and uncanny calm that suggested a far superior spirit to
those I usually met. But there was nevertheless a glimpse of the cloven
hoof somewhere in it that made me shrink within me. What an absolute
sorceress she was, a superb mistress of the black art and, if provoked, of
the blackest crimes.

And yet as she faced me there I confessed I thoroughly liked her. Though
absolutely at bay, beset by open enemies and still more by slippery friends,
she had the aloof and sovereign air of someone better than all the rest.
After all, her crimes – and I did not doubt them – were only in self-defence,
pathetic when I thought of her sister, almost splendid when I thought of
herself. Yes, she had something askance in her being, and yet I liked her.

I told her all that had happened and she listened without flicking
an eyelid. Even when I mentioned Lambert's vile suspicions she kept her
cool uncrooked look and faced me as impassively as though I had asked
her to pass the salt. Not a tremor, not a blush, not a whisper of a protest.
Only when I had finished came a change in her expression, slight and
instantaneous, as was usual with her when weighing up her words. Her
eyes went strangely dry as if she were looking beyond me.

'So he mentioned no names at all?'

'No.'

'Not one of the committee?'

'No.'

She kept looking at me as though trying to probe my mind, but, perhaps
realising that I could never harbour a vile suspicion of her and her sister,
she got up.

'Remember, you know nothing, not even the most innocent things.'

'Nothing whatsoever.'

But Lambert was not to be baulked. We were sitting a day or two later in
Rachel's sanctum by the garden window when a ringing bell in the street,
with the sound of steps and voices, attracted our attention. Frau Boden and
Rebecca hastened to the front-room window, which looked out on to the
street. I remained with Rachel, who shrank at the slightest noise from
outside, and tried to reassure her.

'They believe the worst about us, the very, very worst.'

Her hand trembled in mine, and mine must have trembled, too. Somehow she must have found out or guessed about the sinister threat of the Lambert affair and assumed that it was behind the noise outside. I decided to find out what was going on, but the others were coming back, Frau Boden, pale and trembling, Rebecca, as stonily indifferent as ever.

'It's the town crier,' was all she said.

'Yes, the town crier,' added Frau Boden. 'He was offering a reward from Lambert. Hundred marks. For information about his aggressors. There was a great crowd at his heels.'

She cast a panic glance into the garden where the pram with the baby stood. But all was quiet there.

'Children for the most part,' added Rebecca drily.

She sat down as though there was nothing more to be said and, to avoid any further talk, suggested coffee. She knew that Frau Boden, who was very sensitive to the needs of others, would volunteer. Sure enough, up she sprang, and there was a tender light in her eyes at the idea of doing a service when suddenly the sad look came once more and she asked: 'But what are they gazing at? Some chalked message on the wall?'

'Perhaps.'

'Mere children,' Rebecca repeated, and took up her needlework.

Despite a warning word from Rebecca, I went out to see. A group of children stood outside, together with Matthias and a few of his customers and one or two passers-by. They were all looking agape at the house as though something were about to happen. Down the street the town crier was calling out his message and now and then ringing his bell. Then I saw what it was. A poster offering a reward had been pasted on the house. It was Lambert's poster and the paper glistened with the fresh paste. There was a dead silence in the street as I carefully took the edge and peeled it off.

My audacity was greeted by shouts of laughter from the Matthias group as I screwed up the poster and turned back to the house, where Rebecca took it with the tips of her fingers and bore it off to the bin.

'Not a word,' she whispered. But Frau Boden, who had watched the scene, told Rachel what had happened before we could stop her. The poor girl was wildly distraught and slumped in a heap on the nearest chair, but, with just a word of reproach to Frau Boden, Rebecca set to work to bring her sister round and motioned me to go.

It was a scene that haunted me for many a day. What shadow lay over Rachel's mind, what hidden dread, for her disproportionate distress suggested something more than the Nazi terror, something more than the betrayals of Blankheim, some pestilent blast from the burial of past years that was a blight on her normally exquisite spirit. I always felt that the radiance of her smile was a really revealing gloss on the darkness it sought to conceal.

I was glad when Tilde wrote to me and relieved my mind for a while of all these mystic fascinations. She wrote in her eager, girlish way, her thoughts and feelings racing along and the words all tumbling after; a really thronging letter, gay but anxious, too, for things were going the wrong way and Hermann was showing the cloven heel.

Among the works to ease unemployment a road was to be built across her father's farm, as yet only a proposal, but having all the Nazi force of Hermann and Zeller behind it. The compensation would be only a fraction of the real value. There were other worries, too, so would I come, if only for a day or a week? I packed up at once and went.

That evening I was sitting with the Weicherts and wondered at my wonderment of Tilde and her mother. Perhaps something in the dark oak setting of the room, in the stained boarded floor, in the low beamed ceiling and the subdued glow of the lamp, enhanced the vision of light blue eyes and golden hair. But more than that there was a pure transparency of soul, a simplicity that almost overawed me.

For weeks I had been living with the Wolffs, and grown used to their dark and inscrutable ways, to their muffled views of life and shrouded antecedents. And then their jet-black hair and eyes. Indeed, to look Rebecca in the face was to peep into problematic deeps. And even Rachel, too. For though her eyes glinted with confidences and her lips often trembled with avowals, it was like the silvery ripple of the wind over water that blinded one in its glitter to the unseen fathoms beneath. Bewitching mystery all of it. But how forbidden it seemed after a glimpse of Tilde's mother, a peasant woman of simple ways and homely speech and spirit. My eyes sought again and again her kindly glance and golden hair.

I looked at Tilde, too, who seemed to be a very princess in this little domain of hers. Then I thought of Rachel Wolff and I could not keep my question back.

'Tilde, what was that ghastly rumour that went round about the Wolffs? Murder, theft, what was it?'

All the radiance went from Tilde's face; her mother blanched while Herr Weichert, removing his pipe, cast a pained glance at his daughter. There was a sinister silence, as though the door had been wrenched off and the demons from the outer darkness were waiting with bated breath on every word.

'I confessed to spreading that rumour,' said Tilde.

'Yes, she confessed it,' added Frau Weichert, 'and now it's over and done with as far as we are concerned. I refused to hear it in this house.'

'She thoughtlessly picked it up and just as thoughtlessly passed it on,' said her father. 'It was wrong, very wrong, especially as the Wolffs once spent a week with us.'

'And she did penance,' added her mother, 'going over every day and doing them a service.'

'Defying the village, in fact.'

'You'll excuse me,' said Tilde, and rarely have I seen her look so troubled.

228

I felt rebuked to the very bones. I had been living for weeks with the Wolffs, an honoured guest with the liberty of the house and a share of their society. I switched the topic hastily. How was it with Hermann and Zeller? And what was this conspiracy against Herr Weichert?

It was the old story of the scapegoat, that sinister device of tyranny whereby every man's hand is turned against his neighbour. Herr Weichert was the chosen victim and the whole village breathed a sigh of relief at being spared the blow. He was to pay, not they. It certainly paid to side with Hermann and Zeller. So the Weicherts, who were once so respected, had no longer a friend in the village.

'Come on, I'll show you what their plan is,' said Herr Weichart. 'We shall not be noticed so much at night.'

A few minutes later we were standing at the upper edge of the farm where we commanded a good view of the village and the surrounding fields. The sky was clear and the moon was full. Along the road were the lights of the inn and half enshrouded in the night haze the darker mass of the church. Not a soul was on the road or seemed to be. Herr Weichert looked round before he spoke, and even then his voice was only a whisper.

'They want to build a bypass across this field of mine, levelling those apple trees I planted many years ago and which are giving a very heavy yield. It's a great blow.'

There lay the orchard and, lower down the road, his little house with its pricks of light through the shutters.

'Couldn't they avoid it?'

'They could, but someone else would catch it then. I suggested taking that waste patch and removing the rocks that cumber it. Do you see it towards that clump of trees? That would harm nobody and would give no end of work.'

It was a dark tract sloping up to a clump of trees, but owing to the night haze I could hardly discern its surface. A road over it would be somewhat roundabout and Weichert's farm lay right in line.

'I can appeal against it and I shall, but ...'

He broke off and shrugged his shoulders. He turned off towards his little orchard which lay not far from the road and stared at the trees in silence. He was thinking of the days when he planted them, years and years ago. He was talking to himself.

'Excellent trees, excellent apples, all of them.'

Wrapped up in his own thoughts, he went down on to the road. Someone was going to the village and passed in front of us without a word. Had he failed to see or hear us as we came down over the grass? But Herr Weichert was equally silent. Strange behaviour for a villager at night. I made a comment. He looked round and spoke in a whisper.

'That man's my nearest neighbour. Once my best friend in the village. Sat on the same bench together at school. And now? You see, if the road doesn't go over my field, it might have to go over his. So he has palled up with Hermann and Zeller. Treats them in the inn, up there. And echoes all their revilings of me. We have not exchanged a word since, not even a wrong one, strange to say. Apart from Hermann and Zeller he's my biggest foe in the village.'

All the while he was speaking I gazed at the retreating figure. Had he really seen us or not? And then, I can swear to it, despite the slight haze, for the road was clear and the moon full, the man stopped and looked back. At us, I am perfectly certain. For on seeing us at a halt by the wayside, he abruptly turned away and went on.

'He saw us.'

'Of course he did. And knew who I was as well. And then there are other things.'

'And they are?'

He did not answer me. Leaving the road as though to make sure of something in the field he took a circular way to the house. But before entering he stopped.

'You see, we used to send our stuff to Cologne and sell it as we liked. Now it must go to Brühl where it is sold by public auction. If you are a party man your stuff is sold first when the bidders are many and the prices are good. But if you are not a member of the party the stuff maybe will remain on your hands.

'Not another word, though. We're home. Let's forget it.'

Chapter 22

The Terrorists Also Afraid

A few days later I was bidding goodbye to Tilde on the station at Neuenahr. I was on my way back to Blankheim to my sombre Jewish home with the Miss Wolffs, and the more I avowed its fascination and peered into its over-private reserves, the more I was won for the free and open ways of the simple girl beside me. There was no one on the platform and even the stationmaster had retired for a moment to his office, so that her whole society was mine. As the time approached for the train she handed me the basket of fruit I had put down while we waited.

'With my kindest regards to the Miss Wolffs.'

She read my thoughts and I read hers, and I confess for a moment that I dabbled in the dark.

'I apologise for my question about the ladies,' I said.

She looked at me as though to recall me from my lapse. The sheer integrity of the girl seemed to work on me like a whip. So I was still hankering after some answer to my suspicions!

'Well, don't forget me,' she said. The train moved off and she was soon lost to view.

Forget her! Years and years have passed since those farewell moments on the station, but the vision of them lives with me still in simple glimpses as clear as then. The curl of her fingers as she touched her hair, the slight swerve in her figure as she turned away from the wind, the way she raised her eyes when she spoke but, above all, the occasional slur with her heel when she touched some flaw in the ground. I often hear it still, and see that falter in her step. A slur, a halt, the slightest pause to adjust her heel, and the impulse throbs within me, as it throbs up now when I write these lines, to offer her my hand and to give all I have to help her on her earthly way. Mere flicks which might be forgotten in anyone else, but memorable in her. For there are moments that never leave us and, despite the flight of years, remain companions to the grave.

It was Rachel who met me at the door and her face thrilled up with joy when she saw me.

'Thank heaven, you're back,' she said, and clapped her hands in delight when she saw the basket I had brought from the Ahr. 'Such lovely fruit, from Herr and Frau Weichert, of course, with a touch of Tilde in every piece.

'We've been so alone and afraid!' she said as she led me into the sanctum.

'Afraid? Afraid of what?'

'Afraid of being alone, so alone. Just look at that abandoned house over there.'

She was pointing towards my old home, which rose up beyond in the night; dark, silent, shuttered up, with the big weather-beaten flag drooping down like a sodden rag. I could not actually see the house, of course, for our own blinds were drawn, but the dead deserted form was engraved on both our minds.

'We felt so safe when Herr Engels lived over the way and you were there, and Tilde's pleasant face used to look out through the windows and bring joy to our hearts when she slipped across. It's different now. It's as though your old home has set its face against us.'

She grasped both my hands as she spoke and I felt the tremble of fear quivering in her frame. Frau Boden came hurrying in. She was equally glad to see me. Her face was almost white with anxiety and fear.

'I'm bringing in supper,' she said in her eager way. 'Rebecca is in Cologne. I have had to send the baby away. If it had not been for Rachel I should have gone too.'

A few minutes later she brought in the dishes, and we lingered for a time over that supper, cosily screened from all the outside world, my presence reassuring them. Not surprisingly, they ate well; it was, after all, their first real meal for many a day. But both ladies had delicate manners and in some prettily furtive way the daintiest bits on the table stole their way upon my plate, the freshest tea into my cup, the replacements of knives and forks being swiftly and stealthily effected before I was aware they were there.

And then by the light of the table lamp, which left the rest of the room in darkness, they whispered their fears to me. The house, so they thought, had been shadowed by certain Nazis, and Klassen had called on them to enquire about David Cohen.

'David Cohen? The boy?' I asked.

'The boy.'

'But why?'

'He was seen talking to Else Klebert and denounced to the Nazi Party here. And Else as well, of course.'

'By whom?'

'By Dr Boden.'

It was Frau Boden who spoke. It was typical of this refined lady that she mentioned her former husband's name without the slightest reproach or look of contempt.

'And what has happened?'

Both threw up their hands in blank despair. Their voices fell to a whisper and both moved their chairs up to mine.

232

'To avoid arrest, the boy has fled.'

'At least they can't find him,' added Rachel. 'He must be in hiding with friends.'

As if Rachel didn't know! She cast an appealing glance at Frau Boden for confirmation.

'Must be,' echoed Frau Boden. 'So they arrested his father.'

'Dr Cohen?'

'Dr Cohen. Spirited away in the night and nothing further heard, of course. We've been so afraid.'

'And those men hovering round the house,' said Rachel. 'We felt every hour would be our last here. It's all so still at night.'

I felt it at that moment as I had never felt it before. Here we were, softly whispering together in a lamplit nook of that spy-shadowed house, with nothing but the slow tick of the clock as our company in the deathly silence.

The dread of it stole upon me. Now that my old home lay in lonely darkness over the way, with all my once-happy life there fading away, the windows a faceless blank, my rooms an unlit emptiness, the stairs without one hearkened step of those I had loved and known, I felt myself alone in a foreign land. Above all, when I sat with the Miss Wolffs, who, despite their fascinating ways or rather because of them, seemed mysteriously remote from my own simple views of life. And then the nook in which we sat, so cloistered away from the rest of the house and so secluded from all sound of the village beyond, was filled with the low undertones of the wind that moaned from over the Rhine. It sighed past the windows in the darkness, and the flap of the foliage on the panes was like the tap, tap, tap of some fingertip from the beyond.

When Rebecca returned I went up to my room and felt the fear that pervaded the whole house. I was alone, weirdly alone, in a solitude, which the presence of the ladies only deepened and in a shadow from which every face and glance had fled. I threw open the window and looked out into the night. My old home lay in darkness without one recognising glimpse, the street below with hardly a starlit glitter in the pools, the line of houses all asleep save where, in the distance, an edge of light revealed the window glows of the Golden Hind. Not a voice, not a footstep, not even the betraying shadow of a spy.

I turned to my table and found a note from Hillesheim. Would I call on him as soon as possible in Bonn. He had received a mysterious parcel the nature of which I might be able to explain. A mysterious parcel? The nature of which had baffled him? And then I remembered the parcel I had once put into his care. But that had been returned more than a year ago. What was this mysterious parcel? And from whom?

I sat down and wrote letters to Tilde, to Else and Paul, to Herr Engels and to Hillesheim. Not that I needed to write, but I felt I must escape into the night and seek the freedom of the open sky if only for an hour. And posting letters was a pretext, one which would quell the alarms of the anxious ladies below. So I wrote my letters and went off to the post.

There were people coming from the Golden Hind, first Klassen, then Kollass, then Boden, all of whom passed me without one sign of recognition. But when I reached the Golden Hind who should come out but Brechner and Zimmermann? They answered my greeting in a formal way, and I hurried on into the night. But in a minute or two I heard a voice and a hastened step behind me. It was Brechner. He was clearly anxious to see me. I halted in the shadow of some trees.

'Heil Hitler, Herr Arnold!'

'Good evening.'

We shook hands. I asked about his health and about his wife, whom I had not seen for a long time. He replied in a mere word or two. He clearly had something on his mind which he wished to relieve at once.

'I should like to have a word with you.'

'By all means. About Else Klebert?'

'No, though she is in a very awkward position. She was up before our committee, on Boden's charge, you know, and all went very well. In fact she was so funny, we laughed the matter off. But that damned Boden ...'

He spat on the ground to express his disgust.

'Yes?'

'He's going to take the matter further and if he has his way she will land in some re-education school.'

He broke into a flood of curses that ought to have shrivelled Boden for evermore.

'She ticked him off very nicely, and by God we laughed. Boden will never forgive her.'

There was a step on the road and Brechner crouched back into the shadow of the trees. It was Zimmermann, who looked round and stood in doubt for a moment, but espying us came over. He seemed as anxious as Brechner and greeted me in a most apologetic way. They were really quite humble, and far different from the blustering, swaggering Nazis of the radio and the films.

'I was telling him of Else Klebert,' whispered Brechner.

'By heaven, she carried it off.'

'Took the whole committee by storm, but I am afraid of Boden.'

'He doesn't mean us any good.'

'No. Now look here, Herr Arnold, there's something we want to ask you about. It means very much to us, especially when Boden's against us, and Klassen and that damned Lambert.' Here he spat on the ground again and uttered a volley of curses to which Zimmermann said amen. He looked round to see if we were alone and then seized the lapel of my coat.

'Look here, Herr Arnold. You are the best friend of the Miss Wolffs. Their home is your home. You doubtless hear much that's hidden from the rest of the village. And you are seeing things from the inner side of the wall, so you could relieve our minds a little.'

I cut him short.

'My dear Brechner, you are asking me to betray my trust, cheat my hosts and play the spy. As a straightforward man you would scorn to do these things yourself and I shall model my conduct on yours. But to relieve your minds I shall say something I could repeat before the ladies themselves. I am not in their confidence, I know nothing of their business and it is wholly against my principles to pry. To you, to the committee, to the police, I can in all honesty say nothing.'

It was dark under the trees and I could hardly see Brechner's face, but he was clearly ill at ease. I felt it. He stammered a few words, walked away a few steps to look down the main street towards the Golden Hind and then returned.

'You see, we are in a fix,' he said. 'Our positions are everything to us and we feel that something has been said that might bring us both to ruin. We don't want to return to the bad days before Hitler took over, but Lambert is set on ousting us both.'

'Brechner, Zimmermann, listen. There are two women in this village, two highly respectable women whom I should do all in my power to help.'

'We don't doubt it,' interrupted Brechner, 'but you as an Englishman . . .'

'A moment. I am not speaking of the Miss Wolffs. I am speaking of Mrs Brechner and Mrs Zimmermann, two excellent women who deserve a better lot in life. I shall never – and this I swear to you both – say or do anything that would make them unhappy, and certainly nothing which would send our dear little Ursula, whom we all love and admire, to beg again for bread and cheese at the Jews' door.'

Zimmermann was profoundly moved. He muttered his stammered thanks and offered me his hand. And Brechner took my hand as well.

'I'm satisfied,' he said. 'But is there anything you *do* know that could help us?'

'Impossible. You are assuming I am in the know, and I'm not. But I've made some shrewd guesses. One man you've got to fear, Lambert.'

'Yes, he's trying to shoulder us out.'

As Brechner said this I realised he did not know where the true peril lay. He was thinking of the committee and his little position there, of the greater education of Klassen, Boden and Lambert and then, in comparison, of the modest figure he cut in the eyes of the whole village. And so with Zimmermann. I decided to reveal what I had long since guessed.

'Yes, shoulder you out, that's clear. But there's something more. He has been prying into the affairs of everyone in the village, their incomes, money transactions and deposits at the bank.'

I could see that both were wincing, but I continued.

'And the blow would have fallen long ago on all the worthies of the village, but unfortunately the evidence disappeared.'

235

Both gasped and I realised that a sudden light had flashed across their minds.

'So it wasn't money they were after, not a common theft,' said Brechner.

'No. It was carefully sifted evidence and with it a record of all his dealings too. So he has been silenced for a time. But a muffled war is going on and, believe me, it will stop at nothing, not even robbery and murder. Now do you see?'

They gazed at each other aghast. Had I said too much? The silence of the two was most uncanny, as though both had been walking in darkness on the edge of some dizzy abyss and had suddenly sensed their danger. Their eyes had been brutally opened to a subtle and silent war to the knife in which others were involved. It was gloomy under the trees, but even there I could see that all the steely hardness had gone from Brechner's eyes, and all the impassive sullenness from Zimmermann's face. Brechner clutched towards my lapel again.

'Look here, Mr Arnold. Don't leave things like this. Are you certain of all you've said? I mean certain, black on white, oath on it, certain.'

'No. It's all an inspired guess. I have got two eyes, two ears, and a brain to put two and two together. Now who thugged him and robbed his safe? Did you two?'

'By God, no!'

Both broke out into hot protests and both stumbled over the tussocks of grass in order to seize my coat and arms and face me up to their denials.

'Exactly,' I said at last. 'But don't you see how rash you've been? You both have a burning interest in scotching that chap, Lambert, and you're proclaiming the fact to all you meet. Can't you keep quiet on the point and act in such a way as to allay suspicion about you?'

There was a step on the road from the Golden Hind and we moved off into the darkness. A figure passed. It was Heinrich. The bent shoulders and shuffling gait were not to be mistaken. But he could not have seen us exactly. He trudged off into the night while we three cowered into the shadow of the trees. And so after a time we took our leave.

Had I said too much? I began to think I had. I had given them both to believe that I knew more than I confessed, that what I knew the Wolffs knew, and that these silent, subtle ladies had a mysterious, underhand say in all the family affairs of the village. Had I compromised Rebecca? Perhaps. For Brechner knew, the committee knew, everyone in the village knew, that she was the mastermind for miles around. I admired her for it and had she appeared before me, self-confessed with all her plunder, and convicted of every crime of which suspicion had accused her, I should have admired her even more.

As for Brechner and Zimmermann, I cannot say I disliked them. They were Nazis, out-and-out Nazis who had terrorised the whole village, who had dispossessed men like Dorlich, and held the whole village to ransom by their enforced levies of cash. Yet they were normal, likeable men, with highly respectable wives and lovable children. However, they were yoked to the chariot wheel of the devil by their jobs. And how frantically they clung to their little salaried positions, and how they abased their characters to stand in well with their superiors! For, if once they lost their jobs in a state where the state was the sole employer, they were done for evermore.

Their case was the case of millions. But, strangest fact of all, they had somehow ceased to be Nazis. Now they had got their jobs, and were living in a normal way like the rest, the need for Nazi shibboleths had gone. Without realising for a moment how they were betraying their party they were ready to consort with Catholics and Jews, to be proud of their standing with the Engels family and even to protect the Miss Woffs from insult and attack. They were all Germans now, a unified nation of brothers, and in this new fraternity all political distinctions were lost.

Yet I had my misgivings. On my way back from the post I espied the two on the main road leading to Brechner's house. I halted in the shadow and observed them. They were engaged in earnest talk, Brechner making great play with his hands and Zimmermann, who was taller, bending down to catch what he said. They were clearly conversing in whispers. Had I put an evil idea into their minds?

Chapter 23

Questions of Heredity

On my arrival in Bonn whom should I meet on the station but Else herself? It was a joy to see her. There was always a touch of ecstasy in any glimpse of Else, and I felt the thrill as she stood before me as colourful and sparkling as ever, her red pullover and blue ribbon enhancing her fresh cheeks and golden hair. And yet despite her blithe look she was graver, more subdued. Clearly, she had suffered. Her mother was demented, her father a renegade, her old home seemingly lost for ever, and she herself under a cloud. Perhaps something in that station at Bonn helped to add a further shadow, the piercing wail and sighing exhaust of the engines, the disregarding throng of people whose only concern was the clock and who came only to go, but, above all, the sense of utter farewell in the disappearance of faces which would never appear again. Everything seemed to emphasise the absolute loss of home.

We went into the restaurant and over a cup of coffee she opened her heart to me.

'You can guess what we've been through,' she said, 'and yet the deepest cut of all has been from Grandpa.'

'Your superlative grandpa? You are surely not speaking of Herr Engels, whom I love and honour as my own soul?'

'Yes, Grandpa. Mind you, I say nothing against him personally for he is all in all to us, but I wonder if I'm right.'

Her voice trailed away and tears came to her eyes. She was looking towards the counter where a disgruntled counter-maid was pushing trays over to a waiter and selling coffee for cash. 'But how, child?'

'Well he can't forget that we are the children of our father. At least I think that's it. It's something we feel bitterly. And we love him so much, so much. And it's hard when Uncle Joseph runs my father down as a "ghastly rat". But is there ...'

Her voice trailed away again.'Is there what, child?'

'Is there any – taint in us?'

'Taint? In you and Paul. Rubbish!' I exclaimed. And then I suddenly realised how both of them had suffered. Day after day being bombarded by Nazi genetic theories, by talk of heredity, blood and race. By compulsory researches into the family genealogy, even as far back as the fourth generation. Normally, Else would have laughed it all to scorn, but after losing her father and mother and losing her old home she could not bear to be slighted by one who meant so much to her. Had her nature really inherited the perversities of her father? Had she, after all, the bacillus of evil in her blood? I burst out into a laugh. Though tears were glistening in her eyes, she burst out laughing too.

'It makes me think,' she continued in her old roguish way, 'that I'm an immoral germ carrier and that my veins are coursing not with blood but, excuse the Nazi term, sheer sewage. Above all, when Grandpa shies away from me.'

'Come on!'

I had to burst out laughing again. I was glad of the old sparkle, though I could not help but feel there was a touch of gallows humour in her sally.

'Well, it's the system of thought we live in. There's a flaw in the family line, John, a taint, and if all these theories are right, the apple falls not far from the tree, what's bred in the bone and so on, then I seem to see dear Paul as the ancestor of so many Borgias and myself as the unfortunate forbear of so many bashi-bazouks. It's enough to drive me to a nunnery.'

Else in a nunnery. I had to laugh again.

'Well, you know where I'm going to now?'

'No, you haven't told me yet.'

'I'm going to the only spot that is really home to me now. Just for two or three weeks and with full permission from Uncle Joseph and Grandpa. And I'm longing and longing to get there.'

'I know, to Neuenahr.'

She clasped her hands for joy and pursed her sweet face up for sheer pleasure.

'Yes, to Neuenahr, to dearest Tilde and to lovely Frau Weichert. And those pretty little rooms that look over the Ahr valley.'

But though the theme was inexhaustible I had to get to Hillesheim and she had to buy some things in the town.

'If I've time,' she called out as she sped away from the station, 'I shall drop in and greet Professor Hillesheim.'

A few minutes later I was standing in Hillesheim's apartment, studying the mysterious parcel, which he had not yet ventured to open. I had expected to find him in his usual pleasant mood, but he was rather grave, and looking all the more so in the solemn setting of his study, with its long shelves of books, its ancient desk and dark leather upholstered chairs. And the carpet seemed to deaden every tone in the room. Hillesheim, the blond and buoyant Hillesheim, as I had always known him, seemed a little out of place. So there was the parcel and there beside it lay a note signed with a mere scrawl and giving no address. It announced the sending of a parcel with a request to preserve it intact until further notice. In a word, the parcel had been put into his safe keeping. He thought that because I had entrusted a parcel to him before I might know something of this one.

'I know nothing of it.'

239

'The postmarks are rather obscure, but I make them out as Wilhelms-haven. Perhaps you would like to see them.'

Wilhelmshaven! My heart gave a start. So the Captain had sent it. Not to me, of course, who lived under some suspicion, not even to Tilde, who might also cross the police, but to one who had kept a parcel before, Hillesheim. I had not the slightest doubt. It was a parcel from Rebecca. To be smuggled away on a vessel abroad? For safe deposit in a foreign bank? Papers? Documents? Jewellery? What? And why had they been sent back? What a dangerous game for the Captain? What perils for Rebecca? Something surely had gone wrong and the police were on the track. I gazed at the postmarks in dismay.

'Yes, Wilhelmshaven. I personally know nothing about it. But perhaps you would like to leave the parcel with me?'

'I wonder.'

His doubt threw me into a turmoil. I thought that he would have passed it over to me without question. I could then have consulted with Tilde, with Rebecca, with – I ran through my list of friends. And Hillesheim looked so grave.

'But why not?'

'I thought that I must hand it over to the police.'

'But why?' I protested.

'Look at the postmark. Wilhelmshaven. Has this parcel been smuggled from abroad? I could make a number of guesses,' he said with a quizzical look.

'Hillesheim, Hillesheim,' I pleaded, 'hand it over to me. You have no aim or interest in bringing disaster on others.'

'On your Jewish friends, you mean?'

'Your former hosts, and on me.'

'You? Look here, Mr Arnold. I am now a professor, a state employee, and thus under a strict oath to the government. I have reasons for believing that this parcel is one to which the police must have access. I refuse to be a party to the underhand traffic of the Jews.'

'But you received my previous parcel.'

'Because it was your own property, or so I thought. Papers or the like which might be unsafe in the vac. I have a clear conscience on the point, but not on this one.'

'Hillesheim, Hillesheim, hand it over. The responsibility is mine and no one will be the wiser.'

'Do you think so? The post office can track a parcel and if it tracks this parcel here I am done for. The gates of my own homeland will be slammed on me, perhaps for ever.'

'And they will be slammed on others as well.'

'You can suffer no harm at all, at the very worst expulsion. As for your Jewish friends, they are in the soup as it is. There is no one else as far as I can see.'

240

'No? Doesn't Wilhelmshaven suggest some connection?'

'Captain Klebert?' he said after a pause.

'Yes.'

'The traitor!'

'And the father of one who is extremely dear to us all, Else Klebert.'

He looked at me with a start.

'Yes,' I went on, 'Else Klebert. She'll be coming along in an hour or two to bid you good day. She has suffered enough in the past few months, and if you, Hillesheim, bring a further pang to her heart ...'

I did not finish the sentence for who should burst in but Bürger, as bluff and sardonic as ever. As we cheerfully shook hands he took up my sentence.

'If you bring a further pang to her heart you'll be murdered, Hillesheim. Do you hear? But who is the distressed dame? Your friend, Rebecca Wolff?'

'No, Else Klebert.'

Bürger gave a low whistle.

'Ah, that alters the case. Unlike the God of the Jews I am a respecter of persons, certain persons of course, untainted by the perfidy of Albion and Jewry, but what's this talk of pangs to Else Klebert's heart?'

I told her troubled story, at which both were very moved. Then we came back to the parcel. Bürger, who had settled in an armchair, agreed that the case was awkward, but supported my plea for possession.

'Who'll know?' he said lightly. 'There'll be nothing of this in a hundred years. And besides, what's in the parcel? It's all a wild assumption that it's contraband material, notes and bonds and precious stones. It's not only a riddle to you, but also one to the police until they open the wretched thing.'

'But look at the postmark, think of the Wolffs and then remember the Captain.'

'Exactly. Think of the Captain. Think of all the love letters and all the locks of hair that he has collected in every port. There is enough to fill a score of parcels with stuff he'd like to bury deep before he sails away. All your suspicions of contraband are just so many leaps in the logic and slips in common sense. Sheer guesswork, all of it. Even supposing the Captain sent it, a flimsy supposition at the best, why shouldn't the contents be letters from Else he wishes to hide from his ladylove. Lovely innocence, all of it. Hand it over to me.'

Under the blustering attack of Bürger, Hillesheim began to recover his more normal and happy mood. He was somewhat worried about the Gestapo, who might land him into a scrape.

'Hang the Gestapo,' cried Bürger with his most triumphant smirk. 'To hear you talk, dear Hillesheim, one gets the crazy impression that they've an eye in every cupboard and a finger in every pie. A mere smoky myth. It's your own spooking fear that sleeps under your pillow, hovers at your door, follows you with padded foot wherever you try to escape him, noting your words and reading your thoughts. The truth is, my dear Hillesheim, you are not a National Socialist. You are trembling behind a mask. The Party is good for a temporary post, but not for a permanent belief.'

'Permanent belief? How could it be?' said Hillesheim. 'Politics is not a religion. It is an affair not of morals but of mere expediency, and what is expedient changes with person, time and place. It is thus a matter of personal adjustment, and what wonder if your adjustment is a little different from mine?'

'You confounded sophist!' laughed Bürger, who was about to renew the attack when the housekeeper peeped in and announced lunch. In we went to the dining room where the gaily papered walls, the light curtains and carpet, as well as the spotless tablecloth and sparkling service, seemed to bring us to a more cheerful mood. I rallied Hillesheim on his difficult frame of mind. I was at once consoled by Bürger.

'Wait until the man is fed,' he said, breaking his bread into the soup, which he tackled with great gusto. Hillesheim was more sedate and seemed very reflective.

'Yes, wait until after the meal. I shall speak more freely when my ...'

He broke off as the housekeeper entered with the next course and the silence was a little awkward. Frau Blass cast a quizzical look at us all as though challenging some complaint. She was wrinkled, critical and perhaps a little suspicious.

'No, it's excellent fare, Frau Blass. But we are discussing a state secret, which even you mustn't hear.'

She looked unconvinced and it wasn't until the meal was over and we were left alone with wine in the study that Hillesheim opened up.

'To tell the truth, it's all your fault, dear Bürger.'

'That's right, counter-attack!' Bürger, raising his glass, toasted us both.

'Yes, your fault,' continued Hillesheim, 'for what you said about Reuben Wolff has influenced all my thoughts about his daughters. They are cultured ladies, I admit, the younger one being really charming, but not only are they Jewish, which puts them under a cloud here, but also the daughters of a plausible villain who was condemned for conspiracy and murder, and not murder in a fit of rage but cold-blooded murder for cash. Now what was your inference, Bürger, when we dined and wined with the ladies in question? We were received in the most exquisite way in a most exquisite setting, and we ought to have been really grateful. Yet neither of us, try as we would, could get our minds off Reuben Wolff. His eye seemed to glint in every corner of the room.'

'Ha, ha,' laughed Bürger, 'that fellow, Reuben Wolff! I heard his chuckle like a death-rattle whenever they clattered the plates. And no wonder in such a room. You remember it, Mr Arnold. It had all the sinister glamour of an Ali Baba cave, pillage here, plunder there, cheek by jowl with the top-bid spoils of bell-and-hammer battles. And excuse me, Mr Arnold – I know you are fond of the lady – the more sweetly Rachel smiled, the more uneasy I became. For behind all that varnish of refinement, behind all that masquerade of courtesy, culture and taste, I saw, or thought I saw, two softly speaking, pretty-featured, pussyfooted harpies, ensconced in a shameless wallow of absolute loot. You Delilahs, I thought, you ...'

But he got no further. Our burst of laughter at his extravagance drowned the rest. I had been shocked by what I'd heard, but there was a touch of farce in Bürger's remarks, which tempered the effect. I was about to venture a word when Hillesheim broke in.

'Exactly, Bürger, exactly. That's your picture of the sisters and it certainly influenced mine. Now that parcel is from them, and being from them, dear Bürger, it is something murky. And dangerous for me.'

'Assuming, a whopping assumption, that the parcel is from them.'

'And assuming,' I added, 'that they are the daughters of the criminal in question and that they have inherited his bent for crime. Two big assumptions that I am not prepared to let pass.'

'About the first,' said Bürger, 'there is not the slightest doubt. I come from East Prussia and my people knew the family by repute. But a proof.'

'Or an indication,' said Hillesheim, who seemed to know what Bürger had in mind.

'Well, an indication. We went into the garden that night and I mentioned Insterburg, the place where they lived and where their father was arrested. Rachel was badly taken aback. You remember?'

'I do.'

And at once a deep vista of her unhappy life was revealed. For more than thirty years she had lived forlorn, by stealth, and where her charms were a mere mask for the incurable canker beneath. I no longer wondered at her pathetic efforts to please, at her gracious smile for any kindness, at her fear of public interest and private report. A coarser soul would have forgotten the past, but she had borne it in her heart year after year. And my heart went out to her as it went out to Else, who had a similar cross to bear. But even if her father were the blackest of thugs and held up to scorn as the biggest monster of the human race, I would hold her as high as I have always done in my love and esteem.

'So you see, Mr Arnold,' said Bürger, with a smirk more triumphant than ever on his black-bearded face, 'there's a criminal streak in the two ladies from which we both shrink. Firstly, they are of an accursed race which, even on their own showing, spread plagues and pestilence among the Egyptians and were finally driven into the desert; and, secondly, they come of a specially evil stock with the natural virus of crime in their very blood and bones.'

Bürger had a truly ladling way when serving out abuse and this always diluted the venom of his remarks. We hailed them with a burst of laughter so loud and prolonged that Frau Blass knocked and peeped in with a silent look of enquiry. After Hillesheim had dismissed her with a casual wave of his hand, I took up the challenge.

'My dear Bürger,' I replied, 'your opinion of the Jews is a mere mental warp of the Nazi Party. The Jews may be abnormal, but this abnormality of theirs does not imply crime. Besides, crime is an affair more of environment than of character and I can imagine very virtuous sons of very evil fathers. Look at the children of those monsters of the Reign of Terror in France, Couthon and Lebon. And so with Rachel Wolff. Is it a sign of evil character that she is deeply ashamed of the past and that she is so disturbed by memory of the evil past of others? In my mind she's far nobler than those with a normal past.'

'Let us put it bluntly,' said Bürger. 'Would you, knowing her past, marry such a lady as Rachel Wolff?'

'Why not?'

'And be responsible for a family with such a criminal streak in their blood?'

'I would, if they have no worse criminal streak than that of Rachel Wolff. She is a refined and gracious lady whose qualities ought to be passed on to posterity.'

'Blindly unrealistic,' was Bürger's comment.

'How?'

'You are living in a world of dreams.' And he waved his hands despairingly while Hillesheim filled his glass once more.

'Yes,' added Hillesheim, 'in a world of dreams, in a world of poetic fictions such as those of the Greek dramatists and Goethe.'

'Goethe?'

'Goethe and his Iphigeneia.'

'Explain.'

I was resigned to hear prosaic and brutal views from Bürger, who always palliated them with plenty of burlesque. But to see Hillesheim on the same side, hallooing him on and voicing the views of the street, rather disturbed me. Hillesheim had poetry in his nature, a certain refinement and reserve which suited his handsome features. But his reply was in the best vein.

'Goethe's Iphigeneia is a sheer poetic myth. She is portrayed as the pearl of her sex, a pure and nobly minded girl whose sterling virtue relieves the family from the age-long curse of the gods. In Goethe's play she is a far finer character than that of the Greek plays. She stands for *das ewig Weibliche*, that quintessence of pure womanhood which redeems the human race from all its evil. She symbolises a certain moral truth. She is none the less a pure poetic myth, a flouting of all principles of heredity.'

'How?' I interrupted.

'I shall put it as bluntly as Bürger did. Here is a girl whose sister is in a remand home, her brother in a criminal lunatic asylum, her mother in gaol, her ancestors, every one of them, a rightful prey of the gallows, and yet she, a daughter of this blood-besodden house, has not one single trace of the family curse.'

244

'But it's possible.'

'Not in this life. But supposing it were. To put Bürger's brutal question, would you marry her? Would you marry into a family where everyone had been a condemned criminal? If physical defects are transmitted, surely moral ones are. Rachel may seem to be a very gracious lady, but she has within her the seeds of future degradation, which she would pass on to her children in the third and fourth generation. It is according to Mendel's law and, incidentally, to the law of the Jewish God himself.'

'It all sounds very convincing, but when I see Rachel herself I know it's all wrong. Iphigeneia is hardly a parallel. In her case the whole family was involved in unspeakable crimes, but in Rachel's case only her father. So his crime was owing not to inherited sin but to some flaw in his upbringing, some evil in his environment, some force outside himself for which he was unprepared. One crime does not ruin a man's life. He may recover his balance and repent. And he certainly does not ruin the rest of the family. If that were the rule the human race would never have survived, even though the bad ones are gradually weeded out. There's a tendency towards stability, towards the normal in human life and to my mind in Rachel stability has been reached.'

'And there's a tendency towards evil,' burst in Bürger, 'and it is easier to go wrong than to go right. Once on the slippy path you go down. Goethe's Faust, the man who sinks into all temptations and finally rises above them, is another romantic myth. With every fall you are weaker, and nature finally weeds you out. And take his Iphigeneia. She was the forerunner in every sense of Christ. In order to prove his divinity and to set us the best example he was also born of the worst stock, namely the Jewish kings, monstrous debauchees like David, Solomon and the rest, and thus he comes into the world with all this sensual riot in his bones, and he proves to be a paragon of all the virtues. Sheer myth and moonshine.'

And so we went on. I had heard the Nazis' reflection on Christ before. What a morbid story to them was the story of the Cross. Here is a man of lowly birth, poor, born of the worst stock, a mere wandering Jew, and he meekly preaches self-effacement, peace, goodwill. He founds, or tries to found, a kingdom of shepherd and sheep, and ends up alone – for his cowardly followers fled – as a tried and convicted felon on the cross. What a tale for women and children, what a sentimental tale for the effeminate people of the east!

No wonder Nietzsche said that religion was the philosophy of the poor. And the Nazis used to recall the Germans as described in the Germania, the brave, pure-living and independent Germans who were always ready to appeal to the sword and who aspired not to a sheepfold but to Valhalla. What a superb example of right living these ancient Germans gave! What a contemptible one this ancient Jew with his plea for self-abasement, penitence and prayer! The Nazis shrank from this grovelling philosophy with a feeling of utter contempt.

We might have gone on for hours but for Else.

She peeped in at the door and gave us first a glimpse of her tart and roguish smile. She slipped in and her presence effected a lightning change in our society. Slight and simple though she was beside the black-bearded Bürger and the academic Hillesheim, she at once assumed the centre of interest, and sat down as assured as the chairman of the company.

'So I meet you again, Professor Bürger?'

'You do.'

'The utter rogue, as a lady said the other day.'

'Utter rogue!'

'Yes, she goes to your lectures. She thinks your stage-asides so rich, your comments in the margin, you know.'

'Ah, my impromptu glosses.'

'Yes, and she's always waiting for the next one so that she misses what you say between. Not that *that* matters, she says.'

We all laughed at this.

'But how does she know if she doesn't listen?'

'Instinctive guess, I suppose,' said Else gravely. 'No need to hear the whole sonata to know the piano's out of tune.'

'Oh!' laughed Bürger. 'She'd like to string me up, I suppose.'

'Oh no, no,' protested Else with a sidelong glance at Bürger. 'Professor Bürger is such a wag that no one would ever dare to approach him with earnest intentions.'

This was really too rich. Earnest intentions in German means with hopes of marriage, and Else said this in such a waggish way that we all three laughed our hearty appreciation.

'And what does she think of *my* lectures?' asked Hillesheim.

'Sh!' said Else.

'Just a confidential whisper,' pleaded Hillesheim, and he put his hand to his ear.

'Not even a whisper. It might set all the bells a-ringing.'

Else was now in her element. She went through all the phases of long-range emotion, mimicking the forlorn lady and panting out breathless and hush-hush enquiries. Was Else a little cruel? No, I do not think so. In another it might have been malice, but in Else it was pure humour, humour without a barb. There was not one drop of acid in her girlish soul.

'But what's all this affair about you and Dr Boden?' asked Bürger.

Even Else went grave at this and all her laughter died away.

'That man, Boden?'

'Yes, what happened?' persisted Bürger.

'Oh, he called on us in Cologne and began to pay me attentions. Sent me presents, which I sent back. One day he met me in the street and invited me to Blankheim and naturally I sent him packing.'

'What did you say to him?'

'I looked him in the face and told him he wanted his prettier side smacked.'

'And then he denounced you before the committee in Blankheim?'

'Yes, for speaking to David Cohen, a friend of childhood days. But I carried the committee with me; above all when nettled at one of my gibes he told me I was impertinent.'

'And you answered?'

'Yes, *bodenlos*, but I'm none the worse for that.'

We shrieked at this for, though *bodenlos* means shameless, it also means without Boden.

'And that was the end of it?'

'No. I told them quite frankly that if I met David Cohen again I would speak to him. The committee simply laughed; they all know me, Brechner, Zimmermann, Klassen and the rest, but Boden – who was very annoyed – denounced them in Cologne. In fact I had a summons for today. But I don't intend to go.'

We gasped. Trivial and silly though the matter was, it had taken a serious air. Boden, a Catholic, once member of the Centre Party and husband of a Jewess, was determined by hook or by crook to expunge his past. Clearly, he would stop at nothing and goodness knows what lies he would invent to besmirch Else and do down the committee.

In vain we besought Else to drop her trip to Neuenahr and return at once to Cologne. In vain we pointed out the perils, separation from her people, school of correction and the like. I thought the matter serious, and Hillesheim and Bürger were alarmed. They pleaded with her, consulted together, refused to let the matter drop. Suddenly, Bürger rushed out and a moment or two later we heard him at the phone. He was trying to get in touch with the committee. Meanwhile, Hillesheim and I renewed our pleas, almost on bended knee, but in vain. She laughed our fears to scorn, though all the while I knew it was really gallows laughter in which I heard an undertone of helpless despair. She had lost her mother and father and home, and she was longing to get to Neuenahr and hide herself in the society of one she dearly loved. Then Bürger burst in.

'Else, I'm going to Cologne, for if *you* don't go, *I* shall.'

That shook her. She collapsed in her chair and sobbed as though her heart would break. Such sobs as brought us all to tears, even the cynical Bürger who knelt beside her and hugged her and consoled her as best he could. Then he hurriedly got up and went.

By the time Else had recovered he was well on his way to Cologne. But it was time for Else, too. She retired to wash her tear-stained face and on her return bade goodbye to Hillesheim. However, on reaching the door she turned back.

'Oh, that mysterious parcel, may I see it?'

Hillesheim started, looked at me and Else for one embarrassed moment, and might have asked a question if I had not interposed.

247

'I mentioned it and she would like to see it. The script might be familiar.'

There was an awkward exchange of puzzled glances, but Hillesheim gave way. He brought the parcel, which Else studied in a non-plussed way.

'No,' she said at last. 'I do not know the script. But the postmark ... Oh, that's why you ask? From Wilhelmshaven. Ah! Perhaps from that ... '

As she blurted this out there was a break in her voice and a trace of tears in her eyes and Hillesheim softened at once. He understood and I understood she feared it was from her father's woman.

'You'd better take it, Mr Arnold, but mum's the word.'

So off we went, Else and I. But on arriving at the station I did a very wrong thing. I yielded to Else's pleadings and opened the parcel. She had some justification for she was fretting about her father and I, well, I must know where I stood. So we opened it and peeped in. It wasn't very light in the waiting room, but we saw at once what was in that mysterious parcel. Sealed envelopes, for the most part, and bundles of documents neatly tied and labelled. We bent back the loose leaves and saw notes of sales and mortgages and contracts and other what-not of the legal trade, with bonds and securities. Sheer innocence, apparently, all of it.

'So it's nothing to do with Father,' said Else with a sigh of relief.

'No, just legal documents about which I shall enquire. Just pass them on to Tilde to keep them safe for me.'

So I bade her goodbye, and it was only after she had gone that I realised the horror of what I had done. Every one of those papers had the seal and stamp of Lambert, in a word every one had been stolen as the result of a murderous attack. What right had I to dump them on Else and Tilde and involve them in a murky deal which might mean the ruin of both?

Yet what could I have done with the parcel? Take it back to Blankheim and perhaps be held up as I had been held up months before? Or hand it back to Rebecca and risk a raid on the house by the police? My mind was in a turmoil. Clearly the Captain was in a fix, perhaps already arrested and the parcel had been seized by his ladylove and sent to us for safety. He had been smuggling stuff abroad, bonds, securities, jewellery, of that I felt sure. But was it for Rebecca? Or was it for Joseph Engels? Or both? I had involved myself and others in high treason.

That night I had a call from Bürger who asked me to meet him at the station on his return from Cologne. He would break his journey at Blankheim and go on by the next train. So I met him. We sat in the darkness away from the lights of the station. All the bluffness had gone from his face as he told me his story.

'I had it out with the committee there and I blackened Boden for evermore. But Else!'

He gave a low whistle and I began to fear the worst.

'No, she's all right for the time being, but I told a bare-faced lie and did something that might land me in a fix. You've got to support me, you understand. We've got to keep Else away from the committee.'

'Why, what did you say?'

'I told them that Else had gone to Bonn to discuss her engagement with Hillesheim, the most Nordic man in the Rhineland.'

'The devil you did!' I exclaimed. 'But what will her people say?'

'I called on Herr Engels. He could hardly speak for indignation, because being a strict Catholic he is against all fooling with engagement and marriage. But his son softened him down, Else's uncle you know.'

'Well, as long as it goes no further there might be no harm done.'

'But it will have to go further. On my way to the station I put an announcement of the engagement in the local paper. I mentioned it to the committee and they asked me to send them a copy.'

'And Hillesheim?'

'I sent him a telegram of congratulations with a cryptic note to wait for me.'

'You rogue!'

'Rogue! What else could be done?'

Yes, what else could be done? I pondered the question as I went home that night and shuddered at all the perils that might befall a girl in the hands of Nazi re-educators. I was in the gloomiest mood. The street at Blankheim was very dark, the ruts and pools more treacherous than ever and, as I passed the Golden Hind, Fenger was standing at the door, staring at me in the most sinister way. In his Nazi garb and with his insensate expression he symbolised for me the whole political movement. On I went into the darkness and, though he did not move, I felt his boorish presence behind me, staring from that telltale spill of light on the cobbled street. It seemed to shadow me all the way and, to evade it, I turned to the left to my old home. But suddenly its darkness, its dead and silent emptiness, struck a shudder to my bones. I hurriedly went over the way and halted at the barred and bolted door of the Wolffs' house without daring to knock or to ring the bell. Far down the street, still standing in the light of the Golden Hind, was the ominous Fenger, but before me was someone more ominous still, Reuben Wolff or the wraith of him and the stealthy shadow of night crime. How should I meet Rebecca?

Chapter 24

A Morally Bad Position

I was now not only uneasy but beset by some fundamental dread. Hitherto, with regard to the police, my conscience had been clear. I might, by concealing parcels, have broken a regulation or defied the unwritten law of the Nazi regime. But what of that? The act was morally innocent and I was doing my friends a service. But this was different. This was a clear case of robbery and attempted murder, and I was a party to it, perhaps only an accessory after the fact, but none the less an accomplice and guilty under any law, human or divine. And there was no doubt at all about the culprit, Rebecca. She had paid some thug to rob and perhaps even to murder Lambert, to seize his papers and to scupper his plans against her. Acting in self-defence, she had no scruples whatsoever in a land in which she was an outcast and beyond the pale of the law. But the plea of self-defence, which was possible in her case, was impossible in mine. What had the parcel to do with me? I had drifted into a morally bad position.

Worse than that, I had involved my dearest friends in the same shady deed and exposed them to the rigours of the Nazi penal law. I faltered with my flimsy self-excuses as day after day went by, and I still said nothing. For though I wrote to Tilde I was afraid to mention the parcel or to allude to its guilty contents for fear I should involve her more deeply in the affair. Leave her in her innocence, I said to myself, it is her best defence if caught.

Tilde's photo was on my table before me, and many a precious moment I used to spend in communion with her, for her exquisite look of integrity was a truly splendid offset to all the stealthy evil around me. Else, delicious rogue as she was, might steal a peep into the parcel, furtively lift the folders and afterwards heroically fib to the police, but Tilde never. The faith she had received from the confessional and the altar was beyond all the batteries of the Tempter.

And then her mother. I had a photo of her too, one taken years before and which had stood by Tilde's bedside during all her stay in Blankheim. And when she left she gave it to me, a simple gift which I still fondly preserve. I was studying it one day, subtly aware of all the love which Tilde must have lent it, when Rebecca came into the room and a sense of the striking contrast struck the greeting from my lips.

She sat down without a word and looked at me with her dark eyes as she would look at the merest boy. I felt subdued. She had a quiet, commanding way, wondrously cool and self-possessed, and with her black, glistening, satin dress, flushed cheeks and glossy hair she made a colourful impression in that sober room of mine. I admired her, I must admit, but my admiration was tempered by a deep and sinister fear. As she looked at me in her penetrating way I felt that all my secrets were trembling on my lips. Yes, she knew all right. Those papers, she seemed to say, where are they? You have seen them, I suppose, and know their guilty story. And you pretend to be our faithful guest. It was thus I read her thoughts, but she simply picked up the photo I had laid aside when she came in.

'Frau Weichert,' she said after a pause, looking at the photo in a vague way and balancing it between her fingers.

'Yes.'

'You are very fond of Tilde and her family.'

'Very fond indeed.'

'I like them too.' Here she pursed her lips a little. 'Quite nice in a way, but very simple peasant people and ...'

'And lovely souls, all three,' I interrupted.

She looked me straight in the face and I felt all the power of her deep and subtle understanding. Was there an innuendo in her words? An undertone of rebuke for my love of mere peasants? I thought of her and her sister, their superior social standing, their education, culture and all the desirable whatnot of polite society. For a moment I confess there was a battle in my blood, but the battle went against Rebecca. A glimpse of Frau Weichert's face was decisive.

'Yes, lovely souls, as you say, but be careful.'

'Of what?'

'Oh,' she said, ignoring my question, 'have you seen your friends in Bonn lately?'

'Yes, a week or two ago.'

'Did they, or rather Professor Hillesheim, at any time mention a parcel entrusted to his care?'

'Yes, and he passed it on to me.'

'You have it here?'

'No, I passed it on to Tilde with instructions to preserve it until we heard more from the unknown sender.'

Rebecca was weirdly calm. Her only sign of nervousness was that she picked up the photo again and twirled it between her fingers, but her eyes never left mine. At last she spoke again.

'He didn't say what was in it?'

'He didn't open it. We assumed it was a parcel of private papers. And Tilde's honour in that respect is absolute.'

The worst of lies are those which pass for truth. Under the cloak of Tilde's honour I had sidestepped the sly Rebecca and deceived her. As Rebecca's guest I felt most unhappy. Perhaps I betrayed my own uneasi-

251

ness for my glance seemed to waver and she twirled that photo more contemptuously than ever.

'I was not the sender,' she said at last, so slowly and deliberately that I felt she was groping her way behind my obvious reserve. 'And, by the way, the papers were not mine.'

What a nerve! I felt I was facing a subtler liar than myself.

'I thought they were. Or why were they sent to Hillesheim? He had your previous parcel when I was on vacation.'

'Quite. I mentioned Hillesheim once to certain friends of mine and they must have acted in an emergency on that casual indication. You can truly say if asked that neither the parcel nor its contents came from me.'

So that was it. She was squaring my conscience to a police enquiry. I felt uneasy. Even she was afraid that the parcel might be traced.

'You'd better take charge of the parcel then.'

'Well, leave it for a few days until I find a safe depositary.'

So off she went. Day after day went by, days of tense uneasiness, of anxiety and even fear. It was very hard to study. Time after time, especially at night, I found myself at the window, peeping out into the dark street, startled by every footstep or nervously waiting until the sounds of a distant car had died away. My old home over the way seemed lost in lethal darkness, a thing of repellent gloom, sullen, malevolent, hostile, so that I used to turn away to the lights of the Golden Hind with its memories of the Kevelaar Club and of the civilities of pre-Nazi days.

Hillesheim was most unhappy. He was facing not only a flood of congratulations, but also the general surprise that his unknown fiancée was nowhere to be seen. The shifts and evasions to which he had to stoop played on his nerves. As for Else, she simply shrugged her shoulders, wrote a letter of apology to Hillesheim and dismissed the matter from her mind. Frau Klebert was too ill to receive news or to give advice, and no one in the family thought of writing to her father.

Would the trick Bürger had played come to light? Boden was sure to make enquiries, sure to ask point-blank in his blunt and boorish way what and when and where and why. He even stopped me one night. I was passing the Golden Hind to go to the post when he came out and hailed me. His stocky figure crossed my path and for an instant I halted.

'Just a moment,' he said, holding out his left hand like a policeman stopping the traffic. The gesture was rather discourteous for his head was thrown back and he seemed to be looking down at me in a supercilious way. As he took some time to find his words I edged away.

'A moment,' he repeated.

'Another time,' I said, avoiding his hand and moving off.

'About that girl, Klebert.'

But I was off, leaving him speechless with anger in the glow of light from the porch. So the matter was still rankling in his mind. On my return he was still standing at the porch talking to Lambert. I waited for a time until

252

they both went up the street and followed slowly afterwards in the shadow of the houses. Yes, Lambert would also have his doubts and make some close enquiries. The two men were going slowly and I no longer wondered at the murderous assault on Lambert. I felt my blood throbbing and surging up against him. Without a pang of conscience I could have hit him with an iron bar. Suddenly both of them stopped outside my house. It could have been only for a moment or two, but it seemed to me an hour. Their heads were close together, they were talking very softly and motioning with their hands towards the house. And then they resumed their way. I felt afraid.

Rebecca let me in and she met me at once with a question.

'What did those two fellows want?'

I told her what I knew and she heard me with a silence which boded neither any good. She set her lips and made no comment, but if Boden had been brained that night and his house sent up in smoke I should not have been surprised. We said nothing to Rachel of course. She was waiting for us with a little supper and we spent quite an hour talking pleasantly of Neuenahr and above all about Tilde, of whom Rachel was very fond.

She slipped something into my hand when bidding me goodnight, a pretty present for Tilde. Perhaps she was making amends for what Rebecca had said about 'simple peasant people', or perhaps she felt deeply for the Weicherts now beset by the Nazi regime. It was a very handsome purse, and, on the principle that a large gift never offends, it was filled to the brim with notes. I took it with a pang, for it seemed to be fraught with penance or even with a premonition of coming disaster. There was such a farewell look in Rachel's eyes when she whispered Tilde's name, as though she had finally lost a friend she would never see again. This seemingly parting gift moved me deeply, so that I became oblivious of Reuben Wolff, of all the theories of polluted blood, of even the faintest reminiscence of the attempted murder of Lambert.

I took it to Tilde next day. She now had a job in Neuenahr with a dressmaking firm and I met her just after hours when she was leaving the shop for home. She stepped into my view like an exquisite reminiscence of one I had loved when a boy. Her face, her form, her simple ways, had stolen all my childhood dreams and illumined every memory with a glint of untouchable gold. As befitting her new post she was now more elegantly dressed than when I knew her first, but she was none the worse for that. Indeed she was one of those rare girls whose features and expression would even set off rags to advantage.

'You come as though called,' she said, clasping her hands in sheer pleasure.

'Why, what's the matter?'

'Going home, going home,' she exclaimed. 'I'm so anxious, so anxious along that lonely road. Now that Father is under a cloud and Hermann has sworn to ruin us I go up that lonely hillside road in fear of some attack. I feel that someone is shadowing me or lying in wait ahead, just as it was last Christmas when we heard some stealthy step behind us at every turn in the road. You remember?'

'Of course I do. Despite the stealthy steps behind us I have never spent a happier time.'

'Nor I, either.' And she clasped my hand in sheer pleasure at the delicious reminiscence.

So off we went over the valley and up the hill, lingering at the places where we lingered months before and looking over towards Neuenahr, which was fading away in the dusky haze.

'You remember Albert Gerster? He met me again, not far from here, and asked me if I should like to go to Switzerland where he has settled down.'

'And you accepted?'

She broke into one of her merry laughs, but soon went grave again.

'He was seen by one of the villagers, who reported it to Hermann. Anyway, he and Zeller came storming to our house and denounced me as a spy and a traitor. I had to go to the police again. Fortunately, they told me that all would be well.'

'So Albert Gerster is still here in Germany?'

'Well, just for a flying visit, I suppose.'

Dusk was setting in and the road when bordered by steeps or trees looked ominously dark. Shadows seemed to lour by every bend and as we approached each one I wondered what might be on the further side. And it was silent and lonely and out of view of the lights of the village.

At one of the lonely, silent bends I asked her about the parcel. She assured me it was safe and beyond the reach of the police. I felt I must tell her all, but after an inner struggle I told her only that the parcel would be off her hands within a few days. I would only disturb her conscience if I told her more. But Tilde seemed to sense that I was wrestling with some secret and we stood for many moments face to face in silence. The integrity of the girl was like a flail to my soul.

'Never mind,' she said, 'in a few days time we'll be rid of the thing.'

And so we reached home. The strain of the day was over and Tilde, by way of reaction, began to laugh and behave as though she had drunk some heady wine. Else, too, was there in her most delicious mood and sent us again and again into peals of laughter. Was it only gallows humour, the hysterical, devil-may-care merriment that often ends in tears? I thought so. For after supper, as we sat together, there was an undertone of anxiety no gaiety could subdue. Herr Weichert puffed uneasily at his pipe and failed to keep it alight, while his wife fumbled with her sewing, missing stitch after stitch and finally letting it drop. Would they have to sell their home and leave the village? It was only when I drew the purse and handed it to Tilde that I managed to recall their wandering thoughts.

'She misses you, Tilde,' I said, 'and thanks you for all the kindness that you showed her.'

We all stared in silence as Tilde opened the purse and scanned the contents. We gasped on seeing the roll of notes wrapped in a letter which Tilde began to read. It was a tender letter, such as only Rachel could write, and which Tilde read, half to herself and half aloud, for her eyes were filled with tears and her voice broke in the last few words:

I am alone, dear Tilde, very alone in this hostile village, now that you and Herr Engels have gone. I miss you deeply, your happy face at the window, your brave visits to us and your moving offers of help. I feel more than ever that my happiest days are over, but when I recall them, as every day I must, there is always, dear Tilde, some glimpse of you within them, the dear, sweet, exquisite you who meant so much to me.

Was it the strain of the last few months, the thought that her happy home was lost, the feeling that poor Rachel was in a deeper plight than she was, or was it perhaps the gnawing remorse at having repeated the base slander of the unworthies of the village? Perhaps each, perhaps all, but Tilde burst into such bitter sobs as were distressing to hear. I stood up to console her, but hardly had I touched her hand when she suddenly sprang up, clasped me and kissed my cheek. Her whole frame was convulsed with sobs.

'Kiss her from me, John, kiss her.'

Just as suddenly she turned to her mother, kissed her, then her father and Else, and rushed sobbing from the room.

'Tilde, Tilde!'

But Tilde no longer heard, and her mother, with anxiety in every feature, turned to me and begged my pardon.

'Forgive her.'

'But there is nothing to forgive.'

'Then forget it. Her nerves are very much on edge and she feels our position here. She has been fretting like a sick child, although she's a brave girl and will face any misfortune. Forgive her behaving like this, for she is a good girl and means no harm.'

'There's no need to talk of pardon, Frau Weichert. What Tilde does is always for the best.'

'That's true,' broke in Herr Weichert. 'But come along outside and see what they've done. Come on, Else, the fresh air will do us good.'

He reached for his cap, which hung by a peg on the door and put on his coat. Frau Weichert picked up the purse and the letter and hurried off to Tilde.

Outside it was very dark, save for the pricks of light from the village and the glow from the village inn. But here all was in shadow and we followed Herr Weichert in silence as he went up to the spot that had been commandeered for the road. All the top end of the estate had gone, the orchard of cherry, apple and pear trees, leaving an unsightly clearance of mounds and holes where the roots had been. Even in the darkness we could sense if not see the desolation. Herr Weichert was too full for words. He made some gesture with his pipe-stem, turned in a vain attempt to speak and then went on his way, skirting the ravaged track without a further word. Presently he halted and gazed over to the east into the darkness. He was so lost in thought that I was afraid to disturb him.

He went on staring into the darkness and I began to wonder and wonder when, almost by inner response, I felt Else's hand in mine. She drew me gently aside.

'They've given him an indemnity,' she whispered, 'that plot over there, a rocky, barren waste which would take years and years to reclaim.'

'And he'll never do it?'

'Never.'

'But he seems to be considering it.'

'Ach, no. He just likes to go out in the darkness, right away from the eyes of the village and to pretend that everything is as it was and to live in his little dream. I've come to like it myself, just pretending in the silent darkness that everything is as it was long ago.'

There was a break in her voice and I could feel from her trembling hand how bitter was the loss. We turned and went back home.

Tilde met us at the porch with the traces of tears still in her eyes. Motioning Else to go on, she took my hand and whispered an apology.

'In my distress I forgot myself.'

'But, my dear Tilde, I think none the worse of you for that.'

'Yes, but?'

'But what?' interrupted Else, sidling up and giving me a most malicious wink. 'As far as he is concerned, everything you do is right, simply because *you* do it.'

'Sh!!' I exclaimed.

But she playfully snapped her fingers in my face, laughed at Tilde's blushes and mimicked her shamefacedness with the most comic exaggerations. And she poked her fun at me.

'Sh, yourself! It's all as plain as day; in your eyes she can do nothing wrong.'

'Oh?'

'I think I can,' gasped Tilde.

'Well, what of it?' laughed Else. 'What you do wrong is dearer to him than what all other people do right.'

I did not deny it, for when Tilde's glance met mine, and it was only for one blushing instant, I felt the touch of soul to soul in a truly dazzling way. She must have felt it too, thrillingly, irresistibly, for her eyes fell as swiftly as mine and for the rest of the evening we sat apart, barely aware of anyone else, yet failing and failing for sheer fear to steal another peep. Of course, we couldn't be vexed with Else, whose gladsome ways put us all in the best of humours. I had to turn the tables and deride her weird engagement to Professor Hillesheim.

And so we passed the evening in laughter and pleasant banter until finally Herr Weichert entered the room and sat down in a wistful way as though all his thoughts were abroad. Only once or twice, when footsteps fell on the road, did he show the slightest awareness of what was going on. He started up and we all went weirdly still. Not until the steps had died away did we resume our talk, and then for a time only in whispers. The thought of Hermann seemed to lie like an ominous shadow over the house.

I lingered on until next day, and after working in the library at Bonn I arrived by the last train in Blankheim. Going up the dark street I fell in with Rektor Barth whom, save when at mass, I had not seen for months and months. He told me his news. He had been to see Frau Klebert who was too ill to receive friends but who was clearly getting well. As for Herr Engels, he was longing to return to Blankheim and probably would do so when Herr and Frau Nauheim were ready to come. For Herr Nauheim, the Cologne chef, had often cooked for him and the Miss Wolffs.

We reached the rectory and, while we were talking in the shadow of the trees, someone passed on the road beyond. It was Hamann. We paused in our talk to follow his retreating form as he went by the Golden Hind. As he passed the glow of the inn he deliberately went to the darker side and we saw him look right round.

'He's not going home,' said the Rektor, 'or he would have gone down Station Road.'

'I wonder if he's the man who tried to fire the Wolffs' house two years ago?'

'I would not suspect him without definite proof.'

Hamman was soon lost in the distant shadows, but almost mechanically we stepped out into the road and found ourselves going past the inn and straining our eyes to make out his vanishing form. Sure enough, he came in sight near a street lamp not far from the Wolffs' home. We saw him enter the shadows again and as we hastened onwards we felt sure he would not escape us. He was bound to enter the glow of the next lamp if he kept on his way up the street.

'Stop,' whispered the Rektor, drawing me back into the shadow of a porch. Sure enough, Hamman was crossing the street. Moving along the shadowed walk, he had passed the barber's shop and had arrived at the Miss Wolffs'. He seemed to knock at the window, but then kept on his way for a time. We were about to come out into the open and follow him when we saw him turn back. We slunk back into the shadow expecting him to pass by. But on reaching the house again he simply pushed the door and went inside. Rebecca had let him in.

'So he's paying a midnight visit to the Jews, he the arch-Nazi terroriser of the village!'

'I hardly like going home now,' I said. 'I don't want to probe into secrets and cause any embarrassment to him or her.'

So we went back to the rectory where the Rektor made some peppermint tea. Strangely solemn it was in the Rektor's study that night as we sipped tea and discussed Hamann in subdued voices.

'He has been going down and down for the past year or so. The *Landwirt* is a failure; all the subscribers are dropping off and he can't keep the office going. He has offered it for sale.'

'It's his own?'

'Well, he bought it for a mere song after the confiscation, you know, and a sale is his only way to a little money. That and blackmail money from Rebecca.'

His voice fell to a whisper, but even then I wondered at the Rektor's over-frankness. He was usually as close as the grave, but perhaps he thought that, as a guest of the Wolffs, I might know more than he did.

'Blackmail?' I asked.

'What else? The whole of the Nazi movement is a tale of blackmail from first to last, from Hitler himself down to the youngest Hitler Youth. You saw the decorations in the porch?'

I had seen them, the little tokens or insignia that served as a receipt for gifts to the Nazi charities. There was an array of some twenty or thirty pinned to a piece of cardboard near the door. All the Rektor's own charities – and they form in the Catholic Church an integral part of its discipline – had been declared illegal.

'Yes, Hamann is a desperate man and I've reason to be afraid. Thank goodness, he is joining the SS. He'll perhaps be drafted away from the village. Zimmermann and Brechner are all right for they are men with excellent wives. I am not afraid now, at least of the men in the village.'

He added this with a meaning look as I stood up to go. He kept on gazing at me so that I felt some alarm.

'And beyond it?' I asked.

He paused before answering, and then whispered slowly.

'There's such a thing as a breakdown gang. And you live in the Jews' house. Beware!'

I went home in a most uneasy state of mind. Yes, that was the method. A horde of thugs brought in from outside to do the dirty work. After which they vanish with the loot – and no questions asked. I thought then of a fire and of myself trapped on the top floor. I shuddered and halted. But surely they would pillage the house first. I went on with hesitating steps.

I was nearing the house when Hamann stepped out. I slunk into a porch and waited. He slipped along the side walk and I could see that his fists were clenched. He was shaking them convulsively, not at the house, not at anyone, but in a fit of sheer vexation, or so it seemed to me. He turned back and I thought he might see me. But he halted, remained for a moment in silent thought, then resumed his way up the street. I did not stir from my place for at least ten minutes.

Rebecca let me in. She was a little paler than usual, but calm and almost phlegmatic. In her eyes, however, there was a steady, critical look which made me feel ill at ease. Such a look she might have given me if she had thought of firing the house herself and of engulfing me in the flames. Poor innocent Englishman! It would certainly be a pity, but of course it could not be helped.

I went upstairs aware of some desolation. Yes, the walls of the hall and staircase were bare and the two Dutch paintings I had often lingered over had gone. As I noticed the empty space I realised in a strange way that something of myself had gone, something beyond recall. I stopped at the first bend as though to adjust my shoelace while Rebecca stood silently below and followed my every step. There was a most uncanny silence in the house, a breathless pause, a halt. Yes, the observatory clock had stopped or had gone the way of the paintings. Step by step I seemed to be mounting to my doom. Usually when I came in late I was offered a snack in the sanctum. Why not now? As I closed the door above I felt that I had closed it on all my earthly days. I was clearly in for a fit of nerves.

She came up later with a snack and her eyes never left mine as she brought it in and laid it down.

'We are having a clean-up downstairs. You'll have to take your meals here for the next week or so.' Was it true? Or was she quietly preparing to leave? Securing all her treasures before the outbreak of the storm? I felt very unsafe, but then I thought of Rebecca, cool, calm, collected, and felt ashamed, but none the less uneasy. I comforted myself with the thought that Herr Engels would soon be back and I should be home once more.

Chapter 25

A Superlatively Honest Liar

The next few days were the most disturbing I have ever spent. Not that anything happened. The power of a police state lies in its deep unruffled peace. There were parades, bands and flag days, of course. And there were bellowing harangues by Hitler and the beating of drums by boys at drill, but when the applause had died away there was not one solitary murmur. No anxious crowds, no knots of whispering people, no seething spirit of even private protest. But day in, day out, the same humdrum everyday mood, the same breathless silence at night, the same portentous absence of any obvious power. But there was an underlying tension, above all at night when the streets were still, when the last light had gone from the windows and the final steps had died away on the pavement. The nothing that happened was far more nerve-racking than the descent of a horde of police.

So, when the alarm was sounded, it was almost a relief. I was lying in a doze one night when I was roused by the clang of a distant bell. It was ringing through the night, compelling, incessant, soon to be joined by other sounds, the indefinable hum of moving people, the opening of windows, the release of shutters, the creak of doors, the growing scurry of steps on the pavement below. I threw on my clothes, for the fear of fire was in my blood, and rushed to the window.

Yes, it was fire all right. There was a glow above the housetops as bright as day, a glow of billowing ash and smoke that deepened the terror and tensity of the blackness beyond. On all sides the village was waking up. I was conscious of anxious faces at the casements, of calls and enquiring voices, of shadowy figures speeding along the street. Obsessed by my own peril, I dashed downstairs where I found Rebecca in the hall, fully dressed as during the day, quite elegantly in fact, but calm, almost indifferent and perhaps a little contemptuous of my alarm.

'It's just a fire in the village,' she said.

'But where?'

'How should I know?'

And she shrugged her shoulders as though the fire hardly concerned her. Why should it? A fire in a hostile village? Perhaps I was misjudging her, but her icy self-possession was almost chilling.

I insisted on going out, though I wilted under her dry eye. She drew the bolts with studied delay, halting at each motion as if about to change her mind. I stepped out at last, but it grated on my soul to hear the creak of the bolts and the rattle of the chain as they locked the house against me. I stood still in the open street, forgetful of the fire and of prying eyes as question after question went racing through my mind. Why was she up at so late an hour? On such a day? In such a place as Blankheim, where it was folly to dress up for visitors who never came? If she could plan robbery with violence, why not a fire or worse? Then a thought of Rachel crossed my mind, and I realised I was really too suspicious.

So off I went up the street, now lit up with gleams from the windows and astir with enquiring voices. Glancing neither to right nor left I made my way to Lambert's house but – and I stopped in surprise – it lay there in darkness without one solitary glint through the shutters to show that he was up. The fire was more to the left where the glare was flushing the side streets and billows of illumined smoke were drifting towards the Rhine. I made my way through the fumes with a deep suspicion in my mind. Of course, of course. I had guessed aright. It was there on the edge of the village, no other than Hamann's place, the house and printing office of the *Landwirt*.

I stood stock still. The whole building was engulfed in flame, from top to bottom, as complete a blaze as I have ever seen, so that the form of the house was lost in the roaring streamers of fire. In fact the buildings hard by, so intense was the glow, seemed to be involved in the one all-embracing conflagration. I might have known. Of course. No casual look about that blaze! No hint of a chance spark there as the cause, some flaw in the wiring, some smouldering match or cigarette-end fanned into flame by a gentle draught. So thoroughgoing a furnace, such a scorching swelter of fire and smoke, such eerie leaps and pinnacles of flame had an all-out purpose and plan in every spark. So Hamann had blazed it up. But at once my mind was brought to a halt. Why Hamann? Why not his enemies? Rebecca? Lambert? Albert Gerster? And others whom I could name? Perhaps after all it was just a phase in that muffled feud or fight for power of which we had just had a fearful glimpse in the murder of Röhm, the SA leader who had dared to say Hitler was going soft.

The fire threatened to sweep across to some houses over the way. They looked doomed in the sinister glare of the flames that waved and tossed above them or wholly involved them again and again in banks of lurid smoke. Their tenants scampered about hastily moving their things, and I could see them in dark silhouette dashing to and fro at the back and heaping up their stuff in the neighbouring field. I ran to help them, taking their goods at the door while they rushed back into the house. Fast and furiously we raced, because the heat was intense and clouds of hot paper and ash were floating over the scene and covering the ground with a greyish film.

I was half choked and was afflicted by an almost unbearable thirst. But the fire brigade was at hand and the neighbouring buildings were saved.

Gradually the flames sank. We were able to take a breather, to quench our thirst and wash ourselves and then to return the evacuated goods. Darkness settled down on the spot, but Hamann's house, with its toppled walls and collapsed roof, was a mere smouldering heap.

Despite the pungent smoke that drifted over the scene I stayed at a house and had some coffee with the peasants. They were silent about the fire, just nodding their heads to any questions or replying by a vacant glance. Even in the privacy of their homes they had to be discreet. Later, I saw Hamann in the road talking to the firemen and the police, explaining how it happened and how narrow had been his escape. Strange how the villagers passed him by and ignored his obvious gestures as he vainly looked round for an audience. He could whip up no interest for his pitiful story. He stood there like some common tramp with an old coat over his pyjamas. He was being left to stand in the night. He looked like a wraith of a man amid the drifting smoke from the darkening ruin of his home.

'He made a good job of it, anyway.'

It was Frenzel, the land agent, who spoke. He stood there, an idle spectator, with an overcoat over his night attire. I hardly knew him. He was not as florid as in pre-Nazi days. Moreover, with the coming of the Nazis he had retired from the life of the village.

'You mean?' I asked.

He smiled and shrugged his shoulders, and as we walked away he echoed his own words.

'A very good job indeed.'

He gave me a querying look, but I was very much on my guard.

'If you mean it was a thorough blaze, I don't wonder. The house was half-timbered, the beams would burn like tinder and then, of course, it was packed with paper.'

'Doubtless.'

We walked on in silence for people were looming out of the gloom every moment and I was determined not to gossip. But suddenly he stopped me and addressed me in a whisper.

'This Hamann, what do you think of him?'

'I do not know him.'

'Come on. Do you remember that speech you made to the committee?'

'Speech?'

'Of course. You know what I mean.'

Frenzel was getting impatient and began to raise his voice.

'Of course you do. Was Hamann one of the men you saw?'

I laughed and left him stammering his questions behind me. But the next few nights I spent in a very nerve-racking way. The blaze at Hamann's house seemed to flare up in my sleep and to startle me into panic fears. I would spring from my bed in the utmost alarm, trembling, all of a sweat, yet plunged into sheer wonder at the darkness and silence of the night. For a moment or two I would stand in a daze, then I would rush to the window. Outside all was calm and in shadow save where, to the north, soft lights flitted across the sky like mysterious pointers into ominous nothingness. Or I would go on to the landing and listen, or peep down into the well. The whole staircase was in darkness and the house was so still that I wondered what stealthy doings were afoot there or what breathless whisperings were going on between the unseen somebodies below. I thought, I must leave the house even if I offend my friends. And yet I remained.

As for the guilty packet that was still in Tilde's hands, it began to weigh on my mind like a swelling load of debt. Supposing the police found it with her? But then I would dismiss the thought or decide to go to Neuenahr to burn the thing or post it to God knows where. All day and every day my mind was in turmoil, and often under the strain of alternative thoughts I was brought to a halt in the street or found myself on the wrong path or forgot important appointments.

At last, in desperation, I resolved to face Rebecca. One morning she brought up my breakfast and I was about to broach the subject when she laid a letter on my plate. It was from Neuenahr and I wondered at the address for it was not in Tilde's script. I postponed my ultimatum and read the letter.

My eyes went dark as I read it, and the whole of my being seemed to crumble under the blow. I doubt if I read it all for the letter fluttered out of my hand and left me vainly staring at a blur of black and white. What a blunderer I had been! The police, so wrote Herr Weichert, had suddenly appeared at the house, searched every room for letters and then taken both Else and Tilde away for private interrogation. Why they had been taken, where to and for how long Herr Weichert did not know.

Two days and nights had passed, and still they had not returned. He had asked the police at Neuenahr, but they could give no answer, nor at Ahrweiler where the main station was. But the news had spread to the village and, doubtless at Hermann's instigation, they had been jeered at and molested by certain irresponsible youths. 'Traitors' had been chalked on the walls and certain things had been stolen and damaged. The villagers as a whole were above this sort of thing and many had sent private notes expressing their sympathy and regret. Frau Weichert was very distressed and had suffered a nervous crisis.

So they had searched the house for letters. My own heart cried out against me and my first impulse was to go to the police and make a clean breast of the whole business even at the price of betraying Rebecca. But the thought of Rachel crossed my mind, of her who had befriended me and had an absolute trust in my sense of honour. I could not betray her.

I was walking along the street, muttering aloud to myself, going forward and turning back and then going forward again. I might have dithered this way and that for the rest of the day, but for a voice that pulled me up and brought me back again to a sense of the things around me. It came as a counterblast to my own conscience.

'Aren't you able to make up your mind? Heil Hitler!' It was Kemp, the sanitary engineer, now a full-blown member of the Party as well as an SA man. All his former loyalties had fled and it was strange to see the élan with which he had flung himself into the new order of things. No wonder. With the plea of easing unemployment he and Wessel and the rest were dunning the whole village to have central heating in their houses, bathrooms, boilers and modern toilets, all under the subtle threat of brutal pressure from above. Brechner's Danegelt was nothing to this.

Kemp was cleverly playing not only on their fears but also on the jealousies of the people next door. To be without a bathroom, when your neighbours proudly had one, was to brave the contemptuous whispers of the whole street.

On he went, nodding in a superior way to people right and left, with a peremptory call to some and a reminder to others, and often so flinging out his arm to make the Nazi salute as to knock me half-spinning to one side. No apology, of course.

'You are doing good business now,' I ventured.

'Naturally. There is order in the land now, absolute order and discipline. No unemployment, no idleness, no doles, no wasteful something for nothing. The Führer has shown the way. Work, hard work and more hard work. That is the remedy he has given us. Germany is great now, Mr Arnold, and every day it's getting greater. We shall soon be chasing your country off the map. Heil Hitler!'

He shot out his arm and left me. With my thoughts again in turmoil I reached the police station. Fischer was standing on the step and eyed me in his silent superior way. Make a clean breast to him? Never! I intended to go to Neuenahr, but got no further than Bonn. What was the use of confessing things that might never come to light? Things that might embarrass my friends and plunge them into further enquiries? And how about Else? Tilde, a veritable Joan of Arc, would tell the truth or hold her peace. But Else might tell a fib. Though sterlingly honest to all her friends, she certainly would not shrink from tipping the devil into the ditch. So in my desperation I even went to Hillesheim's house to ask him to intervene. But on reaching the door I turned away. After all, he knew too much and the evidence he would give might be more than was required. But before leaving Bonn I had another counterblast to my conscience.

I met Hans Reimer at the station, the student who had served me in the bookshop at Cologne. He was also an SA man, but unlike Kemp he had a whispered apology.

'No other option,' he said, with an anxious look to right and left, 'if all my years of study are not to be thrown away.'

Far be it from me to misjudge him. He was miserably poor, in failing health and, unless he bowed the knee, had a black future. But he was not so

264

nervous now. The blink had almost disappeared. He looked fuller in the face and more resigned to things. He was wearing a wedding ring.

'I've passed my states exam,' he said, 'and I'm doing my practical year.'

'And you're married?'

'Just the civil wedding, of course, until I've finished training. Ah, here she is.'

His wife came up, a simple peasant girl and a very likeable one. Her grammar was not of the best, as Reimer had once observed, but what of that? She was a good, homely, honest girl with a truly Madonna expression. After all, life with an educated wife is often just a mere armistice. Reimer's wife was a guarantee of domestic harmony. Moreover she was a guarantee of his loyalty to the new order. As we sipped coffee in a restaurant I congratulated them.

I spent the day in the library and returned at night to Blankheim, having accomplished nothing. As I went up the village street I seemed to be entering a nightmare. I halted opposite the house and looked up to my room, that dark, silent and isolated room.

And then I noticed something. It was a light in my old home, just a luminous rift through one of the shutters, but a light and the sign of return. Perhaps it was the police, however, or the insurance agent who had charge of the house, or the cleaner who came in once a day and kept the place in order. Or was it thieves? I rang and almost at once the door was opened. For one startling instant I thought Frau Klebert had returned, the fair face and golden hair, the same dazzlingly white blouse which seemed to flash into my sight. Then I saw my mistake. It was Frau Nauheim who, with her husband, was to run the house when Herr Engels was ready to return.

'So Herr Engels is coming back?'

'Yes.'

She looked embarrassed, above all at my further questions, to which she gave evasive replies. She knew nothing, neither she nor her husband, who appeared and nodded his head in the same negative way. I was surprised for I stood well with the Nauheims and had expected a more welcome response. Still, Herr Engels was about to return and, elated by the news, I was now able to face the worst on the other side of the road.

Rebecca was there as unperturbed as ever. Clearly the police had not called nor had I any further news from Neuenahr or Cologne. There was thus an edge of doubt to my joy. We looked each other straight in the eyes, and I felt she was probing my innermost thoughts. I wondered what were hers, what purpose pervaded those dark mysterious eyes that seemed to be probing mine all the time she was closing the door until I left her at the foot of the stairs. I felt desperately alone as I went up step by step, though I felt her presence behind me right up to the door of my room. Perhaps she felt lonely too.

Frau Boden had left the house, at least that was my impression, and Rachel had gone into seclusion, whether behind the screen or to stay with friends, I never knew, and it was impossible to ask Rebecca. She had a very aloof way and left nothing to be overheard. Yet, as I went up the stairs that night and felt her following gaze behind me, I knew that something had happened which touched us both, something that was babbling behind her silent lips and trembling mutely in my ear. She was waiting for me to speak, and I had nothing to say.

I was to know in a day or two. I was returning from Cologne, and all the way home from the station I was aware of a more than normal stare, a more than normal hush as I passed by various people so that my footsteps resounded in a loud and tell-tale way and everyone seemed to halt and gape in wide-eyed wonderment. What a one-man procession it was, what pin-drop applause, above all when I reached the barber's shop and did a mute and solemn march-past before the concentrated gaze of the whole group. They were looking at my old home, which was standing there as it had stood for years, without one solitary change to warrant such an interest. But something had happened, something that held the breath of the whole village, something that made me the hub and pivot of the gossip for miles around. A note from Herr Engels was awaiting me. He had returned and asked me to come and see him.

Next morning I went over with some foreboding. 'Traitor' had been chalked on the walls and two of the lower windows had been broken. The coarse scribble, the shattered glass, along with the grimy flag that slumped from the attic window, lent a touch of disrepute to the once distinguished front of my old home. Something of Matthias, something of the mere mob, had drifted across the cobbled street. I seemed to be taking his gaze with me, right into the little hall.

Fischer the policeman was taking his leave, and I guessed he had called about the hooligan attack on the house, but I was corrected by Herr Engels's parting words.

'No, I've no interest in the body, nor has my daughter. As for the children, they are too young to express a wish. It's entirely an affair for the state.'

Fischer gazed for a moment in silence and was about to turn away when Herr Engels spoke again.

'And it would avoid all further scandal. He would be buried in un-consecrated ground and that would reflect on the children. It would be a nodding of the head and a wagging of the tongue to the whole village. No, let his name and his memory be buried where neither he nor we are known.'

He said all this as though he were passing the time of day. No sign of an inner tremor, no trace of emotion. My blood ran cold as I thought of the Captain, breezy, effusive, hail-fellow-well-met, with the gust of the sea and the clink of a glass in every word he said, the great lion of the bar parlour and caller of the toast in every local company, now lying a stark, neglected corpse awaiting goodbye with the shovel from some demolition squad.

266

The shock struck every question from my lips. I mutely followed Herr Engels into the sanctum where the portrait of Uncle Joseph, an equally wayward soul from over a hundred years ago, seemed to wave a triumphant welcome to the Captain. What had happened? To be interred in unhallowed ground suggested some disgrace, perhaps suicide, perhaps worse. The iciness of Herr Engels seemed to imply all that and more. It would be a sad reflection on Else and Paul, a dishonour to their mother and her father. No wonder the village was agog with the news, and that the main street was agape on both sides when I passed.

We sat in silence for a time while my old friend gazed in a far-off way at that portrait of long ago.

'You know the whole story, of course?' he said at last.

'No.'

He gazed at me for a moment or two, stood up and motioned me to follow him into the hall. He took his seat in one of the niches while I sat down on an old chest. He nodded towards the sanctum as he lit his pipe.

'Not there, not there.' He shook his head as he spoke. 'The echoes of it would linger there for the rest of my earthly days. It's a tale for a bar parlour or for some lamplit alley corner. Something for the gawps and gossips to muddle and to puddle in.'

'If it's far too painful,' I suggested, 'we can drop the whole subject.'

'No. Better a plain tale from me than some cocktail disclosures from the village. Truth is a precious drop, Herr Arnold, but it is soon evaporated in the froth and fume of small talk. The facts are simple, so far as known. To save the good name of the service he was given a pistol to shoot himself. And he did so.'

'For treason?'

'For what they call treason. Smuggling stuff abroad. Secrets, jewellery, valuable papers, something of the sort. I should face the facts dry-eyed, but Joseph has been arrested, for aiding and abetting him. And Joseph swears he is innocent, though the facts are seemingly against him.'

'Against him?'

'Yes, bills, receipts, signatures and so on were found among the wrappings. They were not discovered until the Captain was dead and the Captain divulged nothing.'

My heart leaped up and I felt my face ablaze. Surely it was all Rebecca's doing, ensnaring the Captain for her surreptitious purposes, cloaking her own guilt by misusing another's name, trafficking in secret with puppets, pawns and men of straw and trampling on them ruthlessly when her safety was involved. She had salted those packets with Joseph's name and I was about to blurt out my suspicion when the realisation that I knew nothing, or at least nothing decisive, froze the words upon my lips. And then I thought of the packet and of my own entanglements, of Tilde and of Else, who were also implicated, and of Rachel, a true friend. No, I must keep silent even at the expense of the innocent. And with this word

267

innocent in my mind I blurted out a question about Else. Yes, she was at home, though under a restriction. And Tilde? He had heard nothing further and I sat there aghast as I thought of the poor girl, a truly heroic victim of my folly and neglect.

Yes, I could have my rooms again and I hastened across to face Rebecca, who opened the door to me. At the first glance I stood abused and shrank within myself. Was it the contrast with Herr Engels, with his rugged, lionlike face, his bushy brows and intractable, aggressive beard, that struck me mute? Or was it the tangle and jangle of my own ragged nerves that made her so smoothly superior, so attractive and yet as coldly aloof as a marble image in a glass bell? She appeared beyond all imputation and the challenge of her lustrous eyes simply hastened the crumbling of all my resolutions. Every question trembled away in incoherence on my lips.

What had seemed obvious in the presence of my old friend was a disappearing blur in the presence of Rebecca, a mere evil breath from the fuddle of the Golden Hind, such a fume of pipe and can as the fresh light of day would disperse.

'I shall be up in a moment,' she said, nodding towards the staircase.

A little later we were sitting face to face and our eyes met for the most quelling seconds of my life.

'You have some news,' she said without dropping her eyes from mine.

I told her of the treason of the Captain, his suicide and the arrest of Joseph Engels.

'That all?' she said at last.

'It's enough for one bulletin,' I replied, trying to summon up some little opposition.

'But not enough for the village, which has far more to say.'

'Maybe,' I said, 'but whatever the guilt of the Captain, Joseph Engels is innocent.'

'You know for certain?' she asked calmly.

'We have his word.'

'Which anyone can give. No, Mr Arnold, a man who goes in for smuggling today cannot be too careful. He must take more than ordinary precautions. Joseph Engels is doubtless the victim of his own folly.'

This was too much. We were trifling on the edge of the subject and I felt that I must now speak out even at the risk of rudeness.

'And how about your own parcel, which might involve us all in peril?'

'My parcel? The one that Tilde has? I'm not afraid of that. The police can have it for all I care. The contents could only redound to my credit.'

I gazed at her dumbfounded. Little did I know then that she had made a substitution, that Lambert's files had been replaced by a book on navigation with little guides to ports abroad, all inscribed as Christmas, Easter and birthday presents, and that nothing remained of the original parcel but the duly stamped wrapper. Who was to know? The Captain's ladylove, who had sent the packet, had been silent to the police; for her own sake in the first place and in the second for Rebecca's cheque. So let the police find the parcel. And all the secrecy would be explained by some tender letters in it addressed to 'My dearest Karl', all in Rebecca's script and now returned to her as the sender, and all in full response to missives from the Captain who had expressed his deeper feeling for the handsome Jewess.

But it was only later that I learned all this. At the moment I knew nothing.

'So Tilde and Else are safe.'

I could only gaze my thanks at Rebecca, oblivious of the serpent and aware of nothing else but its subtle fascination. I looked in wonderment over the no-man's-land between us, over impassable barriers of alien race and blood, while she from her wholly different world seemed to flout the same untouchable taboos and beckon to every fibre of my being. What a bewilderment she was. And so she sat and looked, probingly, suspiciously. But how should I divine her thoughts? Perhaps she had some liking for my youthful turn of mind. Or was it pity?

'So they are safe,' I repeated.

'They were never in danger.'

'But if the parcel had been found?'

'Their being arrested in Neuenahr had nothing to do with the parcel. They were arrested on suspicion of being involved in Hamann's fire.'

'Tilde and Else?!'

'They had both declared that the office should be blazed over Hamann's head.'

I suddenly remembered Tilde's outburst, and Else's too, when she mocked at Hamann on the stairs. So that was it! All my distress had been for nought. And Rebecca had known it all along and never breathed a word. The Sphinx!

'And they had been meeting Albert Gerster who *was* guilty of the crime.'

The tone of this last remark and the probing look she gave me convinced me she was telling a lie. I did not believe Albert Gerster was guilty. Surely, Hamann had made the blaze to get the insurance money, and Rebecca in some subtle way had prompted the idea. He had been dunning her for money to finance his bankrupt schemes and, when she refused to support him, he had turned to the blaze as last resort.

Had Rebecca no fear at all? Here she was, opposed to the Nazi desperados of the village, with the whole force of the nation to facilitate their crimes, and she a mere Jewess condemned, defenceless, and exposed at any moment to a brutal attack. What were her feelings when alone in that house at night, severed from her people, with the drums and tramplings of the anti-Jew fanatics sounding ever louder in her ears? Even at that distance she could hear their furious outbursts, the whoops and cries from the autobahn's lorryloads of Brownshirts speeding to Cologne. A great

269

national rally was being planned for the weekend there, and every street in Blankheim was draped with Nazi flags.

I saw her walking under them that night, each a symbol of death to her and all her race as she made her way over the cobbles, tightly holding the shawl that muffled up her shadowed face. And so she went along, slowly, silently, stealthily, with death and darkness drooping round about her. In a moment or two she was lost in the night haze and I wondered what the following days would bring.

Chapter 26

The Breakdown Gang

As the day for the great rally came we all had a sense of impending crisis. For, behind the fever and flourish of all these demonstrations, there was another and further purpose of which only we in Germany were nervously aware. Every rally was a rehearsal in lightning mobilisation, a slamming of countless thousands at some fixed point, an adumbration of the surprise attack on the peace of Europe. How festive it all seemed to the Nazi demonstrators, how purely propagandist to the observers from abroad! Mere flags, parades and fiery speeches, just to whip up support for the Party. But we knew better. We heard in every rally the rumble of approaching war.

Even Herr Engels was anxious, he who was always so steady and resigned. Some vague fear possessed him so that in the midst of our talk he would stop and listen and muse with the answering shadow of his own thoughts. I grew anxious, too. No wonder then that, hearing an uproar in the distance, we went out. We crossed the old yard to the far wall and looked over the fields to the north-west. Night had set in and the only relief in the darkness was the little red gleam from the restored wayside shrine that shone from over the road, some pricks of light in the distant farms and away on the far horizon the dull glow of Cologne. There was a deep stillness, too, that almost ominous stillness that tempts one to listen and become even more tempted to hear the all-pervading undertones that remind us we are not alone. I was aware, we were both aware in a truly inaudible way, of a moving world beyond us, the hubbub of voices, the rumble of traffic, the tread of parading thousands. Was it only an illusion, some phantom of our inner feelings? Or are there soft vibrations, unknown to the waking ear, which assert themselves in a subtle way at night?

'Do you hear it?' I said to my old friend. He laughed softly.

'I always hear it. Even when the sounds have died away. All this Nazi uproar, these speeches, plaudits, fanfares, parades, all this pandemonium, is playing on my trembling brain and trampling through my sleep. And we are all in the same boat. That fellow is shouting at us even when his mouth is closed. And he is never so much with us as when he has said goodbye. But look!'

The searchlights were on and the beams were flitting silently under the dark clouds. For a long time we stood with our elbows on the wall and watched the mute play of the beams in the night sky. To us it was the first stealthy step of war, and all around us the land lay deep in sleep.

'So you think we are coming to it?'

'Certain. Hitler's policy is one of mounting crises, each one bigger than the last.'

'And the last of all, a European war?'

'Exactly. You see, Hitler is like a chamois scampering along the cliff face. There's no lingering on any foothold. For each jut is only large enough to give purchase for the next leap. In fact it is just a bouncing point. So there's no looking back, no reflection on what is past. The only question we ask is – what next?'

'So you think that Hitler's policy is deliberate?'

'In a certain sense, yes. It is the policy of a gambler who pays one debt by contracting another and who makes us forget our troubles in others very much worse. So every year he casts a bigger stake and the last and biggest stake of all is himself and the whole of Germany in the lottery of universal war.'

'And he can take the nation with him?'

'As long as he's successful. And so long as we all have the jitters, all of us agog as one man and ready to move en masse when we feel the final push. You see, we are a nation in blinkers. Like the scampering chamois on the cliff face all our eyes are screwed on what's ahead.'

There was a movement in the lane, voices and approaching footsteps, so we went back into the house, filled with forebodings.

Even Hillesheim, who had called while we were out, could not dispel them. He was now a frequent visitor. He liked my society and held Herr Engels in high esteem, but he revealed the real reason he had called when we met him in Cologne next day. He had been touched to the quick by a look of humiliation in Else's once so pleasant face and he felt in some way honour-bound to restore her self-esteem.

'I felt it like a lash upon my conscience. There is no more gracious girl than Else Klebert, and to see her rebuked expression, her stealthy look of shame at being her truly lovable self made me wince in every fibre of my being. I have decided to pay her all the honours at my command.'

'Excellent. I have felt the same with regard to someone else and it has haunted my conscience for years.'

'You mean Rachel Wolff.' He had looked round before pronouncing the name.

'Yes, poor Rachel Wolff. Sometimes I feel she has never outlived her early years, but still lingers in them as pure and innocent as when the blow fell. For she is afraid to move beyond them, afraid to leave her refuge, afraid to face her fellow men in every glance from whom she sees a rebuke. And so she has lagged behind in the timorous subjections of childhood, unable to be free, too ashamed to be independent, too diffident to believe in the feelings of a friend. She is as stricken as a trodden flower, too stricken ever to bloom. Have you not felt it?'

Hillesheim looked reflective.

'Now that you have described it, I do.'

'You must. That's why, despite her years, she has all the appealing prettiness of a young girl. She has the loveliest and yet the most pathetic face I know. Heaven save Else from it.'

'Yes, but Else is a far more buoyant spirit and will prove, I am sure of it, superior to any blow. Still, she has a conscience quite as delicate as that of Rachel Wolff. Her soul might be encumbered for many years to come. We must help her.'

As he said this, the forms of Lambert and Boden seemed to loom up gloomily before me in a truly menacing way. Did Else realise her peril? She had openly rejoiced to the police at the blazing of Hamann's office and when asked about David Cohen had mockingly snapped her fingers at the committee. She had a very winning way, but what really saved her was her supposed engagement to Hillesheim, who had gallantly intervened. His academic standing and his straight political record more than outweighed the dubious character of Boden. But for how long? One active Nazi could override a thousand passive opponents. And the bulk of the people were passive. Indeed they were almost paralysed by the doings of a demoniac few. This was borne upon me that very day in no uncertain fashion.

We were in one of the halls at Cologne, in one of the meetings pre-liminary to the great Nazi rally. It was an assembly of Rhenish teachers, all duly summoned from the schools and clocked in at the door. It was to be a real storm of a meeting, a sheer cavalry charge against the academic inertia of the whole Rhine province. The platform was ablaze with colourful banners and bunting, while flags and slogans and placards from the Nazi papers covered the walls and windows or swayed in challenging fashion from the gallery ballustrades.

From outside roared the familiar Nazi fanfares, the blare of trumpets, the thud of drums and the tread of parading thousands. And yet those teachers sat there, women for the most part, doubtless all of Catholic out-look, speechless, passive, unresponsive, without a single spark of the usual expectancy and all with 'eyes front' as though on parade. A palsy had fallen on them body and soul. Or was it sheer fear?

'Not very much fervour here,' I whispered to Hillesheim. We were sitting on chairs at the back, somewhat away from the press of the audience.

'Well, what do you expect? All those men on the platform are the Nazi officials of the union. And do you see those men at the ends of the rows?'

'The SA men?'

'Yes. They are the nominees of the party. They have shepherded their colleagues here and have them under watch and ward. You see, everyone here is under a spying eye.'

273

'Good Lord, and they don't rebel?'

'How can they? They are all state servants like myself. We are all of us fettered by our salary and our pension. If you English were in our position, all of you in socialised jobs and under the thumb of the state, your liberty would vapour away. You are no more brave than we are. And another thing. You must not equate the German public with a Hitler meeting.'

This was the true Hillesheim. To him the Nazi system was the better of two evils, the better of two dictatorships, the alternative to mob rule. He would naturally have preferred a tyranny of the intelligentsia, the absolute rule of those who know. After all, he was a university don. The Nazi regime to him was something very bad and yet it was the next best thing, the one and only assurance against Moscow.

The meeting that followed was the most curious fiasco I have ever known. I felt sorry for the speaker. He was a young man, uniformed, blindly enthusiastic, who had studied Hitler's methods to a T. He began in the approved style, bragging, arrogant, cocksure. It was an exact copy of a Hitler speech, above all when driving home his points. First, the seemingly indifferent tones, then the gathering fervour and finally the shrieking crescendo. But there was an important difference from a Hitler, for the Führer never spoke as a single voice.

Hitler spoke as a band conductor with the audience in full halloo around him, all of them cheering the accompaniment, and all roaring in on the chorus which gathered weight and momentum with every rising shriek. How often have we heard it, the slow fierce words that served as a cue, then the hastening tones and soaring pitch. Heavens, how his crowds responded. With a loud murmur and with arms outstretched, the whole assembly rose to its feet and, as he streaked into his crescendo, the applause went surging round him, frantic, tremendous, irresistible, sweeping him up to his top C, finally losing itself in a deafening salvo of cheers. Sheer hysteria, all of it, hysteria en masse, but with a triumphant feeling in every tone that the whole of Germany was listening, and not only the whole of Germany but Europe and the world.

Alas for our man of Cologne. Unlike his bellowing master, he did not talk to the converted, to a packed claque of his own supporters who passed his fervour on to the whole nation. He spoke as a lone voice, a still small voice crying in the wide wilderness. First, the low ominous tones and then, amid deepening stillness and under a dull impassive stare which made his raging paroxysm all the more grotesque, he raved his way to a climax, the awful hush of which left us wondering what it was all about. Not a wink from the audience, not a whisper, not a glimmer of approval in any face, as his ascent, like a rising spire, tapered off into silent nothingness. And the men on the platform were equally mute, benumbed as they were by the paralysing silence of the assembly. Then there was a clap from the chairman, the nominees took it up, and then the audience, after an irresolute pause, added a tame ovation. I had to suppress a laugh.

274

'Sh,' whispered Hilleshelm, giving me a violent nudge. But all at once the audience, misled by a move of the chairman, clapped at nothing at all. How uncertain those teachers looked, especially the women. There was a nervous glance to right and left, some desultory claps from here and there. Then a bravo started a general acclamation, which stopped as suddenly as it had begun. The poor speaker gasped, stammered a word or two and then, losing control of himself, attacked the audience.

'It's a conspiracy,' he shrieked, 'a conspiracy of the whole pack of you!'

Hillesheim whispered a word and we slipped out. The whole city was in a fever in expectation of the coming rally. We went up the Hohestrasse, which was draped from end to end with flags, while the blare of military music and the tread of demonstrating thousands were keeping every nerve on edge and inspiring all with hope or fear of great events to come. We saw it in the faces and bearing of everyone we met; in the streets, shops and restaurants, and even in the once phlegmatic peasants who anxiously clasped their parcels and ushered their children before them. There was the same inner tension, the same sense of growing crisis, the same quiver and vibration that blurred all calm reflection and later goaded the nation on to the Gadarene rush to total war. The hysteria of Hitler's meetings was simmering throughout the country and everyone in Germany was responding willy-nilly to its tremors.

The Sunday passed in a strange state of unrest. The vast army of Brown-shirts was now returning home and, away on the autobahn, we could hear the exultant calls from the lorries as they rumbled on their way to the south. At times they came roaring through the village, lorry after lorry of excited youths yelling their slogans to the villagers. But they, without the slightest response, gaped from the doors and windows or stood outside the Golden Hind in expectation of a brawl.

I thought of the scene a few years before when the Nazis stormed through the village, broke into the Kevelaar meeting and fired a sinister shot through Klassen's window. It was just the same again, the same excited lorry-loads of youths, the same uproarious career to the Golden Hind, the same flouting of the law, the same – but no, not the same but far worse, for there was no one now in the village who would dare to stand against them. Not one. I looked at my village neighbours as they stood idly in the street and I thought of the teachers at Cologne. How dumbly they belied all the flamboyance and flourish around them. They had looked dull, subdued, resigned, waiting for what might be in store.

While I was standing at the door, who should stroll up the street but Lambert, Boden and Klassen. I greeted them, very discreetly be it said, as they sauntered slowly past. Lambert cast me not a glance. Boden, with his head thrown back, gave me one of his insolent stares. He stumbled along over the cobbles in his stiff and square-built way, ignoring every greeting of the villagers as they passed.

Suddenly thinking of the Miss Wolffs, I looked over the street. The house was shuttered up with no betraying chink of light at the windows. Were they at home? Was Rachel cowering there in the shadows of her nook behind the screen? Was she trembling at every outburst from the street? I really ought to go over and give her a friendly word. But night had not yet fallen, so perhaps I had better wait for an hour or two.

I had never felt the full peril of her position until then. Not only was the law against her, but not a finger in the whole village would be raised on her behalf. Years ago one might have presumed some sympathy in Blankheim, overheard a whispered protest or even espied a helping hand in defiance of the law. But not now. I seemed to see the two hapless sisters being trampled and bludgeoned to death. And the fear that had frozen their hearts was not of the absolute Nazis such as Brechner, Hamann and the like, but of all the backsliding perverts like Boden, Lambert and Klassen who, in their scrubby scuffle for power, would stop at nothing to belie their telltale past.

The three had halted at a bend in the road and were now looking back, following Boden's pointed finger and nodding, so it seemed, their approval. Was he pointing at me? Or at Matthias who was standing outside his shop and observing them in a vague way? Strange to see Matthias so alone, but I caught the glimpse behind him of one or two peering faces as I went into the Engels house.

Shortly afterwards, Hempel and Müller called. They were both in Nazi attire, having just come back from Cologne and, after an absence of years, had decided to call once more on their old friend Herr Engels. Their massive forms seemed to fill the sanctum and, with their sprawling limbs and fresh-air faces, they looked and perhaps even felt a little out of place. Some embarrassment was apparent on both sides. Herr Engels came at once to the point. Lighting his pipe he gave them both a quizzical look.

'Strange events have strange causes.'

'You mean?' stammered Müller.

'Oh no, Herr Engels,' interrupted Hempel. 'You've been away a long time and we have come to pay our respects.'

'Thanks, many thanks. You are welcome, Kurt, Friedrich, if only as a reminder of former times.'

There was a touch of irony here, which was lost on the two visitors. Frau Nauheim had entered with a bottle of Rudesheimer, and with it a certain peace was sealed. The two enlarged on the events of the day, the parade, the rally, the great speech, and finally the dispersal of the host of demonstrators. Somehow, the conversation dragged, even when they broached more personal and familiar themes, Frau Klebert's health, the perils of Else's position, the underhand intrigues of Lambert and the like. They were concerned about all these things, but I sensed some further theme beyond all these, some underlying fear, something which made them start at every uproar in the street. Strange to see these two men, well-to-do, of splendid physique and in the safest garb the land afforded, shrinking from their own shadows.

We were soon to learn the reason for their unease. I had invited Bürger and Hillesheim to supper and they were just coming in at the front door when a fearful hullaballoo with shouts, blows and crashing of glass announced a sudden putsch against ourselves or the Jews.

Sledgehammer blows on the door sent tremors through the whole house. Hempel and Müller were up in an instant, rubber truncheons in their hands, and out they dashed into the hall as my two friends surged in, thrust on by a yelling horde behind. What a crowd they were, young, yelling, excited Nazis determined either to wreck the place or to lay hands on something – was it papers or jewellery supposed to be in my care? In they rushed, but they had not expected such a strong reception. Down they went like ninepins before the skull-cracking thwacks of Hempel and Müller flinging themselves into the fray. Out the young Nazis went, stumbling over each other and leaving a huddle of struggling bodies in the passage. There they lay, writhing, groaning, helpless.

But Hempel and Müller carried on past them. Leaving us to tend the injured or to drag them into the street, they made for the Wolffs' house without a glance behind.

I had to follow. But what a sight met our gaze! The Wolffs' house opposite had been raided. The door was down, the windows smashed in, the curtains bedraggled and torn, floating in the wind. From the upper windows Nazis were shouting warning cries and pitching stuff into the street, pictures, pots, vases and then with a fearsome crash a chest of drawers. Their comrades below were hallooing them on amid the whole-sale wreckage that littered the street. Young fellows they were, excited, red-faced, the worse for drink and all strangers to Blankheim. Their lorry stood to the right, masking the barber's shop.

And Rachel and Rebecca? With a pang I thought of their fate as I rushed out into the street. Hempel and Müller felt the same and pitched into the opposing crowd like two furies. A sudden light flashed into my mind. So that is why they had called, why they had brought the rubber truncheons and had talked and listened and waited until the crisis came. They had sensed the coming of the breakdown gang, had pondered it and prepared for it and were now fighting like demons to disperse the rabble. The raiders, taken by surprise, quailed and wilted, crouching down, turning tail and stumbling over the wreckage to get away. Back and back they went, their youthful figures contrasting with the broad frames of their two opponents. Still by sheer force of numbers they might win. They rallied, and were closing on our friends when help arrived.

I could hardly believe my eyes. Brechner, Zimmermann, Hamann, Kollass, all the left end of the committee, emerged like a bolt from nowhere to throng against the foe. There was a fearsome melee round the doorway, but the issue was not in doubt, and away went the crowd in a fright as Müller and Hempel forged their way into the house.

I tried to follow, but was held up. In the turmoil of friend and foe, for they all wore Nazi garb, I stood wedged in the corridor, crushed and buffeted by both sides as they forced their way inside or out. It was a blind uproarious scrimmage where all who had elbow room were wildly striking right and left or yelling out their protests at every blow received.

At length, by sheer pressure, I was borne into the sanctum, the first glimpse of which left me aghast. It was stripped of all its treasures, strewn with wreckage, and in the far corner the door of the big safe gaped open. Near it Hempel and Müller were talking in a most excited way.

At their feet lay Rebecca. Blood was streaming from a deep gash over her brow, her face ghastly white against her dark satin dress and her glossy black hair. She was fully dressed as though about to go out and had clearly been a moment too late. I knelt down and felt her pulse. Yes, she was alive, though badly stunned by some cowardly blow of the raiders.

'They've got all the papers,' cried Müller.

'Every mortal one,' blurted out his companion.

They were both standing there, wholly oblivious of Rebecca, casting hasty glances left and right, through the smashed garden window and down the whole length of the room into the street. The papers, all her records of dealings with the people of the village, with Hempel, Müller, Brechner, Zimmermann and the rest. They fiercely clutched their truncheons and their eyes flashed furiously from their badly bloodstained faces. What next?

'Let's hold up the lorry,' cried Müller.

They were out in an instant, while Brechner and Zimmermann tended to Rebecca, reviving her with water. She muttered something. Brechner knelt down and listened. It was something important for he motioned me away. Eventually he looked up.

'Let's get her to the car,' he said.

They helped her up and escorted her to the street. Here there was a fresh uproar. Hempel and Müller had boarded the lorry and flung the driver into the street. Out he shot into the roadway where he lay sprawling on his face, his limbs writhing in agony as though suffering from broken bones. Meanwhile, Hempel, to prevent any escape in the lorry, was wrenching at the controls. And then, as if by magic, the hubbub died down.

A strange hush fell on the scene as Brechner and Zimmermann, those two brownshirted Nazis, slowly escorted Rebecca down the street to the waiting car. The white face, the streaming blood, the helpless gait of the hapless Rebecca seemed to strike the people mute. Not a step did they take to help her, not a word of pity did they utter, not a look of sympathy illumined their quietly awestruck faces. They just stared in silent fear as she was carried to the car. And what of Rachel?

I could only pray that she had not been in the house, for there was no trace of her in the days that followed.

Meanwhile, Hempel and Müller raised the hue and cry for the missing papers. Their idea was to round up the raiders and to search them one by one. They went about their task with a will, waving their truncheons and lining up their youthful foes against the wall. Another fracas was in the offing when, at that very moment, the state police arrived, three car-loads of them, and swiftly brought the rioters to order, some rounding up the combatants, some entering the raided house, some collecting the badly injured.

As the first evidence was being taken I went back to my own home where I met another scene of ruin. Some of the raiders had got in again, only to be met by Bürger and Hillesheim who, with the help of Matthias and the Nauheims, had finally driven them out. But the old clock was toppled in the struggle, some of the quaint engravings smashed and a few relics of the chase swept from the wall. Even old Herr Engels had not escaped injury for he had refused to give up the keys.

'They wanted the keys of the safe,' said Hillesheim, 'and we had some ado in clearing them out.'

'And one actually went up to your room,' said Bürger, 'but happily in the course of the struggle I toppled him over the balustrade. He must have broken a bone for we had to carry him out.'

'But why into my room?' I asked.

'And why into Rebecca's room?' rejoined Herr Engels, who was still visibly trembling from the excitement of the past half-hour.

'Why to her safe? Why to the all-important papers? It wasn't a sadist raid but a raid with a purpose.'

'Led by someone in the know?'

'Or directed.'

'Aye, by someone in the village,' suggested Bürger. 'Someone who knew the ins and outs of the Wolffs' house and yours. You might make a guess, Herr Engels.'

The culprit was surely Lambert, but I refrained from saying so. In the meantime, the debris was cleared away, and before supper was announced in came Paul and Else all agape at the stirring news. The police came shortly after and took some depositions. But where was Rebecca? Where had she gone?

It was days before news began to filter through that she had sold the house a year before and that – though this was rumour – she had now smuggled herself and her wealth abroad. But the mystery of the stolen papers deepened with every hour, because the police seemed to have no interest in their theft. Perhaps the police were loth to prosecute. Such a case could bring only scandal on the party. And so, at a whisper from above, the whole affair was closed.

Chapter 27

Lambert Pays the Price

I felt that no papers had been stolen and that Rebecca, on leaving the house, had left not a single trace of her business deals behind her. To me this was all self-evident. But it certainly was not evident to any member of the committee. They all began to spend both restless nights and anxious days in expectation of the coming blow. For Rebecca had written proof of their secret deals with her, and this she had preserved as a protection and a threat, as a trump card against them in case she were betrayed. At least that was their thought. That she would be loyal to them when her use for them was over, that she would respect their families who had never respected hers, was more than they could hope for. They were all clearly guilty of bribery and blackmail, of jobbery with the hated Jews, of betrayal of the Nazi cause. Where was Rebecca, where were those papers, where was the thief? Despite the indifference of the police, these were the questions that harassed them and kept their minds in thrall.

They all felt, of course, that I was in the know. Why had our house been attacked? One of the gang had raided my room, the police had called upon me, searched all my cupboards and bags, and finally subjected me to a close examination. I was hand in glove with Rebecca, it seemed, and had been the go-between of her and her nameless friends. And now she had gone abroad. What more likely man than myself to have helped her over the border? Surely I knew her present address, received letters from her and her sister, and served as an agent in her affairs? So thought the people of Blankheim. The police must have known all about her and left me strictly alone, but the committee thought differently, and I did receive an enquiry from Lambert.

To me the situation was uncanny. The wrecked house over the way with its boarded door and windows, the silence, the emptiness of it, the feeling, when I looked across, that a phase of life had passed away and that something of myself was now no more, preyed heavily on my mind. The stares of Matthias and the neighbours seemed to deepen in penetration, and long after I had passed I felt their transfixing gaze.

On one occasion, Fenger brought me almost to a halt. He stood right in my path and set his eyes upon me as I approached. I had to step into the roadway as he turned slowly round and eyed me in his brazen way. And Herr Engels endured an equal scrutiny.

Poor Herr Engels. The raid seemed to echo and re-echo in his mind. Often as we sat together he would halt in his speech and listen, his hand to his ear, his eyes intent, his whole being possessed by the fear of an unexpected blow. After which he would breathe a deep sigh and take to the soothing influence of his pipe.

'I'm afraid I've lost my footing on earth and am rambling amid the blurs and empty bubbles of my own brain.'

He said this in a tone of self-reproach; he, the absolute realist, the most self-possessed man I've ever met.

Was he hinting at death when he went on, 'I hope I'm not peeping over the brink, nor adding my soul to the shadow of things. But I'd like to close the door on all that's going on and retire to my dreams of a happier long ago. For the walls have fallen down from this little nook of mine and I'm sitting in the odious draughts of the open street.'

The members of the committee continued to dog my every step and surprised me in many an unexpected way. I was returning one night from the station when a frail figure approached me from the shadow of the trees. It was a woman. Her face was muffled in a shawl, and she looked stealthily around her as she spoke.

'Mr Arnold, Mr Arnold!'

'Good evening. Well?'

I had nothing to fear, nothing, and yet I felt afraid. I could not see the woman's face and yet I felt I knew her.

'Do pardon me, pardon me, but may I talk to you for a moment?' She said this in such a breathless and apprehensive way that my fears vanished.

'But who are you, and what do you want?'

It was Frau Brechner, the frail and trembling Frau Brechner, and she beckoned me into the darkness of the lane that led to the Rhine. She faltered in her step, her speech and her story, lapsing at times into sobbing incoherence. We were out of all earshot and the lights of the Golden Hind were obscured by the distant houses and trees. Yet she gasped out her plea in almost inaudible whispers.

'Mr Arnold, do help us. You alone can save us, no one else, and it will cost you nothing.'

And so she sobbed out her story, her fears for Alex and his position, the house, the secret mortgage, the threat of eviction, prison, disgrace, the underhand dealings of Lambert, the spitefulness of Boden, the jealousies of Klassen and the committee. Surely I could help her. I knew Rebecca, I had influence with her, I stood high in Rachel's esteem, I enjoyed their full confidence in business affairs.

I soothed her as best I could, but why was she so prostrate? Frau Brechner was too pious a woman to be ravaged by mere earthly fears. I was seized by a sudden doubt.

'There's no call for such distress, Frau Brechner. Alex may have taken a bribe, but he has done no moral wrong.'

She suddenly seized my arm and struggled amid her sobs for an answer. 'But supposing he has?' she gasped at last.

'Has? What?'

'He tells me now it wasn't a bribe. He simply refused to pay. He stole it.'

She said these last three words with such a wail that I realised the full horror that had driven her into the night. Anything, anything, anything but the fleck of crime on her name! Of course, to Brechner himself the defence was a good one. He had simply refused to pay the rent since payment to a Jew was almost treason. In fact, his rent-free house would be to his credit in the Nazi view, and he need make no bones about it. He had told his wife the rent was a gift, to spare her Catholic conscience. An excellent defence, indeed, and yet I suspected a wink from Rebecca. It was all far too subtle for Brechner's primitive mind.

'Hush, Frau Brechner, don't worry. This new defence of Alex is a helpful hint from – now say it to no one else – Rebecca herself.'

Coming from me, the explanation was decisive. So I pooh-poohed her fears and assured her of all my help in clearing Alex. I could really do nothing, of course. I did not know where the Wolffs were. But she felt truly relieved by my consoling words. I accompanied her home, but she did not close the door when she entered. Long after I had left her and was well on my way to the village I could see her in the lamplit doorway still straining her eyes after my retreating form.

Frau Zimmermann was next. She came one night with Ursula, for she knew how much I admired the little girl. Though twelve years old she was as small as ever, with the same sweet modest look as when I saw her years before dancing with joy in the roadway at the sight of a piece of bread and cheese. I admired Frau Zimmermann, too, and my heart went out to her when I saw her care-worn face and read in every line the drab battle of the years and the haunting fear of those yet to come. But there was a charm as well in her pleasing features, the charm of a good conscience, of pure innocent thoughts and of troubles nobly borne. I felt a favour in her presence.

Ursula left after a minute or two, blushing her shamefaced thanks at the gift of a box of sweets. I accompanied her down to the door and something of the lilt and lyric of things went with her as she left the house. I lingered at the door as her radiant little form went speeding down the street.

Frau Zimmermann was awaiting me anxiously. Her deep distress as she opened up her heart to me meant that I was won for her plea whatever form it chose to take. She hid nothing from me, apparently in the belief that I knew all. Hans had taken a bribe, the rent of his little house. He had taken it on conditions prescribed by Rebecca and signed by himself so that evidence was lying against him in case he should prove false. And now the papers were stolen and perhaps in hostile hands. The blow could fall at any minute.

'So you are living in a house to which you have no title?'

'As far as ownership goes, no. But we have a rentbook, signed up two months in advance, though we have paid no rent. She used to sign the book as though we'd paid it. The book protects us, but the contract? What of that? We are staring ruin in the face and you can help us, Mr Arnold.'

'How, Frau Zimmermann?'

'Write to Rebecca and tell her to put us right. Ask her about the contract if only for little Ursula's sake. You would not see her plunged into ruin. Do help us!'

She went on with her plea without allowing me a word. But eventually I spoke and gave her what assurances I could. As far as I knew, the papers, if any existed, were not in hostile hands. Moreover, her husband, so I had heard, had now an excellent defence. It would meet the charge at every point. She suddenly went white and then blazed up as red as fire.

'You mean ...?'

'Yes. From the very outset he refused to pay the rent.'

'And robbed Rebecca of the money! Never! Yes, he has talked like that, but we are not thieves, Mr Arnold. It is a gross untruth. I would never have stood for it, not even at the price of my life.'

The thought of a smirch on her good name was more than she could stand. So I assured her once more of my high esteem and goodwill. She went at last, but only after imploring me with tears in her eyes and finally taking my hands and pressing them to her breast.

Then Klassen. He sent word to me to visit him and, when I declined to go, he came to me. No pleadings with him. He sat down at my table as though the room were his and I, simple schoolboy, were at his beck and call. What a martinet he was! Assuming his most cutting expression he told me in staccato tones that he had come on behalf of the committee. The committee, did I understand? The committee! The greatest power in Blankheim and the strong right hand of the government in those parts! And the committee would stand for no nonsense. I, as a foreigner, had allied myself with the Jews and was aware of certain things about which the committee must be informed. So I had better answer his questions and answer on the dot. As he rapped out all these threats his sharp features and pointed beard seemed to stab the air and add an ominous point to his words. But I remained unmoved.

'Nothing doing, Herr Klassen. If you, as a private person, require any information ... '

'Private person?'

'Private person. Brechner is the group leader here, not you.'

'What do you mean?' he shouted. 'I am as answerable as anyone in Blankheim.'

'Tell Brechner that, not me. In any case, if you require any information you had better go to the police. They've already examined me twice and have my full and honest replies. Apply to them. And if you want to usurp their functions get their permission first – and Brechner's.'

I have never seen a man in such a rage. His face went white. He rose from his seat, clenched the table as he leaned across and hissed in the most detestable way.

'You'll appear before the committee!'

'Most gladly. At their invitation, of course – and Brechner's.'

That extra bit about Brechner, added after a slight pause and with a certain touch of malice, made him wince. He said much more in a blustering tone, but I declined to listen. I stood by the door the whole time, prepared to bow him out. He went, casting back a hateful glance as he reached the foot of the stairs.

So a few days later I met the committee, though only after a prior word with Zimmermann and Brechner. They met me at the station in Bonn, and asked me to be careful, to say nothing that would lead to anything else, reminding me that Boden, who had had no truck with Rebecca, was ready to oust them all. In accusing one I would indict the rest for, as Herr Engels used to say, the one rope would do for every neck.

I met the committee in the room of the Golden Hind where I had met the Kevelaar Club some years before. I thought of that assembly as I sat down at the foot of the table, that scene of generous fellowship, that free exchange of jest and laughter, the inspiring presence of my noble friend and, above all, the worthy purpose with which they had come together. As I now looked round the room my heart sank. Brechner, as the chairman of the meeting, sat at the far end of the table, a somewhat inferior figure, aloof, suspicious, out of place, uncertain in his thoughts and stumbling in his speech and clearly at loggerheads with his more educated colleagues. Yes, Klassen, Boden, Lambert, the renegades from the Catholic Party, these were the men who bestrode the committee and plied the decisive word, while he, Brechner, the only true Nazi in the room, was overshadowed by these turncoats and reduced to a hostile silence. I felt I had to hold my own and if possible counter-attack to restore the balance of power. For Klassen sat to my right, Lambert and Boden to my left, while Brechner was sitting afar off, quite out of touch with the true centre of debate.

Klassen opened the meeting and I at once cut him short.

'Excuse me, Herr Klassen, I am not here at your instance but at that of the committee. Herr Brechner, you are the chairman, would you kindly tell me why I'm here?'

My interruption took Klassen aback, but shook Brechner out of his torpor. He gave a short gasp and then asserted himself. Of course he was chairman. Who was Klassen to thrust him aside?

'Quiet, Klassen!' he insisted as Klassen began to attack me. 'I am chairman here, not you. You'll speak when I give you the word.'

'Bravo!' cried Hamann and Zimmermann. 'Brechner is chairman here.'

'In affairs of the Party we are all equals,' said Klassen, 'and I shall speak my mind freely, whether chairman or not.'

'Equals!' shouted Brechner, whose blood was now fully up. 'Equals, do you say? I, an old member of the party, one of the veterans of the movement, and you just a crisis convert who ratted the Catholic position at the last moment.'

The meeting was now in an uproar and, but for the arrival of Hempel and Müller, it would have been broken up there and then. They were not really members of the committee, but their presence was essential to preserve order. They were in sympathy with neither side, but they wanted clarity about Rebecca and the papers. They were both on bail in connection with the raid. Their massive muscular presence soon subdued the meeting. They gave Brechner the word.

'Well, Herr Brechner, why am I here?' I asked.

'To tell you the truth, Herr Arnold, I don't know. You've been before the police and that ought to be enough. But some people seem to think that you know more than you've admitted, Rebecca's whereabouts, the mystery of the papers and so on.'

'Perhaps,' said Müller, 'you could throw some light on the matter.'

'None whatsoever,' I replied.

'But there's a very strong rumour in the village that you can.'

'But if rumour's to be believed you might address your queries to others. I know nothing, but there are pointers, you know.'

'And they are?'

'You've no need to ask the police. They are as plain as a pikestaff.'

They all went silent at this. They gazed at me with their greyish faces, each revealing its private secret and its general suspicion. Did each think that he alone had taken a bribe from Rebecca or did they guess that they were all involved? What did each know and each suspect?

'Well tell us what is plain,' thumped out Lambert. His face was as grey as any, and his eyes glinted.

'Need I say?'

'You must.'

'It's as plain as any pikestaff that the raid on the Wolffs' house was no mere chance. It wasn't an outburst of the SA against the hated Jews. As Herr Engels said, each raider went to work like a dog on the lead. They went for the safes and papers. Now who in the village has an interest in those?'

'The raiders,' blurted out Lambert, 'acted as National Socialists against the hostile Jews. Who can blame them for that?'

'And the attack on our house?'

'They mistook your house for the Jewish one. They were misled by the chalk marks on the wall.'

'And the attack on the safes?'

'Nothing was stolen. Naturally they would look for incriminating papers. But nothing was taken away. They were searched and nothing was found. Who are you to cast suspicion on zealous SA men? Do you, a foreigner, accuse our brothers of brigandage? You must answer for such malicious talk. And I, a man of the law, will see that you don't escape.'

I had to let fly at that. Lambert was a man who clearly would stop at nothing. The raiders, as SA men, were not likely to be punished. Their guilt would only reflect upon the movement. A scapegoat would have to be found. And what better scapegoat than me? By hook or by crook some whitewash would be found for the party.

'Congratulations, Herr Lambert. It's something to have found a scapegoat. But as a scapegoat I don't fit the facts. There was a purpose in that raid and that purpose was for papers. And let me tell you to your face that *that* purpose was yours.'

'You liar!' He thumped the table with both his fists. I thought he was going to strike me, but he turned round in fury to the committee.

'You all heard that, that damnable slander. I call you all to witness what he said. You dare,' he thundered, standing up and shaking his fists in my face, 'you dare to sling such mud at me!'

I stood up, they all stood up, all loudly calling for order. I was prepared for a fight, but Hempel and Müller intervened. They came between me and Lambert.

'Just move up two. We are sitting here.'

They pushed Lambert up the table, and settled down in the chairs between.

'Now, no wild statements,' said Müller to me. 'Just say what you can vouch for. And you,' he said, turning to Lambert, 'sit down quietly and listen.'

'I refuse to listen.'

Hempel forced him into his seat. I resumed.

'I say that the raid was organised by someone who knew the houses and the position of the safes. It was a raid for papers. Were you looking for the ones you had lost, the ones that were stolen months ago? Or were there others on which you thought you would like to lay your hands?'

'I refuse to listen to such slanderous stuff,' shouted Lambert.

'Slander? By no means. You are the biggest intriguer in Blankheim. Have you forgotten that you invited me to your house? That you tried to bribe me? And make me a tout on Rebecca? Reporting to you the details of all the people who called? As a man of the law you ought to have been more careful. As an honest man I refused. And have you forgotten the dastardly way you revealed Herr Engels's private affairs to the committee? You, a man of the law, who are pledged to discretion. Yes, you, who would like to have your finger on every paper in the village.'

There was a rumpus after that. Lambert stood up to go, shouting out his threats and promising legal proceedings for unlawful detention. But my blood was up. I threw further fat on the fire by shouting: 'If any papers were stolen they were stolen by you to be used against every notable man in the village. You've been amassing evidence for a long time. You might have struck before, but Rebecca was a bit too clever for you!'

This was a thing I should never have said. It sent a shock through the whole company. Even Lambert was taken aback and gazed at me dumbfounded for a moment. All the others gasped enquiries. How? What? Explain.

Lambert, seizing his chance, broke away to the door and, as the others turned to stop him, rounded on them with a pistol.

'Back! Back! Or I fire!'

'Put it down, put it down!' The cry came from all sides.

'I shall not,' stuttered Lambert, who was shaking with excitement and waving the weapon in a truly reckless way. Perhaps he might have fired at us in his fit of the sheer jitters for he had lost all control of his hands and tongue.

'I bought this,' he shrieked in jerky outbursts, 'after the attempt on my life some time ago and I'm taking no second chance. Back there, back there, or I fire!'

Suddenly Müller leapt forward and seized his wrist. There was a deafening report as the pistol went off and a loud cry from Klassen who fell back struck in the arm. Then another and another, which sent Boden and others scuttling under the table. But Müller held fast and bent back Lambert's wrist until with a sickening crack the bone broke. Down he collapsed like a sack.

Did Lambert fire in earnest? I do not think so. He was too great a coward to take deliberate aim. There he lay on the floor, white, helpless, in a dead faint. And there lay Klassen too in an equally helpless plight. As Stenzel, the proprietor, peered in, Müller offered him Lambert's weapon.

'Hand that over to the police and let us get these men to hospital.'

By the time we got out, almost the whole village was assembled in the street. We were escorted by the police to the town hall where our evidence was taken. It lasted hours and hours, and it was midnight before I got away.

My nerves were all of a jangle. I had mentioned Rebecca's name and had made a hint of things that should have remained concealed. The police had harped on this very remark, returning to the question again and again to elicit what I knew. I was stubborn in the one reply.

'It was just a bow drawn at a venture. I knew the two were at loggerheads and that Lambert was trying to pry into the Jewish affairs. From hearsay and from words half-heard I felt that Rebecca would thwart his attempts. But I knew nothing for certain.'

'Had Miss Wolff any part in the rifling of Lambert's safe?'

'I know nothing of that. Miss Wolff was always clever enough to keep to the right side of the law.'

'How do you know?'

'By the very fact that you left her alone. Though a Jewess and outside the law she was never under arrest.'

'But she might have engaged in illegal acts and you as her guest might have known it.'

'And you as the police would have known it as well. Or were you such fools as to be bluffed? I shall assume you know your business.'

They smiled grimly at this and I gave them a tart wink. This put our talk on a better footing, but it was not without a meaning glance that they said they would see me again. And so I left.

To soothe my nerves and to avoid the crowd, which still thronged the main street, I went a roundabout way home, along lanes and over fields via the other end of the village. It was long after midnight. The streets were now deserted, though lights in one or two windows showed that some were still out of bed. A car passed me as I strode on in the darkness, but it stopped about a furlong ahead outside Lambert's house.

I felt certain it was Lambert's. Someone was getting out, slowly, painfully. He was talking to the driver, who took him carefully across to the door and gently helped him in. Yes, it was Lambert's house all right and that was Lambert who must have just returned from the clinic after receiving attention there. I slackened my pace and halted so as not to be seen by either of them. The driver went back to the car, started up and drove away. I did not move, however. I still held back in the darkness lest prying eyes should see me.

The street was strangely quiet. There was no movement in the opposite windows, and from those on my side came no light. So all was well. Or was it? One, two, three, I might have counted ten, and was about to resume my way when I heard a sudden sound, the tearing open of a door, a scurrying rush that drove me back to the shadows, and the scurry of retreating feet. I caught a hasty glimpse of two men racing away at top speed, two familiar forms, and away I hurried too, instinctively, blindly, at a truly panic pace, down one dark alley and then another for I felt some crime had been committed and that I might be involved.

Lambert had been attacked before in his home and now at this ominous moment he had perhaps been attacked again. I made my way to the towpath, the dark, deserted towpath where the barges slept at their moorings and where their little lantern lights rippled peacefully over the Rhine. How soothingly still it was, with the cool night air fanning my heated brow. I was glad to be alone and I lingered for more than an hour unravelling my tangle of thoughts.

What I had surmised in the silence of the towpath was fully confirmed next day. Assured that Lambert was not at home, two men had entered the house and rifled the safe. It was a very hasty raid and, to save both time and trouble, they had thrown everything into the stove, documents, deeds, rolls of notes, every paper they could find, whether it concerned their case or not. The files and records for at least three years had met with the same fate, thrust pell-mell into the stove, which was filled with glowing ashes by the time the police arrived. They might have saved the smouldering remains but for their preoccupation with Lambert. He was found dying in the corridor, his skull cracked by a blow from a heavy weapon. He was in no condition to be heard.

Clearly, robbery was not the object, nor was murder. The raiders had been surprised by Lambert's unexpected return. They had lain low when he entered, but on discovery had attacked him. In the assurance that dead men tell no tales, they had struck at Lambert to kill, fired thereto with desperation, hatred and fear. Who were the culprits? I spent hours waiting for news of arrests, but the question was not as easy as one might have supposed. Lambert had enemies everywhere, not merely in the village but also in Cologne and Bonn, and just as thugs had raided Rebecca so perhaps thugs had raided him, in each case blackguards hired from outside.

Then came another theory, rumoured widely in Blankheim and just as widely believed, that the police themselves were involved. Were they, too, afraid of exposure? Had they also had dealings with Rebecca? Accepted gifts for favour? And played fast and loose with the law? Rumour reached such a pitch and assumed such persuasive power that within two days of the event there was no sure witness in the village. The plainest of facts were smothered in the sheer haze of hearsay. Indeed, there was no extra peril in guilt for even innocence was a ground for suspicion.

The whole village was present for the funeral, man, woman and child. They lined the streets, they packed the church, they thronged the grave-yard, hundreds of earnest faces, hundreds of bared heads, hundreds of clasped hands, but never a tear. It was weird to see. One felt that with all their horror of the crime there was a deep undertone of inner relief. The plea: at least I am innocent. The sigh: there but for the grace of God. The question: I really wonder where my neighbour stands?

Six men shouldered the coffin, including the two familiar forms I had seen on the fatal night, two respectable family men who were now at one with society, and fulfilling with a real dignity the most solemn of its behests. With bowed heads and clasped hands they heard the final words of the priest, muttered the due responses, and crossed themselves in God's name. I thought none the worse of them for it. And yet, when Ursula met me at the gate and made her little curtsey, I felt an inner rebuke.

Yes, it was hard to face her, and hard to face Herr Engels after the events of that night. My mental reservations lay like a blurring shadow between us. I had seen the two culprits; I had made a hasty guess; and I might in an honest outburst have enlightened the police. Instead, I told them a half-truth, slurred over the essential facts and played with hints and inklings to lead them to a false elsewhere. And this not only with the police. To all I met I told the same misleading story, and every time I told it I felt the same drop in my own esteem.

Worst of all were my meetings with the police. I had to brazen out my false version, which threatened to crack under the ever-increasing strain. The taxi-driver who had taken Lambert home picked me out as the man whom he had seen upon the road. At first he was decisive, but under the stress of my questions he became a little vague. But the threat was there. Time and time again the police returned to the theme.

Luckily, Herr Engels was no longer alone. Joseph, his son, had been released, having proved that the jewels, which were to be smuggled out by the Captain, had never belonged to him. And then Frau Klebert was expected to return. These developments crowded out the story of Lambert's death, but still I felt uneasy. The police were wearing me down, they were pressing the committee hard and the rope seemed at times to be tightening round the doomed men. But no decisive move was made. More evidence was needed. Some unexpected factor was heading them off the main track, some influence perhaps, some force or, what seemed to me most likely, some smuggling up the back stairs. Under a tyranny everyone has his price.

Chapter 28

I Am Beaten Up

My only escape from all these trafficking thoughts was to go to Neuenahr. I had to apply to the police, of course, who held me, in effect, on bail. After all, I was the man with whom Lambert had last quarrelled, whom he had threatened to prosecute and who had threatened him in turn. And then I, or someone like me, had been seen near Lambert's house, within minutes of Lambert's murder. According to the police, I had been playing a darkling part and knew more than I confessed.

Nevertheless, they let me go, but I had to report to the police when I arrived at Neuenahr and keep in touch with them throughout my stay. I was grateful for the concession and felt that the murk was lifting from my part in the whole affair. So I was very happy as I packed my bag to go, depressed a little later after a farewell word from my old friend. He assured himself that the door was closed and gave me a quizzical look.

'I'm grateful to the police,' I said.

'Well, beware of their being grateful to you.'

'What for?'

'For another witness.'

'How's that?'

'Well, Tilde's an excellent girl, but two tongues are longer than one and even the shortest story grows in the telling. So beware! Do take a seat.'

We sat down and he resumed. 'A mere whisper to that simple girl may return as a thousand echoes to those who are straining to hear them. And I know you'll utter more than a whisper. Infinitely more. What fills the heart flows over at the lip ... and remember, you might control what's being said, but not what's being heard. A private tiff in the kitchen becomes blood and thunder in the bar parlour. So be silent.'

He said all this between the puffs of his pipe and with such intensive glances as revealed his deep concern. Though as mentally alert as ever, he was not as calm as he had been and I felt some quiver of anxiety in all he said and did. The events of the past few months had taken toll; his daughter's nervous breakdown, the suicide of his son-in-law, the un-wavering threat to Else, his son's arrest, the brutal attack on the house and, finally, Lambert's murder in which we seemed to be involved. Each and all these things had impaired his self-possession and left him halting at his

291

own fears. I think he was afraid to let me go, and I mean afraid for himself. He felt stronger in my presence.

My heart was heavy with the thought of him when I arrived at Neuenahr, but it was heavier still at my glimpse of Tilde when she wonderingly opened the door. Her sad face lit up as she clasped my hand in hers and led me in. I looked at her in silence, vainly trying to find a word. She was silent too, paralytically so, for her eyes were tense with suppressed tears and her lips were trembling with a sob of sheer sadness. So we stood for a whole minute with my hands firmly clasped in hers while my heart strove in vain to ask her what was troubling her so. Then she started to speak, but immediately broke down in an outburst of tears. I helped her into a chair.

Her mother was deadly ill in a nursing home with little hope of survival. Indeed, every moment now was shadowed by the end. It harrowed me to hear poor Tilde speak, for her hands were clasped in prayer before her eyes and her whole being shook with the spasms of her grief. But she was brave. She thanked me for my consoling words and for one tremendous moment I felt her tear-stained cheek against my own. I could have crumbled to the ground in my own unworthiness, and even now I am chastened at the gracious recollection.

How often after all these years I return once more to the scene, to that simple room in the Eifel with its panelled walls, its boarded floor, its heavy oaken beams. Yet, topping the splendour of all my early days is that glimpse of her sad face near mine, that trustful touch upon my cheek, that clasp of a hand. But the instant passed, and away she went to freshen her hands and face and to prepare some coffee for me.

I did not follow her, nor even peep through the door she left open. I was afraid to speak, deadly afraid of intruding on her thoughts or of stealing on feelings wholly due to her mother. I sat in silence and waited, listening intently to every little sound, her step, the clink of a cup, the plash of water, the familiar grind of the coffee-mill, all of them sundered by deep mysterious pauses. Those quiet moments of waiting were the most wistful I had ever known.

She came at last with the tray and the room seemed to light up in her presence. She was smiling through her tears.

'You know,' she said, as she set down the tray and looked me steadily in the face, 'all the time I was making coffee I was listening and listening and listening, and you never made a move.'

'No, I was too busy listening to you.'

'Oh! To every sound?'

'To every one, including the slur of your heels.'

She laughed out joyously.

'I did it on purpose,' she giggled.

It was now my turn to laugh. Tilde was like a princess in the simplicities of her peasant home. Something of her charm pervaded every part of the room, as if a glance of hers had entered each, and all were peeping back in silent glee. We lingered indulgently over the coffee, or fondly toyed with the slices of bread or trifled with the fruit and biscuits until dusk suddenly broke upon us and painfully surprised us still treading the air of a dream.

Some time later Herr Weichert came in. He looked pale and thin, indeed so thin that his clothes hung loosely about him and his collar seemed a size too large. And when he sat down he drooped, slumping into his chair as though unable to stand erect. I tried to entertain him with my news, when he had washed himself and changed, but his eyes assumed a far-off look and his thoughts seemed all abroad. In the midst of my talk about Blankheim he suddenly interrupted me with an outburst on his own affairs.

'And they threaten to give it to one who's more worthy if I don't keep it up to the mark. More worthy, think of it, more worthy,' he cried, 'after taking away my best plot and forcing me to look for a job in the valley.'

I was totally at a loss for a moment to understand what he meant, but Tilde peeped in and explained.

'It's the new entailing law,' she said. 'If our farm is not kept up to scratch it will be taken away and given to another. Father's got to work at Neuenahr as the farm now does not pay and we have had to let things drift. So they threaten to turn us out.'

'And to give the house and land to Hermann or to one of his nominees,' said Herr Weichert. 'As if they haven't done harm enough.'

Tears gushed to his eyes as he made this reference to his wife, whose health had broken down under the ruthless persecution of the past two years. It was Frau Weichert's house, the place where she and her father were born, and the thought that it might be lost and fall into the hands of such a ruffian as Hermann had driven her to distraction. I thought of Herr Engels and his almost religious attachment to his quaint ancestral home. How would he face such a threat?

'Why not sell up first?'

'Sell up, sell up!' gasped Herr Weichert. 'Sell what has been ours for all our lives, sell our home for mere money.' The profanity of such an act seemed to leave him completely aghast. Tilde broke the stillness.

'Sell up! We shall blaze it up. Send the whole thing up in smoke and ashes before Hermann gets his hand on it. We have only one hope, John, that Uncle Franz will take it over.'

'Yes, the only hope, the only hope,' said Herr Weichert in a brooding tone, after which he seemed to sink into a torpor and to be deaf to all we said. He would have left his supper untouched but for remonstrances from Tilde. And even afterwards when he took to his pipe by the stove he dawdled so long between the puffs that he had to light up again and again. Eventually he got up with a jerk and went out for a glance at the stable.

To escape his gloom we went into the garden and walked across the little field. From the stable door on our right, which threw a dim gleam on to the

293

yard, we heard a grunt and the scrape of a rake. Herr Weichert was busy and we could see his shadow flitting to and fro on the inner wall. A dog appeared in silhouette with head alert and ears erect, stared at us for a moment and then began to speed in our direction. But at a call from Herr Weichert it halted, and on we went.

It was dark in the field and, save for the whistle of the wind, very still. Even our steps on the soft grass seemed to sound away over to the road. We stopped at the top and listened. There was a faint noise of voices coming from the valley, the snatch of a song, a whistle and then all went still again. Away in the distance against a background of sheer darkness were some indications of the village, mere pricks of light from the cottage windows and the village inn.

'It's the only time I like to venture out,' whispered Tilde. 'I do not see the changes to the farm or the people of the village.'

'But how about the livestock?'

'Oh, we've got rid of that, save for the hens, two or three pigs and a cow. A boy comes over to help us since father does not have the time any more. Oh, father's going in again.'

I looked. The light had gone from the stable and I heard the closing of the door. At that moment voices came round a bend in the road, youthful voices it seemed to me as they called out into the night. Herr Weichert was calling too. But he was addressing not the youths but the dog, which was now growling fiercely by the roadway. A hubbub was flaring up. I guessed they were pelting the dog with stones and that Herr Weichert had intervened.

'I hope they are not pelting father,' gasped Tilde, running towards the road. I followed her. Despite the hail of stones she ran right up to the dog and seized it by the collar. The youths continued to shout, but Tilde did not answer.

'Come in, Tilde,' said Herr Weichert quietly.

I can say little of what happened next. I was just aware of a crowd of youths, all shouting out abuse or casting stones at my retreating hosts, but the moment they caught sight of me they raised a great cry. As one man they rushed upon me and before I could raise my arms they were showering blows on my defenceless head. I was battered to the ground in an instant and, amid the loud confusion of sounds, I could hear the growl of the dog, the high-pitched voice of Tilde and the shouts of her father. I seemed to be whirled away on a mighty flood of forms, deeper and deeper into a most unearthly stillness, where I was lying wholly alone staring dreamily into a void.

Now I am not going to blame the Nazis for this attack. I admit that Nazi shadows were lowering over the Weicherts and that a certain political animus played a part. But the Nazis in the main were a very disciplined body and were not easily involved in mere riot. Their violence was always prompted from above. No, it was not the Nazis. I was an intruder in the village, the favoured friend of Tilde, and this these country youths could not forgive.

They had beaten up Albert Gerster in a similar way, and that was before the Nazis came. However that may be, I was laid up for weeks in a nursing home suffering from concussion and three broken ribs. It was small satisfaction to know that two at least of the attackers were severely mauled by the dog, since Tilde was also injured and Herr Weichert did not wholly escape. In fact, Tilde was so badly injured – for she did not spare herself in the fight – that she was unable to attend the funeral of her mother.

I awoke from my coma to face the police. Not the police of the Ahr but of Blankheim, for the mystery of Lambert's murder was still unsolved. Three of them trooped in, three typical German officials, and sitting at my bedside they subjected me in their relentless way to a close examination. Sticklers they were, plying the same questions again and again, so hammering at every detail that my brain began to flag and my memory to waver until I had to ring the doctor for relief.

I was granted a rest at lunchtime, but three hours later they returned to the charge. In they came again, silent and relentless as ever, sat down, drew out their notebooks and, after an understanding nod to each other, began once more. But in my desperation I resolved, as far as my strength allowed, to play a more active part. Brushing aside the first question I blurted out my protest.

'Excuse me, gentlemen, but what are you after? I have answered these questions again and again, and apparently my answers are not enough. Tell me what you want to hear. In other words, what do you want me to admit?'

'The truth. Therefore answer the questions as we put them.'

'I refuse. You are not trying to elicit evidence but simply to enforce admissions. I cannot carry on. My brain is getting blurred and I may be saying things which, in a normal state, I should deny. Be frank with me. I shall be equally frank with you for I've nothing to conceal.'

Though I uttered the last few words without a qualm I wondered at the ease with which I lied. Whether the police sensed the lie I do not know. They just continued to dun me until the doctor intervened. Frankly, I was puzzled. What was stopping the police from making an arrest? To me the problem was a simple one and ought to have been easily solved. But it was simple only to me. There were complications beyond my ken, facts that led enquiry to places far from Blankheim and involved numbers of people who had been evading the law. Here I suspected Rebecca's influence.

Of course, they questioned Tilde and went carefully through my letters. They found nothing, so absolutely nothing that they grew suspicious. Something must have been held back, something concealed, and their reaction to this verged almost on the comic.

'Some evidence is missing.'

'How do you know?'

'Because we haven't found it.'

To their great surprise, I laughed outright. The three were in deadly earnest, indeed in such deadly earnest that they called me to order at once. I tried to explain, but they frowned me down. On and on they went, asking me the same or nearly the same questions, noting and noting and noting what they had noted a score of times before, pausing only for an exchange of nods or staring me into compliance when I referred them back to my previous replies.

I breathed a sigh of relief each time they closed their books with a snap, stood up and bade me goodbye. But an end to all this came at last. One day after a long session they shook hands with me most heartily, wished me a swift recovery and went off never to return.

The same day in came Tilde. She, too, had been a hospital case and had been laid up for weeks, weeks which had wrought a change in her. I hardly knew her at the first glance, so pale she seemed, so subdued, so sad. And then she looked older too, indefinably older, as though her mind were lost in a shadow and all her happy childhood had followed her mother to the grave. She just sat down and looked away for a moment, playing with her trembling fingertips or smoothing away some fold in her black dress, which made a mournful contrast to the white enamel of my room. Her first words were almost a whisper. She asked me about my health and revealed her distress at being, though only in an innocent way, the cause of my troubles. I laughed. I thanked her for her sympathy and reminded her of the girl in Goethe's poem where a violet, though trampled under foot, rejoiced because the foot was *hers*.

She brightened up at this and a glimpse of the old Tilde made me forget for a moment the sadness in her grey-blue eyes and pale cheeks. She was able to give me her news. Her uncle had bought the house in which her father could still have his home. As for herself – but here she gave me a strange look.

'Yes, you yourself Tilde, what are you going to do?'

'I am keeping something from you, John.'

'Oh, and why?'

'I am under a solemn promise not to mention it, not even to my father. At least for the time being. But to ease my conscience towards him I am mentioning the fact just as I am mentioning it to you.'

'And the fact concerns your future?'

I was puzzled, but I had to respect her silence. After all, in view of the attentions of the police, my own lips were sealed about many things. And this made me uneasy. For a secret is the ready-set-go of all deceit.

So Tilde was keeping something from me. The police had interviewed her, that was certain. I felt their presence now, as we had felt the presence of Hermann stealing softly behind us in our wanderings on the Ahr. So in our days of convalescence I felt a following shadow, a warning voice, a whisper. This time we went along the Rhine, not along the bank, but over the wooded heights by Rheinbreitbach. In the heart of the forest is a little wayside shrine, Auge Gottes or the Eye of God, and perhaps the sense of being observed led us to this lonely spot, away from the prying peeps of the police and into wider and diviner views.

The shrine is a simple block some seven or eight feet high with a niche for a picture of Christ, while the eye of God, who sees all things, is portrayed on the gable above. The whole is enclosed in fir trees with a gap serving as an entrance to the triangular space beyond and with rustic seats facing the hallowed stone. And all around are the silences of the forest, a stillness such as broods over the reft recollections of past years. After the tiring walk up the hills Tilde sank into one of the seats, removed her hat and fanned her heated cheeks. For a moment I stood there lost in thought.

The scene lives on within me. I have a view of it before me, which I made then and still preserve. I was pondering it only an hour ago, and by the light of my lamp the scene took on a deeper tone. The shrine, the girl, the rustic seats, the touches of sunlight on the turf, even the pathetic droop of the grasses.

I still preserve that scene, for to lose it would be to efface my days, to disperse the light that was, and to darken the spacious skies above the heights of Rheinbreitbach. I could return to the very stones in the picture, to the wild grasses by the rustic seats, to the stray flowers peeping up from the turf or to the soft and elusive shadows of the leaves.

After so many years, I ponder these vanished forms and wonder at the breathless presence that lives even in the very least of them. For in every one is also some touch of my companion who adds the delight of her society to all my memories of the Rhine. In such a glimpse I am once again on the heights of Rheinbreitbach, amid the russet tones of the forest, which was then deeply tinged with the brown of the autumn fall, with views of Bruchhausen, of distant clouds and the Rhine, of those long carefree hours when the sun was yet high and the heather still green on the hills.

An hour later we were sitting on the heights above Honnef with the Rhine far below us and the proud outline of the Drachenfels ahead. How steeply it rose from the sloping vineyards by the river, right from a bluff of bare rock to the bold and steadfast ruin on its brow. But my eye was not on the old keep, nor on the rising trend of the hills behind, nor on the sombre mass of the Rodderberg which lay in deep shadow on the further bank of the Rhine, but on the long and slender island of Nonnenwerth with its nunnery and chapel half-enclosed in leafy trees.

I knew the island well, and I was lingering in the view of the gardens and the walks when, all at once, I realised that I was not alone in my thoughts. Tilde was also lost in the view, wholly oblivious of all the grandeur around her yet so responsive to my inmost meditations that she turned round to me as though I had spoken.

'You were about to ask me something,' she said simply.

'Yes, I was.'

I hardly knew how to go on. I was honour-bound not to ask her a thing, but a question rushed to my lips. For there, with the view of the nunnery, was, perhaps, the answer to my question.

'Did your mother express a last wish she hoped you would fulfil?'

'Very many.'

'Did she mention Nonnenwerth?'

She gazed at me for a moment, but I tried in vain to guess the thought behind her troubled look.

'John, you are probing my secret.'

So we dropped the subject, but I wondered whether the dead hand lay on all her future days.

Chapter 29

The One-Man Parliament

On returning to Blankheim a sense of something lost and gone beset me. No one seemed to know me as I walked along the street, and those who did just looked askance or gave me the merest nod of recognition. On they went, intent on anything but me, and yet their following glance when I had passed revealed to what a pitch I held their thoughts.

Did they really suspect me of murder? I think they did, for the taxi-driver's story that he had seen me on the fatal night not far from Lambert's house was known to everyone. And then, when things were looking black, I had vanished Heaven knows where. That had certainly set them talking!

It was a relief to them to feel that the villagers were innocent, that a foreigner was to blame. It was all as they had suspected. I was just Rebecca's lackey and tarred with the same brush.

Then I met Brechner turning into Station Road, not far from the Golden Hind. He started a little, but had to stop though it was only after an obvious delay that he shook my outstretched hand. As I saw from his bluish garb, he had lost his official position and was now a railway worker. I made no comment about it, nor did he. To my questions about himself and his wife he gave the most halting replies. He had become a weakling. He, the once insolent Nazi who would have browbeaten the best in the village, kept turning his eyes away as though unwilling to meet my gaze.

He was glad to get away and, knowing he had something to conceal, I bade him goodbye. How embarrassed he had been! How embarrassed they all were! Thinking I had left the village for good they had backed up the gossip against me just to clear themselves of suspicion. And now they met me as strangers, as gloomily aloof as the Jews' house, which stood so lone and desolate over the way.

It was Else who opened the door and the very first glance made me forget my sense of loss. She was colourful as ever, with enough of the old sparkle to quicken my heart and to gladden my eyes after the gloomy looks of the village. For one brief second I was back in the glint of happier days when a lurking smile of hers always kept us on the quick qui vive or trembling on the imminent brink of a laugh. But suddenly her finger went to her lips and, with a jerk of her thumb towards the sanctum, she motioned me to silence. We tiptoed in, stole our way upstairs to my room and softly closed the door. She halted to listen and then sat down and faced me.

'What's the matter?' I asked in a whisper.

'Boden,' she said, pointing downward.

Now, as 'Boden' means 'floor', I naturally looked down, whereupon she suppressed a laugh.

'No, not this Boden,' she added with a malicious smile, 'I mean the Boden under the Boden. I wish he *were* – for evermore.'

Of course she meant 'under the ground', dead and buried. So Boden was in the room below in conclave with Herr Engels. This was serious. Perhaps Else was not so gay after all. Perhaps her humour was of the gallows kind, just a devil-may-care outburst, a flippant snap of the finger in the face of unhappy fate. It must be so. There was a feverish tremor in the cheeks, which revealed some deep disquiet.

'What's he doing here?'

She explained. Her mother had gone to Switzerland to complete her convalescence, but Else, who had also wanted to go, had been held up. A veto had slipped in somewhere, not from the police but from the party, and from whom of the party but Boden? He had succeeded Brechner as chairman of the committee and great white chief of the village. And, moreover, he was Kreisarzt, or the medical officer of health, a state official.

I looked aghast at Else. The gravity of the situation began to weigh upon me.

'Soon after my applying for a pass he asked me to come and see him. An official order on official paper officially stamped.'

'So you went?'

'God forbid. I replied I should come in the company of Hempel and Müller or, if he liked, of Frau Boden.'

'You didn't! You have handed him the justification to take action.'

'Yes, he has threatened to do so. Insult to an official is the charge he intends to bring.'

'Heavens, and what are you doing about it?'

'I wrote that, from what I knew of him, he hadn't the ability to be insulted. So he has called. He is down below, talking to Grandpa.'

I was afraid. Boden was a man without conscience, so blockish, so obtuse, so beyond all reason, that any plea for justice would thud against his ears in vain. Blind to any rights but his own, he would trample over the common law without reck of friend or foe.

I went down just as he was leaving. He did not deign to meet my glance.

'You'll be receiving a summons from the committee,' he said, without a glance at Herr Engels, who was showing him out.

At the sound of the closing door Else raced down the stairs and approached her grandfather, who was returning to his seat.

'What did he say?'

Herr Engels settled quietly down and lit his pipe before replying.

'That you are to stay here and that I am responsible.'

'But I shall go,' cried Else, 'even if I must cross the frontier without a pass.'

She quivered with passion. She set her teeth and clenched her fists and, had Boden been there, she would have set about him with a knife. I had never seen her like this before. All her sense of humour had gone. I recalled her to her better self.

'Else, you lower yourself by shaking your fist at such a man.'

'I should stick out my tongue, I suppose.'

'It would be more in keeping.'

'Exactly,' said Herr Engels in his quiet way. 'Leave fury to the Nazis.'

'Why?' cried Else, still unappeased.

'Well, you have only your fury. They have fury and the big stick. And when the big stick is raised we shall be at the wrong end. It is all very well to be furious when you've the harder skull and the thicker hide. And you've little of these, I reckon. If it came to a struggle they'd crack us like an egg and leave us nothing but the empty shell. For we'd lose not merely the fight but a lot besides.'

'For example?'

'This house of mine.'

We gazed at him aghast.

'He hinted that there were families here in dire need of a home and that I was anti-social, living alone in a large house. At my time of life I ought to be content with less. I suppose he wants me to make my will and leave every copper to the party.'

'The shameless rascal,' hissed Else.

She gazed for an instant at us both and without a further word went out.

After further talk with Herr Engels I went to find her. But she had gone. I even hurried to the station, but the trains had just left and I peered along the platforms in vain. Nor did she return for the evening meal we took in silence. Herr Engels was wrapped in his own thoughts and I in mine, while Frau Nauheim, who served the meal, went in and out in her mute impersonal way. She made no reference to Else, nor did we. But the emptiness of that empty seat between us grew deeper with every passing hour.

As night set in I felt uneasy and the house went very still. I tried to tell my old friend what had happened on the Ahr, but my story was too remote from our present thoughts. After a time I felt he was listening beyond me, perhaps to some footstep in the lane, to the faint horn of a ship on the river. We both lapsed into silence. So to pass the time, without saying a word, we started to play chess, the wondrous chess of men who wait in vain for the other to move and so move out of turn. How often we overlooked the check! Or queered the diagonal of the bishop! Or failed to see a plain *en prise* of the queen! And still the night went on, and still we waited and waited and all the time I wondered – but for what? I started up.

'We shall have to see the police.'

'No. She has probably gone home to Cologne.'

'But she said nothing about where she was going.'

He looked at me in his steady quizzical way.

'No. She ought to have said where.'

So all the time he had not been worrying about Else, but thinking of something else, of the possible wreck of his house, of the raid on the Jews' house, of Lambert's murder, of the long illness of his daughter and the suicide of the Captain. Yes, he himself would be next in this long trail of disaster, he and his world of memory in which he had lived for so many years.

We had just stood up when there was a ring of the bell. It was loud, prolonged, urgent, as though from the police. I heard the ominous throb of a car.

'The police?' I guessed.

'Show them in.'

I went to the door. I had no time to peep out for, the moment the door yielded, in walked Hillesheim, who shook my hand and then asked for Herr Engels. He seemed anxious and in great haste.

It was about Else. He had met her by chance near the station at Bonn, determined to travel to the frontier and to cross it without a pass. In vain he had tried to dissuade her, telling her how perilous it was to avoid the controls. To gain time and to consult with us, he had offered to take her by car to the south, while she had agreed to spend the night with a school friend in Bonn. So he had gone to Cologne, had seen Joseph her uncle, and had now called on Herr Engels for his advice. He could not bring her back by force, but he could keep a watchful eye on her until she got to the frontier.

'I should be ready to intervene at the critical time.'

He said this in such a serious way that he startled us into silence. And then we saw how it was to be done, for he had loosened his greatcoat and we could see that he was in uniform, not the mere brown shirt of the rank and file, but the regular dress of the higher ranks. He was taking a dangerous risk himself.

'And should the worst come to the worst?' asked Herr Engels.

'I shall have a most plausible story, which I shall have to rehearse with Else herself. In her pretty way she is a bit of a rogue and as far as bluffing goes she certainly will not let me down. But you never know.'

'No,' said Herr Engels. 'Even the safest paths in life are cumbered with a "but". And when we stumble over it, let us be glad that the "but" is no worse. We have to take a risk, and I think Else is well advised. She is better abroad than here, exposed as she is to the malice of a Boden and to the dangers of an institution. In Switzerland she will be with her mother, to the benefit of them both. Let her go. Godspeed, Herr Professor.'

'Many thanks, Herr Engels.'

Hillesheim was most relieved. He was more committed to Else than we had thought. She was as much his concern as ours, but he was anxious about the old man.

'But you'll have to face that fellow, Boden, and face him alone, Herr Engels.'

'Well, I shall face him. What of it? If I've had my time, I've obviously nothing to lose, and if I haven't had my time I must have been wasting it. Don't worry. At my time of life I'm beyond his power. He cannot rob my earthly past nor spoil my spiritual future. Both are now in the hands of God.'

'So you're really not worried?'

'Why should I be? He is a very, very ordinary man with a very ordinary mind, and it would be sheer impiety on my part to forget God by thinking of him.' With that, Hillesheim went.

We saw him off at the door and watched as he drove away along the cobbled street to Bonn. Herr Engels stepped into the road and went on gazing after him long after the car was lost to view.

'Grand man, Hillesheim,' he murmured more to himself than to me as he walked in. He set his watch by the old clock and for a while seemed to be lost in thought.

'Yes, grand man,' he repeated, as he bade me goodnight. 'He seems to have stepped out of a dream I once had about my daughter. It was my dream and hers, Herr Arnold, an illusion which the light of day at once dispersed. But now what only might have been is set to be.'

His words took me aback. He had never spoken so clearly in favour of Hillesheim. Else was but a girl, yet he was placing her decisively in his hand. Her sham engagement with Hillesheim was now a real thing, and indeed her only protection against the hidden hand.

And with that he went to bed. But I went up to my room and, throwing open the casement, looked out towards Cologne and gazed at the ghostly searchlights as they flitted over the night sky. For an hour I followed their vagaries in the distant darkness and then went to bed filled with fear and foreboding of what the morrow might bring.

But nothing happened. Days passed by without one word from Hillesheim or a call from Boden. Naturally, Hillesheim could not write direct for fear of the censor, who went through all my post and even through my copy of *The Times* before it was delivered. Any letter to me would have to be passed by private hand. It was brought ten days later by Bürger. He also brought a code to translate the proper names, for every one was carefully disguised. Hillesheim had devised it on the morning of his departure. His lengthy letter read:

I am writing this from Zollikon, where I am staying for a day or two with your friends, the Baumann family. Your daughter, Frau Klebert, is at the window beside me, and let me say straight away that she is in the best of health, without a trace, as far as I can see, of that unfortunate breakdown that harassed her for so long. She is brimming over with good spirits, overjoyed at having her children here and looking as though every shadow has been lifted from her mind save one, your loneliness at Blankheim.

You are never far from her thoughts. But would you be shocked to hear that she may never return to her old home, to the place which so frayed upon her soul that she must forget her immediate past? The Baumanns insist on her staying and I think they are right. But you are a philosopher, Herr Engels, a wise man and an excellent father, so to know that your daughter is in safe keeping will be a sufficient solace for her being far away.

And Else and Paul? They are also here, after a certain excitement on the way. The rogue never told me that she had a secret plan to carry out, one which would land me in Queer Street if it should ever be known.

She had determined to rescue a Jewish boy, formerly of Blankheim, David Cohen by name, who was hiding in Waldshut on the wrong side of the Rhine. The news put me in a pickle, I can tell you. Had the boy been able to help himself all would have been well, but the poor fellow was a nervous wreck after being months and months on the run. He was in a terrible state when I saw him, trembling, feverish, perspiring and afraid to put one foot beyond the door. There are bridges at Waldshut, but they are closed to all without a pass and the only way was across the river. He could swim it or go by the ferry. But he was in too shattered a state to do either.

A month or two ago it might have been easy. There's a bathing pool here and the bathers are able to cross by ferry in their simple bathing kit. That is, boys and girls, who have nothing more than a mac and towel. But Cohen missed his chance. He jibbed and jibbed until the bathing season was over and there he was left, a hesitating wreck of a boy, most piteous to see. As for swimming across, he had again missed his chance. The water was too cold. There remained only one chance, by canoe, and the people with whom he was staying had bought one. But he knew no more how to handle it than the man in the moon.

But Else, as you know, is an excellent paddler and had considerable practice on the Rhine. On the very first day she took the canoe to the river and in an hour or so had it afloat. I had to play the stranger, of course, and observe her from afar. She hovered round the ferry, conversed with the officials on either side, rowed round the island between Koblenz and Waldshut, and thoroughly spied out the nakedness of the land. It seemed to me a very easy task to cross the river. The Swiss end of the ferry was just deserted countryside, a stretch of bare fields over which the path ran to the boat. The town of Koblenz lay well behind the island, out of view. It was child's play to row across and just disembark.

For two days Else paddled about or basked in the boat. She made friends with the boys and girls who were idling on the front, taking them across or letting them take a paddle so that to ferry Cohen across would not strike one as suspicious. Believe me, Herr Engels, it was a great strain on my nerves to

304

keep on watching and waiting and to pretend not to know her and to feel that I was flouting the party and risking not merely my career but my life.

She decided to take the risk early on the Friday morning and I received a private note to that effect. By the time I had got to the promenade she had launched the canoe and moved off as some people came along. It was Cohen supported by two friends and I could see by his stiff and jerky gait that he was in a bad state. Else called out, made a motion with her hand up the river and after a moment or two approached the bank and took Cohen aboard.

I breathed a sigh of relief as Else paddled away from the bank, though Cohen cut an awkward figure, crouched as he was in front with Else paddling behind. It looked an unnatural sight, but it was early morning and few about and the canoe moved swiftly away from the bank to the other side. I breathed a deep sigh of relief and sank on a seat, believe me, in sheer exhaustion. And then I got the shock of my life.

They were not far from the edge of the island when suddenly a canoe shot out from the shade and hallooed Else to stop. They were not officials, either German or Swiss, but from their dress I saw they were two Hitler Youths. They swept on to Else's boat, while she turned a little to the right to enable them to come alongside. So she was lost, and the boy as well. I could have cried aloud. And then something happened which took away my breath. As they swept alongside the first youth laid aside his oar and raised himself to grasp the fleeing boat. But Else was up at once and thrusting her oar right into the fellow's throat tossed him over into the water. The second fellow also raised himself as the boat listed deeply, and with a second thrust he was toppled out as well. And then away she paddled to the Swiss side where she landed Cohen.

Things might have been more difficult, but for the hopeless collapse of Cohen. He staggered some distance towards the town and then fell in a swoon. He had to be taken to the hospital, where his condition spoke for itself and where he was at once accepted as a genuine refugee. Else's case is still undecided, but no difficulty is expected. Her part in Cohen's rescue is in her favour. And then her mother is here and Paul. He came over in a normal way. But he does not intend to come back.

Their only fear is that pressure will be put upon you to enforce their return. Boden will certainly suggest it and try either to oust you from your house or quarter undesirables on you. And he'll make you responsible for what has happened here and accuse you of aiding and abetting. We must try to thwart his plans.

So much from Hillesheim. There was also a letter from Frau Klebert and a long one to me from Else thanking me for a thousand things of which I was hardly aware. She was only a child when I met her first, but I gave her all the courtesies I use to those much older. She recalls them one by one, for the purely pretty purpose of saying something nice to me.

305

Bürger stayed for supper and kept us in excellent humour with his sardonically witty remarks. Later, when sipping his wine, he made a brisk suggestion.

'May I stay with you to help when Boden comes?'

'By all means,' said Herr Engels, 'but let me warn you. The man's an impregnable blockhead. He no more responds to your thoughts than a dollop of sodden blancmange. You shake the sluggardly stuff and after a palsied tremor or two it settles down just where it was. He wearies me, Herr Professor. The more I try to enter his thoughts the more I find myself on the wrong side of the door.'

Boden came a few days later. Frau Nauheim announced him, but in true Nazi style he pushed past her and was in our midst before we were aware of him. But he stopped short on seeing Bürger. Raising his brows, he looked at him in a mute unrecognising way. Bürger addressed him.

'Bürger, by your leave. Have I changed so much for the better that you don't know me?'

Boden turned to Herr Engels, who was observing him with a sardonic look.

'May I speak to you in private?'

'In private? You mean I should expel my guests and entertain an intruder. Perhaps you think, Herr Doktor, that this is the bar of the Golden Hind, with a public right of entry from the street, where drinks are at your call and the landlord at your bidding. But this is my home, dear sir, and kindly remember in future that here the first respects are due to the doormat.'

Boden stiffened up, only too aware of Bürger's malicious smile and my obvious nod of approval at every remark.

'I didn't come here to be insulted,' he blurted out at last.

'Nor we to be outraged. But now that you are here just kindly declare your business. I have no secrets from Professor Bürger nor from my English friend here, both of whom you know. I am glad of their presence. Perhaps they may go on hearing when I have long since ceased to listen.'

Boden was white with anger, though not in the least embarrassed. He was far too cloddish for that.

'I refuse to speak until they go.'

'We had better stay then,' smirked Bürger, 'and save much futile talk. In any case, you've no right to speak here at all. This is not the committee room, nor, as Herr Engels has pointed out, the bar of the Golden Hind.'

'I am the Ortsgruppenleiter, the chairman of the committee.'

'Yes, the one-man parliament of Blankheim; upper and lower house, assembly and speaker, president and Führer all under the one hat,' laughed Bürger. 'One member of the committee does not make the committee, no more than one swallow makes the summer. No wonder the resolutions you pass are unanimous. They are all proposed, seconded and put to the meeting when the meeting has been dispersed. And then they are passed by the show of one hand in silent acclamation. And that goes as the voice of Blankheim.'

'I am not here to speak to you,' stuttered Boden.

'But to me,' broke in Herr Engels. 'And if you've come here to repeat your threats you may save yourself the trouble. Drop all talk and do your worst. If you've got a bolt – shoot it, and if you've got a gang – send it, and if you want a safe to crack – then crack it. The police and the insurance company have both been warned of my fears, so beware! And as for Else Klebert, you must now apply to the Swiss police. It would certainly help her plea for refuge if you would put up your case against hers. Now go.'

Boden stood for a moment near the door, white, stiff, suffocated with rage.

'You will hear from me further,' he said at last.

'I don't doubt it,' rejoined Herr Engels. 'Whoever heard the last of the devil, from the hour when he cumbers our cradles to the years when he squats on the grave. I am prepared for his worst, and for yours, Dr Boden, from now on to that final hour when perhaps I shall sense in the muffled drums his tattoo on the coffin lid. But his coming again will leave me cold, just as yours will, Herr Doktor.'

'You will hear from me further,' he repeated.

'Well, as long as it is only from you,' said Bürger, 'we shall peacefully sleep in our beds. Just let me show you the door.'

It was a relief when he went. We felt that the door had closed on the outside world and that we were at home once more. Wine was brought, the best from the cellar, and after the first sip Herr Engels lapsed into the most genial mood I had seen for many months. The sanctum was again itself, quiet, secluded, dignified. And whenever the clock struck the hours we all seemed to linger in the chimes.

Before he left, Bürger said he would like to accept the offer from Herr Engels of a couple of spare rooms in his house until he got fixed up again in Bonn.

'It will be one way of keeping Boden out.'

'Thank you, Herr Professor. Be assured that when you come the last of my fears will go. You will help me to hold the fort and stop Boden from taking the place with a rush and a cheer. Your presence will certainly halt him and make him feel at least that a front door stands between us. Now all that's needed to complete my pleasure is to have Tilde here again.'

He thumped the table at this and turned to me with a smile.

But I had received a letter from her that afternoon and had not yet told him the news. She had sent it from England, enclosing the kindest letters from Frau Boden and the Wolffs. So that had been her secret. She had faithfully promised Rebecca to reveal the plan to no one lest Hermann should get to know and perhaps prevent it. So there she was in England, a very daughter of the family, and almost as much at home as with her father on the Ahr.

307

'I thought I should be in service here,' she wrote, 'but no. Fraulein Rachel and Frau Johanna take the dishes from my hand. I have my own place at the table, whatever the occasion; they have made me part of the family.'

And did I know what fervent friends I had in the two sisters, she asked. They had told her how, in their old house, whenever evening came, harrowing fears beset them. Hardly daring to speak or even to turn on the light, it had been an immense relief whenever I arrived home.

'My dear Herr Arnold,' wrote Rachel, 'I used to feel years ago that the most moving sounds I had ever heard were those in a piece by Mozart, in one of the last cadences of *Die Kleine Nachtmusik* where he assembles all the despairs of his soul. But now, let me confess, though music has its lovely tones, the sound of your returning footstep at the door in such fraught times was more lovely still, and lends a haunting echo to every hour I live.'

So I wrote to Rachel assuring her that my returning footstep would not be delayed any longer than I could avoid.

Only Herr Engels was sad. 'It will be lopping the last branch when you are gone,' he said. 'And when the greenery is shorn away I shall finally be left as a mere stick, giving shade and shelter to no one. What a thousand pities, Herr Arnold! For when you go away something of me will go with you, not only some of my yesterdays but many of my tomorrows. You are young, dear sir, you are young. You are a green leaf of mine, so to speak, a glimpse of spring in my wintry days and a promise of blossom to come. But enough. You must not let me detain you.'

'But Herr Engels', I reassured him, 'I've still a year to go at Bonn, and my thesis is not yet finished. That means I shall be with you for some time, and you will have two allies in the battle against Boden and the rest of the gang.'

And with that, he smiled again.